# after Care

## L.B. DUNBAR

*Keep reading,*
*darlin'*

*L.B. Dunbar*

www.lbdunbar.com

*Happy Festivas!*

L.B. Dunbar

After Care

Cover Design: Shannon Passmore/Shanoff Formats
Cover Image: iStock
Edits: Kiezha Smith Ferrell/Librum Artis Editorial Services

# Other Books by L.B. Dunbar

**Silver Fox Former Rock Stars**
*After Care*
*Midlife Crisis*

**Rom-com for the over 40**
*The Sex Education of M.E.*

**The Sensations Collection**
*Sound Advice*
*Taste Test*
*Fragrance Free*
*Touch Screen*
*Sight Words*

**Spin-off Standalone**
*The History in Us*

**The Legendary Rock Star Series**
*The Legend of Arturo King*
*The Story of Lansing Lotte*
*The Quest of Perkins Vale*
*The Truth of Tristan Lyons*

**Paradise Stories**
*Paradise Tempted: The Beginning*
*Paradise Fought: Abel*
*Paradise Found: Cain*

**The Island Duet**
*Redemption Island*
*Return to the Island*

**Modern Descendants – writing as elda lore**
*Hades*
*Solis*
*Heph*

# Dedication

#cancersucks
For those taken.
*Grandma*
*Aunt Joan*
For those who survived – twice.
*Mom*
And for those who hopefully will never get it.
*MD, MK, and A*

# 1
## The Introduction

"Is that your daughter?" A pretty blonde sat next to me on the edge of the pool. I fidgeted with the scarf wrapped around my head and smiled.

"Yes." The beautiful brunette was mine, and even though she was eighteen, she was child-like in spirit, laughing as two little girls splashed her. Watching the younger two frolic in the water reminded me of my own children at that age. Life was much different then.

"Both yours?" I asked, shifting only my eyes to the twenty-something woman, adjusting the scarf once again on my head, waiting for her to notice it. There wasn't a way to miss it. The thin material made no sense in the heat of the Hawaiian sun, but the traditional paisley patterned bandana in bright yellow made sense to someone like me. I was a breast cancer survivor. If you didn't know, the head wrap gave it away.

She nodded in response to me and we remained silent a moment.

My eyes closed as I faced the brilliant blue sky, soaking up the sunshine, a welcome reprieve from the frigid temps we left behind in Chicago. I desperately needed this vacation. *Party of three, please.* I looked forward to the family time with my grown children. We had much to celebrate, the doctors told me. I smiled despite myself as I looked back at the two babes dousing my daughter.

"She's good with kids," the young woman remarked, and I stared off at my own child on the verge of womanhood. She'd make a great mother one day. Tears prickled my eyes. I didn't want to think dark thoughts, but they often crept in. Silently, I hoped I'd get to see the day she mothered a child of her own.

"Cannonball." A loud male screech erupted from my other baby—more a child than a man at the age of twenty-two. He catapulted into the huge, oddly shaped pool, covering his sister in a tidal wave of water, and drowning the two little girls.

L.B. Dunbar

"Caleb," I shouted but the mother next to me laughed. A man with dark, chin length hair caught one of her daughters under the arms, hoisting her upward from the vigorous aftershock of my son's jump. Masie held the other. Tiny arms wrapped around my daughter's neck, holding tight like a second skin. Laughter surrounded all of them.

"That's Ava," the woman pointed to the dark-haired one matching her apparent father. "She's six. And the blonde, choking your daughter is Emaline. She's four."

My eyes drifted back to the collection of young people but froze on the man with rock star looks. Deep set eyes, a thin scrap of scruff around his jaw, and the midnight color of his wet hair, added to what I imagined was a brooding look on an average day. Smiling at his child made all the difference in his appearance.

"You can ask," the woman said. "Yes, it's him."

I turned to her, fully facing her equally striking appearance. Softer than his, her face held a playful look in her blue eyes. Puffy, pink lips conjured images of them kissing each other passionately. Passionate enough to create two small daughters. I sighed. It had been a long time since someone kissed me like that. Even the man who created two children with me had fallen out of practice years before everything happened.

"He's Gage Everly."

I blinked at her, shaking my head in confusion. "I'm sorry. Should I know him? Do I know you?" My eyes opened wider, a tingle of fear that somehow, I didn't recognize him when it should be obvious. Not only had the cancer taken my hair, it had taken my memory, I chuckled, knowing that couldn't possibly be true.

"Gage Everly, lead singer of Collison?" Her brow rose in question, as if I should recognize him or the name of the band.

"I'm so sorry," I said again, cursing the terrible habit I had of apologizing for everything. *I'm sorry, I wasn't younger. I'm sorry, you no longer love me. I'm sorry, I got cancer.* "I don't..." My head shook to acknowledge I didn't recognize him.

6

She chuckled softly, clapped a hand, and covered her cheeks. "Oh my, how refreshing." Her blue eyes beamed brighter than the sky overhead.

"I think it's just because I'm old," I weakly smiled, reaching for the bandana once again. My hair had moved from the stages of peach-fuzz to crazy C-shapes and kinky, curly Qs, going in all directions. I didn't need the material covering my head, but sometimes, I felt safer wearing it. My hair color hadn't returned to my natural fading brown, but a mixture of white and dirty blonde.

*You can dye it whatever color you want when approved*, Nurse Marjorie had told me. *Purple's very popular for people your age.* Her sweet, innocent voice intended to encourage me. Instead, I wanted to erase the smirk on her lips.

*Your age.* I was forty-three. I should have been in the prime of my life. Where was that sexual libido return everyone promised me would happen? Oh, right, it walked out the door with a younger model—blonde, thin, and cancer-free under her skin.

The new hair combination caused conflicting emotions. On one hand, the brilliant color reminded me of my growing age. On the other hand, the change from lackluster to vibrant aided to the new personae I wanted to adapt. It was time for a change.

"Oh." My companion's eyes opened wide, "Oh, I wasn't implying…I mean…It's just that…" Her hands waved in front of her as she swung her thin body toward me. "It's just everywhere we go people know it's him. It's nice to meet someone who doesn't recognize Gage."

I smiled. I didn't know how to respond. A child squealed and I turned my attention to the pool, noting my son in a deep conversation with her husband. Masie still held one girl while the other tried to climb her father. Caleb wanted to be a guitarist when he was younger. It was his life's ambition, until he discovered baseball. The sport became my ex's dream for our son. Watching Caleb, his body straightened, his awe trained on the man before him—someone I didn't recognize, but surely Caleb did.

A gruff voice behind us bellowed, "Please step away from him."

L.B. Dunbar

My body twisted to face the sound, rich in baritone, tough as a boulder, and rugged like gravel under bare feet. I shivered despite the heat. Two thick arms crossed a midnight colored T-shirt stretched over the barrel chest of an older man, rightfully in his forties with silvery hair curling at his neck and salt-and-pepper facial scruff. He wore black pants, balancing himself with a wide stance of thick legs. Regardless of tinted aviators, the weight of his eyes bored into me. Rock star sprang to my mind.

"It's okay, Uncle Tommy," the woman said. "They're only talking."

"Well, we all know where talking can lead." His knuckles met his neck and he scratched at the hint of hair under his jaw. The sound traveled to me, and a thrill tickled over my sun-heated shoulders. His pouty lips crooked in one corner as I sensed him teasing the girl. It was obvious he knew her secrets. "But seriously, he's on vacation. He doesn't need a groupie and some wannabe—"

"Excuse me?" I interjected, attempting to make my voice as knife sharp as his but failing miserably as he removed the aviators. Two deep set circles of coal returned his focus on me and the will to breathe escaped me. He stole my breath, literally, as he'd noticed the scarf. There was no way he couldn't, but he kept his eyes pinned to mine.

*Out of respect*, I told myself.

*To hold me prisoner*, my mind whispered.

*Take me*, I foolishly screamed, and then the deepest blush I've ever experienced crawled over my skin, prickly, tickly, tingly like the tiny tap of a million feet. I shivered again. The motion snapped his attention and he turned away.

"Tommy, this is…" the young mother paused. "I'm sorry, I didn't catch your name."

"Edie," I said, holding out my hand while the other fingers found security in touching the fabric just above my ear. "Edie Williams."

"This is Tommy Carrigan. He's the band's manager." She turned to look up at him over her shoulder, her smile affectionate. "He's a giant teddy bear when he isn't acting like a grumpy eagle." She pouted as she spun back to me.

"Don't be ruining my reputation before I make an impression, sweetheart," he teased with a hint of Southern drawl, his eyes redirected to the pool but his shoulders loosened a little. Oh, he'd made an impression all right. A deep one, right between my thighs just from the sound of his voice.

Then I noticed my hand still lingering in the air, waiting for him to reach out and shake mine. When he didn't, I awkwardly lowered it, fussing with my scarf one more time.

"Don't mind him," the woman said. "By the way, I'm Ivy. Ivy Everly, and I'm happy to meet you."

Her smile put me at ease. For some reason, I was just as pleased to meet her.

Funny how a random introduction changed everything.

# 2

## A sane woman would never

*The headscarf isn't there*, I reminded myself.

Reaching for it had become a habit, but I didn't wear it that night. *You don't need it*, Masie told me as I got ready for the evening and I agreed. This was the first step to a new me, I encouraged myself, only my heart hammered at the thought as I pulled open the solid club doors. The tropical air tickled my neck while the wave of air-conditioning hit my face. The humid caress was a welcome feeling as I questioned once again, how had I gotten myself into *this* position.

Within hours of meeting, Ivy had invited me to join her for cocktails. At first, I hesitated knowing we were on a family vacation, but my daughter encouraged me to go. She also agreed to babysit Ivy's little girls. And just like that, I was going out for drinks with Ivy Everly and her famous husband, Gage, lead singer of Collision, a band I knew nothing about.

My son told me they were something. *"Mom, how have you not heard of them?"* His voice echoed in my head. Suddenly, my arm was enveloped by another, and my face shot up to find Ivy's arm looped around mine. Her big, blue eyes widened like a smile.

"Ready?" she asked, tugging at me as I smoothed my black dress over my hips with my free hand. I was still a little bloated from the treatments—everyone responded differently—although my body shape was getting better. However, I'd never return to the shape I was twenty years ago.

Without thinking, I reached up, my fingers finding soft hair unhidden by a scarf, reminding me once again of how far I'd come.

"You look beautiful," Ivy said, and I looked at her again, my brows pinching at the compliment. Her eyes saddened for only a second before she let the sympathy pass and a smile brightened her face. She squeezed my arm tighter. "There's Tommy."

L.B. Dunbar

wheel to their passionate display of affection. Attempting to free myself from Ivy's grasp, my opposite hand was clasped, and I spun to find Tommy holding it. His fingers spread and without thinking, I laced mine with his.

The thick digits brought an instant comfort and distraction. A strange ripple traveled up my wrist, increasing my pulse and ratcheting up my already pounding heart.

"Gage," Tommy barked, and the lovers broke apart. He shook his head, and I looked back to find a wicked smile on Gage's lips and a dazed look in Ivy's eyes. "Don't make me have to babysit," he commanded, and Ivy turned to face him. Shaky fingers came to her lips and they curved into a smile.

"Chill, Care," Gage snapped, wrapping an arm around his wife. The nickname startled me.

"Sorry, Uncle Tommy," Ivy mocked, but there was a certain teasing familiarity when she spoke to him.

"Let's get you guys to the VIP section." Tommy still cupped my hand in his, and while every fiber of my being wanted to press my palm firmer to his, I tried to keep it aloft, separate. Only…it wasn't working. My hand started to sweat and panic spread. I hadn't held a man's hand since…I couldn't remember when. I couldn't think of the last time David held my hand—not even bedside, during the worst of times. I wanted to melt into the warmth palming mine. Heat flushed over every inch of my skin with thoughts of that same hand skimming my body. The image screeched to a halt. *My body.* He'd discover parts of my body weren't mine anymore. What was I even thinking? A man like him would have no interest in a body like mine or a woman like me—older, settled, boring. Scarred.

My arm flinched, hoping to loosen my fingers, suddenly feeling dragged instead of led to the roped-off VIP section. But his hold tightened, forcing our palms together, suctioned with the warm dryness of his and the dampness of mine. *Nope, never going to have interest in a sweaty, middle-aged woman.* I sighed.

12

"Take a seat," he offered, nearly whipping me into a chair, while Ivy climbed on Gage's lap when he sat on a couch. Tommy pulled a chair next to me, his body angled to where he could watch the boys in the band. His back toward the crowd.

"Are you their bodyguard or something?" I asked, snorting at the thought, even though his stature suggested it. His brooding stance earlier in the day gave me the same thought.

"Nah, their manager, but I might as well be a bodyguard. These boys can be a pain in the ass, especially Jared." He nodded in the direction of a lounge chair and I twisted to look over my shoulder. Brown hair, blue eyed—he looked so all-American to me, but the most innocent could sometimes be the guiltiest. Tattoos laced his arm. In contrast, thick rimmed-glasses covered his eyes. I didn't know who Jared was any more than I recognized Gage when I met him by the pool, and my age was certainly showing in that lack of knowledge. The feeling of being out of my element grew ten-fold, and I shifted in my seat, tugging at the hem of my suddenly too-short dress, willing it to reach my knees.

I didn't know why I even brought this dress with me on our vacation. I supposed I'd hoped for a little family-of-three dinner celebration. I was a survivor of many things, and the Hawaiian trip was proof of it. Still, a form-fitting black dress wasn't my typical wear, and I was suddenly self-conscious in it. It could have also been the way Tommy's dark eyes narrowed on my fist at the hem and followed the struggling along my thighs. In the dimly lit bar, his eyes were silky black ink, matching the streaks in his hair. Taking a deep breath, his nostrils flared and he looked away from me, his knuckles stroking the heavy scruff on his jaw—not enough to be a beard, but more than a dusting. It was more silver than black, and the contrast with his hair was mouthwatering. I'd noticed this contemplative motion when we met.

My eyes followed his to a group of women drawing closer to our section. *Of course*, I thought, *younger women*. I glanced away in time to find a waiter headed toward us and held my hand up for a drink. He ignored me.

"Whatcha want, darlin'?" Tommy's gruff voice startled me, and I turned back to find him staring at me. Twisting a discarded napkin in my fingers, I was about to speak when he continued.

"Something fruity? A frozen something-something with an umbrella peeking out the top?"

"No," I chuckled. "Why, do I look like a fruity drink kind of woman?" Where did the flirty tone come from? I didn't flirt. I still couldn't believe I even spoke to him. He hadn't spoken to me earlier in the day, and I sensed I was just one more person for him to babysit.

His eyes roamed my body, starting at my exposed knees. He licked his top lip then rubbed his tongue over the lower one as he rode up my thighs with intense eyes and skipped over the hem to my breasts. My chest heaved, and that's when I looked away. He was only teasing me.

"Actually, you look like a fine wine, aged to perfection, sweet on the palate and lingering on the tongue long after you've been swallowed."

I gasped.

"What?" A nervous laugh escaped, half thrilled, half deflated. He had to be teasing me, but the richness of his words, the essence of his description, lapped over my skin as if he drank me in, inch by delicious inch, and swirled me in his mouth like a wine sample before swallowing me whole. Just like he'd described. Ignoring my horrified gasp, he lifted two fingers in the air, and the waiter immediately returned.

"A bottle of…" he paused, his eyes shifting sideways to me. "Red for the lady."

"Actually," I interrupted. "I'll take a glass of Moscato, please."

"Hmmm," Tommy murmured. "My skills failed me. You seemed to balk at the sweeter things."

"Really?" I laughed again. "You just thought I'd like a fruity drink." I reminded him, pausing as I tilted my head. "What did you have me pegged for then?" Maybe I wanted to be fizzy and funny, like someone young and frivolous.

"*Actually*," he smirked as he emphasized my word, "I had you pegged as—"

"Tommy, don't you just adore Edie?" Ivy squealed from behind me, and I spun around to find a girl drunk on love, holding a light pink drink in her hand with her husband's arm wrapped around her midsection. I sighed again. Oh, how I hoped life would always remain this way for them. My heart pinched, knowing it wouldn't. Marriage was hard work. One in two marriages still ended in divorce. I wasn't a statistic; I was a trend.

I smiled up at Ivy.

"Edie." Tommy snapped his fingers next to me. "I thought your name was Debbie."

I nodded slowly. Once again, any thoughts of attraction to a man like Tommy Carrigan were futile. It was as if I was a kid again, starstruck by the aura of rock star around him. Only, getting struck by a star would hurt, like an asteroid hitting Earth. *Kaboom.* I was spiraling out of my orbit, and I'd already been hit by that kind of heat—something I never wanted to experience again.

"Care," Gage sighed, shaking his head at Tommy. It must have been short for Carrigan, his last name. "Try to be a nice guy." Sarcasm dripped from his tone as he peered down at his manager.

"Edie. Like E and D," Ivy smirked, glaring at Tommy.

*What's with these two?* I thought, but ignored any questions when my wine arrived. The entire bottle was placed on the table and a glass poured. The sweet bubbles tickled my mouth, and I quickly swallowed the prickling cool refreshment. One glass, then I'd excuse myself, I decided. This was over my head. The pulsing lights. The rhythmic beats. The dim corner for VIPs. I didn't belong here, and Tommy, not remembering my name, confirmed it.

"Take Edie dancing," Ivy cooed, and I spun to gawk up at the blonde getting nibbled on the neck by her husband. I turned back to Tommy, and something in my expression made his eyes widen.

"I don't dance," I blurted, gripping the back of my chair with one hand, the cool glass of wine in the other. I never danced. *Never.*

"Everyone dances," Tommy replied, looking incredulous.

"Not me, but go right ahead." I nodded to the filling dance floor and the rising number of girls nearing our section.

Commotion to our side made Tommy twist in that direction. A few girls had crossed the barricade, and Tommy stood to speak with them. Jared got up as well, patting Tommy on the back as he took half a step toward him. Another band member joined the small montage of men holding back the young girls in their low-cut, too-short, slim-fit outfits.

"I think I need the bathroom," I said, jumping up too quickly. I drained the wine in my glass as I watched Jared smile, Tommy's arms flap in exasperation, and the blond band member reach for a girl, bringing her into the VIP section.

"I'll go with you," Ivy offered, but I shook her off. We weren't college girls needing to tag team. In fact, I didn't know why I was there. I was a forty-three-year old woman, and she was...what? All of twenty-eight, if that?

"I'll be fine," I said, holding up a hand after steadying myself.

"You'll come back, right?" Her voice squeaked in a yearning lilt. My shoulders sagged. My plan had actually been to use the restroom and escape, apologizing later by feigning a headache.

"I'll be right back," I acquiesced, patting her arm in assurance.

In the bathroom, I gave myself a pep talk. *You can do this*, I encouraged, as I stared at my too-wide blue eyes and pursed my bright red lips.

*You don't need to dance.*

*Just have another drink.*

*He bought the bottle for you.*

*This trip was to celebrate.*

I sighed as I tugged at the wrinkled skin under my chin. The folds sprang back into place after releasing them. My tan skin was striped with rings of a lighter mixture because of the folds, reminding me of an okapi leg. I had to laugh at myself. What else could I do? I didn't need to impress these people. I wouldn't ever see them again. Ivy seemed to latch onto me, but I didn't understand why. She was sweet, though, and I decided I could hold the bold face for another hour. I washed my hands, patted my warm cheeks, and exited the bathroom.

Upon re-entering the club, my eyes landed instantly on Tommy, dancing. Well, maybe not dancing, but standing on the edge of the dance floor with a woman leaning into him and another pressing playfully at his chest. As I crossed to the VIP section, he turned to face me, possibly feeling the weight of my eyes boring into his broad back.

It wasn't fair. How is it men aged well, while women just aged? If I was fine wine, he was a bottle of whiskey, his flavor ripening as the years passed, aging him to perfection over time. Nervous fingers swiped through my wayward curls, and I spun away from his glance. Eyes focused on Ivy, I stalked toward her.

"Are you all right?" Ivy asked. "You look a little flushed." She rose and wrapped slender fingers around my arm, guiding me to take her seat.

"I'm fine," I replied, and as politely as I could, removed my arm from her grasp. "I think I'm going to call it a night, though." I pasted on my best false smile. Her eyes pinched, and her sweet face fell a little.

"Are you sure? I'm sorry if something happened." I didn't even know what she could mean, but her genuine concern warmed my insides.

"What could have possibly happened?" I teased. "Honest, honey, I'm all good. This really isn't for me, but you have fun. I'll check on your girls." Without a care, I reached for her, pulling her into a quick hug. "Thank you for inviting me."

"Maybe Petty should walk you to your room." *Petty?* Was that the blond band member's name? I glanced over my shoulder to see him whispering into the ear of the girl he pulled forward from the crowd.

"I don't think that's necessary," I laughed. Petty wasn't going to willingly step away from his momentary interest.

"I'll go with you then." Ivy stepped toward me as Gage reached for her waist. "Babe?"

As a young couple, him a rock star and her a mother, I bet they rarely had time out together. I couldn't begin to comprehend the life of fame, so I didn't try.

"Ivy, it's only across the way." I rubbed up and down her arm, gave Gage another false smile, and turned for the exit.

I hadn't made it down the hallway for the lobby before the sound of heavy feet followed me.

"Whoa, where you headed so fast?" The gruff voice startled me, as did the hand that gripped my bicep, and I spun, ready to fight off an attack.

"Tommy?" I gasped, completely shocked that he held my arm, pinning me in place.

"Why'd you leave so quickly, darlin'?" His hand slipped to my wrist before releasing me. A trail of heat trickled where his palm blazed against me. I shivered at the sensation.

"I'm heading back to my room. The bar isn't really my scene."

His eyes narrowed on mine, and his lips twisted in a way that made him look like he contemplated something. He took my elbow and started tugging me in the direction of large double doors.

"What the heck?" I muttered, struggling only slightly under his grip. He pulled the door open with ease, drawing me into what appeared to be an empty ballroom. Tugging the door shut behind him, we were submerged in momentary darkness. "Are you insane?"

"Maybe," he murmured before stepping closer. The assault of the air conditioning disappeared the moment his body came near mine. Heat emanated from his presence. "Why did you leave?"

"It wasn't my thing," I repeated.

"And what is your thing?" His arms crossed, glaring at me as our eyes adjusted to the dim lighting. I wasn't about to tell him *my thing* was a good book and maybe a rerun on Passionflix. Reading passed the hours, filling my heart with adventures I'd never experience. I was good alone, even if I didn't always like it. Lonely most nights, but it wasn't something you spilled to a stranger.

I crossed my arms to match his stance. "What do you think is my thing?"

"Do you always answer a question with another question?"

"Why?"

"See, you did it again." The hint of a smile filled his statement, and I relaxed my shoulders. I reached for my head, then tried to disguise the nervous habit by twisting a too-short piece of hair around my index finger.

"I would have danced with you," he said, as if he'd do it for my sake—do *me* the favor. The hairs on the back of my neck rose, hackles bristling like a dog ready to bite.

"Well, thank you for that generous offer, but as I said, I don't dance." My hand lowered from my hair and fisted at my side.

"Why not?"

"Why does it matter?"

"You did it again." He chuckled, and I huffed. I hadn't noticed the habit, but with my previous condition, asking questions was a necessity.

"It's still early. Let me guess where you were headed." He paused, considering me for a moment, like he did when he was trying to figure out what wine I drank. He scratched at his neck, something I found strangely seductive, and a spark flickered inside me. "Clandestine rendezvous with someone?"

"No." I laughed, thinking he was more capable of such a thing than me.

"Off to read the latest mystery thriller?"

"No," I scoffed, trembling. He was getting closer to the truth.

"That leaves washing your hair or a good time with Mr. Bob." He motioned toward my lower regions.

"What?" I barked, but he ignored me and continued.

"Or are you going to call your cats at home, check up on how they're doing?"

"Thank you for making me feel even older than I already feel about myself." My eyes narrowed. I didn't own cats. I didn't even like cats. And none of this was the point.

"What's that supposed to mean?" His arms uncrossed, and he stepped toward me. Our chests rose and fell in opposing rhythm, until slowly, our breathing regulated, falling into a pattern with one another, but I couldn't say who followed whose lead.

"I saw that girl leaning on you," I snapped, shifting the conversation completely and sounding like a jealous girlfriend, but I couldn't be jealous, not really. "I get that you're used to younger things."

His dark eyes widened in disbelief, then narrowed to black slits. "You know, darlin', jealousy is an ugly shade of green, but on you, the color is beautiful."

I straightened. Was there a compliment in that statement?

"You know what your problem is, though?" A hand came to my hip, and I should have swatted it away. Any sane women would have done that. Any woman trapped in a dark ballroom, standing too close to a stranger whose body heat was higher than ninety-eight-point-six degrees would have pushed him away. But he made me want to be a little crazy. Maybe the treatment had damaged my brain cells after all.

"Please, enlighten me," I bit out, wanting to cross my arms as a shield, but he stood too close. My hip was tugged forward.

"You need to be sexed up, and often." His voice lowered, his tone dropping like pebbles plopping into a pond.

"Did you…Did you just try to quote *Gone with the Wind?*" I stammered, appalled that he'd ruined one of the greatest quotes of all time, but thrilled at the same time, that he misquoted it on me. Flutters rushed through my lower abdomen in a way I hadn't felt in a long, long, *long* time. His eyes sparkled and another thought occurred.

"Sexed up?" I choke-barked.

"I'd use a different word, but I'm sensing you're too much of a lady, and you'd be offended by it."

Suddenly, I felt more offended that he couldn't say what he wanted to do to me. I didn't think I was that uptight. That old.

"Try me," I whispered through gritted teeth.

"Nah, I think sexed up is good enough for you, darlin'. Anything else would be too much."

My heart dropped. He was correct in many ways. I was well past the point of wanting my body parts crassly labeled or physical interactions demeaned. On the other hand, I also wanted someone to want me *that* passionately, just once in my lifetime. To clarify, I wanted someone who just wanted to fuck me, like being with me was the greatest moment of their life. Like they would never get enough, deep enough, connected enough—to me. It was a silly fantasy.

"I see," I offered, my voice quiet. My shoulders fell, defeated. I knew what he meant. It was nearly the same thing my ex-husband said. I wasn't fun anymore. Tommy's hand remained at my hip, but the other hand brushed back my barely-there hair, caressing around my ear. There were not enough locks to curl behind it. It was another reminder of how incomplete I felt.

"Actually," he teased. "I don't think you do see. You're that fine wine. Perfected and waiting to breathe. And I'm sensing you're ready to be uncorked and sampled."

My mouth fell open, a popping sound filling the space between us, and that's when his mouth descended.

Two warm, large, plump lips melted over me.

And I stilled instantly.

It had been nearly two years since I'd been kissed, and it definitely had not been like this. His mouth moved over mine, too harsh at first, too aggressive, until he realized I wasn't responding. Thick fingers combed into my short hair, and his hand at my hip tugged me flush against him.

"Kiss me back, darlin'," he growled against my mouth.

My lips followed his lead, tentative at first. A tug of the lower lip. A suck on the upper bow. A lick across the seam, and I opened for him. My body crushed against his, arms sliding up his firm biceps to grip his shoulders. My tongue met his, curling and colliding, crashing with his as I breathed him into me, willing him to get closer. My breasts remained firm against his chest, and I nearly cried at the lack of sensation, but the rest of my body responded. The drumming between my thighs beat triple time, making up for other areas.

Our mouths moved together, and he tipped my head for better access. We were making out like teenagers—lips exploring, hands slowly groping, an energy building around us that took my breath and shook it like glitter in a glass jar. Then his palm came to the side of my breast, and I halted, releasing his lips so quickly, a soft pop echoed between us.

"I can't..." My voice trailed off. Oh, God, this was embarrassing. This was the worst thing. I didn't know how to say it. "I can't..."

His thumb caressed the side of my breast, rubbing harder, pressing firmer.

"You don't think I've felt a fake tit before, darlin'?" The query stopped me. I hadn't realized I'd curled up on my toes to reach his height. My feet fell as flat as my heels would allow at the question. My hands slipped from his shoulders, drifting over the hills of his biceps and skipping to his chest. I palmed the firmness of his pecs. Solid. Strong. Real.

"How did you know?" The question was stupid. Of course, he'd touched other women, most of whom, I assumed, were younger than me. Of course he had. Groupies surely had implants. Some women had them for funzies, enlarging what wasn't there or enhancing what God already gave them. Either way, my situation was different. "Don't answer that. Never mind."

"Jealousy just shifted to a different shade. Still like you wearing it, beautiful." The words brought tears to my eyes, and I rapidly blinked. I couldn't be jealous. Of course, he'd been with other women. *Look at him,* I screamed to myself. Although, I was more upset over the fact he called me beautiful, and I didn't feel that way.

"I think I should go," I whispered, lowering my head and almost resting it on his chest, but I held back. The thick pad of his finger tipped up my chin.

"Tell me what just happened here."

"You kissed me." I giggled without humor. In fact, my whole body shook with the after effect of what we'd just done.

"When I touched you," he clarified. My face shot up to look at his. His dark eyes beamed down at me, but there was a softness to the edgy black. His eyes shimmered like ink instead of granite.

"I can't...I just can't let you touch me there."

"Why not?"

I sighed, taking a step back. Two large hands caught me on my shoulder blades and brought me back to him. He massaged along my bra strap, thumbs circling in a way that would make a normal woman relax. Instead, I tensed.

"I have breast cancer. *Had*." The doctor's words echoed in my head. "I have no sensation in my..." I choked on the word. *Nipples*. I didn't have any. Masie had convinced me to get nipples tattooed just to make myself feel better, but they were two dimensional. It wasn't the same thing.

He didn't respond, but his hands slipped to my hips.

*This is it*, I thought. He's going to thank me for the night. Or worse, not thank me at all, just step back and walk away. My head lowered in shame. Cancer wasn't my fault. I wasn't even embarrassed I had it. It wasn't contagious. It wasn't that kind of disease. But I also didn't want it to be a crutch. The last thing I needed was his sympathy.

Preparing myself mentally for the blow to my ego, I took a deep breath, closed my eyes, and...

The sides of my dress rose up my thighs. The thick, tight cotton swept upward, revealing more skin to the air conditioning and the roughness of his jeans. My knees already brushed denim, but my upper thighs were feeling the softened fabric as well.

"What are you doing?" My voice was so low, it struggled with the words. My brain fought to comprehend what was happening. The pulse between my thighs beat faster than my heart, speeding toward a finish line without knowing when the race started. Dampness pooled on my cotton underwear, and the faint scent of my sex filled the sliver of space between us.

"You have other areas that are sensitive," he offered. "I'm sensing they have uncorked needs as well."

The sound of his gravelly voice nearly undid me. I clenched, suppressing the tremble in my knees and the urge to lift a leg and wrap around him like a tree. My core sought friction. He was what I needed. His thick leg would be perfect. Better yet would be the mass straining against his jeans.

His fingers climbed—up, up, up—scrunching the material of my dress to my hips until…

*Shit.*

"What the fuck?" His finger found the high-cut band at the leg of my underwear. Since it had clearly never, ever crossed my mind that anyone other than me would see these panties, I'd forgotten about them. High-cut *and* high-waisted, they covered my lower abdomen, landing at my true waist to flatten the loose baggage of my lower belly. I suspected he was more familiar with thin lace and racy strings, and I had on the grandmother of all underwear in hopes of keeping a few things tucked into place.

"Oh my God," I muttered, pushing at his wrists to lower my dress and cover myself. Could things get any more embarrassing?

*Yes, actually.*

He had slipped two thick fingers under the elastic band at my hip and trapped me by my underwear. Fingers clenched in the fabric, pinning me against him. I couldn't budge his strength, and he wasn't releasing me despite my protest.

"This is embarrassing," I murmured.

"You think I care about your underwear? I'm more interested in what's under there," he growled. Literally, it was a groan of an epic man-bear.

I felt like a rag doll, jostled by the tug of my underwear, as I pressed at his chest to free myself. Then it happened. Two thick fingers crossed over my sensitive skin, so slick, so achy, so repressed. We both stopped struggling, and he repeated the motion before entering me. My breath hitched. Had he violated me? No, this was more like visceral pleasure to the *nth*-degree. My core clenched tighter than it ever had. I was so turned on, I couldn't think. My surprised eyes found his just as shocked by my response. Was this really happening? Wasn't this every woman's fantasy? A random, sexy man in a dark ballroom during a vacation, who you'll never see again?

Not mine. Not here. Not like this.

His fingers stopped moving, his arm frozen in a position that pinned me to the wall and connected me to him. My hand returned to his wrist, wrapping around the thick trunk and clutching at it to remove his fingers from me.

"I'm not going to lie. I want you…but I can't do this," I choked out, sounding weak, desperate, and lame. Why couldn't I just let him finger me? Why couldn't I be carefree and open to experimentation? To one-night stands? To a fling? *God, maybe I should have cats.*

One hand on the wall near my head steadied him as our breaths mixed, twirling over each other's like our tongues had moments before. He pushed off the wall and stood taller, a paw of a hand rubbing at the heavy strain in his jeans, pressing seductively up and down with the heel of his hand.

"Don't tease me, darlin'. I'm too old for this shit."

No teasing. I wouldn't even know how to tease. I'd been married, divorced, and alone for three years. Teasing was the last thing I knew how to do.

"I…" My voice faded as his fingers slipped down my channel, tiptoeing to my entrance for an exit, and that's when I did the unthinkable. My traitorous body betrayed me.

I clenched.

My thighs slapped together, and our eyes snapped to one another.

"Oh, you're definitely teasing me, beautiful, and that buys me a free sample." His fingers plunged upward, retracing their retreat, and filling me enough I had to tip up on my toes. An animalistic groan settled between us, and I realized too late the sound came from me. My lids closed, and my forehead lowered to his shoulder. It was as if I was drugged. His fingers danced to the edge again, then leapt upward into my depths. I was too far gone, too wet, too wanting of his touch *Because. You. Want. This*, my body screamed. My hips curled, and my teeth bit into his shoulder.

"That's what I thought, darlin'. You were ready to breathe." He sniffed at my ear before pressing his lips to my neck. I squirmed at the sensation and danced over his fingers as they increased their pattern,

25

thrusting deeper, harder, thrilling me in a way I couldn't remember being thrilled. He was right. I wanted to breathe, and I was taking my first breath in a long time. The air was thin, the fragrance thickening. I heard the slick sound of my sex being touched, tender yet tantalizing, and I rocked with each stroke, silently begging to reach the tipping point. I gritted my teeth. I concentrated on the pleasure of his fingers. I fantasized a little that he said something dirty to me.

*I want to fuck you,* whispered in my head, and I detonated. Champagne uncorking had nothing on the release that escaped me. I overflowed with foamy bubbles and crisp crackles and sticky moisture that smelled sweet, tasted divine, and made me drunk on Tommy Carrigan. My head lulled back and tapped lightly on the wall behind me. Stars of silver light flittered behind my closed lids.

"That was something, darlin'," he muttered to my neck. *You can say that again,* I thought. And then panic struck. Oh, my God. *What had I done?* The sound of his fingers slipping out of me made me cringe. I…I just let someone finger-*f…* me. I couldn't even think the word, although the thought triggered me over the edge mere seconds ago. A trickle of dampness slid down my thigh, and I reached for it without thinking. Swiping my wet fingers on the wall, I used my other hand to straighten my dress and maneuver my underwear back in place. I couldn't look at him.

"Now," he whispered, his voice gravelly and strained. "Uncork me." His belt clinked, and a zipper unzipped. I was suddenly in over my head and rolled mine against the plaster behind me. Sensing something from eyes avoiding his, his thumb and forefinger tenderly gripped my jaw.

"Just touch me," he said, and I was reminded once again of pebbles plunking into a puddle. Smooth, plopping splats. I'd never been spoken to like that, in a voice like that. Hesitantly, I reached for the open seam of his jeans. The tips of my fingers tickled over the smooth head, rounding the mushroom shape to discover a mass so thick, so firm, so hard that my mouth watered. I closed my eyes and let sensation guide me, plunging forward as he had, to fit my hand within his jeans and

My eyes flipped instantly to a man I had no business staring at, or thinking about, although he'd filled every thought since we were introduced earlier in the day.

Tommy Carrigan.

Not Tom. Not Thomas. Tommy—even at age forty-five or so. His salt and pepper hair gave his age away, but more accurately, the slightly longer locks curling at his neck were shimmery silver and black satin. My mouth dried when he looked in our direction. My cheeks heated, and I was thankful for the dim light covering the teenage-like feeling of embarrassment. I was only embarrassing myself with thoughts I shouldn't have had of a man whose very essence said player. His solid, barrel chest and thick biceps under another black T-shirt proved what I already knew about him. He wasn't a young man, but all male. There was a certain sexiness about an older man, one no longer lean with a six pack, but firm, with a rounded chest and tight abdominal muscles. Tommy's T-shirt showed all that off, leaving not much to the imagination. Unfortunately, my imagination was running rampant, as was my heart. I was doubly grateful for the pulsing beat of the bar music drowning out the organ in my chest drumming three times faster than usual.

When we met earlier in the day, Tommy had the same effect on me and I credited the shiver up my spine to being out of practice in the art of attraction. I was instantly overwhelmed by his dark looks. Yet his defensive vibe of crossed arms and refusal to shake my hand left a salty impression on me. His standoffish presence set up a wall between us, and I scolded myself for overreacting to his rock star hotness.

As Ivy and I crossed the night club, I was conscious of people watching us, wondering myself how *she* ended up escorting *me*? Despite her innocent look, Ivy walked like she owned the room, and many eyes followed her every move. The stares could have also been intended for the man making a bee-line for us. With dark, chin-length waves and even darker, intense eyes, Gage Everly's focus was solely on his wife. Within seconds, he cupped her cheeks and kissed her like he hadn't seen her in years. Ivy's arm was still looped with mine, making me the literal third encircle his stiff shaft. Coarse hairs tickled my knuckles, and I drew upward, caressing the trail leading to his belly button while stroking his length.

"Fuck, darlin'. Slow is good, but fast is better." I repeated the motion, and he swallowed. "Okay, slow is good, too," he muttered, lowering his mouth to my neck.

"Might need you to sample me. Give it a taste," he murmured as I continued to tug him, increasing the pressure as I squeezed. His hand covered mine, guiding me. I knew one thing. I couldn't taste him. That was too much. Wild thoughts threatened to ruin it. *Where had his...been? Who had he been with lately? How many? How often?*

"Stop thinking," he murmured as his lips parted, and he sucked at my skin—the same skin that had ripples and folds, a testament to my age. My head tilted, allowing him more access. I was ridiculously drunk on this man, letting him intoxicate me with gruff words, a scruffy jaw, and wicked fingers. His hand palmed my backside and squeezed, pressing me toward him as my palm increased in speed.

"Mouth, now," he demanded.

"No," I said, my voice weak. I might have misunderstood, because his lips crushed mine, commanding I open for him. I faltered in surprise as I stroked, but he squeezed my smaller fingers within his large ones, forcing me to continue jerking him. My thumb caressed the slit on his tip, and moisture seeped outward, lubricating the pad of my finger. I used it to increase the beating, the stroking, the rhythm. All the while, his mouth moved over mine, a haphazard pattern of kissing and nipping.

I worried I was doing it wrong, taking too long, but pressed on his chest, guiding him to turn and lean on the wall. His stance relaxed, and his legs spread. His back held him upward as his head fell to the plaster behind him. His hand continued to work with mine, and I snuck a peek at what we were collectively doing. That unfamiliar flutter rekindled, filling my lower belly as I stared at what I considered a scandalously delicious vision. I was helping him get off while he was working on himself. *Oh my.*

My heart beat as rapidly as my arm moved.

"Right there, beautiful," he hissed. "So close."

With strength I didn't know I had, I increased the pressure, the speed, the dexterity of my grip, and warm liquid spurted from his tip. My fist was covered in hot stickiness, slipping through my fingers and coating our collective palms.

"Enough," he whispered, stilling my fingers. His eyes closed, and he tapped his head against the wall. His clean hand pressed against his face and rubbed downward. Something was wrong. Shaking my hand free of any residue, I stepped back from him.

"Darlin'?" he questioned, his eyes suddenly on mine. My heart plummeted to my stomach. I didn't understand what I was feeling. I couldn't believe what I'd just done. I…I had to get out of there. So, I did what any self-respecting women who just fulfilled a fantasy with a sexy strange man in an empty ballroom on a long-overdue vacation did—I ran. Wayward thoughts raced through my mind as the click of my own heels matched the thudding in my chest.

When leaving the hospital, aftercare was always part of the experience. What you did *after*—the procedure, the treatment, the incision that cut deep. However, nothing could have prepared me for how I'd take care of myself after Tommy Carrigan. There was no list, no instruction manual online at patient dot com for matters of the heart. No checklist. Nope, the aftercare sheet was a blank page. How did you treat tingling lips, skin rough from scruff-burn, and an ache so fierce your heart felt like it might burst?

# 3

## Morning Delight

Shame washed over me at how I ran from Tommy Carrigan, a man ridiculously sexy for over forty. It wasn't fair. And neither was how I treated him. Running had never been my thing. I was committed to the core—to my children, to my marriage, to my job. Then my marriage failed, and I got breast cancer. It put things in perspective for me. Life was short, and I was only forty-three.

This led me to a yoga class the next morning with Ivy and Masie. I still didn't understand the young rock star wife's obsession with me, but she was sweet, and she'd included my eighteen-year old, Masie, in the invitation.

"A girls' morning," she cheerfully said as she texted me. "Breakfast afterward."

I allowed myself another torturous indulgence. Seeing Ivy would remind me of my previous night's escapade in a vacant ballroom with the band manager of Collision. His life was rock stars. Mine was pearls and cardigans. We were polar opposites, and yet, for a few heated moments, we lived on the same planet.

"Isn't Ivy da bomb, Mom?" Masie asked as we walked to the north side of the resort. A grassy area was shadowed by the towering building and provided a serene space for morning yoga.

"Yes, da bomb," I replied, wondering what that meant. I chuckled to myself. Kids and their euphemisms, I couldn't keep up.

"Her life seems so awesome. Gage Everly as a husband, and her two girls are so sweet." Masie couldn't stop sharing humorous stories of her babysitting adventure the night before. At one point, the fourth band member visited the Everlys' penthouse condo, and Masie had more misadventures to share with me. I was worried she was a little star-struck by the whole aura of Collision, particularly their youngest member, Weston Reid. I didn't need her having a vacation fling with someone she'd never see again.

The thought stopped me.

Wasn't that exactly what I'd done? Although allowing someone to finger me couldn't actually be labelled a *fling*. It was more like a one-night stand, of sorts, kind of, maybe…Actually, it hadn't been any of those things. It had been mind-blowing, and my thighs still hummed from the heat. A pulse beat at my core with the memory. Of course, I couldn't sleep after I returned to my small rented condo. Thank goodness, the kids had their own room. I tossed and turned, my thighs clenching, my fingers twitching, yearning for a repeat of what Tommy had done to me. But I cursed those thoughts repeatedly, putting myself in my place with reminders that he was affiliated with a famous band, and I was just…me.

Mother of two. Breast cancer survivor. Professional assistant.

"Edie." Ivy's voice echoed across the lawn as people gathered for yoga. A walking path was at the edge of the property, connecting resorts and allowing visitors access to the ocean side scenery. My boss had covered part of this vacation to Hawaii, calling it a bonus. Despite the previous days off for medical leave, he told me I deserved a break with my family, and as the Christmas holiday was a slow time, ten days of vacation were allotted to me.

A scarf covered my hair again, although admittedly it was warm in the early heat of the day. I didn't have the typical skinny girl yoga pants, or a cute work-out shirt, but wore a spandex skort and a tank top, possibly a size too small as it was Masie's. Ivy's eyes fell to my chest before smiling and lifting to mine.

"You look sexy for a workout," she teased, and I blushed, glancing down at the swell of cleavage peeking over the red shirt.

"She always looks good," Masie added, a touch of support in her proud daughter voice. She'd been so reassuring when my hair fell out in clumps and my body bloated. *You're still you, Mom*, she told me over and over again. It was too much for a teenage girl to witness. *It wasn't fair*, I often screamed, as she was my sole supporter when it should have been David, my ex.

"Ready for this?" Ivy teased, spreading out the mandatory beach towel over the grass.

"Ready as I'm going to be." I'd never done yoga, but I had started working out regularly. It was a way to combat the swelling of my body and improve my mindset. I had to do something. The routine stuck long after the treatments ended. I reminded myself that no one was looking specifically at me. Women come in all shapes and sizes, and despite the public place, this was nothing.

We sat as instructed, legs crossed and minds emptied, only mine refused to go blank. I continued to see Tommy's dark eyes, inky and concerned as he spoke to me. I had to chuckle when I thought of his surprise at seeing my underwear and the ridiculous struggle that took place before the shock of him entering me with his fingers. The mere thought made me wet, and my core clenched. Sitting cross-legged was not a good position for the images in my brain.

We stood and followed a series of stretching and twisting and balancing, until finally, we leaned forward, bracing palms flat on the ground, shoulder width apart, while our feet separated, forming an equilibrium of arms and legs, with backsides in the air. The downward dog position. My head lowered to center between my elbows and I had a perfect view of the walking path behind me when I should have been concentrating on my form.

A man in dark shorts and a sweat-laden white T-shirt walked slowly on the wooden path, one hand on his hips, his barrel chest rising and falling with exertion, as if he was winding down a long run. With earbuds in his ears, his fingers scrolled over a phone. He paced a step or two before stopping and facing our direction. I became acutely aware that my ass was in the air, pointed at him. I couldn't see far enough to know if he saw me, but heat rose up my chest. My arms shook, and my hamstrings ached as the instructor told us to press backward. I noticed the man begin to walk forward toward our yoga haven.

"Oh no," I muttered.

*He's not looking at me*, I argued with myself, but Tommy—yes, of course it was him—stalked straight for the collection of yoga participants. Always preferring the back of anything—a classroom, a theatre, a bus—I was at the back of this group, and when he stopped short at my side, it was obvious he recognized me.

"Uncle Tommy," Ivy hissed, clearly annoyed at his intrusion but keeping her focus on her position.

He dropped down to the standard form for downward dog, making it look effortless as he bent forward and stretched out next to me.

"Didn't take you for a yoga expert, darlin'," he greeted me.

"How would you know?" I quietly snapped, leaning forward to support myself. He chuckled.

"Always a question."

"So, you're Ivy's uncle," I interjected, ignoring the jab. My legs shook. My arms ached. I couldn't concentrate.

"Yeah, she's my niece." His voice softened, the gruff smoky sound lighter, drifting, like the thought saddened him. I ignored the fact he basically repeated what I just said and swung my head so I could look at Ivy on my left before rotating back to Tommy on my right. I noticed no resemblance between them.

"Back to yoga. Do you do this often?" he asked, a teasing curiosity in his tone as his mouth twitched while he spoke. His head was turned to look at me behind his elbows. He was breaking form.

"First time for everything," I mocked, and felt my face redden. Last night had certainly been a first.

The curl of his lips told me he knew where my thoughts were—in a dark ballroom, with his fingers…*Oh goodness*, I couldn't think of that, flinching as moisture seeped between my legs in this awkward position.

"You're breaking form," he said, noting my thighs that momentarily pressed together. My knees bent.

"I can't do this with you watching me," I snapped, humiliated at being caught thinking of him and stretching my body in such a way it brought on lurid, luscious thoughts of him doing things to me. My face reddened further, possibly even purpled. I was nearly suffocating with dirty thoughts of Tommy.

"What happened, darlin'?" he teased, the question reminiscent of my momentary freak out from the night before when he reached for my breasts. The reminder forced my eyes to my cleavage, blatantly on display as the leaning position lowered my top, accentuating the curve of my breasts. I'd had them restored to my 36Ds as best I could after the surgery.

*Go away*, I wanted to mutter at the same time my brain cried, *Take me*. I was ridiculous.

"I just can't do this with you staring at me," I said, peeking around my elbow at him.

"Why not?"

"Because..." I'm self-conscious enough as it is, I wanted to add, but the instructor's mic crackled.

"Lady in red," the instructor said. "You're breaking form, honey. Straighten the legs. Tuck in your abs. Accentuate the backside."

My elbows snapped, nearly collapsing me, and I wanted to bang my head on the ground. She was speaking to me. Tommy chuckled beside me.

"Okay, I'll leave you to your struggles. But you know what seems better than this position, darlin'?"

I was afraid to ask. "What?" I grumbled.

"Bacon and eggs with me." My head swung to face him. He'd folded down to his knees, looked at his phone, and spoke to it as he addressed me.

"I'm not done here."

"I know where you can finish your work-out."

"No," I said, but my body screamed *yes*.

"Room 413. Half an hour." He rolled up on his toes and stood as if unfolding an accordion. His eyes met mine as I remained in my awkward position. Dark orbs flicked to my raised backside.

"No," I repeated, but he smiled slowly and walked away.

+ + +

I couldn't believe I was doing this. I hadn't even waited fifteen minutes. My concentration was completely lost. I folded back on my ankles, excused myself from Ivy and Masie, and headed for the lobby. I told myself, I would knock on his door, and he wouldn't be there because I was early. Then I told myself, I was stupid *because* I was early. It made me look desperate. Then I internally argued, I was being ridiculous, and making up the whole thing; he never invited me to his room for breakfast. So, I knocked once, waited, and then spun for the elevator. Defeat filled me instantly even though I'd been self-deprecating anyway.

I hadn't taken one full step when the door flung open. Eyes appraised me as I stood in my make-shift yoga get-up. I hadn't bothered to shower or change. I figured he could take me as I was. I meant, take me for how I was dressed. I…oh, forget it, I cursed myself.

"Edie," he said, eyes roaming back up my body. "I'm glad you're early. I'm starving." Did I imagine his teeth snap on that second sentence? Could I believe I was about to enter a strange man's resort room? As I stepped forward, I realized Tommy didn't feel like a stranger. I didn't have thoughts of him being an ax-murderer or something extreme. He managed a group of young men, whom I imagined could be unruly. His niece was part of that mix, and I'd seen him react to her daughters on our first meeting. This man was…a man…not a killer. My heart raced, nonetheless.

Then I noticed his attire. He stood before me dressed only in a towel.

"I couldn't concentrate," I replied, my eyes wandering over the firmness of his body. Abs. Pecs. Biceps. Oh my.

He nodded slowly, noting my appraisal. "I can help with that concentration."

"I can come back later," I stressed, my voice squeaking as I pointed over my shoulder for the elevator, but my eyes refused to pull away from the trail of hair leading above the curl of the towel wrapped low around his waist. *Mother of all things holy.*

"Breakfast is coming," he said, reaching out for my arm and tugging me into his room.

*Breakfast*, my mouth watered. *Coming*, my throat swallowed. Oh goodness, I was a mess.

I walked forward on stumbling feet. His room was a king-size suite. The large bed was the focus, but a couch with a small dining table for two also filled the room. It was a breezy space for one. The balcony door brightened the room, as the curtain was drawn wide, and the glass door stood open allowing in the subtle resort sounds and the whistling winds.

He stood behind me, his presence emitting the heat of a shower. I took a deep breath, preparing to speak, when he spoke instead.

"Didn't finish your workout?" He paused. "I can help with that, too." Thick hands came to my hips and his breath tickled my neck. Instantly, I tilted, allowing him access to my skin. *What was I doing?* I wondered only momentarily as my body started to tingle with his nearness and the flutters in my lower belly took flight like a flock of seagulls. "I didn't take you for a yoga girl. We need to talk about your form, Edie."

"You seem to have a check list of things you don't take me for," I said, not recognizing my own voice. "What do you take me for, then?"

He huffed against my neck, kissing me in a place I noticed this morning had a tender mark of broken skin. He'd given me a hickey. Not a full-fledged bruise, but enough of a purple scratch to mark me. I had a hard time explaining it to Masie, who eyed it suspiciously as we walked to yoga.

*"I think something bit me," I said, "and I reacted to it."* It was almost too close to the truth.

"Hmmm…" He hummed against my skin, and it prickled in anticipation of his lips meeting mine, which hadn't happened yet. He simply teased me with his closeness. "I'm not sure how to take you yet." His voice purred with the double entendre.

Thick hands caressed up and down my sides, curving over my hips and tugging up the skirt on my skort.

"Now, what the fuck is this?" He chuckled, and I should have been embarrassed, but I had to laugh. If I was getting an education in stranger sex, he was getting one in older women's apparel.

"It's a skort. It's like a skirt over shorts."

"What the fuck?" he repeated, lifting it higher as he stepped back to appraise the contraption. I swatted at his hand, laughing as he peeked under the skirting, trying to find an opening. "Take it off," he demanded.

"What?" I choked.

"Take. It. Off," he repeated slower, lower, as if I couldn't understand basic English.

"Why?"

"Always a question," he muttered, shaking his head. He crossed his thick arms over his bare chest. He hadn't bothered to dress or even suggest it. There was something in the way he looked at me. Something in the way his arms stiffened over his chest and his widened stance that pissed me off just enough to do as he said. I forced my skort down, kicked out of my tennis shoes and stood before him in low-cut purple panties. His eyes widened, and I tugged at the hem of Masie's tank top. In the light of day, the slight bulge of my stomach rested over the waist of my underwear. I was pear-shaped at best, but the underwear dissected me in the wrong places. Maybe I needed to rethink trying to be a tough bitch in response to him. I wasn't one of those women, anyway.

My fingers folded into the thin material and I began to stretch it toward my thighs. Tommy stepped forward so quickly he startled me, and I bumped into his bed. His hand cupped my face to stop me from tumbling, and he kissed me. The full onslaught again, but this time I was better prepared for the intensity. His mouth opened immediately, and I followed his lead, loving the confidence he expressed in kissing. His plump lips were assured, experienced, and surprisingly tender. He sucked and sipped and slipped his tongue across the seam, taking me to another level. He tipped my head, and our tongues tangled deeper, stretching for connection. He swept the inside of my mouth before drawing back.

"We need to work on your technique," he said, and I thought he meant my kissing, but he spun me to face the bed, and I pitched forward. "Your downward dog could use practice."

*Oh, Lord.*

"I didn't know you were a yoga aficionado," I said, though the statement was breathy.

"I have many skills," he said, guiding my upper back to lower to the bed. "Stretch your arms forward." I did as he said. My backside raised in the air. My arms flattened on the bed cover, and he stroked up and down my spine, rubbing a line down the bone before massaging my sides. Then he pressed forward, the stiff length of him meeting me square between the cheeks of my ass.

"I seem to have developed a problem when it comes to you, Edie," he said, his typical puddle-plopping sound dropping to a handful of gravel dumped into water. "I can't seem to figure you out." His thick hands continued to caress up my sides, while tugging me gently backward, forcing my backside to meet his hard length in short, steady beats. If I wasn't so turned on, it might be reminiscent of a bad comedy movie. The rhythm continued, like a quick puff of air. *Uhn. Huh. Uhn. Huh.*

"Ever have sex like this, Edie?" The crass question should have given me pause, but my mind was fogging on the rhythm he set, the pulsing of my core, and the liquid pooling at the apex of my thighs. I was wet, and the damp material of his towel aided the moisture forming on my cotton underwear.

"Rarely," I stammered, not wishing to recall the few times David and I mixed up our sexual encounters. My response elicited the sound of a towel unravelling and the wet fabric hitting the floor. Bare skin hit the back of my thighs as he returned to his steady hammering. *A tap. A tap. A tap.*

I was coming undone, the fiber of my being beginning to unravel. The flutters in my belly had progressed from the flock of seagulls to a storm of flapping birds. My fingers gripped the duvet.

"This will be a better work out," he groaned before saying my name. I didn't know if my name was a question or a statement, but all I could answer was, "Yes." My underwear slid to my knees, and I pressed inward, forcing them to my ankles. His foot held them down and he tapped my heel to step out of one side. His fingers caressed over the cool globes of my backside and I couldn't believe I was about to do this. I also couldn't imagine stopping. I was so wound up, I was ready to snap. Tears welled in my eyes. I wanted this so badly I ached.

The nightstand drawer opened, and I heard the rip of foil. I almost laughed. It was a sound I hadn't heard in nearly twenty years. How did I get here? How did I get in this position?

All thought escaped me when a thick finger slipped inside me, and I gasped.

"Fine wine," he muttered, before removing his finger, and I whimpered. "Ready to breathe again, Edie?" I rolled my head against the bed cover. I didn't have the breath to speak, afraid I'd crack if he didn't enter me.

"I need the word, darlin'."

"Yes," I exhaled, and he slammed into me so hard I pressed forward on the mattress. I yelped, and he stilled. His hands rubbed down my spine, steadying me before drawing my hips backward. He filled me so deep the sac of his balls pressed against my entrance. A strange sense of completion rippled through me, as if I'd never had sex before, and I practically cried at that thought. It hadn't ever been like this.

He slid to my entrance as he had the night before with his fingers, but I clenched my thighs, attempting to hold him in. Thrusting forward, he chuckled.

"I like how you're a little greedy even though you want to deny it, Edie." He pressed a kiss to my shoulder blade before repeating the near exit, only to fill me almost instantly. The pace increased, the sound of slapping skin becoming a metronome of music. He pressed at the inside of my thigh, forcing my knee to rise from the bed. The position opened me up.

"You're breaking my form," I tried to joke, but his deep thrust cut off the words.

"I'm hoping to break many things," he muttered, and my heart pinched in my chest, because I knew Tommy Carrigan was going to break not just my heart, but all of me.

His fingers slipped to the spot I needed, paying attention as he stroked and parted and circled while he entered me. I screamed into the duvet as I came and felt a second wave instantly as he pulsed his release. The jolt of him, stiff and vibrating deep inside me, set off subtle aftershocks but not enough to cause an eruption.

"Sorry, darlin'," he said, as his forehead came to my back. "I sensed you needed another minute to get there again, but I couldn't hold on any longer." His forehead rolled back and forth on my damp skin. "What are you doing to me?" he muttered before pressing a quick kiss to my back and standing. He pulled out of me slowly and moisture seeped down my thigh, but I collapsed on the bed. *I just need a minute*, I thought, closing my eyes.

I heard him step away and return with a towel. He startled me as he wiped between my thighs. Then he stretched behind me. We lay sideways across the bed. His chest hit my back and an arm curled over my waist.

"Feel good, darlin'?" he murmured to the skin on my neck.

"Just need a minute," I said, my voice drifting. He chuckled and that's the only sound I heard before I slipped into sleep.

+ + +

It didn't feel like enough time passed before a knock came to the door. I jolted upright, wondering only briefly where I was and why I was still partially naked. However, I was covered by the duvet, and a pillow had been placed under my head. A resort server entered the room and set a large tray on the table. He smiled down at me and I rolled to cover my face as he walked out of sight. I didn't want to think about how many times he entered this room to find a woman in this bed. The subtle click of the door set me upright. Scooting for the edge of the bed, I found my underwear and skort right where they landed on the floor. Further embarrassment set in, and heat colored my cheeks.

"Hungry, darlin'?" Tommy asked, reentering my view, now dressed in jeans without a shirt.

"I should go." My voice rasped from sleep, and I searched for a clock. "What time is it?"

"You only slept a half-hour." I reached for my scarf to find my hair. Somewhere, it had slipped off my head. "You look beautiful," he said, and my eyes lowered. I couldn't look at him when he complimented me.

"I didn't sleep well last night," I offered, ignoring his kind words. I remained at the edge of the bed, and he stepped forward, cupping my chin. His eyes examined my face before he spoke. "Breakfast is ready."

I followed him over to the small table and sat while he removed metal lids for two plates. Scrambled eggs, crisp bacon, and fruit. I inhaled. "Smells delicious. Thank you."

The gratitude surprised him, and he paused mid-air with the coffee carafe in his hand. I waved him off from pouring me a cup.

"I don't like the flavor."

"Huh, another thing I didn't have you pegged for." I noted the tease in his voice.

"How poorly you've perceived me so far," I countered. He sat and stared at me a moment.

"Yes, I think I have." I didn't know what to make of that statement. If I thought there was a compliment in there, I couldn't find it.

It should have been awkward. Two random adults having sex in the morning. I couldn't even call it a one-night stand. The walk of shame was supposed to happen in the morning, not the actual sexcapades. I didn't know what else to call what we'd done. Make love? Nope, the term did not fit. Sex, definitely. A slight tingle returned, my imagination leading me to ask him for a second helping. And I wasn't referring to the eggs. However, I took a hefty bite to rid my thoughts of the bed.

We ate for a moment in silence.

"How long?" he asked, and I swallowed the piece of bacon in my mouth before chewing it properly. "How long did you have it?" He looked up at my hair and instantly my fingers went to the wayward curls. I didn't have a clue what I might look like, and I started combing the edges near my ears. His hand reached across the table to stop me.

"I've been cancer-free a few months. I had months of chemotherapy before that. Aggressive. I just wanted it out of my body. I had a single mastectomy and then added the implants to both sides to balance me out." I offered a weak chuckle at my vanity. I didn't consider myself vain, but I also couldn't fathom anything other than the decision I made. "This vacation was a celebration of sorts. I had survived. For now." I sighed.

"Why the sigh?" He asked, his eyes still focused on my face.

"I guess at one point, I thought I might die, sooner rather than later. It was an awful period in my life. Worse than the divorce."

He sat back in his seat, but took his coffee mug with him. After a sip, he said, "Just confirming what I already assumed. So, you aren't married."

"No," I blurted with a laugh, and then focused on him. "Are you?" My voice cracked. Hadn't I heard these horror stories of men who worked with bands, sleeping their way through the tours, while their wife raised children back in some small-town?

"Nope," he said immediately, chuckling at the expression on my face. "Not my thing. Never plan to be." The statement wasn't an admission. It wasn't a threat. It was a declaration—*don't get any ideas in your head, Edie; it's only sex.* I nodded, smiling weakly as if I understood. As if I were cool with it, as my kids would say.

I took a deep breath hoping to redirect the conversation.

"So, a band manager," I began. He stared back at me a moment, then confirmed. "A band manager."

My eyebrow rose, hinting I wanted more detail than a parrot response.

"I took over the boys when they were still raw talent. They were an opening act for a band on the edge of their retirement."

"I didn't know bands retired."

"Ever hear of Boys II Men? New Kids On The Block? NSYNC? Bands retire," he adamantly stated.

"Wow. Never pegged you for a pop culture, boy-band kind of guy."

He laughed in response. "Oh, what kind of guy do you have me pegged as?"

I thought for a moment, tapping my chin. "My first thought, Rolling Stones, unequivocally. But the more I learn, I'm not so sure. I think under the hardcore rock star manager might be something a little softer." He choked on his coffee, laughter filling his expression.

"Now, now, don't be pinning me as some soft rock freak, but I do like me some Stevie Nicks." I laughed as he referenced the female rock queen.

"Annie Lennox?" I raised a brow.

"Her, too."

"Madonna," I suggested.

"Blasphemy." But his soft chuckle told me he might like a song or two of hers as well.

"Music is your life, isn't it?"

"Of course," he said, setting his cup down.

"Do you play something?" The shift in his seat and the glance out the window answered the question. He did. But I sensed the subject wasn't one he was going to share with me. Silence swirled between us.

"So," I drew out the word. "If I were a song, what would I be?"

"Something classic," he stated immediately and my lips twisted.

"You really think I'm boring, don't you?" My voice fell as did my shoulders. I must be so plain Jane compared to who he usually slept with. He tilted his head and then motioned toward the bed. "Uhm…no." I giggled and his head spun back to me. He stared at my eyes, travelled down to my lips, and fell to my chest.

"'Barracuda'." His face was dead serious, but I barked out a laugh. "What?"

"You had me down on my knees when I saw you again." He misquoted the song, but his voice lowered, and I shivered under the deep tenor of his voice. The seductive song was certainly not me. I was no temptress like that. I continued to laugh, shaking my head.

"What do you think?" One eyebrow rose on his playful face.

"For myself?" I sat forward for a moment. "Maybe more 'Landslide'."

His face lowered. "How old are you?"

"Forty-three."

He stared at me. "You're not dead."

"Not yet," I chuckled without humor, and an awkwardness fell between us.

"I don't mean that," he corrected. "I mean, that song's about change. What are you reflecting on?"

"Life," I said, adamantly, letting my eyes drift to the bed.

"Darlin'," he said, leaning on the table. Why did the way he say that endearment make my skin tingle? He had a touch of Southern drawl, but it was the way he purposely rolled the *r* that made my insides leap. "How many one-night stands you have in life?"

I sat up straighter at the question.

"Why?" His hand lowered, and I prepared for him to smack the table in frustration. "None," I answered. He swept his hand outward toward the bed, and I lowered my eyes. "It's morning," I justified.

He laughed. A hearty, rock the table, belly full of laughter.

"Okay, so what about me?" he asked.

"'No More I Love Yous'." The Annie Lennox song spilled out of my mouth. He sat straighter, his eyes not even blinking. I smiled to soften the odd choice of words. "I mean, who wouldn't love a song that uses the word *woebegone*?"

"Is woebegone how you see me?" His voice sobered, and I didn't want to ruin the playfulness of this game.

"No," I tapped my chin, lying, because there was a sadness just under the surface of him, just under the tattoo over his heart, that I couldn't read. "I think 'I Put a Spell On You' might be more fitting."

"You think I put a spell on you, darlin'?" He questioned, his mouth curling at one corner.

"Definitely," I said. "Most definitely," I added, nodding. The flirtation smoldered between us. "Actually," I paused. "I was going to name you a Bee Gees' song, but you don't strike me as a Bee Gees kind of guy." I lowered my tone to match his, as he kept telling me I didn't seem one way or another.

He laughed again, drumming his hands on the table and making his coffee mug rattle.

"That reminds me. You owe me a dance."

# 4

## Walk of Shame

Breakfast had been sweet, and parting did include sorrow, but as the flirting ran dry, it was either to bed again or exit. As I seemed to be in a pattern of flight, I opted to leave, but not before Tommy questioned me.

"Why'd you run last night, darlin'?" he asked. I didn't have a good answer. Did I tell the truth that I panicked? Did I lie and say it was my normal response to awkward situations? I'd seen his face when we finished, and I couldn't read him. I didn't *know* him. I was caught between shame and thrill.

"I don't know." That was the best answer I could give him. We stood at his door after I thanked him once again for breakfast. Was I supposed to thank him for sex as well? I had no idea how to do this sort of thing. I'd been with David for twenty years. When we finished sex, we rolled over, each to our own corner of the bed. Sometimes, we didn't even say *goodnight*.

Tommy stroked my cheek with the thick pad of his thumb. His eyes searched mine, and I realized there would be no words between us. He kissed me softly, tenderly, sweetly. It was a kiss of goodbye, and I wanted to cry as his mouth covered mine, pulling at my lip as if to say, *take care*, and *I'll think of you*, and *this was fun*. The last one cheapened the experience just a little, and I lightly pressed on his chest to signal I couldn't take any more.

I returned to my room, showered with quiet tears, and put on my bathing suit to brave the walk of shame in front of my children. Masie texted me to say she was already at the pool. Caleb hadn't even gotten out of bed until I entered the small condo. He called out a sleepy hello, and I answered with, "I'm showering." He left me a note, he was pool bound as well.

I quickly found Masie in the middle of the hubbub of rock stars. Surrounded by subtle bodyguards I hadn't noticed the day before, Gage and crew had a small section of the pool deck quarantined. Ivy waved me over, alerting the pool security I was with them as I drew near. To my surprise, Tommy sat in a lounge chair, laidback and relaxed as if not a care in the world. As if he hadn't rocked my world with mind blowing sex in a position I'd practically never experienced. I sighed, attempting to hold my head high as I passed the chairs filled with lazy rock stars to an empty one next to Ivy.

"How are you?" she asked, a touch of concern in her tone.

"Where did you disappear to?" Masie interjected, even though I texted her to say I was using the resort gym instead of finishing the yoga session.

"I worked out," I said, and Tommy coughed from his end of the line.

"I went to look for you," Masie said. I hadn't counted on that, although I knew that her nature was to worry about me.

"I went for a walk." I hated lying to her. She was a good girl and a great daughter.

"But you're okay?" she asked, and I sat in the lounger with a huff.

"I'm fine." I might have said it a bit too brusquely, but I didn't understand the inquisition. So I was missing for an hour, hour and a half tops, big deal.

"Leave Mom be," Caleb said, appearing out of nowhere and sitting at my feet. He was a good kid, too, albeit wrapped up in his own world. He hadn't been home during the worst of the cancer treatment. I didn't want him missing college to come take care of me, as his protective nature would have wanted to do. I lied to him often, saying I was fine, but I know Masie most likely told him the truth. Some days were rougher than others.

I laid back and listened, the conversation filling with chatter from two little girls, groans of hungover twenty-something adult males, and the occasional teasing of a young married couple. It was heavenly and mind numbing, and the dialogues flowed around me, lulling me into a comfortable state of lazy.

The heat was stifling, despite a swift breeze, and I stood to enter the pool. I wore an orange strapless tankini with a black polka-dot bottom.

Not the sexiest, but I was well past bikini days like the slim bodies of Ivy and Masie. As I entered the pool, an older woman stood at the end of the stairs.

"You have a lovely family," she said to me, and I stopped one step from the pool's bottom.

"Thank you," I said, glancing over at my two children, proud of the compliment. Masie had my original hair color, brunette, but streaked with gold highlights from the sun. Caleb was tall, his body filling out, on the verge of manhood, with subtle chest hairs. His hair matched his sister's, minus the golden streaks. I loved them both unconditionally.

"Your husband is a fine catch," she offered, and I turned to face her. Following her line of vision, she focused on Tommy who sat forward on his chair, staring in the direction of where I stood. Dark aviator glasses covered his eyes, though.

"Oh, he's not my husband," I nervously giggled, glancing back at him before addressing this shrunken raisin of a woman who obviously had eyes for Tommy.

"Oh my, unfortunate man," she said, patting my hand, and I smiled at the hidden compliment. I twisted slightly to see Tommy shake his head, but I assumed he couldn't have heard the woman from this distance.

"Are those little ones your granddaughters?" So much for compliments, I decided, as I looked at Ava and Emaline, Gage and Ivy's daughters.

"Uhm, no," I chuckled to lessen the sting. How old did I look?

"Didn't think so, but you never know. Grandparents are getting younger and younger these days." She smiled sweetly, and I guessed her age to be almost double my own. Just out of curiosity, I had to ask.

"Who did you think was my family?"

She chuckled as she responded. "The whole lot of them. You look like one happy family on vacation together. Those two girls look like sisters." She nodded at the huddled Ivy and Masie, who were whispering to each other. "Thought you and the man might be celebrating something special, as you both look so happy. My husband and I took our family on a vacation to celebrate our wedding anniversary." She paused. "That was back when it had been fifty magical years."

"That's sweet," I said, trying to process how she thought I'd mothered all those boys and girls and was married to Tommy. Ava and Emaline saved the day by entering the pool, followed by Gage, West, and Masie.

I didn't want to notice West paying extra attention to Masie. It had heartbreak written all over it for her. She was only eighteen, and he was a twenty-two-year-old rock star. As the newest member of the band, I assumed he was still trying to find his way amongst the older three, who seemed like life-long friends. Caleb had tried to fill me in, telling me that Collision was one of the hottest bands out there with their alternative rock sound, sultry ballads, and raging songs. After sharing a few titles with me, I was able to admit I'd heard them, but I couldn't say I knew anything more about its members, or their manager. He was a music buff, and playing guitar would have been his dream, had his father not driven him toward baseball.

I exited the pool to find a margarita by my seat.

"Tommy took the liberty," Ivy said as I sat. I held up the tempting drink, ready to tip my head in thanks, but found him speaking to a young woman on his right. She wore a red bikini. I sighed as I took a hefty sip of the salty sweet lime combination.

"It must be hard to fight off all the women," I muttered, referring to Tommy, but thinking of Gage as well. "I don't know how you do it."

"Oh, you get used to it." Ivy chuckled. "Although I'm not the one with a jealous streak. Gage is rather...possessive. I don't worry. Gage would never cheat. Tommy would kill him."

I wanted to believe, for her sake, that her man would never stray. I wanted to believe it with my whole heart, but knowing what happened to me, I found it hard to have such faith in complete loyalty. Her comment about Tommy gave me a thought as well. It must be nice to know she was protected from all sides—a sort of checks and balances for her trust.

"Tommy told me you're his niece," I said, hoping to learn more about him and her relationship. Ivy didn't open her eyes as she lay in the Hawaiian sun.

"Yep. My mother was his younger sister," she whispered without offering more information. "So, what do you do for a living?" she asked, blatantly redirecting the conversation.

"I work for a manufacturing company."

"Butt plugs," Caleb coughed, and Petty sat forward on his lounger a few seats down.

"What?" Ivy giggled.

"We manufacture—"

"Butt plugs," Caleb coughed again, and Jared started laughing as well.

"Caleb!" I admonished. "They do not make…" I lowered my voice. "Butt plugs." This set Jared laughing and Petty cracking a mischievous smile. "They manufacture plastic parts and pieces for a variety of companies."

"One of which makes butt plugs," Caleb said, wiggling his brows, and then squirming in his seat.

"Stop it," I laughed. "I don't know that."

"Mom, please." Caleb laughed. He'd researched my company for a business project in college, finding all the subsidiaries and retailers who purchased products we supplied. One happened to include a sex toy manufacturer who specialized in…butt plugs.

"Do you get samples, Edie?" Petty asked, and Tommy reached over and swatted the curly blond in the back of the head.

"Be respectful," Tommy demanded.

"Just asking," Petty grumbled like a petulant child.

"You didn't answer," Jared stated, and fell into another fit of laughter.

"No, I don't get samples." For some reason, my eyes flipped to Tommy's, but I couldn't see his eyes behind his dark lenses. Besides, he had returned to his reclined position, and another girl had joined the first at his side. I decided I needed another drink. We weren't family, but we were too close for comfort to this group of band members.

Standing at the bar, Gage came up beside me. The dark-haired, dark-eyed singer looked every bit a rock star, or a tortured poet, with his layers of leather necklaces and a wrist full of bracelets. I noticed that all the guys, including Tommy, had the same set of two: a solid silver band and separately, a row of brown beads.

"Hey," he said, looking over his shoulder at his wife before turning back to me. "I wanted to ask you to back off a little." The comment startled me.

"From Tommy?" I blurted, looking over Gage's shoulder at a man clearly busy with other women.

"Tommy?" he questioned, brow crinkling. "No, Ivy."

"What?" I asked, looking back at the young musician.

"Yeah. It's just…she's become sort of instantly attached to you, and it isn't good for her."

I blinked in surprise. I'd noticed the same thing, but I certainly hadn't pursued a friendship with someone nearly fifteen years younger than me.

"I don't—"

He cut me off. "Ever since her mom died, it's like she's always searching for her. Missing her. I don't know what it is about you, but she's latched on, and stuck hard. You're all I've heard about for the past twenty-four hours."

I stared at him in disbelief. "I don't think I understand. I didn't mean to do anything to Ivy. In fact, she spoke to me first. She asked me to join you last night, and included me this morning for yoga. She invited Masie to the pool. I'm just here with my daughter."

"Look," he said, brushing long fingers through his chin-length hair. "I just mean I think you should step back. Even if she asks, maybe tell her no."

I blinked again before speaking. "Why?"

"Her mom died of breast cancer." His eyes shot to my head scarf and away. "I'm not implying—"

It was my turn to interrupt, and I raised a hand to stop him. "I'm not sure what you're implying, but I do have breast cancer." I sighed. "*Did*. And anything that has happened with Ivy was never meant to hurt her, or mislead her, or anything else you might think. She's a sweet girl, and my family has enjoyed her company, but if you don't want us around her, we don't need to be." With that, I stepped away from Gage despite the protest of my name that echoed behind me. I neared the row of chairs, guarded by security but not protected well enough if those girls kept talking to Tommy and the woman Petty pulled into the VIP section last night currently sat on his lounger.

"Where's your drink, darlin'?" Tommy asked me, as I returned empty-handed, and I almost snapped that it was none of his damn business. Instead, I wondered how he even noticed I walked to the bar and returned without one, as his concentration had been on the suddenly *three* women next to him. I didn't directly answer him as I continued walking.

"I passed," I said, reaching my chair and picking up my bag as I slipped on my flip-flops.

"Mom?" Masie questioned as Tommy said, "Your bathing suit should be green, honey. It's a color that suits you." He referenced my jealousy last night, and called it beautiful. I exhaled as I fought to get my cover-up over my head. My scarf slipped within my dress.

"Care," Gage growled, returning to our cove of seats with a drink for his wife and one for himself.

"Where are you going?" Ivy asked, and I looked up at her husband before answering.

"I have a headache," I said, a bit too harshly.

"Mom?" Masie questioned, sitting forward on her seat, pressing Emaline upward. The four-year-old blonde sat between Masie's raised knees. "Are you okay? You haven't gotten one in a while, right?"

"I'm fine," I snapped, trying to control my voice.

"Do you need something?" Ivy asked, concern growing in her voice as well. "I can run to our room and get you something."

L.B. Dunbar

"Babe," Gage growled low, and I looked at him again. The pressure of Tommy's eyes weighed on me, his direction insinuating he watched Gage and me, but I refused to glance up at him.

"I'll come with you," Masie said, scooting Emaline forward. My heart raced with all the attention, and I just wanted to get away from all of them.

"No," I snapped, and the world stilled. Emaline peered up at me. Masie stopped moving. Ivy stared. Gage looked away, and Tommy's eyes weighed heavier despite the reflective lenses.

"Leave her be," Caleb said to no one, but implying Masie. Always my protector, guilt riddled inside me.

"Look, old lady," I laughed, waving up and down my body like a fashion model. "Hot flash or something."

"You're too young for that," Tommy growled from his end of the chairs and I wanted to say, *who asked you to speak. Go back to talking with your little girlfriends*, I thought but my mouth remained clamped shut in response to him.

"Maybe it's just the heat," I said to Masie, avoiding eye contact with Ivy. "Or I didn't get enough sleep last night. I'm okay. I just need a nap. That's what vacations are for." I was rambling. "I'm just going to lie down for a while. I'll be fine." I lowered my tone as I spoke, trying to lessen the attention on me and assure my daughter at the same time. "Dinner for three at six, okay?" I reminded her with a smile.

"Oh, Ivy asked us to join her and the guys for dinner at—"

"No," I bit. "No, thank you, honey," I said, redirecting my gaze to Ivy, but quickly looking away. "Family dinner for three tonight," I repeated to Masie and then looked over at Caleb. He shrugged and sipped a drink.

"I'll see you later, baby," I said to him before glancing back at Masie, and she nodded to agree.

+ + +

The condo door slammed and I was pissed at myself for running away again. Rather, being chased away. I had done nothing wrong. I had not led Ivy on in any way, whatever that would even look like. And who was Gage to speak to me as he had? I didn't care if he was the greatest rock star that ever lived; I hadn't done a thing to his wife. In fact, I was suddenly feeling like his wife was the one sucking my family in, lulling us to act in ways I would normally never condone, and taking up the time I wanted to spend with my own children.

I sighed, swiping at my hair, realizing I lost another scarf. It must have slipped into my dress when I struggled to tug on my cover-up while I spoke to Masie.

"Why am I here?" I said to the empty condo living room. It was a beautiful day. It was Hawaii. And I did not have a headache. I didn't want to pretend, and I didn't want to hide, but I wasn't one to make a scene, so there was no way I would return to the pool. Remembering there was a long hallway leading to stairs on the side of the building, I decided I could exit the area and head unseen to the beach.

The resort was originally a hotel, housing hundreds of rooms. Over time, an additional two buildings were added, providing condos for rent. Ivy already told me they had the penthouse suite on the top floor of the original hotel, and I knew the rest of the band was a floor below. I couldn't understand why Tommy would be on the fourth floor, other than a need for some separation, which was exactly how I felt.

I crossed the blacktop walk and cut through the scraggly bushes to get to the beach. A large set of boulders stood in my path and I climbed over them because the tide brought the ocean too close for a path. On the other side, I found a clear strip of white and walked a bit before spreading out a double-wide beach blanket. Flopping onto the mini-haven, I fell back, deciding I didn't have the concentration to read. I drifted into a hazy, afternoon nap, heated by sunshine but cooled by a swift ocean breeze. Time peacefully passed.

"Where the fuck have you been?" The harsh words startled me, and my eyes opened to be blinded by the brightness of the sun. I had no idea how much time had passed, but by the position of the sun, I guessed it was late afternoon, nearing evening. I sat up instantly at the strong reprimand and twisted to look up at the person casting a shadow over me.

Squatting to rest on his toes, his knees cracked. "We've been looking everywhere for you, darlin'." He sighed, swiping a hand over his silver and black hair, which curled at the nape of his neck in the heat. His eyes were still hidden by the aviator glasses and he wore only crazy tropical board shorts. He looked like an older surfer and the athletic build of his body proved he might be able to handle the sport.

"Excuse me," I bit, my voice groggy from sleep but also offended at the tone of his. He looked out at the ocean as I wrapped my arms around my raised knees.

"Masie is going crazy, so is Ivy."

I snorted, looking out at the sea myself. Reckless waves rolled and crashed into each other. I hadn't braved the ocean yet. Deep water frightened me.

"What time is it?" I asked, ignoring his comments about Masie and Ivy. I twisted to reach for my bag and pulled out my phone. It was almost 4:30 p.m.. *Shit*. I had been gone a while. I sent Masie a quick text telling her I was at the beach, and I was fine.

"Where'd you go, darlin'?" Tommy asked, helping himself to a seat in the sand. His position copied mine briefly before his legs stretched forward and his arms fell back to brace himself upright.

"I came to the beach," stating the obvious. He waited but I didn't offer more.

"About ten minutes after you left, Masie went to check on you. She came back frantic that you weren't in the room. Ivy got involved, wondering what to do. When Gage told her to chill out, you maybe wanted some alone time, she freaked out." Tommy paused and peeked over at me. I'd been listening to him, but I refused to meet his eyes, keeping mine lowered to my toes digging in the sand. "I saw Gage talking to you at the bar." He paused again, waiting. "Noticed the tension, too, when you both returned from it."

I bit my lip. What could I say?

"Ivy asked Gage what he said to you. When he gets nervous, he swipes through his hair. She instantly knew something was up. She wouldn't let it go until he told her that he asked you to back off. She went ballistic."

I huffed. I didn't see how any of this had anything to do with me. Shifting, Tommy fell to his side in the sand. One elbow perched him upright while his legs remained stretched forward and crossed at the ankles. He looked like a bathing suit model for older men. His fingers dug tunnels into the sand. He seemed to contemplate something as he watched his excavation, then looked out at the ocean before returning to furrow in the sand.

"Ivy's been around music her whole life. God knows it's a miracle she's turned out as normal as she is. A bit innocent still, but not naïve." For some reason, my heart beat faster in my chest, as if I had been the one searching for a missing person. "Her father, Bruce, was a bassist in a band. He was a drug addict, and after getting her mother pregnant, he killed himself. Overdose."

That racing heart plummeted to my stomach, and I swallowed the instant lump in my throat.

"She mentioned you were her mother's older brother," I said softly, wishing for him to continue.

"I am." He scooped up sand and let it sift through his fingers. "When her father died, the band needed a new bassist, so they asked me to join." I sat up straighter, remembering that I sensed he played an instrument during our breakfast conversation.

"My sister was the lead singer of the band." I didn't understand where this history was going, so I remained quiet. "I'd been in a band myself. One that had all kinds of trouble and was falling to pieces before we got started. We merged with my sister's guys and became Chrome Teardrops."

My mouth fell open.

"It was a time when female lead rock bands were on the rise and rapidly hitting the charts."

Was he kidding me? Chrome Teardrops was one of the best bands of my twenties, and the female lead singer was gorgeous. Every girl wanted to be her, dress like her. *I* wanted to be her.

"Kit Carrigan is your sister?" I gazed down at him.

"So, you do know a bit of music history," he scoffed, the laughter not filling his throat like I knew it could.

"Just that I idolized her. Her voice was amazing. I copied all her song lyrics in a notebook. 'Broken Wings' is one of my favorite songs ever." I sounded like a teenage groupie, which was exactly how I felt about finding out one of my idols was his sister. Then another thought came to me.

"Didn't she die?" Before I gave it a sympathetic pass in my brain, the words tumbled out of my mouth. "Oh my God," I muttered, my hand covering said mouth in shame.

"She did," he replied, looking out at the water and throwing a handful of sand away from him. "Breast cancer. Eight years ago." I felt sick. The pieces were slowly coming into place. Kit Carrigan had one of those public deaths where she became a strong advocate of mammograms and self-examination. She died too young and still in the prime of her career.

"Ivy was only twenty. She needed Kit. They were two peas in a pod, but Ivy was in college. Kit was adamant that Ivy would be something other than a rock stars' child. When she got sick, Ivy was lost. She became a parent when she was still a child, in more ways than one. I became her guardian, but she didn't need me. She's strong-willed. Thankfully, she finished college, but never used her degree." He sighed, returning to rake the sand with his fingers.

"I know what Gage said to you. He admitted it to Ivy in their rather publicly displayed argument." He shook his head, obviously upset with whatever had happened. "The tabloids will have a field day." He sighed. "I actually disagree with Gage. I think you being around Ivy is good for her, but I don't want her having any false hopes either. I think Ivy's smart enough to know no one can replace her mother. However, it never hurts to have female role models." He took a deep breath after those words.

"She's surrounded by a lot of men and poor examples of women, always throwing themselves at the band for cheap thrills. Ivy knows some women will use her to get to the band. She's smart enough to *not* play along with those shenanigans."

Silence swirled between us for a moment as my mind processed all that I'd learned. Kit was Ivy's mother. Ivy didn't have a father. Kit Carrigan was Tommy Carrigan's sister. Tommy had been in a band.

"Is this what you think happened? That I was talking to Ivy to get to the boys or you?" My voice rose, and I shifted to face him. "I didn't even know who the boys were. I still don't even know who you are," I added incredulously.

"I'm just me," he said, sounding somewhat defeated as he didn't meet my glare. "Just Tommy." His eyes remained on the sea, and I sighed.

"Yeah, well, who is Tommy?" I asked, because I was learning he was hiding things from me. He didn't answer me, and I shifted back to face the ocean, my ankles crossed and my arms braced me upright. My heart hammered in both anger and empathy. His story was sad, but his accusations unwarranted.

"With everything I just told you, I should have made you sign a NDA—nondisclosure agreement."

I gasped. "What?"

"You wouldn't believe how much that story would sell for."

"Are you kidding me? That's despicable." I hissed, wanting to collect my things and run away from him once again. Instead, I scooped up a handful of sand and threw it weakly away from me in my disgust at another accusation and the thought of such behavior—money at the expense of someone's personal history.

"Wait. You don't think—" A raised hand stopped me but my voice was filled with disbelief.

"You may not know me, but I'm getting a sense of you," his gruff voice responded. "I don't take you for someone who would do that." He paused. "I don't want to believe you would do such a thing."

L.B. Dunbar

"You *don't want to believe*?" I choked, irritation fully filling my throat.

"It's only been forty-eight hours," he reminded me, and I paused a moment, swiping at my hair.

"Fair enough," I sighed. "I'll sign something if it would make you feel better, because I would never share that story with others." My shoulders fell, matching the heavy pit tumbling to my stomach. I still felt physically ill at the thought.

The weight of his stare forced me to face him. "The fact you just offered to sign something is good enough for me, darlin'."

"Why?" I blurted, although warmth filled me with the return of his drawled endearment.

"There's something about you that I trust."

We let that statement sit between us a moment.

"Want to sit on my towel?" I offered, noting the deep tan of his body and the sand sticking to his arm and leg pressed into the white grains. He smiled slowly at me, eyes roaming over my body.

"My view's good from here."

I blushed as I looked back at the rolling waves. In the distance, white foam shot above the surface—the tell-tale sign a whale swam beneath the water. Suddenly, it breached, exploding above the ocean to expose half its glorious body before slamming back against the water line.

"Did you see that?" I squealed, clapping my hands and bringing them against my chest in my excitement. I turned to look at him, but his eyes were still on me. "That was amazing." My voice rose like a kid on a Ferris wheel. Tommy shifted and scooted closer to me, resting his body on my towel after all. I looked at him over my shoulder. Lips to my sun-kissed shoulder were the only warning I received before his mouth found mine. Truthfully, his mouth seized mine, rolling over my lips like the reckless waves of the ocean. His tongue plunged forward, crossing the surface, as if catching a large breath, like the whale. His arm straightened to hold himself upright while his other hand cupped the side of my face, keeping me connected to him. He kissed me like the devil had a purpose and it included devouring me.

58

Whale breaching was possibly a mating message, but the messages I kept getting from Tommy confused me. One thing was evident: I'd mate with him again if he asked. The morning still lingered in my mind, and damp heat pooled between my thighs as his mouth continued to take mine. Tommy kissed like a master, like he practiced frequently. His crafty kissing brought my thoughts to the girls at the pool. Sensing something, he pulled back slowly, dragging my lower lip within his before releasing me. His eyes glowed a rich chocolate brown color, dappled with flecks of green and gold.

"Now that was amazing," he said, and heat rushed over my skin, which had nothing to do with the sunlight beaming down on us. "Know what else?"

"What?" I asked, setting myself up as his lip twitched and curled at one corner.

"This morning. That was amazing."

# 5

### Party of three

Having dinner with adult children isn't much different than younger children. They still wanted to be on their phones most of the meal, until I told them I'd confiscate them like when they were teenagers. Caleb chuckled, and Masie sent one final text before placing it in her purse.

Spending time with my children was still one of the greatest joys of my life. I stared at these two miracles across from me. They had grown so fast. When did Masie turn into a beautiful woman on the verge of going to college? When did this young man take over Caleb's body, turning him into a budding minor league baseball player? I sipped my wine, marveling at the strangeness of life. I never imagined spending the next phase of my life alone, but that's exactly where I was going to be when Masie went to school.

Letting the thought pass, we ordered. Duke's Restaurant was a highlight along the boardwalk between resorts, and I couldn't wait to dig into fresh-caught seafood. It was good to be with my kids. We had a pretty open relationship, maybe too open about a few things, but I did my best to be supportive and honest with my opinion. I worried about Caleb and his decision to play ball. I worried about Masie and her choice to become a nurse. She'd grown up too fast over the last two years.

"Okay, West said he's at the Pink Flamingo," Caleb announced after I paid the bill. "I'm going to meet the guys there." Caleb hesitated a moment. "If that's okay with you?" How could I tell a twenty-two-year old no? He was a man, even if he would always be my little boy. As he left the table, Masie stared after him. She wanted to join him, but being eighteen, she wouldn't be admitted into the bar.

"So, West, huh?" I started, sipping the last of my wine. Masie's head spun to me.

"Mom." Her voiced whined in that way when she didn't want to discuss something, or I'd embarrassed her, but the pink flush of her face proved she agreed. She'd noticed him.

"Well," I replied, answering in the same elongated sound. He was a nice looking young man of twenty-two, even if he was too old for Masie. I didn't want her to get hurt. "He's a little old for you, though." I spoke softly, knowing I tread in dangerous waters. With daughters, any slip of the tongue could lead to unintentional drowning.

"Mom," she pealed again, before her shoulders sunk. "I know. And he's a rock star, but he seems so different than I thought. I mean, he seems normal, like a guy I might meet at college." The admission seemed to bother her.

"You're going to meet lots of boys in college," I said, reaching over and rubbing her arm. "You're too beautiful for your own good," I added. I was biased, but she was striking, and I was jealous, just a little. I never looked that good when I was her age.

"I know, it's just…" Her shoulder shrugged, and I waited. "I don't think I can talk about this with you."

"Oh." I sat up straighter. "Oh, okay." Was I hurt? Maybe a little. But did I know what she wanted to say? I think she wanted to tell me a girl could have a little fun.

"I mean, I know I might never see him again. It's not like I'd marry him," she scoffed. "It's just…he is a rock star." Her face brightened, and she giggled a little, euphoric at the possibility of hanging out with someone famous. I could only hope it wasn't more. As if she thought about it a moment, her face fell, and she added, "I mean, he's more than a rock star, of course. He's just…a really nice guy."

She was the farthest thing from a shallow person, and I smiled to myself.

"Masie, we're on vacation. I don't mind you spending time with him. He seems like a nice guy, but I don't think you should do anything more. I don't want to see you set up for heartbreak."

Masie nodded agreeing with me. "I know. I get it. I do." She paused, brushing back her long brunette hair. "But I like him. He's fun. There's nothing wrong with that, right?" She wasn't looking for me to answer, but I did.

"Of course not. In fact, I think it's great that you and Caleb found people your own age to hang with. I didn't expect you to hang out with your old mom the whole time."

Masie sat up, eyes widening. "It's not that, Mom. You know if you wanted us to spend all our time with you, we would. I mean, this is your vacation." Panic set in her voice, and I saw the stress covering her face. The purpose of this vacation was to remind all of us to be thankful and celebrate. I wanted my kids to enjoy themselves, to be worry free.

"It's *our* vacation, honey. Just keep things in check," I said, hoping it would be enough of a hint without spelling out that I didn't want her sleeping with him.

*Hypo-meet-crite.* Guilt washed over me. With each passing moment of the day, I became more and more reflective of what I'd done, and how I'd done it with a virtual stranger. A stranger who still kissed me on the beach like we were celebrating something special. Maybe not a golden anniversary like the older woman mentioned, but something momentous, at least for me.

"You know, Mom." She hesitated. "If you met someone, and wanted to spend time with him during this vacation, that would be cool, too." Her eyes lowered to the table and she stroked the rounded edge, nervousness filling her voice.

"Oh, honey, I don't think that will happen for me." Sadness filled me as I realized I didn't have plans to see Tommy again. While his attention had been refreshing, revitalizing even, I didn't expect to spend time with him.

"I saw the way Tommy looked at you," Masie said, turning a sheepish smile on me. "I think he might be interested."

"Masie," I laughed, mock-scolding her. "I don't think so, baby." I patted her hand.

"Well, if he did ask you out, I think it would be cool for you to spend time with someone as well." She lowered her brow and narrowed her eyes at me in a teasing manner. "Just keep things in check." Her voice deepened as she teased me, and I swallowed. *Too late.*

We ended up having a mother-daughter movie night where I let her drink wine in the condo and we laughed at the shenanigans of *Bad Moms*.

"Thank goodness, you aren't like that," Masie said when the single man stripped the single mother on the kitchen counter. Yes, I thought, thank heavens. Being stripped and taken on the counter would be so…heavenly, but I kept my thoughts to myself.

Her phone continued to buzz and ping with messages throughout the movie, which she took on the sly, but she didn't ask to leave and I silently thanked her for giving us this private time together.

"West says Tommy wants to know if you want to join them." My heart skipped a beat and I found myself containing the excitement that he wanted to see me. It struck me as ironic that Tommy didn't even have my phone number after all we'd done. I looked over at Masie, and despite her expectant look, I couldn't leave her alone.

"Tell West thank you, but I'm good here with my girl." Masie smiled, and relief washed over me. I'd made the better—the smarter—decision. She typed, hit send, and set the phone on the cushion once again.

"You know, I feel kind of sorry for Ivy. She doesn't have a mother to spend time with. I don't think she has many girlfriends, either." Masie said, thoughtful a moment. "Probably because everyone wants to get close to her to be close to the band."

"Is that what she said?" I questioned, feeling a pinch of sorrow for Ivy myself. After all Tommy told me, I knew Ivy missed her mother and didn't have many female influences.

"She just told me I was lucky I still had you. She also said she was sorry that you had cancer." She looked up at me. "I didn't tell her, I swear, but Ivy knew. The headscarves are a giveaway." Masie wrung her fingers together, twisting them as she spoke. Her phone pinged again but she ignored it.

"Honey, you don't have to be ashamed to tell anyone."

"I'm not," she cut me off almost instantly. "It's just, I hate how people look at you sometimes, and I want them to know you're okay.

You're still you." I smiled at my daughter. She was going to be a great nurse one day.

"Speaking of scarves. I lost mine today. I think it fell off when I was putting on my cover-up."

"Yeah, Tommy took it," Masie said, looking down at her phone again. "He was so pissed off at Gage. I can't believe Gage wanted you to stay away from Ivy."

I sat up a little and twisted toward Masie. "What happened?"

"I didn't find you in the room, and I was telling Caleb when Tommy instantly jumped in. Ivy did, too. Tommy turned on Gage, asking him what he said to you, as if he knew something. Ivy started getting upset, and finally Gage admitted he asked you to stay away from her. It was so awkward for Caleb and I. Ivy immediately started apologizing for Gage and trying to assure us she wanted to spend time with us and you. Caleb was still pretty upset, though, and suggested we leave. West tried to convince him we should stay. Finally, West decided he'd leave with us."

"Where did the three of you go?"

Masie laughed. "We went to the shuffle board court and played with an older couple."

I couldn't help myself. I laughed, too. Caleb could befriend anyone. The fact West tried to shield Masie moved him up a bit in my opinion. The fact he played shuffleboard with old people pushed him even higher on my ladder of approval.

+ + +

We didn't see any of the band members the next day. Caleb explained they had practice and then some excursion on the island. Either way, I found myself poolside, but restless. Thoughts continued to wander to Tommy and what happened between us. I'd been married for twenty years and divorced for nearly three. In that time, I'd had less than a handful of dates and a heaping scoop of cancer. I had no time for relationships or even experimentation. I didn't know how to date in the modern age, and I wasn't sure I wanted to, but some nights were extremely lonely.

I did own a Mr. Bob, as Tommy referenced, but I didn't use it often. I always felt weird using it alone, which was exactly its purpose. Unfortunately for me, I wanted actual sex. I wanted a man, and not in a take-care-of-me financial and spiritual kind of way, but more of a physical and emotional sort. I wanted to feel loved, not be told I was when I wasn't. I wanted to have sex that meant something more than two bodies getting out a release.

I was pathetic, I decided. It wasn't going to happen. I'd had random sex with Tommy. How did I feel about that? Overwhelmed. Out of body. Orgasmic. There was no doubt I'd been more aroused than I'd ever been. Just kissing was an experience with him, and when I thought of it my lips tingled. I wanted more. I wanted another round. I wanted him.

And that was not a good decision.

That night, I was invited to come to the penthouse suite. Ivy stressed that she wanted Gage to apologize in person. I told her there was no need, that I understood his motives, but she insisted. I was nervous, and I asked my kids to come with me, more as buffers than anything. Caleb said he had people to meet, and Masie said she was going to work on some reading for her winter break homework. As weak as these were for excuses, I had no choice but to go alone.

The penthouse had a sprawling private balcony, and the band was in a relaxed state of mind, scattered around on outdoor couches and settees. Ava and Emaline were already in bed. Gage lazily strummed a guitar over his legs, despite their earlier band practice. Ivy had greeted me with a warm hug and another round of apologies.

"He's just…stupid, sometimes," she offered weakly as she led me closer to the group. Tommy sat in a chair with his legs sprawled apart, his arm resting over the wicker arm. A beer dangled between two fingers, one of which wore a large silver ring. He didn't greet me, other than a head nod, like I was someone he recognized but didn't know.

L.B. Dunbar

"Gage," Ivy demanded, crossing her arms and staring down at her husband. He propped the guitar next to the couch and stood slowly, wiping his palms on his jeans.

"I'm sorry, Edie." Silence followed the statement, and I swore I heard a whale bellow in the distance. It was painfully awkward for both of us.

"And?" Ivy said icily. Gage swiped his fingers through his dark hair, looking away from me.

*He's nervous*, I thought.

"I didn't mean what I said, that you should stay away from Ivy." The silence again filled with the tick-tock of an unseen clock.

"Keep going," Ivy snapped, lowering her crossed arms to two fists at her sides.

"I'd like you to spend time with Ivy, especially because she doesn't have many friends."

"Gage!" she growled, almost as if she were warning him.

"What are we?" Petty interjected, sounding hurt. Tommy sat forward to cuff him on the shoulder. "What?" Petty whined.

"*Female* friends," Gage amended in response to his wife.

"And?" Ivy repeated, her foot tapping. Literally. She tapped her sandal-covered toes like a scolding mother.

"Jesus, fuck, Ivy," he hissed, glaring at his wife.

"Is that couch comfy, Jared?" she questioned the other band member sitting on an outdoor sofa.

"N—"

"Don't answer that," Gage said, holding up a hand to his friend.

"You know, this is kind of bullshit," West said, glaring at Gage before standing from his chair, excusing himself from this painful scene. Ivy's foot stopped tapping, but her fists clenched harder. Gage and she stared at one another for a few moments before Gage looked away. I couldn't believe this powerful front man for a successful band was waffling under his wife's gaze.

"And I'm an idiot for saying what I said." He rushed the words out, then sat with a huff, picking up his guitar and placing it back over his knees.

"Close enough," Ivy sighed. Then she stepped forward, took the guitar out of his hands and straddled his lap. She kissed him so passionately that I grew wet watching them, and then I looked away, ashamed at staring while they were so intimate, so private, so blissful. I caught Tommy watching me, and I had to look away from him as well.

"Get a room," Jared groaned, picking up Gage's guitar.

"Get out of mine," Gage muttered against his wife's mouth. There was no mistaking the *I love yous* that followed before Ivy shifted to curl up on her husband's lap. The love between them was so intense, it vibrated in the air, and while I felt weak at the knees from the display, I wanted to cry as well.

"Take a seat, Edie," Jared offered, and I sat opposite him on another couch. Petty was to my left, but suddenly Tommy was trading seats with him. The blond fell into the single chair and tipped his head back to stare at the stars.

"I need to get laid," Petty moaned to the dark sky overhead. I giggled at his bluntness, but Tommy sat forward. He prepared to fist Petty's leg but Petty was too quick, bending one knee toward the other, forcing Tommy to miss his target.

"Don't be crass," Tommy said.

"Since when did you become so uptight?" Jared asked of Tommy.

"Since *he* doesn't get laid," Petty sighed, looking back at the band manager with a gleam in his eye.

"Who has time with you assholes to babysit?" Tommy mocked, taking a long sip of his beer.

"That's okay, Tommy. You don't need to defend yourself. We know you're A-sexual."

"A-sexual?" I snort laughed.

"Dude," Gage warned, but Jared explained, "Against sex."

"Fu…" the *k* sound followed without Tommy completing the word.

"When was the last time you got laid, old man?" Petty teased.

"None of your damn business," Tommy grumbled, finishing his beer and then peering into the bottle as if more would magically appear. Ivy stood to my right.

"Always getting hit on, but never up for the occasion," Petty mocked, stroking his imaginary appendage above his jeans.

"Okay, that's enough," Tommy said, standing.

"Dude, shut up," Gage barked, directing the warning at Petty.

"What?" the blond mocked, arms raised to protect his head in a fighter's stance. I hadn't seen Ivy leave, too enthralled by the playful but telling banter between these men. She returned with an armful of beers.

"Babe, don't serve them, especially him." Gage pointed at Petty, who just laughed and helped himself anyway.

Something in me sensed the frustration rolling off Tommy. While I thought the words exchanged seemed jovial and carefree, Tommy sat rigid next to me. I don't know where the boldness came from, but I felt the need to defend him.

"Don't you think that's a little unfair?" I directed to Petty. "I mean, Tommy's an attractive man. I suppose he could get laid if he wanted to on the regular."

Jared's mouth fell open, repeating, "On the regular," while Petty's teasing expression dropped. Silence followed my statement. Then a burst of laughter rushed between the two band members. Even Gage chuckled a little. I looked at Ivy, who had returned to Gage's lap. She shook her head and smiled, dismissing the guys as acting like boys.

"Why is that funny?" Suddenly, I wanted to know what I'd said to make them laugh. They continued to chuckle, dropping the tone down a bit at the seriousness of my question. I felt like I was defending mankind instead of a man.

"I mean…" I swallowed preparing for what I said next. "He's sexy."

Silence fell again. Birds chirped. The wind blew, and then a slow rumble began. A snicker. A chuckle. A gasp.

"Tommy?" Jared shrieked.

"Sexy?" Petty howled in humor.

"What?" I defended again. All eyes were on me, except Tommy, who sat slightly amused himself at this conversation. His lips curled.

"You don't think you'll get old one day?" I addressed the group, but Tommy's head swung to face me at that question.

"Darlin'," he started, but I continued by placing a hand on his arm.

"What will you look like?" I said to Petty defensively, growing bolder in my need to prove that Tommy was a sensual man.

"Portly," Jared snickered, cutting his gaze to Petty.

"Will you have sexy silver hair?" I said, eyeing Tommy's head. "Wrinkles from laughter? Eyes that have seen too much? A heart that stays strong for others?"

Tommy sat forward at this comment, his elbows coming to his knees as I assessed him.

"Scruff on your face, if you can grow any," I teased, as Petty's blond features didn't lend to facial hairs. I was hoping to lighten the tension around Tommy. Jared laughed.

"You don't think your body will shift? You'd be lucky to have the strength to carry the weight of others." I squeezed Tommy's arm and he rolled his head to look at me over his shoulder. His hands tented, fingers linked to support his chin and this accentuated his firm bicep, but I wasn't talking about his physical appearance despite my description. I was talking about who I sensed Tommy Carrigan was inside. He was strong, and he carried the weight of his band.

"That's a chest full of love, giving up everything for others," I said, scooting closer to him and spreading my palm to rub across his pecs, feeling his heart racing under his white T-shirt. I patted his chest, but my hand slipped downward.

"Those abs are—"

"Enough," Petty squealed like a girl. He shriveled up, curling into himself by raising his arms and lifting a leg as if to shield himself from the sight of me touching Tommy. It was all in jest, but there may have been some reality to his covered eyes, like a child witnessing his parents kissing.

Something flamed in Tommy's eyes as he watched me describe him, caress him in front of these boys he mentored.

"What about his lips?" Gage teased.

"No!" Jared shouted, like a squeamish child, covering his eyes with the heel of each hand.

"Words of wisdom said to a bunch of punk-ass boys," I stated, emphasizing the last three words. Tommy's mouth twisted, and he bit the corner, holding in the laughter ready to escape. I wanted him to laugh. I wanted to hear that hearty sound again.

Leaning forward, I cupped his cheek and pulled him toward me. He met me halfway, and I kissed him. Sweet, slow, tender, my lips nipped at his. The moment we touched, a pulse shot up my middle so quickly, my whole body tensed, but I relished the feeling, desiring it to happen again and again. Still, I kept my mouth soft on his, pulling lightly at his lip and opening mine to gather more of him. My thumb grew aware of the thick scruff under its touch. I might have purred.

"Holy fuck," someone muttered.

"No shit," another male voice stammered.

"I knew it!" Ivy squeaked.

"Mom?"

I pulled back abruptly, dazed from the kiss, muddled by the boldness of defending Tommy's sex appeal. My brain slowly processed that I had just been caught kissing a man by my daughter.

"I…I…" I brushed back my too-short hair, unable to fully face Masie, who stood next to West at the side of the couch where I sat. "I was trying to prove a point," I muttered, my face reddening in humiliation that I'd just kissed Tommy in front of all of them.

"I think Tommy has the point now," Petty snickered, and Tommy reached over to smack him on the side of the head. He changed his mind mid-swing and stood as he grabbed another beer from the collection Ivy set on the low table between the comfy couches. He walked over to the balcony railing and stood with his back to it, watching over the collection of people within the circle. Mortified, I excused myself, after Masie explained she was finished reading and West asked my permission to let her hang out a bit. While I hoped that Tommy might offer to walk me to my room, or even ask me to stay, I'd decided I must have embarrassed him more than defended him. Ivy walked to me the door of the penthouse instead.

"I don't know what came over me," I muttered. "I'm so sorry if I humiliated him in front of the boys."

Ivy's sweet smile curled to full wattage. "It takes a lot to embarrass Tommy. It takes even more to truly upset him. He's fine." She looked back in the direction of the men and Masie. Tommy remained like a statue against the balcony railing.

"I'm so embarrassed myself," I said, my voice lowering. "I've never acted that way before." I brushed a hand over my head, cursing that I didn't have hair to pull in my frustration.

"Are you sure you don't want to stay? Have a beer?" Ivy asked, peering back at her uncle before looking at me.

"I think I've done enough damage tonight," I offered, sweeping a hand down her arm.

"Thank you for not hating Gage," she said, looking down at her feet. I tipped up her chin with my fingers.

"Honey, I don't think there's much that could upset me, either," I lied. In regards to Gage and Ivy, they were like children to me, still young, still grabbing the world with raised fists, hoping to conquer everything. At my age, I knew better. There was always something bigger to be upset over.

$$+ + +$$

I'd fallen into a deep sleep, so I hadn't heard Masie return, or Caleb enter even later, but I couldn't miss the pounding at the door. Caleb actually answered it after peering through the peep hole. The pounding continued as he turned the deadbolt and unlatched the chain.

Tommy stood in the hallway, his eyes a little wild, his hands braced on either side of the frame. He looked drunk.

"I want to sleep with your mom," he blurted, and Caleb's head swung to me. He stood in only sleep shorts, Masie behind him, while I stared in disbelief at the unabashed statement. "Just sleep with her, kid. Sleep," he muttered, his voice lowering.

"Do you know what time it is?" Caleb accused him, always my protector.

"No," Tommy said, eyes trained on me.

"Are you drunk?" Caleb questioned, knowing the answer.

"Maybe," Tommy admitted.

"I don't think so, pal," Caleb said, starting to shut the door, but Tommy stopped it with a thick hand.

"I won't force myself in, but I need your mother." Something in his voice swelled my heart. I'd been in this position before. I knew too well the lies a man told when he was drinking, but Tommy seemed different. *Oh, the lies we tell ourselves as women.* I stepped forward, patting Caleb on the back before pushing Tommy into the hallway, which was an open balcony.

"Just give me a minute," I said to Caleb while I peered at Tommy. The door closed behind me, but remained slightly open by the deadbolt catch, my children waiting on the other side of the panel.

"What do you think you are doing?" I snapped, trying to keep my voice lowered in case any neighbors heard the commotion. If Caleb was home, it had to be after two in the morning.

"I need you," he whispered. "Just sleep. Scout's honor." He lazily crossed his heart then attempted to hold up two fingers. He wasn't sloppy drunk, but he was struggling.

"My ex-husband was an alcoholic, Tommy. I'm not going anywhere with you." The comment brought Tommy's head up, and he stood taller. David hadn't ever been able to admit it, but he drank excessively.

"Darlin'," he said, and I hated the effect that name had on me. My insides curled. My heart skipped a beat, and my head warned me. "It's nothing like that."

I heard noise behind me, and I spun to find Masie with my phone and my room key held out for me.

"Maybe you should just walk him back to his room," she suggested. I couldn't read the expression on her face, but I feared she thought there would be a scene. She'd witnessed a few in her years, and I couldn't put her through it again. Not here. Not when this was supposed to be a vacation from such things.

I smiled weakly, trying to assure her with my eyes that I wasn't frightened, and I'd be back soon. She closed the door on me before I remembered I didn't have on any shoes. I wore only a T-shirt dress as a nightshirt.

"All right, Tommy, lead the way," I demanded, a bit irritated.

"You don't have shoes," he said, looking down at my feet. "I like your purple nail polish," he added, noting the pedicure I'd given myself. "It's a much better color than green."

I rolled my eyes and started walking, hoping the movement away from my door would prompt him to follow me. It did, and we walked in silence down the balcony hallway to the stairwell and then down to the lobby. We rode the elevator up to his floor in the main hotel and he led me to his room. I stood outside as he fumbled with his key. Leaning against the wall, I waited while he opened the door. He paused once he had it open, pressing his body along the door jamb. Half his body was in the room, the other half in the hallway.

"Why'd you kiss me like that?" he asked, his eyes meeting mine and then falling to my bare feet again.

I shrugged. "I didn't like how they teased you."

"They were only playing, darlin', but I'm not going to lie, no one stands up for me." My eyes searched his face, and I saw what I described to them. He had sad eyes that held in tears. He had a strong heart to keep theirs happy. He did everything for the band, everything for Ivy. Tommy Carrigan had a solid, outer shell, but I wanted to know more about what lay underneath.

"I didn't mean to embarrass you. I'm so sorry," I said, and his head shot upward.

"You didn't embarrass me. Fuck, I wanted to beat my chest and claim you as my woman."

I stared at him, my eyes too dry to blink. He couldn't be serious, despite the caveman-ness of calling me *woman*.

"I…"

"And that kiss, Edie." He paused, biting his lip before letting the plump lushness spring free. "I felt that kiss in my toes. To the ends of my hair. In my…" He rubbed his zipper.

"You're drunk," I laughed, feeling a little tipsy myself just looking at him. I shook my head. I couldn't deal with drunk, but he was sexy.

"On you, Edie," he said. "Only on you." He paused, staring me down, roaming over my nightshirt to my bare legs and back up again. "Come inside, darlin'."

"I shouldn't," I said, standing my ground as I pressed off the wall.

"But you want to," he added.

"I can't," I stated, twisting my ankle and letting my toe drag on the cool carpeting.

"But you could," he teased, lifting his chin. "Just sleep, Edie. I promise. I don't trust myself with what I drank, but I want you to trust me enough to know I'd never take advantage of you. Not like this." He paused, lowering his eyes.

"I just want to be close to you," he admitted. "No one's ever talked like that about me, and I just want to capture it for a little while. I want to hold onto it, if I can. For just a little bit." I stared at him and the brick wall of defense I tried to use against him crumbled. I took a deep breath, loosened my crossed arms, and stepped forward.

His wide eyes proved I surprised him, but he readily stepped back, allowing me entrance to his room.

# 6

## Jive Talkin', or rather dancing

The crash of thunder and a bright spark of lightning woke me. My body flinched with the suddenness, and the dark room illuminated a second time with another flash of light. An arm tightened over me, and I settled into the chest at my back despite my racing heart.

After Tommy led me into his room, he pulled back his bedcovers and motioned for me to climb in. He excused himself, stating he needed a moment, and returned to tuck the sheet over me, as a barrier between us. I didn't like it, but I appreciated the gesture. He was trying to assure me he wouldn't take advantage of me.

"I heard what you said, darlin', about your ex-husband." He kissed my shoulder and then breathed into my neck. "Thank you."

I didn't understand his gratitude, but he'd fallen asleep almost instantly, before I could ask him what he meant. I always hated this about men. They could close their eyes and their worries disappeared. I closed my eyes and my mind wanted to race through an endless list of concerns.

As the rain rumbled, and his balcony curtain flew in the rushing wind, Tommy snored lightly behind me. I had to chuckle. I couldn't seem to escape a man that snored. David's nightly nasal orchestra was terrible, and I often joked the neighbors could hear him. But I didn't wish to think of David when I lay precariously positioned in the arms of another man. Unfortunately, seeing Tommy drunk dusted off memories long settled.

*David, accusing me of cheating on him when he was the one to have an affair.*

*David, coming home drunk and acting like I was the love of his life, only to tell me fifteen minutes later I was the worst wife.*

*David, attending activities for our children while inebriated, and my interference, out of fear he'd embarrass us all.*

Life hadn't been easy, and it hadn't always been kind, but I was thankful to have my health. Selfishly, I didn't want to think about how I'd like a little bit more than that.

I squirmed, attempting to remove Tommy's arm from my waist.

"Where you going, darlin'?" He muttered as if he hadn't been deeply snoring less than a second before.

"Bathroom," I whispered, despite it only being the two of us.

"No running," he warned.

"No running," I chuckled, patting his arm as he rolled to his back to release me.

It was early morning, maybe six a.m. or so, but the darkness outside his balcony doors made it feel like midnight. There was something about rain that suggested a return to bed, and that's what I did after using the bathroom. I crawled up the center while Tommy lay on his back, one arm hitched behind his head, his full body sprawled on display. He wore black boxer briefs that accentuated his tan. He was cut, as if trenches were dug along his skin. Not a full six-pack, but definitely dips and curves implying firm muscle. It was his chest that was impressive, nearly two plates of steel. My eyes roamed his form. His abs slowly rose and fell at the waistband as he took a deep breath. He'd caught me admiring him.

I fell to the bed beside him, facing the model-worthy display before me. There was no mistaking the bulge in his boxers.

A peaceful silence fell between us as he rolled to face me. The wind outside the window increased, matching the pace of my heart. There was something in the way Tommy looked at me. Thrill shimmered through my body, causing the ends of my skin to tingle. I wanted him to touch me, but he only stared at me. He looked tired.

"You should go back to sleep," I whispered, knowing that was the last thing I'd be able to do.

"Not what I had in mind," he said, looking down at my lips.

I had to giggle. "I have morning breath," I said, rolling away from him and covering my mouth.

"Let me see," he said, following me, his body bracing over mine as his hand struggled to remove mine from my lips. He was teasing me, not tugging as strongly as he could. "Don't resist me, darlin'," he said as a knee came between my thighs. My legs bent instinctively, opening, begging for him to draw closer.

My movement paused his, and I released my hand. The thick pad of his thumb stroked my cheek before his mouth crushed mine. This was something I'd learned about Tommy and kissing: he came in hard, demanding, but he quickly slowed. In fact, he'd slowed so much, this kiss was different. He took his time after the initial onslaught, pressing soft kisses to each lip and each corner, teasing me more before opening his mouth and covering mine. He sipped at my lips, tugging them to his, holding the lower one captive before opening once again. He was flirting with me, savoring me, and I was getting drunk on him.

Finally, his tongue crossed the seam of my lips, and while I wasn't a fan of morning kisses, I couldn't deny my hunger for his tongue. Sweeping through my mouth, our tongues tangled in a lazy, rainy morning kiss of discovery. He took his time, carving out my mouth and etching into my heart a kiss I'd remember long past this vacation. Our bodies shifted, and Tommy found his way between two open legs. The heavy length of him pressed against my core, and my body squirmed, searching for friction, but he continued to kiss me.

I wanted to sprint. He wanted to stroll.

We seemed to compromise as the kissing intensified. His hips slowly thrust against me, and my response to his kisses increased. Eventually, I couldn't breathe and pulled free. His mouth didn't leave me, though, but moved to my jaw and my chin before travelling down to my neck. A fist gathered my nightshirt at my side and slowly the material rose.

He pulled me to sit upright, and I followed his lead despite my galloping heart and warning head. We hadn't been naked before, but I didn't stop him from removing my dress. Instantly, I covered my chest, arms crossing in a giant X. Within the blink of an eye, my wrists were clasped, uncrossed, and I found myself flung back on the bed, arms pinned to the sides of my head. Tommy was in a sort of half push-up position, and his eyes met mine for a second before he looked at my chest.

"Those are some pretty titties, darlin'." His eyes roamed the firm hills and dipped into the valley between them.

Any woman who has breastfed knows about the letdown sensation. It's a tickle just above the swell of cleavage, signaling what a female body was made to do. It's natural, and strangely sensual, and the feeling crept through me when I hadn't felt it in years. I wanted it to keep crawling, reaching a part of me that no longer existed, but it couldn't. Liquid filled my eyes, and I questioned if I could follow through with what we were beginning. Tommy gazed intently at my breasts, but I had no sensation in them.

"I told you, you're beautiful, right?"

I nodded, not feeling confident I could speak without releasing tears.

"And I bet you had beautiful breasts before," he said, letting his voice lower. "But I don't give two shits if those are fake or real, as long as what we're about to do is real to you."

I sniffed, blinking rapidly, but a tear slipped from my eye and slid to my hair. He released one wrist and swiped at it, rubbing his thumb and forefinger together.

"Want to stop?" he asked, while his tone begged me to continue.

I rolled my head back and forth on the pillow.

"Thank fuck," he muttered, drowning out the *k* sound as his mouth covered mine again. His hips rolled, and I moaned against his lips. Releasing me, he sat back to look at my underwear. Low-cut cotton again.

"Sorry, I wasn't expecting you," I said.

"Where you expecting someone else?" he grumbled, tugging down my underwear.

"No," I laughed. "But I bet you're used to leather and lace, and I'm one-hundred percent cotton."

He flipped the material to the side of the bed and then pounced back, two strong arms caging me in.

"Don't bring other women into bed with me, darlin'," he warned, his eyes darkening as he glared down at me. My euphoria slipped down the meter scale. I nodded to agree with him, and his mouth found mine again. While we kissed, his hand roamed, tucking up under my breast and smoothing over my stomach to tease the coarse hair at the apex of my legs. I was soft in the center, and as he palmed a hunk of skin, my hand gripped his wrist to halt him.

He stopped kissing me and pulled back again.

"Don't play with my fat," I warned, trying to tease him but slightly serious. Squeezing me there was only going to remind me again that I wasn't groupie material.

"Fishing for compliments isn't flatterin', beautiful."

"I'm not fishing. I'm stating the obvious." My voice rose an octave, irritation filling it. A forced compliment was the worst kind of compliment—the obligatory one said after a negative comment. It was so disingenuous.

"What's obvious to me," he started as he slipped to my side and let a finger trail down the middle of my stomach, which I sucked in. "is you don't see yourself clearly."

I wanted clarification, but I didn't want to ask. Anything he said to me was within the realm of the heat of the moment. I needed to get out of that realm and back into thoughts of having sex with him, because I wanted that. I wanted to have sex with him again and again. There was no room for my emotions.

His finger travelled lower, combing through crisp curls before diving in deep. My back arched off the bed at the intrusion, loving every bit of pressure within me. He twisted and released me before torturously entering me again. I gripped the bedsheets in a fist when his thumb hit that spot, the one that triggered all my pleasure.

"You're sweet, darlin'," he whispered as he watched me, my body rolling without control, drawing his finger into me and begging for the friction on that nub. The orgasm crawled up my thighs and crept down my belly, and when the two ends met I detonated, my knees collapsing and pressing together to hold his hand between my thighs. I moaned as my back curled off the bed, and my head fell back. The sensation wasn't ending, but curling and crashing like the waves off in the distance, and I let the tide roll.

"Now that's a sight I want to see again," he said, releasing his fingers slowly and climbing over me for his nightstand.

Foil ripped. Lightning struck again, flashing behind him. The world was dark and murky around us as the storm outside continued, but all I sensed was him. He was thunder, and I anxiously awaited the strike. He held himself outside my entrance, teasing me with the tip, as he parted me.

"This might be quick, darlin'. Morning sex usually is." If he didn't want other women in this bed, he just brought them here, but I quickly forgot them when he rushed into me. I bowed off the bed again as he swiftly filled me to my depths. The missionary position was different from the other day. Some might think it mundane, but something felt strangely intimate about him over me, looking down at me as he filled me. He must have felt it too, because he slipped his knees forward and pulled himself upright. Taking my hips with him, keeping us attached, he lifted me by my backside. I used my feet to help balance myself as he held my hips and pummeled into me repeatedly. Each thrust hit a spot deep inside me that I didn't know existed, tapping it over and over and over until I couldn't take anymore. My body wanted another orgasm, although I'd never had two in a row before.

When his thumb hit my center, stroking me rapidly as he thrust deep inside, tears filled my eyes again. Frustration. I wanted this, this release, this pleasure, this painful tapping deep within me.

"You right there again, darlin'?" He questioned, and I was reminded that we hardly knew one another. There were signs, sighs, sounds people too comfortable with one another expressed if the other is paying attention. Sometimes when you are with the same person for so long, you forget. I'd forgotten the joy in discovery, and I loved that Tommy didn't recognize yet that I was about to come a second time, and it was going to be huge.

I tipped my hips, clenched within and released so large my toes curled. Moisture seeped from my core, and I heard the slapping of our bodies against one another in the wet heat I'd produced. He stilled, and with my hips raised, I felt the sharp jolt of him inside me, pulsing and jerking. My head rolled to the side. I was sweaty and lazy, depleted of all energy.

He lowered my hips, slipping out of me, and removing the condom. It disappeared off the side of the bed and he stretched out next to me. His hand scaled over my stomach as my chest rose and fell with the exertion of what we just did. Propped on an elbow next to me, he looked like he'd barely broken a sweat.

I chuckled, and his hand jiggled on my belly.

"I love that you're like opening a bottle of fine wine," he said. My laughter died, and his finger traced circles on my soft abs. "You're refreshing," he said, swiping his other hand through his hair, but not looking at me.

"Something different for the palate," I suggested. His lips curled as I played along with his metaphor.

"Something different, darlin', definitely."

He rolled away from me after that and picked up the condom from the floor. I still hadn't moved. I didn't know what to do next. Did I dress? Did I ask for a shower? Did I just leave? I sat up as he returned from the bathroom, a towel in hand.

"I guess I should…" I faltered, knowing I wasn't about to clean myself in front of him. I started scooting for the edge of the bed.

"I don't want to leave this bed," he said. "Not yet." His tone matched the one he used the night before, the same one where he told me he wanted to hold on, just a little bit.

He reached for his phone and ordered room service again. He'd slipped on his boxer briefs sometime when he went to dispose of the condom. Reaching for my dress on the pillows, he handed it to me.

"Would you be more comfortable if you put this back on?"

I nodded and took the nightshirt from him, excusing myself from the bed for a moment, and awkwardly covering myself as I briskly walked to the bathroom. Once inside, I collapsed against the door only briefly before realizing I was a mess. Using a washcloth, I cleaned myself, said a silent apology before I used his toothbrush, and dressed. My underwear was still missing.

I returned to the room and found him in the same position as I'd left him: one arm behind his head, partially propped up on the pillows, legs sprawled across the bed. He stared out the open balcony door at the dulling storm. Turning to me, he held out a hand, and I took it. His hands were thick, the tips of his fingers rough. Mine looked so small inside his, veiny and sprinkled with freckles. Beauty marks, my mother called them.

He sat forward, wrapped an arm around my waist and tugged me over him to bounce on the bed beside him.

"You have that look again," he said, staring down at me where he towered on an elbow over me. "No running. Breakfast is coming."

He returned to his resting position, and I sat up.

"We should talk," he said next, and I stiffened. Here it comes, I thought, not even knowing what he could say. *This was nice. Let's exchange numbers. I never want to see you again.*

My chest clenched with each scenario.

"Tell me about your ex-husband."

The command took my breath. "What?" I choked.

"You said he was an alcoholic. Tell me about that."

"Why?"

"You're doing it again." He chuckled, looking at me, but my question was an honest one.

"Really, why do you want to know?"

"I find I still don't have you figured out. You keep surprising me, and I want to know about this."

"I thought you said no other people in the bed," I teased, trying to make light of discussing David and wishing to avoid all messy conversations anyway.

"That was before. When I'm about to enter you, make us one, there's only room for us two."

My breath hitched again. There was something sweet in that statement.

"But now I want the deets on the ex."

This was too strange, I thought, as I shook my head and answered. "He was an alcoholic. End of story."

"Not enough," Tommy said, letting his arm fall from behind his head. He clasped his hands on his lower abs, and I forced my eyes not to linger on the covered package, knowing how large it could get.

"I was married for twenty years. We were young when I got pregnant. We got married. It was the right thing to do, so we did." I shrugged as my mother's words echoed in my head. Twenty-one and a recent college graduate. Pregnant and married wasn't the life plan.

"He graduated college a year before me and had a high-pressure job in an accounting firm. He worked long hours. He travelled. We seemed to circle one another instead of blending like married couples. We had been people who partied, but not partiers, if that makes sense. I guess life just got to him."

"You making excuses for him, beautiful?"

"No," I scoffed. "David had choices. He just chose himself, as he always did." He'd been a selfish man all our marriage. Even the times he tried not to drink, the selfishness was still part of his personality.

"You stayed with him," he stated. This was always where things got sticky.

"I did. I thought it was me. I thought it was the kids. He sometimes told me it *was* me. He mentioned a few times he didn't want to be a father. We did therapy. We tried vacations. But the bottom line was David had a problem that he didn't see as a problem. He lied to me and he lied to himself. I couldn't take it any longer."

"What happened?"

"I turned forty. I was over it. My kids were older, and I didn't like my life. I didn't feel like I had one. I found a new job and asked him for a divorce. When I found out he had an affair, it sealed my determination to take back something for me."

"You seem like an independent woman." It was the first impression I think Tommy got correct.

"I am. Or at least, I like to think I am." I couldn't admit to him that there were many times I was weak. I still wanted to be held. I still wanted

L.B. Dunbar

someone to tell me things would be all right when they didn't seem to be. I still wanted someone to love me.

He took a deep breath, and I continued.

"I got cancer around the same time I served David with divorce papers. He swore he'd change, that he'd be there for me. But he wasn't. It was just one more thing that drove him to drink. I knew I'd be better alone than with him."

"Very independent," he muttered, as if surprised or impressed.

"I just wanted *me* back. I wanted my life," I stated, patting at my chest. "And then I thought I was going to lose it. Lose everything. I couldn't stay with David. I'm forty-three. If I've lived half my life, and was fortunate enough to get the other half, what would that other half bring? It couldn't be a failing marriage, an alcoholic husband, and a very unhappy me."

The air in the room grew heavy, and darkness filled the balcony window, bringing on another round of stormy weather. The oppressive atmosphere matched the one in Tommy's room, and my stomach dropped at how I'd taken our carefree minutes and tainted them with memories of a man I once loved, but who didn't love me.

Tommy hadn't spoken, and I scrambled to the end of the bed, reaching over it for my underwear. I'd said too much, and the weight of it crushed me. If I was going to bare my soul, I wanted my underwear back on.

"I should go," I muttered.

"I don't want you to." The words startled me. "I want to eat eggs, discuss music, and just look at you."

"I…" I had no words. My heart raced. My stomach flipped. I wanted to kiss him. His lip twitched, and he tipped his head as if he read my thoughts. Taking another risk, I climbed over his feet, straddling his legs and crawled up the length of his body. His smile widened as I sat at his lap, painfully aware of what lay just underneath my backside.

"I'd like that, too," I said softly, tracing a nail over his abs, making them suck in. A hand came to my hip.

84

"Kiss me, darlin'," he asked, and I did. I kissed him with the same tenderness I did last night, with the longing I had to be with someone who was rough on the outside like him, but equally sweet. I kept my body still as I concentrated only on his lips, letting the tip of my fingers stroke the stubble on his jaw, shifting to nails scratching through the short hair.

"You like that, darlin'?" he muttered against my mouth.

"I do," I purred, continuing to scratch while I returned to kissing. His lips were plump and delicate when he'd let them be, and the kisses washed over me, cleansing me of thoughts of my ex. I pulled back slowly, taking his lower lip with mine before releasing him. His eyes were closed, and he opened them slowly.

"You brushed your teeth." He chuckled.

"So did you," I replied.

"Is it strange that I like you using my toothbrush?"

"Not if you aren't offended that I did."

"Please, offend me," he said, leaning forward for my mouth and forcing my body to rut back against his growing length. A knock at the door interrupted.

"Breakfast," he muttered, gently pushing me off of him. "I'd rather get drunk on you instead, but I am starving." He said it so casually, so nonchalantly, as if he had no idea how that thought ricocheted my heart rate and sent desire rushing through me.

If he wanted fine wine for breakfast, who was I to deny him?

+ + +

"Your music knowledge is horrendous," Tommy chuckled, pointing a crispy slice of bacon at me. I smiled in response. I described every song by the singer—you know, the one by the short, pixie blonde about being alone—or—the band with four guys and the front one looks like so-and-so. Tommy was good natured about my lacking information.

"Favorite song of all time," he asked. I had to really think about it and then I had to try to clarify without using a movie or television show, which he mocked mercilessly, telling me those references didn't count.

"'Wait For Me' by a band called Colt45." I shrugged my shoulder, glancing down at my plate. "I saw them in a small venue when I was in college. They were amazing, and I just loved that song. It hit the radio, but I remember hearing them before it went public."

I looked up to find Tommy staring at me, bacon still poised in between his fingers. He dropped the bacon on his plate and turned his head toward the balcony window. I had no idea what I'd said, but the air around us dropped ten degrees. He sat back and rubbed at his jean-covered thighs.

"What did I say?" I asked, bewildered. His head turned back for me, and a smirk curled his lips but didn't reach his eyes.

"Nothing, darlin'."

I nodded not understanding what happened. Turning toward the clock, I gasped.

"Oh my gosh, is it really nine-thirty?" This wasn't some play on escape and using the time as an excuse. It really was three and a half hours after we woke, and I could only imagine how my kids might react to my walk of shame across the resort complex. Thinking of that reminded me I had only my nightdress and bare feet to carry me back to the condo. I groaned, standing.

"How am I going to get out of here?" Tommy followed me up from his seat.

"Whoa, whoa, slow down, darlin'. You don't need to rush off."

"But it's nine-thirty. Oh, my God, my kids are going to think…" I let the thought trail off and covered both my cheeks with my hands.

"They aren't going to think anything," Tommy said. "Why don't you call Masie, ask her to bring you whatever you need." He paused and looked around his room. "Where are your shoes?"

"I didn't wear any," I said. "You were making a small scene, and I just wanted to get you back to your room."

Tommy's face dropped. The edges of his jaw hardened and his cheeks angled.

"Don't ever let me do that again, you understand? You kick me to the curb. Tell me to fuck off, but don't walk across a resort without shoes for me." His tone was serious, almost eerie, and I nodded to agree.

"I really need to go, though."

He offered me a pair of way-too-large slides before he tugged on a T-shirt, slipped into his own flip-flops, and escorted me from his room. When we neared my room, after walking through the parking lot instead of the lobby, a sadness pressed on me. Each time I parted from him I felt as if it would be the last time I experienced him. It wasn't just the sex, but sex *with him*. To my surprise, breakfast afterward had been equally rewarding. He was funny, smart, and nice to look at when he smiled back at me.

As we stood before my door, I awkwardly played with my key card, twirling it in my hand.

"I want to give you my number," Tommy said. Although it was only a phone number, the thought warmed my insides. He pulled out his phone, and I realized I'd left mine in his room.

"I'll just text mine to your number," he said, typing in the digits.

"But I left mine in your room," I said sheepishly. He smiled slowly, and I noted this meant we'd have to see each other again. "Come in for a second. I'll write your number down."

He followed me into the condo where I noticed all the lights were still off. The blinds for the balcony remained closed. The door to my bedroom was shut.

"Just a minute," I said, stepping over to my room, and opening the door to find Caleb sleeping in my king size bed. My heart pumped faster as I crossed the foyer, and knocked on the door of the room Masie and Caleb shared. They hadn't minded sharing a room. Caleb said it would be like when they were children in bunkbeds on vacation, only this time they each had a double.

"Masie," I announced, opening the door to see Masie spring from her bed and West roll to the opposite side. I shoved the door completely open.

"What the hell is going on?" I asked, stepping into the room.

"Mom?" Masie questioned, blinking while she ran a hand through her long hair. I'd clearly surprised her.

"Weston?" Tommy said behind me, and my heart dropped. This didn't look good for any of us.

"Nothing happened, Tommy," West defended quickly. He tugged at his T-shirt, straightening it over his abs. "I swear, Tommy."

Masie watched him as Tommy snarled, "If you touched her, you're a dead man."

"Mom," Masie started, turning back to me. "We only slept together."

I gasped, a hand covering my mouth to suppress the whimper.

"I mean…I mean, *sleep*. Mom, we literally only slept."

"Get the fuck out here," Tommy growled, addressing West, who quickly crossed the bedroom, not even glancing in Masie's direction. He slipped past me as if I'd reach out and punch him, which I wanted to do.

"Masie, how could you?" I groaned, thinking she did this because I wasn't present.

"How is it any different than what you did?" If she struck me, the blow would have felt the same.

"Easy, girl," Tommy said behind me, but I turned on him.

"Get out," I bit, swiping a hand over my barely-there hair. "What was I thinking? Get out. Please." I stared at him, then shifted to West, whose head hung while he brushed back his longer bangs.

"Mrs. Williams…." It was the first time he'd called me by my full name.

"West, I'm politely asking you. Leave." My teeth grit with the request.

"Darlin', I'm sure it looks—"

"Out," I cut him off. My heart was in my throat. I was the pot calling the kettle black, and I hated myself even more for it. I'd given my daughter the impression this behavior was acceptable, appropriate.

Tommy glared back at me and then gripped West by the nape of his neck. He tugged his charge and shoved him toward the door. I flinched as it slammed behind them.

Turning to Masie, I saw her horrified face before it hardened. Tears welled in her eyes.

"How could you embarrass me like that? Nothing happened." She slammed the bedroom door in my face. My shoulders fell, and I pinched my own eyes, trying to process that my daughter slept with a rock star in my condo. She was only eighteen!

Crossing to my room, I found Caleb smiling up at me.

"What's wrong, beautiful?" he teased, spreading his arms like a child wanting a hug. I ignored him. "What happened?"

"I just found West in Masie's bed."

Caleb sat up and in mock-surprise shrieked, "What?" A hand came to his chest in an effeminate manner. "How could she?"

"Caleb," I warned. "What did you do?"

"I didn't do anything. Sounds like Masie did." He wiggled his eyebrows and then noticed the seriousness of my stance.

"Oh, fine. He called her after you left. I didn't see the harm. He's a decent guy. Masie said they were only listening to music, and I believe them. Geez, Mom, chill. Masie isn't like me." I found little reassurance in that statement, but knew what my son meant. He shared too much of his manslut escapades, more than a mother should know. Fortunately, my son and daughter were close, and Caleb was protective. He'd never let someone close to Masie if he thought he'd hurt her.

"How could you let him in here when I wasn't home?"

"Uh, Mom. Eighteen," he said, pointing to Masie's door. "Twenty-two." He pointed to himself. "Think we can handle being alone."

Frustrated, I exhaled.

"I'm going to shower," I snapped, heading for the master suite bathroom. When I finished, Masie still had the door to her room closed, and Caleb was in the other bathroom showering.

The day looked like it would remain overcast, matching my mood, and I decided retail therapy was in order. I needed to step away from all my thoughts and deeds.

I knocked on the bathroom door. "Caleb, I'm going shopping."

"Kay," he shouted back.

Grabbing my bag, and slipping into flip-flops, I headed for the parking lot. I wore shorts and a T-shirt for easy access to try on clothes. My credit card was suddenly burning a hole in my wallet. When I stepped out of the stairwell, I found West pacing near our rental car—a Jeep Wrangler my kids demanded I rent.

"West," I said, surprised to find him walking to and fro, typing on his phone. His longer bangs were a mess, parting his hair in the middle with strands blowing in the low breeze.

"Mrs. Williams," he addressed me formally again. "Nothing happened. I swear on my life. On my mother's life. I'm so sorry. I know what it looked like…" His voice trailed off. Something stabbed me in the chest, reminding me he was only twenty-two. His plea seemed sincere.

"How did you get into my condo?" I asked.

"Masie…" he paused, rethinking the direction he wanted to explain. "Masie and I were talking on the phone, and I asked her if I could play her something. I went there…" He stumbled, and I instantly learned West wasn't a good liar. He was definitely covering for my daughter, the little vixen, who I assumed invited him over as soon as I left. Whose fault was that? Tommy's? I sighed. Mine, I recognized.

"West, you seem like a decent guy, and I might have overreacted in the moment. I trust Masie. I think I was just a little startled."

"That's what Tommy said. But I'm still sorry."

"She's only eighteen," I added. "She's still in high school."

"I know," he sighed, combing back his hair. "I know." Frustration filled his face, and I realized this young man had a crush on my daughter.

He was trying to do the right thing, I hoped, because he was just that much older. It was a real struggle.

"Do I need to say you shouldn't see her again?"

West stopped moving. His hand no longer swept his hair.

"I really wouldn't like that request." His honesty was refreshing. "But I'll respect it, if that's what you wish."

I shifted my bag, jutting out my hip.

"I think Masie would kill me if I did that."

West looked at me, a slow smile gracing his lips, and two dimples formed around it. He was really cute, and I could see Masie's attraction to him.

"You need to keep things in check," I warned, repeating the words I'd said to Masie, and feeling guilty once again that I wasn't following my own rule.

"Definitely." West stepped forward and unexpectedly hugged me. The move was so sudden, I staggered after he released me. "Thank you. Thank you so much, Mrs. Williams. See you later," he shouted as he walked away, his voice sounding lighter.

I turned for the Jeep when I heard Caleb call my name from three stories up.

"Mom, hang on. I'm coming with you."

+ + +

My son loved to shop. It was a strange thing, but I assumed he'd grown into it because he was always with Masie and me, until he started playing baseball and guitar. He especially loved athletic shoes, which could get pretty pricey, the larger his feet grew. As we walked the shopping strip, we wandered in and out of touristy boutiques, overcrowded with people who had the same idea as us on a cloudy day in Hawaii.

Caleb also loved graphic tees, and we spent more time trying to get him to make a decision on one or two than anything else. Eventually, he gave me time to visit a few dress shops, and I picked up three new dresses, perfect for summer back home. Most places we entered were

L.B. Dunbar

over my price point despite the hole-burning credit card, but I was happy with the items I purchased, feeling slightly relieved from this morning's misunderstandings.

"Masie called Dad," Caleb told me as we ate lunch. I hated when she did things like that. Not because it was hurtful to me, but because it would only lead to a broken heart for her. I could only imagine how the conversation went:

*What did your mother do?*

*Do you miss me?*

*Talk soon.*

He didn't care what I did, only that I did something to make our children reach out for him. He had no backbone when it came to discipline, so I always looked like the bad parent. On top of that, asking if our child missed him was only reassurance to his ego. He never told them he missed them. Why would he? He had a carefree life, living on a boat on the lake for a bit and then moving into a condo in downtown Chicago. The last statement—*talk soon*—was always a lie, setting the kids up for false hope. David rarely followed through with call backs and visits. He attended what he could, when he could, he said. My heart ached that Masie thought her father would give her comfort after this morning.

"And, what did he say?" I asked, drawing in a deep breath.

"The usual," Caleb shrugged. Caleb didn't really have it as bad as Masie. He was already off to college when the divorce happened, and as baseball was David's number one priority for Caleb, his father hardly missed any of his games. Caleb fulfilled David's dream, but I often worried it wasn't our son's.

Hours passed. We shopped. We strolled. My son was a funny man, and I enjoyed his company. As we neared the Jeep, I saw another man leaning against it, his back to the spare tire, foot pressed to the bumper. He concentrated on his phone as his fingers typed frantically. Approaching slowly, I looked up at Caleb.

"What did you do?"

"Nothing," Caleb said, holding up his hands as if in surrender. "Nothing, I swear." But I knew my son, and he winked. Tommy straightened as we approached.

"You have been so damn hard to find, darlin'," he drawled, inhaling and looking relieved. My brows pinched as I glanced at Caleb.

"Keys," my son said, holding out his hands.

"Wait." Tommy held up his hand. "Did you buy a pretty dress?" His eyes roved to the bags in my hand.

"I did." My brows pinched as I thought of my new things.

"Slip one on."

"What?"

Tommy looked at Caleb and back at me. "Hop in the Jeep and change. We'll keep watch." When Tommy winked at Caleb, I realized my son had conspired against me.

I stepped into the back seat and struggled to pull on a pretty lavender dress. It had thin straps over the shoulder and a deep vee at the neckline. I only wore my flip-flops so the ensemble had a beach-chic look to it. I combed through my hair and applied some lipstick I found in the bottom of my bag. Stepping back out of the Jeep, Tommy stared at me.

"What?" I snapped again, fanning out the dress at my sides.

"Beautiful, darlin'." He hesitated, like he wanted to step toward me, but didn't out of respect for Caleb's presence.

"Keys," Caleb said again, and I handed them over.

After Caleb pulled away, Tommy and I stared at one another. I wasn't certain why I changed my dress or why we stood here, but I spoke first. "I'm sorry about this morning."

Tommy nodded in response. "Did you mean what you said? That you made a mistake."

"I didn't say that." I blinked, taken aback.

"No, your exact words were *what was I thinking*, implying you made a mistake." His lips twisted after he spoke.

"I didn't mean that," I said, looking up at him sheepishly. "I might have…overreacted."

"Understandable," he replied, nodding his head again. "I'd like to talk about that...over dinner."

"Okay," I replied, dragging out the word, trepidation filling me while we stood in a parking lot. Dinner sounded nice, but talking worried me. When he held out a hand, I felt a little better as I wrapped my fingers with his. Tommy didn't just cup my hand. He held it, palm to palm, fingers between fingers. It was as if he would lose me if he didn't hold tight.

We walked in silence a few blocks before he stopped in front of a heavily populated seafood restaurant. I pretended I didn't see some of the glares people gave us as we walked to the front of the line. Tommy offered a name, and we were immediately escorted to a table along the windows with a perfect view of the ocean.

"How did you do that?" I marveled, noting all the patrons waiting for a seat. Tommy shrugged his shoulder. It was the first time I'd seen him use his position to his advantage. We ordered drinks and then Tommy pulled something from his pocket.

"I don't want to assume, but I'm thinking David might be your ex-husband."

My phone was set on the table between us and Tommy pressed the home key. The screen lit up with text after text after text from David.

"If he's not your ex-husband, I want to know if you're dating him, because if you are he needs his ass kicked."

Tension I didn't know I was feeling slowly released as Tommy spoke.

"If he is your ex-husband, he still needs his ass kicked, although I won't do that, out of respect for him once being married to you."

My mouth curled lazily upward.

"But let me add, he sounds like a fucking asshole either way."

A laugh escaped. One sharp bellow. Tingles rippled inside me that the man across from me wanted to defend my honor against a man who promised to honor me all the days of his life.

Tommy slid the phone closer to me and I briefly noted the short quips regarding Masie, and my incapability of being a mother, and making a mistake taking a vacation, and was I dating anyone, which was none of his damn business.

"That last one's my favorite, so let's start there. We're both on vacation, and I'd like to propose we live a little. No promises. No commitment, but I like spending time with you, and I want a little more of it. So…" he faded off to brush the waitress away. "I don't want to share you with anyone else while we're here."

My mouth fell open. Not at the restriction of sharing, but at the implication that I would go out with someone else.

"You do realize that I have hardly dated in the past three years. It's been even longer since I've had sex, and this…" I pointed between us. "…has never *ever* happened to me before. So, I think it's safe to say I won't be going out with anyone else while I'm here."

It was his turn for a curling smile, and a chuckle escaped. He crossed his arms and leaned toward me.

"Three years." He whistled low, as an eyebrow tweaked. His smile deepened. "I've got some work to do then."

The comment sent shivers down my spine, but I liked the sensation.

"To show you I'm serious, I'd like to give you my room key." He slipped a black plastic card out of his pocket. "It's so you can visit me when you can, when you want, whenever…" His voice faltered, and he waved a hand. Was he nervous? I smiled again as I took the offered room card.

"I promise not to be a stalker, though," I assured.

"Phew," he teased, swiping at his forehead. "Already had one of them. Had she been you, I might have enjoyed it, though." He wiggled his eyebrows, and I laughed, but the seriousness of what he said wrestled inside me. There was so much I didn't know about him, and the fact someone tried to take advantage of him frightened me.

The waitress returned, and this time Tommy didn't wave her away, so we ordered, and I decided to let my questions rest. Over dinner we discussed the guys in the band, and Tommy told me more about each of them. I think he was trying to reassure me that West was the most decent of the four.

"Gage is Gage. He's intense, and he loves Ivy fiercely. He almost lost her, because he can be stupid, but he knows he needs her. She gets him because of her mother." Whenever Tommy mentioned Ivy's mom, his sister, there was a certain sadness to him.

"Petty is a male whore, and I have no doubt he'd impregnate someone if I wasn't so diligent about who he's with. Jared's smart. He went to college, but dropped out for the band. He followed Gage's dream. West is the newest addition. He replaced Cash."

Tommy looked out the window as he spoke the last man's name.

"Who was Cash?" I asked. Tommy snorted softly.

"You really don't know music, do you? Cash Bennett. He was the lead bassist, and he killed himself." Tommy sat back and drummed the table. "Damn overdose." He swiped a hand through his hair. I focused on his face. There was more to the story, but I didn't wish to pry. "Anyway, West is probably the best of them all. Talented, but good at heart. Eager and mostly still innocent. He didn't mean anything to be misrepresented with your girl."

"I know," I replied softly. "It was just sort of a shock, and I felt guilty."

"Guilty?"

"If I'd been there, West wouldn't have been."

"Darlin', I know about guilt, but what happened with him sleeping next to your daughter has nothing on what I've seen. He's a good kid." He raised an eyebrow, defending someone belonging to him.

"I know," I leaned on the table. "I said I overreacted. That isn't easy for me to admit."

"Well, let's get to admitting more of your sexual history, as your musical one sucks."

I laughed, and he watched my lips. I wanted to kiss him, or he wanted to kiss me. It didn't matter. There would be more kissing, either way.

When dinner finished, we walked hand-in-hand again, taking our time meandering down the main strip of shops. He asked me about my job, and as I described it, I realized it didn't sound very exciting, but it paid my bills. I was a personal assistant—which meant taking care of other people, kind of like Tommy. The conversation switched to my home, Chicago. He'd been there several times for concerts.

"Collision's dream is to play the big stadiums. Wrigley Field's a rare gig. The guys would love to headline there."

We halted at a corner, and Tommy tugged me to the left. We walked past two storefronts before he stopped in front of what I assumed was a small bar. Neon signs strobed beer advertisements through a narrow window. The place looked like a hole in the wall, shoved between a surf shop and a tattoo parlor. He opened the door, and I was assaulted with music.

"Is that ABBA?" I laughed as 'Dancing Queen' flowed to the sidewalk.

"That it is," he said, placing a hand on my lower back and pressing me forward to enter. Once inside, the lights were dim and the bar long. In the back corner were a jukebox and a strip of wood floor that could potentially be for dancing.

"What is this?" I giggled as Tommy led me to the end of the bar.

"Local hang out," he replied, helping me up on a stool. He raised two fingers without speaking an order.

"You've been here before?" I questioned when two short tumblers with dark liquid were set before us. The dinner wine and rich seafood already made me warm and fuzzy inside. A short sniff of alcohol within the glass told me I was about to be set on fire.

"Something like that." He raised his glass, tapped mine, and shot back the whiskey.

*Oh, what the hell.* I did the same, only I sputtered and coughed and didn't empty the glass. Tommy walked away from me after patting my back a few times, and I watched him cross to the jukebox. Quarters were slipped in, and he pressed a few buttons. Returning to me, he explained, "The locals play this shit disco music to keep tourists out. If you can stomach the 70s, then you can hang without being bothered here."

"How old do you think I am?" I teased, as he suggested I was familiar with 70s music, *which I was.*

"Not old, darlin', but you're not a headbanger, either. You aren't even bell bottoms and tie-dye T-shirts. You've got poodle skirt and pearls written all over you, although you aren't that old either." He wiggled a finger as if sketching me.

"You've just painted an awful image of me," I laughed, but he had me pegged. I loved the 50s although I was a product of the 90s. College years filled with fishnet stockings, shoulder pads, and off the shoulder tees had nothing on my ideal of saddle shoes and a full skirt.

"Not really." He paused, leaning towards me. "I'd like to color in the lines of that drawing and then color outside them just for fun."

I gasped, but my insides tingled.

This place made perfect sense. The band could never enter a bar like regular people. Gage was recognized everywhere. Ironically, Tommy seemed to be noticed as well which was strange as the band manager. Then again, he told me he played in his sister's band, Chrome Teardrops, and I figured that must be the recognition. Some music buffs really knew their band members.

A Bee Gees song popped on overhead.

"They're playing our song," Tommy whispered, leaning closer to my ear.

"How is this our song?" I giggled.

"You said you'd pick a Bee Gees song to describe me."

I laughed as I clapped once.

"Dance." He held out his hand.

"Oh, no. No, I told you I don't dance. I meant that. It wasn't a blow off."

His lips rose and a beautiful smile filled his face. "Oh, yes. You owe me a dance."

Tugging me off the barstool, he pulled me to the small dance floor and spun me dramatically. I stumbled a little and arched a brow to indicate, *see, I told you I can't dance*, but he continued to guide me, pulling me close and moving my hips to match the sway of his. I laughed again, realizing this tough, rock star manager, who swore a little bit too much and kissed like the devil himself, knew how to dance...and to disco.

"You are a wonder, Tommy Carrigan," I said as he pulled me close to him, chest pressed to chest, as we stood in more of a moving embrace than a dance while the Bee Gees' song 'How Deep Is Your Love' played in the background.

"You are a wonder, Edie Williams. One I want to keep wondering about."

L.B. Dunbar

# 7

### Baby, you're a rock star

My fingers delicately traced over lips still swollen and rough from kissing Tommy. After dancing, he brought me back to the resort, where he kissed me in his car and then walked me to my door, kissing me some more. We were like teenagers as our mouths mashed together and bodies pressed against walls. The stairwell. The hallway balcony. The tiny alcove entrance to my condo. Each time we broke apart, one of us would reach for the other and another upright surface met someone's back while mouths returned to devouring each other.

I lay in bed, replaying the night in my mind. Each kiss. Each caress. Tommy had big hands, but he touched me like I was a delicate butterfly, like I might flutter away if he didn't tenderly care for me. It wasn't that he couldn't be rough, but there was a certain control to his hardness. Then I thought of his laugh—husky and rich—like the way he moved his hips. I giggled to myself, recalling how he tugged me into the disco-playing, dive bar, and we danced. I never danced, but with Tommy as my lead, I feared I'd do anything he asked. He made me feel spontaneous, and little more like someone *I* used to know.

I also thought about my daughter. When I had finally made it through my front door, I found Masie and West on the couch in the small living area, watching a movie.

"Night, honey," I offered as a simple way of apology and approval for West sitting in the condo without me present. How could I judge her for wanting to spent time with someone who made her feel special? Here's the thing: Weston Reid was a rock star, but he was spending a lot of time with my daughter instead of trolling the bars with his two wayward bandmates, Jared and Petty. Was her heart going to break when they parted ways? Absolutely, and I'd know firsthand how she'd feel. We'd just have to pick up the pieces together.

When I left my bedroom the next morning, I found Masie already awake, and we decided to hit the pool area early. For a while the silence pressed between us, but slowly she began talking to me. She couldn't stay angry for long, and she couldn't keep quiet long, either. We began discussing the litany of things ahead in her final semester of high school, and her decision-making process for college. Nursing school was going to be a difficult journey, but one I knew Masie would embrace with passion, just like everything else in her life. I didn't want her going far from home, but she needed to branch out and see the world. She was torn between Wisconsin and California, two gravely different areas.

"Think West would come visit me if I went to Santa Clara?" she asked sheepishly.

"That would be fun," I offered, knowing I tread on thin ice. "Might be hard with his schedule. Doesn't Collision have a world tour starting next summer?" Tommy told me some of the plans for the band. The world tour was a huge undertaking to promote their next album, which they needed to cut as soon as this vacation was over. I couldn't piece together why they stayed at a resort instead of renting a condo or a house on the beach. The time of year—winter break—made sense to me, but it seemed strange none of them had gone home to their families to celebrate the holidays.

Masie shrugged. "Maybe the tour will come through the Midwest?" Hope filled her voice while she tried to express with her body language that it didn't matter. My poor girl was falling hard, and the pieces might be harder to put back together after all. As soon as I looked up to find Tommy walking toward the pool area with Ivy and the girls, I knew my pieces were going to be scattered with my daughter's.

"Hey," Ivy said, setting up next to us as if she were part of our family.

"Mornin' darlin'," Tommy said, biting his lower lip and letting it roll from his teeth. He'd already texted me this morning to say the same thing, but it wasn't the same as hearing his voice. I really liked that rolled -r sound.

"Good morning," I replied, a slow smile pressing my lips upward like they held a secret. That secret included the sensation of his mouth on mine.

"Got to get to the guys. Band practice again today. You lovely ladies have fun." He winked at me and bent to pat Emaline on the head. "Ivy, honey, see you later."

"Bye," she sang, holding up Ava's hand to wave at their uncle. He blew a kiss to Ava, which Ivy made her reach and catch. Ava giggled. Tommy was too sweet.

We settled in like women do, chatting and giggling about anything and everything. Ivy talked about the girls, and I answered questions about motherhood. Masie talked about college, and Ivy talked about her own experience.

"I went to college to be a music therapist. Even though both my parents were musicians, and I come from a musical family, I can't really sing." She giggled. "I guess the gene skipped me. As my mom grew sicker, I saw how music helped her and how sad she was that her singing and playing were slipping away from her. I wanted to help those who needed that peace."

"I didn't know your mom was a musician," Masie said, and I held my breath, worried that Ivy didn't wish to share that information with people she hardly knew.

"My mother was Kit Carrigan from Chrome Teardrops. They were popular when…I guess maybe, you were in college," she motioned to me.

"Oh, I've heard of her," Masie said, sitting up excitedly. "I don't remember her from that band, but I remember her solo with the band Colt45."

The name startled me. I'd mentioned that band the other day to Tommy, telling him one of my all-time favorite songs was from a similarly named band. So strange, I thought, to hear the name again.

"Wait, was there more than one Colt45?" In my limited music history, the only Colt45 band I knew of was an indie band when I was in high school. I saw them play at a small bar that allowed underaged patrons on occasion.

"Possibly, but not that I know of—" Ivy started, but then Emaline raced for the pool, and Ivy stood to follow her. We shifted to the edge of the pool so Ivy could get in the water with her daughter and the conversation about her mother ended.

A few hours later we were sunburnt and a little toasted from day drinking. I was on the verge of one too many margaritas when Ivy asked us to dinner.

"It's Sunday, and that means Tommy's pasta night."

I sputtered my drink as salt coated my lips. "What?" I giggled.

"Every Sunday, Tommy makes pasta for everyone, demanding we eat together like a family and not a gaggle of musicians, as he calls them. It's open invite for others, but the band has to be present. He even does it on the road."

"I didn't realize today was Sunday." I'd lost track of the days since we started our vacation, but Sunday meant we were almost halfway through our ten days of Hawaiian heaven.

"All day," Ivy chuckled. "Anyway, we'd love to have you all join us." I appreciated that she was including Caleb, who was mysteriously absent today. He was in bed when we left this morning but hadn't made an appearance at the pool.

Masie looked at me expectantly, but I was already accepting the invitation. "If you're sure, what can I bring?"

"I think Tommy wants you to bring only you," she winked, and I choked on the swallow of margarita I tried to sip after speaking. "You don't need to bring anything else."

+ + +

Hours later, we arrived at the penthouse suite with wine, bread, and brownies. It was the best I could do in the small-scale galley kitchen of our condo. Besides, I wasn't much of a cook, but I could bake. The penthouse was filled with laughter, music, and even some football bowl-game. I loved how my family seemed to meld with theirs, as Caleb immediately jumped into an argument about who would win the Rose Bowl, and Masie joined Ivy to cut vegetables for a salad. I was charged with doing nothing after Tommy greeted Masie and I with a kiss on the cheek, and a firm handshake was offered to Caleb with a pat on the back.

"Mmmmm, hope those brownies are laced with something," Petty inhaled as I walked past him with the piled-high plate. The comment earned him a swat from Tommy.

The personal assistant in me wasn't good sitting still while others buzzed around me, and I kept interfering, trying to taste sauce, cut vegetables, or slice bread.

"Here, I have something for you to do," Tommy finally said, leading me down a hallway and gently shoving me into a bedroom. The door closed behind me, and I spun to have my cheeks cupped and my mouth crushed. I melted into him, relaxing a little as his lips moved over mine.

"Was that the something for me to do?" I teased, when he pulled away, sipping my lips in slow tugs.

"Yes," he muttered before returning full mouth and thick tongue to kissing me. We only stole a few minutes before he said he needed to check the pasta.

"Please," I begged. "Assign me something to do." His eyebrow rose, and a smirk filled his face.

"You have no idea how many ways I want to assign you," he teased and then turned his back to me. I reached out for his back, spreading my hands over the broad breadth of it. He paused, and I bumped into him. Slipping my hands forward, I wrapped my arms around his chest and pressed my cheek to his back. I loved back hugs. His hand rubbed down my arm and he lifted my fingers, pressing a kiss to my palm.

"Is it too much to say that I missed you today?" he said into my hand, not able to look at me. I pressed a kiss to the middle of his back. "As long as it's okay with you that I missed you, too."

He bared his teeth and dragged them against my tender palm. The tingling pain sent pleasure rippling down my arm, and I shivered. More than twenty-four hours without sex with him, and I was a hot mess of desire. Moisture pooled in my underwear, and I rubbed my thighs together. If there wasn't a room full of people down the hall, I might not let him leave the bedroom. My grip tightened on him, spreading my fingers across his firm pecs.

"Darlin', if you don't let me go, we aren't leaving this room, pasta-night be damned."

I released him with pouty lips he couldn't see, as his back remained to me. He opened the door and swatted my backside as I exited. He wasn't following me.

"I need a minute," he said, taking a deep breath, and my eyes shot to the bulge at his zipper.

"Stop looking, beautiful. That's making it worse."

I smiled broadly, my face pinking, but thankful I wasn't the only one affected. I liked that I'd done that to him.

I was assigned to set the table, an extra-large seating arrangement that provided space for everyone. Gage and Ivy sat at one end while Tommy sat as head at the other. I was given a seat next to him while Masie and Caleb blended in the middle. Dinner was a riot of conversation, delicious food and the occasional roll sailing across the table to someone. I was teased by my children that spaghetti was my only specialty, to which Jared and Petty decided I was the perfect match for Tommy, as that was all he cooked.

The comment was said in jest, but my face glowed in shy embarrassment. It implied there could be something more than what we had, but Tommy had already been clear. He was on vacation and wanted to live a little. Matchmaking wasn't on the docket for this trip. The teasing passed just as quickly as everything else, and dessert consisted of my brownies and vanilla ice cream.

"Cleans the palate," Tommy said, holding his spoon between his lips just a little too long and staring at me. Wine was in abundance, and I'd definitely had my fair share by the time I stood to help clear the table.

"Tommy cooks, we clean," the boys chimed together. As a guest, I felt obliged to help.

"Uncle Tommy, can you sing to us before bed?" Ava asked while we were clearing the dishes. I hadn't realized how late it was, and the girls needed to get to bed.

"We have guests tonight," Ivy said, smiling up at me.

"Please," Ava begged, her younger sister echoing her whine.

"Have Daddy sing?" Ivy suggested, to which Gage looked up.

"Yeah, I can sing."

The girls giggled. "We *know* Daddy. You're always singing." Ava rolled her eyes. "But we want 'Jelly Belly.'" Emaline clapped after her sister spoke, and her mouth opened in the most adorable surprise.

"'Jelly Belly'" she cheered, and Ava followed in with a rousing chorus of "Jelly Belly! Jelly Belly! Jelly Belly!"

"What's 'Jelly Belly'?" I asked at the same time Petty looked to the ceiling and groaned. "Not 'Jelly Belly.'"

"It's a song by four probably pedophile guys who couldn't be a real band, so they sing kids' songs instead," Petty answered me.

"Yeah, well, those *four guys*," Jared emphasized, "are freaking millionaires."

"And what are we?" Petty scoffed.

"Close but not quite," Jared added, and my head shot up in surprise. "Okay, maybe a little bit more." He laughed as Petty scowled. Looking around, it made sense. They had the penthouse suite for ten days. Each member had their own room somewhere else in the hotel, but *millionaires*? I was so naïve.

"What makes Tommy singing 'Jelly Belly' so special?" I asked the girls, bending at the waist to be on their level.

"Tommy's voice goes deep, and he makes it deeper," Ava explained, trying to imitate the sound with a froggy croak. She looked at her uncle, and clasped her hands. Small eyelashes batted and her younger sister followed suit.

"How can you say *no* to that?" I asked Tommy.

"He won't," Ivy laughed. Reaching for Emaline and then scooping up Ava, he proved Ivy correct. Carrying one girl on his hip and the other under his arm, he walked down the long hallway and disappeared. I smiled with pride. He was a good man, maybe too good, and he loved his family, this ragtag group of relatives by blood and choice. It was refreshing to see a man act in this manner.

After a few minutes of clearing the table, and forming a huge pile of dishes on the counter, the soft tenor of a male voice drifted toward the dining room. I stopped, perking up like a deer hearing a hunter in the distance.

"Is that Tommy?" I questioned, my head turning toward the sound. My heart ratcheted up a notch, and my breaths increased. Ivy nodded toward the hallway. "Go listen."

For some reason, I walked slowly, as if called to the song, lulled by the voice. This wasn't a song about Jelly Belly, whatever that was, but something deep and sad, like a lullaby. I slowed to a tiptoe, not wanting to interrupt the sound. Pausing outside the door, I peeked around the jamb to see Tommy sitting on Ava's bed, strumming a guitar. His fingers worked methodically, his eyes watching his fingertips stroke a string and pluck a chord. His voice followed, quiet and confident. A presence behind me made me turn.

"His voice is so beautiful," I said to Gage, slightly surprised.

"It is," he said, looking down at the floor. "He's a master." My brows pinched, not understanding his meaning, and I turned to listen in again.

"Sing us one of yours," a sleepy Ava begged, stifling a yawn.

"Not tonight, baby girl," he said softly, but something must have shown on her face because he started strumming again. Instantly, I recognized the melody. As his voice filled the first line of lyrics, I stepped forward, filling the doorway. My mouth hung open. He sounded so familiar. I mean, he sounded exactly the same as…

"You sound like Lawson Colt," I muttered, staring at Tommy as his fingers screeched across the strings, coming to an abrupt halt. He turned to look up at me, eyes wide and a little wary.

"Lawson Colt," I murmured. "Of…of…of Colt45."

Tommy stood up slowly, but I stepped back, bumping into the wall behind me. I looked from Tommy to Gage as Tommy took a hesitant step toward me.

Gage's wide dark eyes pinched his brows. "You didn't know?" He chuckled. "You had to know."

"Her musical knowledge is atrocious," Tommy commented, with no humor in his voice. He stepped closer to me, holding up his hands in surrender as mine flattened against the wall behind me.

"I think she's star struck," Gage laughed, and I heard the soft tap of Ivy's sandals coming toward me down the hall.

"Star struck," I choked, a tinny sounding screech erupting from my mouth. I paused, trying to catch my breath. "You lied to me."

"Now, darlin'—"

"Don't," I cut him off, raising both hands to hold him back from me. "You…" I paused, looking around his side to see two little girls watching us as harsher words tipped on my tongue. *You fucking lied to me*, I swallowed, irate.

"I didn't lie," Tommy defended.

"You didn't tell the truth." My voice rose a little louder. A little too loud, apparently, because Caleb came down the hall.

"Mom, what's going on?"

"He's Lawson Colt," I stammered, waving a hand in the direction of Tommy. "Of Colt45."

"Well, duh," Caleb mocked, smiling his damn dimpled smile. Then his face dropped. "What's wrong?"

My mouth had popped open, but I snapped it shut. "You knew?" I questioned.

"Mom, everyone knows he's Lawson Colt."

"Not me!" I shrieked, and then I paused. *Everyone knew*. My eyes flipped from Gage to Ivy to Tommy. I looked like a fool. My music knowledge was bad, *but this*…not recognizing one of the greatest guitar players of all time? Slowly things made sense. Kit Carrigan and the band Colt45. A brother and sister duet, who sang heart-wrenching ballads about lost love, missed opportunity, and permanent separation. He wasn't just some guy in the band—he was her brother, her partner. Hell, if my weak memory was correct, he wrote all their songs. They broke the charts. Prior to that, he mentioned he played in his sister's band, Chrome Teardrops. They were one of the greatest female lead rock bands of all time. She set record after groundbreaking record for female artists, and he helped her, probably with songs he'd written for her.

I brushed past the small crowd in the hallway.

"Darlin'," followed after me as walked.

"I told you," Ivy whispered, but to who I wasn't sure. Not wishing to make a grand exit, despite my embarrassment, I reached the kitchen and grabbed a dish, pushing Petty out of the way.

"I'll take over. I need something to do." Scrubbing dishes and handing them to Petty, we filled the dishwasher in silence. Jared remained present as well, most likely waiting to catch any dish I started throwing, as I was certain I looked like I wanted to break something.

Tommy lied to me.

And truth by omission is the same thing. He hadn't told me.

*I should make you sign a nondisclosure agreement for all I've told you.* The words rang through my head. Did he still think I'd say something to someone? How little did he think of me? How little did he trust me? How could he give me his room key, unless he believed I'd never find out who he was?

*We only have a few days. Let's live it.*

*Lies*, I fumed, as I slammed the dishwasher shut and then filled the sink with sudsy water to tackle pots and pans.

"Darlin', let the boys do that," Tommy said softly from the door.

*I don't want to talk to you*, I yelled inside my head, but I'd already been embarrassed enough.

"I've got it," I snapped to the pan I circled with the sponge over and over again.

"Boys. Out," Tommy barked, but I turned and glared at Jared, willing him not to leave me alone even though I didn't know him well.

"I don't think—" Jared began.

"You're not here to think," Tommy snapped, and Jared narrowed his eyes at his manager. He didn't move, though, and two warm hands came to my upper arms.

"Darlin'." He spoke softly, as if to a spooked child. I was spooked, but I was also pissed off. I rolled my shoulders forward, pulling my arms

L.B. Dunbar

from his grasp. Refusing to look back at him, I rinsed the pot and started on the large serving bowl.

"You're kind of stubborn, aren't you? I didn't have you pegged for that." I bristled at the comment. How wrong he'd read me. How wrong I'd read him.

Lawson Colt. It didn't make sense, but it did. He couldn't be Tommy Carrigan to his sister, Kit. They would appear like a married couple with the same last name. Sister and brother acts had been a thing of the past. Not to mention, Lawson Colt had already been making a name with his indie band. Then his band disappeared. Had he given up his band for her? My shoulders fell, though not completely relieving the tension. His presence lingered only a moment longer before he stepped out of the kitchen. Jared took the dishes I stacked and started drying them. Petty had disappeared as soon as his duty was replaced by me.

"He didn't mean it," Jared said, speaking low. "I think he might have liked the anonymity. He can't go anywhere without being recognized. It's crazy." Memory flashed to the girls in the bar that first night, and more of them at the pool the next day. The dive bar where he said a local could hide, and the way a name passed us to the front of the line at the restaurant the night before. He was a freaking rock star in his own right.

"I'd like to understand, Jared, but I feel a little foolish. I had no idea, and considering you all did, including my Caleb, and no one said anything…" My voice trailed off and liquid welled in my eyes. I blinked several times. A hand came to my back, but I shook my head.

"I'm fine," I muttered, a phrase I'd said a million and a half times during a marriage of deceit. It was fine that David worked late. It was fine that he travelled too much. It was fine that he used our money to take a trip when he wanted a break from his life. Fine. Fine. *Fine*.

My shoulders fell completely, but the tension still pinched my back.

"Would you mind pouring me another glass of wine?" I asked Jared.

"Anything you want, Edie." He stepped around me for the opposite counter. "He really likes you. I know that. He's never dated anyone your

110

age." He paused, and I looked up at him, eyes narrowed. He was reflective a moment. "That sounded wrong."

Petty's head popped around the corner. "Well, he dated, cough, cough, women your age when he was younger. Then when he got older, they got younger."

"Not fucking helping," Jared yelled with a false laugh, pushing Petty's head away from the kitchen entrance.

"What I mean is—"

"Jared." I paused, blinking back the additional tears in my eyes. "Would you mind if I finished the dishes myself? It's a good distraction. Go watch the game or something." I smiled weakly, but hoped to convey that I really wanted to be alone. I was embarrassed enough, felt foolish enough, and had already created enough of a scene. I needed peace.

Jared nodded and pointed over his shoulder. "I'm right out here if you need anything." Nodding, I swiped at a tear before it escaped and returned to scouring the dishes.

+ + +

"Do you have any idea how fucking long I've been looking for you?" Tommy snapped, crouching down next to the chaise lounge where I lay. I'd texted Masie and Caleb after I snuck out the employee entrance of the penthouse, telling them I was headed to the bar. I didn't mention which one, although I'm certain they both knew why. I took a glass and the bottle of wine from the counter and went to the beach instead. I didn't want to be around people.

My eyes opened fully, as I'd been dozing after finishing the bottle. Impulse forced me to reach out and I cupped his cheek, drawing down to his chin, and then scratching at his neck with my knuckles. That prickly scruff brought me a strange comfort. Releasing his face, I slowly pressed myself upward, allowing him space to sit. He remained crouching a moment, watching me before he set a bottle of whiskey in the sand and took the seat opposite me.

111

"I'm sorry I didn't say anything, darlin'." He paused, and I waited. He was right; I was stubborn, but this time it was justified. I could wait a long time. In fact, I'd been waiting a lifetime for someone like him, yet somehow, I felt like he was already slipping away.

"You didn't trust me," I said, understanding all his reasons why and still not liking the answers.

"It wasn't that. Not one bit. I liked that you didn't know me. *Him*," he corrected. "I'm still me. I'm still Tommy Carrigan."

"I don't understand," I said, lifting my head to look at him.

"My name is Thomas Lawson Carrigan, Jr. My dad is Tommy, so they called me Lawson. I took the name Colt because it sounded bad ass and went with the vibe of our band. We wanted to be something classic, like the old 45 records, although Colt45 sounded *tuff*. A gun. Alcohol. Bad things. *Bang*." He signaled with two fingers towards the rolling ocean. He looked out at the water and I observed his silhouette. His beautiful, silver-streaked hair and matching scruff beard. The buff of his body and the curve of his plump lips. He was gorgeous, while I was me. Short hair, curling in Cs and Qs, streaked with silver and white blonde. We didn't match.

He was a rock star. I was just…me.

I turned away from him, looking down at the hand he returned to the arm of the chaise. He made music with his fingers, music that melted girls' hearts and soaked their underwear. I had been one of those girls. I had stood, mesmerized, falling in love with him and his words, when he played at that Chicago venue all those years ago. Twenty-five plus years ago, and here he sat. He'd made it in life. I'd never felt more incompetent.

"You're a fucking rock star," I said, shocking him with my use of the word. "And I'm a fool."

He rolled his head to face me, but it was my turn to look away.

"I thought you saw me differently than some groupie. I thought, maybe, you felt something for me." Tears I refused to shed clouded my eyes. "You must have laughed double-time at my lack of music history, hoping, *no*, knowing, I'd never figure out who you were. You could keep up the charade." I shook my head, disappointed in myself. My ex lied a hundred times and I never caught on. How had I fallen into this empty feeling again?

"I didn't lie to you. I just left it out. And I'm not sorry you didn't know. Your knowledge of the music industry *is* awful, and I loved it. It was interesting to watch you speak about things you lacked understanding about but were excited to share. Seeing your face light up as you realized you loved a song after I played it for you, or trying to describe one you liked without knowing the artist. It was refreshing that you wanted to impress me, but in a totally unskilled, unbiased way. And not recognizing me allowed you to get to see me without all the other bullshit clouding us."

"Us," I whispered. How could there be an *us* when only one of us was truthful?

"You are different, darlin', that's what I like so much about you. You don't see the other stuff. You only see me." His voice faltered. "Or maybe I just hoped you had." Silence surrounded us for a moment and I shivered with a chill in the night breeze.

"Please, beautiful," he begged. "*Please*, don't let this change anything. Be mad at me, if you want to. But I kept the truth from you so I could feel like a normal man."

"Normal?" I huffed. "You're a rock star," I repeated. "One that girls threw their bras at and showed you their tits. One where girls cried when you sang or fainted when you smiled at them."

He closed his eyes, sighing deeply, the exhale sad. A million sorrows filled that sigh and my heart pinched. I understood his need to be seen for him—a man. It reminded me of me. I didn't want to be viewed as a divorcée, or a mother of two, or a breast cancer survivor. I just wanted to be recognized as an independent woman—one who wanted to be loved and was willing to give love in return. If I forgot about what I *didn't* know regarding Tommy Carrigan, I found what I did know, I liked.

I stood, straddled over his knees, and rested on his thighs. My hands cupped his cheeks, and I stared into his ink-colored eyes.

"You're a rock star," I said softly, the words seeped into me. He was a rock star, and I could see that meant a world filled with pain and hard losses, loneliness and empty promises. He'd done so much for others and I didn't know the half of his reasons.

"So, what now?" he harshly scoffed. "You want to fuck *the* Lawson Colt?" His voice sounded shattered as his arm swept toward his body. He scooted forward so I slid to his lap, his head tipping back like he was used to this treatment. Visions of women riding him, enthralled by his status instead of the man, made me sick.

I reached for his face once again, leaning forward until our noses nearly met. His eyes watched me, skeptical of what I'd do next. My heart raced, wondering where the boldness in me came from.

"I don't want to *fuck* Lawson Colt," I hissed softly. "I want to make love to Tommy Carrigan."

With that, he leaned forward, and I fell against him. My mouth crushed his as I straddled him, pressing the full force of my core over the length of his stiff zipper. My hands dove into his hair and held his lips to mine, slowing the kiss enough to be tender, taking my time to savor each dip and curve of his mouth. My tongue reached out for his, and the kiss returned to burning flames. He sat forward, and I pushed downward, groaning at the position, the connection, the heat of him under me.

Still feeling emboldened, I pressed his shoulders back to the chaise and broke the kiss to remove his T-shirt. My hands skated over the subtle ridges of his chest and around his sides, focusing on the small tattoo under his heart. *Kit Kat*, it said, with a breast cancer ribbon, a small token of his love for his sister. I bent forward, keeping my eyes on his, lowering to kiss him there. His heart beat rapidly as I continued to scatter kisses across his firm pecs, scraping my teeth over his nipples. He hissed in response, muttering his favorite swear word.

My hands continued their exploration, rubbing upward through the short vee of chest hair and rounding his shoulders. While we'd been together, I hadn't taken the time to really admire him in this way. My palms caressed down each arm at an equal pace until I got to his wrist. I wiggled over the thick length of him before reaching for his belt. Other than grunts and groans and the occasional *fuck*, he wasn't speaking. What I hoped was that he was feeling, experiencing, that I cared about him: the person, the man, Tommy Carrigan. While the rest of his life was intriguing, all I knew so far was what he told me, and I liked it. I liked him, probably more than I should.

*Don't fall in love with him*, I warned myself, as I unbuckled his belt and sat back to undo his zipper. Awkward hands reached for his waist and he joined me to remove his boxers and jeans enough to free him. I sat back further, slipping to kneel between his legs, my eyes focused on the length in my palm.

"Darlin'," he hissed, both begging and warning me. I wasn't good at this, but I wanted to try. I wanted a taste. My lips kissed the wet tip, then my tongue joined for a swirl. I opened wide and swallowed just the head, sucking hard before opening to press a kiss to the moist skin. His hand started petting my hair. I opened again and forced him as far as I could. My gag reflex was strong but I hoped I could make up for it at first by licking along the cut ridges and stroking up the vein. Repeating the motion several times, his thighs quaked under my palms.

"Darlin', I want this, but I think I want inside of you more." His hands came under my arms, and he tugged me forward forcing me to release him with a soft pop. As I sat upright, he reached out for my underwear, slowly dragging it down my hips under my skirt.

"Should we really do this here?" I whispered, suddenly conscious that we sat on the dark beach. Anyone could see us if they wandered close enough. Then again, we hadn't seen anyone near our secluded position by the break wall. He reached out a finger, swiping through folds ripe and ready for him, and I whimpered with need.

"Put this on me," he said, holding out a condom he withdrew from his pocket.

"I…" I hadn't done that in nearly twenty years. In fact, I worried I wouldn't do it right. Seeing my trepidation, he decided to give me a pass. He bit the foil and tore the package. I watched him roll the condom downward and hold himself upright.

L.B. Dunbar

"That…" I couldn't say the words, as they caught in my throat. *That was freaking hot.* He patted his thigh, and I stood to wiggle out of my underwear. Then I returned to straddle him, hitching up my skirt, and, positioning myself at his tip. I gripped his shoulders, pausing as he rested just under my entrance.

"Don't ever lie to me again," I said, narrowing my eyes at him, and then I slid myself over his hard shaft. We let out a groan in unison, and his mouth reached for mine as I stilled, acclimating to the thick length filling me. This position was different, deeper, and that special spot on me rested against him. I moved slightly and released his mouth as instant pleasure rippled through me. My nails slipped from his neck and dug into his shoulders.

"Like that, darlin'." He chuckled. "Do it again." I did, slowly losing myself as I rolled my hips over him, holding him deep inside me, and rubbing that spot against him.

"I…" I couldn't speak, and my hands slipped to his hips, where I tugged at his skin, trying to get him deeper inside me. I wanted him to crawl under my skin and stay there, never letting this feeling end. I rocked, groaning, and he let me take what I wanted from him. "I'm coming," I warned, as if he didn't know from the clenching and rutting I did against his body. My hands released him, and I circled my breasts, reaching up to my neck, and slipping my hands over the back of my head. My whole body tingled as I came, falling forward when I couldn't take it any longer.

With that, he wrapped an arm around my waist and began pistoning me over him, moving me up and down, giving him friction that stood him at attention within me. He was so hard, so very hard.

"Touch yourself, darlin'. Get there again."

"I can't," I whimpered as he jostled me. "I don't…I mean…" He'd taken not only my breath but my words. He slowed enough to grip one of my hands with his free one and drag it to my core. He held my fingers there until I pressed against myself, lightly tickling until the tension built. I gasped at the sensation, and he increased the thrusting. Together, we climbed.

"Get there, darlin'. I'm too close." He looked down at where I touched myself, and I followed his lead. Despite the dark night, I could see the outline of our joining. "That is fucking hot," he said, and I giggled, losing a bit of my concentration, but the laughter clenched at him. He stilled, and the pulsing inside me set me off. I stroked myself as he spilled forth with tender thrusts. I came again, though not as strong as the first time.

My forehead fell to the top of his head, and we remained like this a moment.

"You are a wonder," he whispered, and I pulled back.

"I've never..." My voice faded, and the corner of his mouth crooked. "I don't touch myself," I said, looking away, tickling my fingers over his abs. "I've never done that before."

"I'm sensing there are a few things that you've never done before, and I'm happy to be the first, though I'm sorry it took you so long to discover those things." He smiled broadly, and I smacked at his chest.

"It's embarrassing to admit you're the first to give me a double orgasm."

His brows rose. "What the...well, we need to go for three." An aftershock of him pulsing paused us both.

"What was that?" I shrieked, the sound echoing in the quiet night breeze. He chuckled, and I felt it inside me, which is where I wanted to bury his laughter, storing it for after I left. I didn't want to think of parting from him. Not yet.

"Number three in my room," he teased.

+ + +

Once back at his room, I excused myself for his bathroom. When I came out, I found him stripped and sprawled on his stomach across his bed. I admired his backside—two fine globes that would make ancient sculptors jealous. He rolled to face me and patted the space next to him, but something in his slightly opened nightstand caught my eye. Slipping the drawer open further, my eyes widened. Lifting up the fabric, I peered over at him. His eyes didn't leave mine.

"What's this?" In my hand, I held the black scarf I wore, and lost, by the pool the other day. Turning back to the drawer, I found the scarf I left behind when he first took me doggie style against his bed. Red polka-dot material filled my hand. Last was a yellow scarf, the one I'd forgotten after that first introduction by the pool. He didn't respond, his eyes hooded with his silence. My brows pinched but he still didn't speak, only patted the bed once again. Staring back at him, my mind raced. He wanted someone who admired him for *who* he was not *what* he was. Collecting my scarves seemed to be a small statement. Was it possible Tommy Carrigan liked me *for me*? Despite my earlier boldness, I wasn't strong enough to ask that question.

"I shouldn't spend the whole night," I said instead, crawling over him to what seemed deemed as my side of the bed. He remained on his back, facing the ceiling, and we each lay with our thoughts for a second.

"You know that thing you did, when we were at Ivy's?" he asked.

"What thing?" My brows furrowed, completely uncertain what he referenced.

"Where you kind of hugged me from the back?"

My lips curled at one corner. "Sure."

"I liked that. I liked that a lot, beautiful." His voice lowered as if he'd just admitted the world's biggest secret. Pressing a hand to his shoulder, I pushed at him. He glanced at me, and I did it again, signaling for him to roll to his side, his back to me. When he did, I scratched up and down his spine a few minutes and then scooted closer to him, pressing as much of me into the back of him. He reached for the arm I wrapped over him and dragged it to the middle of his chest, flattening my palm under his. I kissed his back a few times and his shoulders relaxed. His breathing leveled, and he drifted off to sleep. Without asking him my question, I answered my own about my feelings for him.

*I like you Tommy Carrigan the man*, I quietly kissed into his skin. *I like you a lot.*

# 8
New Year. Orgasmic Goals.

I didn't fall asleep, waiting until Tommy was deep at rest. Then I stood and dressed. I placed all my scarves back in his nightstand and reached for the bedside light when he gripped my wrist.

"I don't like you sneaking out of my bed," he said, his voice gravelly and gruff.

"Go back to sleep, baby. I need to get back to my room." His sleepy body perched up on an elbow.

"That's a first." And he smiled slowly, groggily.

"What is?" I asked, still keeping my voice a whisper like I'd wake him.

"You call everyone else honey or baby, even that dumb ass Petty tonight, but not me. But now, you did." He smiled like a kid ready to see Santa, and I swiped a hand over that prickly scruff that I liked so much then kissed him briefly.

"I'll see you tomorrow, baby."

His hand reached for the nape of my neck so quickly it startled me and I was pulled to his mouth, returning for more than the brief kiss I'd just given him. With a full onslaught attack, my insides leapt to life. If he kept that up, he'd get that third orgasm out of me, but I decided it wasn't a good idea. I wanted earlier to be about him, not me. I pulled back after a minute.

"I wanted a piece of you," he whispered, his eyes lowering to the nightstand. "Creepy?"

"Flattering," I replied, my lip curling with the hope he wanted to remember me as much as I would remember him.

"There's a concert tomorrow. I want you to be there. I'll send tickets for you and the kids," he offered, sitting upright.

"Tomorrow," I whispered, swiping at his nose, before he stood from the bed. My eyes questioned the movement.

L.B. Dunbar

"I'm walking you back to your room. But tomorrow, beautiful." His wink was my warning, or better yet, my promise.

+ + +

When I returned to my room, I knocked on Masie and Caleb's closed door. Pressing it open, I found West and Masie asleep on Masie's bed. I should have woken him. I should have kicked him out, but they were dressed and he lay cradling my daughter to his chest. It looked innocent enough. All clothes on. On top of the bed. So, I left them wondering about Caleb to find him in my king size one.

"Hey." I rustled his arm. "Hey, go to your own bed," I teased. He rolled slightly, lifting his head from the pillow. "Masie and West are in there."

"So?" I said, reminding myself they looked innocent.

"So, I'm not sleeping with West *and* Masie in the same room," he said in mock horror.

"Well, I'm not sleeping with you," I exclaimed. "Sofa city, babe." I entered my bathroom, prepped for bed, and returned to find he hadn't left.

"Caleb," I hissed. "Out!"

"Mom," he whined. "I'll never fit on that couch."

"Oh, my God." I sighed, making a wall of pillows down the middle of the bed. I couldn't believe I was doing this, but I was drained from all that happened—the moment of truth, the wine, the sex. I was exhausted. Still, Caleb wasn't six years old; he was six-feet-three and twenty-two. As I lay down, my son's hand reached for mine. In a groggy voice he asked, "Did you make up with him?"

*No*, I shouted in my head. *No, I am not discussing this with my son.*

"Yeah," I answered instead, smiling slowly to myself. Honestly, I could only hope Tommy understood my intentions tonight. I liked him, as Tommy Carrigan, I really, *really* did.

"He seems like a nice guy. How did you not know who he was?" Caleb chuckled, sleep deep in his laughter.

"I don't know." I sighed. "I just didn't, and yeah, he is a nice man." Although that older woman at the pool suggested Tommy and the band were part of my family, Tommy had actually made us feel like part of his. He'd welcomed us to dinner and treated us like we'd always been there. It was a warm-fuzzy feeling.

"You know it's okay to date him, right?"

"Oh, honey, we aren't dating. We're on vacation. I might never see him again."

"Why would you say that?" Caleb asked, propping up and shifting as he continued to hold my hand.

"I just mean, we'll go our separate ways when this vacation is over. He's a busy man, a *famous* man. But our time together has been fun," I added, my voice saddening at the reality. I wouldn't see him ever again after five more days, but being with Tommy had been exciting. "Why, what did you think I meant?"

"It's just…I don't know…" His voice faded. "You're okay, right?" The shift in his voice clued me to his concern. Cancer. Death. It's a hard discussion to have with your child, one especially hard for them to understand when they are away at college, living their first taste of independence. Caleb came home immediately when I learned the diagnosis. I sent him back to school, knowing there was nothing he could do about it.

"I'm fine, honey. The doctors say that I'm all good." *For now*, but I didn't add that. There was a chance the cancer could come back. Some day. But maybe not. That was the part I was holding onto—the maybe not.

"Well, you have my permission to date him. Just have fun, Mom." I chuckled.

"You know he asked me if he could take you to dinner, right?"

"No," I laughed, "When?"

"The other night, when he met us in town. He texted me to ask if he could take you to dinner. He wanted my permission." Caleb fell back on the bed, and I stared up at the ceiling.

"That was...very gentlemanly of him." And sweet, I thought. Caleb grunted, falling back asleep almost instantly, like men can do. I rolled to my side, my back to him, with the wall of pillows in between us. Fifteen minutes later, I heard him leave my room, and a few moments after that I heard the front door click open and shut. I smiled, knowing Caleb had been the bad guy. He kicked West out.

+++

The next morning, I woke to a text. **Good morning, darlin'. You look beautiful.**

**How would you know? I'm still in bed.** 😊

**Then you definitely look beautiful, but you'd be prettier in my bed.** 😉

I laughed before texting him back. **Good morning btw. xo.**

**xo?**

**Kiss. Hug. Too much?** Ugh. I wasn't good at this and I fell back on the pillow, holding up the phone while the three little dots wiggled as he typed. They disappeared and then returned, and I held my breath. *Too much*, I decided and flung my hand with the phone down on the bed.

The ping noise signaled his response.

**Shit, I like that almost as much as you calling me baby.**

There was a pause and three dots again so I waited.

**Concert tonight. I'll see you there. Sending over three tickets. Call Ivy and ride with her.**

The concert? I was too old for this, right? My knowledge of Collision was next to nothing, minus one or two songs. My kids were going to be thrilled, but that wasn't the adjective I'd use for me. Not to mention, I had nothing to wear to a rock concert. I flung the phone back to the bed and then remembered to type a thank you. He had mentioned the concert wasn't typically part of their stay in Hawaii. Ivy told me the Hawaiian vacation over winter break was a tradition, and she refused to break it. The concert was unexpected and she wasn't happy about it, but when some publicist found out Collision would be on the island, they asked for a special New Year's concert that was too good for the band to pass up. Checking the date at the bottom of my screen, I noticed it was actually New Year's Eve.

In preparation for the concert, I suggested Masie and I get manis and pedis. I also needed to do a little shopping. In addition, I asked Masie if we could bring Ivy and the girls. After the day at the pool, I had a sense that Ivy didn't do much when the guys practiced. I couldn't imagine her life when they toured. I knew all about a man who travelled often and being a single-but-married parent of young children. It sucked. As Ivy was on vacation, one hijacked by this concert, I thought it would be nice to include her. Masie was excited by the invitation.

We learned about the intensity of a Collision concert when we suddenly couldn't get to the penthouse suite. The elevator doors opened and a security guard met us. We weren't on any approved list so Masie texted Ivy. Instantly, the penthouse door opened.

"Thanks, Sam, but they're welcome. I'll have Tommy update the list." I assumed the guys were gone already for sound checks or something-something, I didn't understand.

"The press probably knew we were here all along, but with the concert, Tommy upped security. The stalkers can get a little crazy and he doesn't like to risk the girls."

"How do you do this?" I asked, concerned for Ivy's well-being.

"I've known this my whole life." She shrugged. "So, what's up? Masie said you had a surprise for me." Ivy's eyes lit with curiosity and excitement.

"Mani-pedis," Masie cheered. Ivy just looked at me.

"I thought you might like to do something girlish. Bring the girls. They can get a polish, too."

"Really?" Her surprise confirmed what I thought: Ivy didn't do these things often.

Gage entered the living room and paused when he saw us gathered. His hair was wet from a shower, and he scrubbed at it, making short waves.

"Babe," he said as way of questioning his wife and the audience.

"Edie and Masie want to take me out for manis and pedis. It sounds fun. Ava and Emaline will go, too." She walked to her husband, and he stepped forward, reaching for her face and drawing her close, kissing her deeply like I'd seen him do before. I had to look away. It was too intimate.

The door to the penthouse slammed and heavy steps sounded across the entrance floor before we heard, "Gage Everly, what the fuck is taking you so—" Tommy's voice cut off when he saw me.

"Darlin'," he said, surprise in his raised eyebrows.

"Edie wants to take me out for manicures before the concert." Ivy addressed her uncle, still enveloped in her husband's arms. "Doesn't it sound like fun?" If I didn't know better, there was a sense of pleading in her voice, as if encouraging her uncle to side with her in the decision to go. Was there something I was missing?

"I want you there with me," Gage said into Ivy's hair, loud enough for us all to hear.

"Stop being a possessive prick and let her go. What do you expect her to do, chase the girls and stare at you all day?" Tommy said, exasperated. Gage looked up at his manager and flipped him off.

"Yeah, well, right back at you. We're late. You have two minutes." Then Tommy pointed at me, the index finger sharp in my direction before curling it towards him, then he started walking away. I looked at Masie, shrugged my shoulder, and walked to the entry way. I was hardly out of Masie's line of sight when Tommy wrapped an arm around me and dragged me into the corner. His mouth crushed mine, surprising me with that way he could, before I melted into the kiss.

"You are a sight for sore eyes, beautiful." He shook his head and started kissing me again. My hands combed through the hairs at the nape of his neck. They curled up a little, and I twisted a few between my fingers. With a little tug, he released me, muttering into my neck. "Fuck, I want you." Excitement shot through my belly like a firework, straight up my core to my heart. I bit my lip as I smiled.

"We're late. Get the fuck in the truck," Gage mocked behind Tommy in his worst imitation of his manager's Southern drawl. Tommy released me and spun, as if protecting me.

"You know, you are the biggest pain in the ass."

"Yeah, well, I'm your paycheck in the ass, too."

"As if," Tommy snorted, and I gripped the back of his shirt. I hadn't seen this side of him with Gage before, but I sensed tensions ran high under the pressure of a concert. My arms slipped around him, and I pressed my cheek to his back. "Play nice," I muttered, like I would speak to my children.

"He's lucky you're here, Edie. I'm getting sick of his grumpy shit," Gage muttered.

Tommy flipped him off like a child. "Well, right back at ya," he mumbled as he rubbed a hand over my arm and then released my hold on him. Spinning to face me, he kissed my forehead. "You know I love that, right?" Implying the back hug I'd given him, but my heart thumped at the word love. I nodded under his lips and he pulled back with a quick smile before holding open the door for his lead singer. It slammed behind them, and I jumped.

Returning to Ivy, I asked, "Are they always like that?"

"They can be. Gage is…needy, and it gets on Tommy's nerves. But Gage also realizes he *needs* Tommy. He knows the business, the people, the perks, the pitfalls. If Gage wants Collision to be something, he needs Tommy." Ivy spoke nonchalantly, as if she herself had a business head on her shoulders.

When we couldn't get into any salons with five people on New Year's Eve, we decided to shop. Ivy found me a sort of hippie-looking dress with wide sleeves and a short hem. We went into a toy store, where I bought both girls an arts and craft project, and then we found a pharmacy that sold cosmetics and bought nail polish. We ate lunch at a place specializing in fish tacos and returned to the resort. I painted Ana and Emaline's fingers and promised them craft time after a nap. Ivy let me put them to bed with a story.

"My mom would have loved you," she said to me as I returned from their room. "She didn't have many girlfriends. It was hard in the business. It was either cutthroat female musicians vying for the top, or groupies throwing themselves at the guys in her band." This comment included Tommy, and I tried not to think about it. "She found it difficult, always having to explain that Tommy was her brother, not her love interest. Eww," Ivy said with a shiver.

"She always felt she was defending herself. Her music. Her love life. She dated, and she was involved, but she didn't want marriage. She said she was committed to me, and she was. I think she did the best she could to try to make my life normal. She wanted me with her, but she wanted me to experience school and sports and clubs like she had as a kid. I don't think it's ever that easy, though, when your parents are already famous." Ivy sighed, as I started painting her nails. "I told you I went to school for music therapy, after she died. It was her dream that I go to college, but I can see in hindsight why she wanted it for me." She paused, watching the brush slip over her nail. "I need something to do. I can't keep following Gage all over the country. The girls are growing. Ava starts first grade this fall. It was hard having tutors and going on tour. I don't want that for them."

She peeked up at me. "And what about me? Is being a mom all I'm going to do while he sees the world?" She shrugged as if stopping herself. "Of course, I've already seen most of it, or as much of it as you can see when you are in twenty-six states in as many days."

"You don't have to work," I said as a statement, but it was more a question. Ivy surely didn't need the money.

"I don't, and I'm lucky because of that." She lowered her voice. "But I want to."

"There's nothing wrong with that," I said.

"I want to feel like I'm contributing."

"You are, honey. You're Ava and Emaline's mother. They need you now." I believed that wholeheartedly. I'd been fortunate to stay home while my children were younger, and David worked. It was only when

Masie started fifth grade that I returned to a day job, more to get out of the house than to be employed.

"But what if it's not enough?" she whispered, and I could see, in her twenty-eight years, the fear most women I imagined faced at some point. Being a mother was a miracle, and a dream, but you lost yourself a little along the way. Children's demands, their needs, their desires all came before yours. They define you, and you don't recognize yourself any longer. In the presence of an absent husband, I imagined Ivy's life was as lonely as mine had been at times.

"What does Gage say?"

Ivy scoffed. "I'm sure you can guess he hates the idea."

"Why?"

Ivy's shoulders fell, and her hand went limp in mine. "So many reasons, but none of them valid anymore."

"I don't think he likes me," I said, sounding like a teenager.

"He does. But he's jealous. He wants to be the center of my world. It was hard when I lost my mom, and I lost him for a few years after she died. He sees you as taking my attention, but he doesn't mean it in a bad way. He just doesn't want me to try to replace her with you."

The words were so honest, so raw, and I gathered they'd talked about this.

"Honey, no woman is ever going to replace your mother. No one. But I'm here for you, if you want me to be. I know I live in Chicago, and you live in California, but if you want my friendship, it's yours." Tears came to her eyes.

"You know, I come here every year at this time. My mother loved Hawaii, and it was the only time of year I had most of her attention. I return in her memory. She loved this resort, and we always stayed in this penthouse. Silly, isn't it?" She swiped at a tear. "But I think she knew I needed something, and I feel like she sent you to me." Wet fingernails or not, she reached out and hugged me, and my heart broke for a girl who lost her mother too soon and was losing herself as a mother. How cruel the world could be while giving us blessings at the same time?

L.B. Dunbar

+ + +

The bar was large. Edged with tall tables, it mimicked a concert venue by providing standing-room-only in the center of the space. I expected the scent of beer and my heels to stick to the floorboards, but several open doors at the back of the room allowed a tropical breeze to swirl throughout, resulting in a pavilion feel rather than a closed-in club. The hardwood floors were thick planked, like a deck, adding to the casual, Hawaiian atmosphere. A long bar filled the wall to the left of us with the stage, perpendicular to the bar, set up for a band. The wide floor space allowed the crowd to participate without furniture in the way, and with the packed house, the place busted at the seams with people eager to see Collision. We had a reserved table, roped off, and guarded in a back corner. I smoothed down my hips as I remained standing, too nervous to sit yet. Although Ivy had me purchase a hippie style dress, Masie suggested I wear something different.

"It's one size fits all, Mom. You can totally pull this off." Convinced, I slipped into her stretchy, black tank dress with thin ribbon straps and one of Caleb's white dress shirts tied below my waist. She shrieked after I told her the dress highlighted my unattractive bump in the front too much, so she added the dress shirt. The shoulder continued to fall, and Masie assured me that was the look I wanted.

"Mom...you look smoking hot. Tommy will drop when he sees you." While I wasn't so sure about that comment, I did feel good. It was a professional-slash-shabby-chic look. Strappy heels completed the outfit, taking it from what could have been a daytime look to a nighttime, dance-club feel. I kind of liked how I looked. Actually, I felt freaking sexy. With my bright-colored nails peeking through the strappy heels, I felt like I could conquer anything, including Tommy Carrigan as Lawson Colt.

However, my bravado stumbled when Tommy was introduced by the emcee, and the introduction revved the crowd to a rousing chorus of chants for Colt. Settling the crowd with his good nature and gentle laughter, he highlighted Collision. Gage entered from the left and his presence mesmerized the audience. He commanded attention, and it made sense why everyone, including Ivy, gave into him. Of course, his attention scanned the crowded bar, seeking his wife, and smiling slyly in relief at the sight of her.

"You're gorgeous," he breathed deeply into the microphone. Apparently, this was his signature address, and the audience went crazy as he eyed his wife over their heads. Then Petty tapped his sticks, and the house came to life with music. They played two songs before Caleb grabbed both Masie and Ivy by the hand.

"Let's dance," he said, wishing to tug them toward the front of the crowd.

"He won't like it," Ivy shouted over the voices joining with her husband.

"Do you always do what he likes, Ivy?" Caleb taunted, and Ivy gave in, following Masie's lead to the stage. Gage did give his wife a narrow-eyed look as Caleb and Masie sandwiched Ivy, forcing her to dance. I sat back at the table and watched with laughter as Gage's irritation grew, but he didn't break the song. He pointed at her once, and when I thought she flipped him off, I realized she had actually flipped up her ring finger, reminding him that the huge rock on her finger meant she belonged to him.

The song ended, and Gage walked to West, stripping off his guitar and handing it to the bassist.

"How you enjoying the show?" Gage barked into the mic. "Collision is my family, but sometimes we have special guests join us for the holidays. Who's ready for a new year?" The crowd went wild, shrieking and screeching, whistling, with hands in the air. "So I'd like to give you all a treat, and call up our new friend, Caleb, to play a bit with the guys." The audience roused again, encouraging my son to hop on the stage and take the guitar offered to him by Gage. Tension stood between the two men, but Gage's stage presence kept him in the entertainer-moment. He clapped Caleb on the back and pointed subtly at his wife. I noticed Ivy heading for the side stage, and I rushed to intercept her there.

"Don't you start with me," she snapped at her husband as he reached her. Instantly, he embraced her, kissing her in that commanding way he had and dragging her behind the stage. I remained on the side, mesmerized by my son, wondering how much he might miss a dream he was never allowed to have. David wanted a baseball player, not a musician.

From where I stood, I saw Tommy exit the opposite side of the stage. He wandered through the crowd, where he was immediately accosted with pats and hugs and women sauntering up to him. Some hung on his arm, another grabbed his ass. One went in for an embrace, jumping up at him. I stayed hidden, watching the scene, torn between watching my talented son perform, wishing he had lived his dream, and not wanting his reality to ever be as complicated as Tommy and Gage's lives seemed. The women. The groping. The jealousy.

Gage returned only moments before the song ended, brushing past me for the stage. He hugged Caleb in that guy way, patting him on the back, and Caleb walked towards me as the crowd roared.

"That was fucking unreal," Caleb shouted, pulling me upward in a bear hug. "He's an ass, but that was awesome." Setting me on my feet, I asked Caleb what Gage said to him.

"'Keep your hands off my wife.' As if," Caleb snorted. "Ivy's cute, but she's not my scene, and I don't play that shit, wanting another man's wife." He huffed, brushing his hand through his brown hair. "His wife. Jesus," he muttered. The sentiment ran deeper than Gage's implication. My son had every right to be pissed, but he was also pumped. The high of performing was so similar to the adrenaline of playing ball, and the buzz of being the center of things rested in his flushed cheeks.

"What a rush," he added, as someone handed him a water bottle and a shot of something. He downed the one and then guzzled the other. Looking over my shoulder, I followed his gaze to find Tommy standing behind me.

"Got talent, kid. And fucking guts, I'll give you that."

"Yeah, well, fuck him," Caleb said, the high still climbing, keeping him amped up. Tommy nodded in agreement.

"Need your mom for a moment." Caleb nodded, instantly dismissing me with a turn for the stage.

"Oh no," I said, the second Tommy tugged my arm, pulling me back in the direction Gage had disappeared with Ivy. "I'm not going anywhere after all those women were all over you."

"Your dress should be green, darlin'. It's a such a good color on you." He smiled as he pulled me into a small, private bathroom. I was on the verge of telling him where he could shove that color green.

"Got underwear on under that dress?" he asked, eyes roaming over me like he couldn't decide which flavor to select at an ice cream counter.

"Of course," I barked, my blood pumping in both agitation and excitement at the way his eyes dilated to black.

"Take them off."

I stared at him, my hands gripping the sink at my back. I shook my head.

"You need to breathe, darlin'. You're all pent up again."

"Well," I exhaled. "It's hard watching women hang on you."

"Oh, it's hard all right," he said, reaching for my hand and forcing it over the thick bulge in his jeans. "But only for you."

Our breaths were the only sound between us as our chests rose and fell like we'd run a marathon.

"Who am I in this bathroom with, girl?" He glared at me, reaching for the small sink and crowding me in.

"Me," I choke-swallowed, his nearness lowering my bravado and the willpower to stave him off. He inhaled at my neck, his nose skimming my skin without kissing me, and my mouth watered.

"That's right. You." He blew on my damp skin as the heat in the tight space shot higher. "Only you." He paused, his nose continuing to trail over my skin, pushing the collar of the dress shirt to fall down my arm. "Now. Panties."

He pressed back, allowing me limited space, and I slipped my hand under my dress without revealing anything and slid the material down my legs. Trying to be a smart ass, I held them up to his face with only one finger, but he grabbed them. Bringing them to his nose, he inhaled, and my mouth fell open. Then they disappeared into his back pocket and a small, square packet appeared instead. I couldn't believe we were about to do this—in a restroom, behind a stage, in a bar—but when he dropped to a knee, I had my answer. We were. His fingers found my core, damp and eager for attention, before his mouth lowered, and he sucked me hard. My hands fell to his hair, and I bucked forward.

*Oh. My. God.* I'd never felt anything like it. I'd had oral sex before, but nothing compared to his plump lips pumping my lower ones, parting me with the force of this tongue and lapping over skin so sensitive, so tingling, so aware of his aggressive attention. My lower belly filled with full flutters and the tell-tale sign of clenching told me I was close, but he pulled back, giving my clit a tender nibble. He stood on a rush and unbuckled his pants, freeing himself as his mouth sought mine. His lips tasted like me, and I lapped it up, reveling in the risqué sensation, just like our precarious location. His hand reached to lock the door and then he rolled on the condom.

"I don't think the sink will hold me," I said, pressing down on it and wondering how I'd balance on such a thin edge. Let's face it, he was strong, but we were older, wall sex didn't work the same as it may have in my twenties, not to mention, there really wasn't any wall space other than the back of the door.

"Turn around," he snarled, animalistic and ready to capture his prey. I did as he asked, and he hiked up my dress, massaging my cool backside with both hands before kicking my feet apart and positioning himself at my entrance. He pressed me forward, and I gripped the sink for leverage before he slammed into me without warning. My belly hit the edge of the sink, and my hand slipped to the faucet, striving for anything to hold me steady as he hammered into me, repeatedly filling me without nearing the exit. One hand held my hip while the other slipped forward without missing a beat and stroked that spot I needed.

I caught his reflection in the mirror. He was watching me, and the expression on his face spoke of an intensity I'd never seen. I looked away. His hand released my hip and awkwardly cupped the back of my head.

"Look at you," he demanded. I peeked upward again, staring at our reflection. "Who do you see in that mirror, beautiful?"

"You…" I faltered, my breath catching as no man had been like this with me before.

"And?" he barked, pressing at the back of my knee so I'd lift my leg, positioning it on the corner of the sink, so he could go deeper, when I already thought he'd gone as deep as he could.

"You and me," I groaned, feeling him hit something that was bringing stars to my eyes. The orgasm built, and it was going to be messy, but feel oh-so-good.

"That's right. You and me. Us. Only us. That's all there is." I watched as he pressed forward with a grunt, and my eyes rolled back as I came big, so big it seeped out of me as he stilled his hammering and pulsed deep within my channel. I clutched at the faucet, legs too shaky to hold me, as I silently begged for the sensation to never end.

He pulled out of me abruptly, and a rush of moisture slipped down my leg. He waded toilet paper and caught the drips the best he could before pulling up his jeans. I hadn't moved; I didn't trust my legs to support me. Slowly, I raised my head to meet my own eyes in the mirror, dazed and wide, and a smile too bright, my lips seeming to glow in the fluorescent lighting.

I still gripped the sink to steady myself as I turned to face him. He worked at putting my dress back in place as my knees trembled.

"Give me back my underwear," I said in a voice equally quaking.

"Nope, it's staying in my back pocket." He patted his ass. "Like your jealousy, tucked away for safe keeping."

My eyes narrowed at him as he backed out of the room so I couldn't reach his pockets. Then he held out a hand for me and led me back to the party.

+ + +

Masie was drunk.

L.B. Dunbar

Despite the orange underage wristband, someone had gotten her drinks that looked innocent enough, like a rum and Coke, or a vodka and Sprite. I don't know what all she had, but just after midnight and the start of a new year, I had to get her out of the bar.

"I'll take her," West said stepping forward as Masie leaned on me.

"You will not," Tommy commanded, his voice harsh and direct. "You can't leave with her."

"He doesn't like me anyway," Masie slurred, weakly waving a dismissive hand at West and answering for him.

West's mouth opened but Tommy held up a hand. "You know why you can't leave with her," he said as he narrowed his gaze on West. Even I think I knew the reason—Masie was drinking underage, but more importantly, she was still in high school. The paparazzi were here in full force, snapping a few sanctioned pictures and stalking the front door for anything else.

"I'll call you an Uber. You'll have to go out through the back." Tommy took care of everything, kissing me quickly as I followed my daughter into the car, begging her not to get sick in the short ride to the resort.

"Why won't he kiss me?" she sobbed, breaking into full-blown tears as she fell against me. I stroked her hair, not having an answer other than West saw the truth of their situation. Masie was still a kid in high school. As much as he might be attracted to her, he was doing the right thing by keeping her at a distance.

I didn't answer her, knowing anything I said would either turn into an argument or bring on more tears, so I just held her close, praying again that she didn't puke on me. I got her to the condo before she rushed for the bathroom. Collapsing over the toilet, she vomited, and it took all my strength to hold back her hair as my own gag reflect kicked in.

*Shit.*

I released her long enough to find a hair tie and wrap her hair at the nape of her neck. There wasn't much I could do for her. This wasn't a sick six-year-old child. This was a girl with the body of an adult who was going to have a wicked hangover the next day.

134

"The room is spinning," she said, and lowered herself to the tile floor. I'd been in that position once or twice. I'd dealt with David numerous times like this. The best solution was a towel for a pillow and the cool tile beneath her. The toilet in close proximity was the smartest thing.

Exiting the bathroom when it looked like she'd rest a moment, I entered my room and sat in a wicker chair near the window. The moon was full. It was a new year, a fresh start, another cycle. Only I didn't want to circle back. I couldn't return to who I had been, when I returned home. Tommy had changed so many things in what I did and how I felt, and I didn't want to give him up. I sighed, stroking my neck, remembering the nearness of his nose, his breath, and the teasing of his lips. When it was time to let him go, I didn't want to lose this feeling.

Deciding to text him, I reached for my phone and returned to the chair.

**Made it back. Masie puking.**

The dots appeared, and he replied, **Sounds awful**.

I waited a beat, wondering if I could ask the next question on my mind, as insecurity returned, recalling all those other women at the bar.

**Still have my underwear?**

The message returned almost instantly. **How does that make you feel?**

I told him to never lie to me again, so that meant I had to give him the truth.

**Painful.**

I could almost see the surprise on his face. His dark eyebrows rise, his eyes brighten.

**Really? How so?**

How difficult could the truth be? How truthful did I want to be?

**I ache for you**, I typed. My core pulsed faster than my heart. Moisture dampened my thighs, and I ached, yes, I ached in a way I never had before.

There was no response, and I stood to undress. I wanted to text again, asking if my comment had been *too much*, but decided against it.

My thoughts ran wild: worry over Masie; recollection of the backstage bathroom; hyperawareness of the racing between my thighs.

Then my phone binged.

**Stay dressed**.

Most women might want to read, *get naked*, but that…that message sent my pulse to near desperate measures. My fingers twitched, and I wondered if I could do the unimaginable. Could I touch myself? Would it feel as good as his thick digits? Could it replace him buried deep inside me? The thoughts alone almost brought me to orgasm, and the answer to each was a resounding *no*. I wanted him with every fiber of my being, and the anticipation heightened the wait.

Fifteen minutes later, my heart skittered in my chest, and I tried to regulate my breathing as a soft knock at the door announced him. He texted as well, but I didn't need to read it. Taking a calming breath, I opened the door.

"How's Masie?" he asked as he entered, and it soothed my anxiety that he asked about my child. I peeked into the bathroom to find her still on the floor, asleep.

"She'll live, but she'll hate life tomorrow," I chuckled, leaving the door open a crack. Without questioning what he wanted, I led him to my room. I stopped in front of a chest of drawers with a flat screen television over it. It stood opposite the bed. My hands gripped the surface as my backside rested against it. I don't know why I was so nervous.

He stepped inside and closed the door. Locking it, he looked at me. "You okay with that?" I nodded, agreeing that the interruption of one of my children would be mortifying. "I don't think you'll see Caleb for a while." He was correct. Caleb still rode the tide of playing on stage, and he had a new collection of his own fans, or at least momentary groupies, but I didn't want to think of him. Tommy sat on the edge of the king-sized bed, facing me.

"Put your shoes back on." His voice was husky, deep and rough, like gravel in a glass jar, and I followed his order without question. Just like him telling me to stay dressed, replacing my shoes on my feet seemed sensual, alluring, and invigorating. I returned to my place by the dresser, and Tommy stood. First, he kissed me. His tough, thick fingers caressed my cheeks and stroked my neck as his mouth took its time to lick and suck and nip. Tugging at my lower lip, his tongue entered my mouth, but not in the aggressive, conquering way he typically took, but more like a casual stroll on a rainy day. He swept inside and covered my teeth, tangling with the hungry muscle.

His hands came to the collar of my shirt and pressed it open, allowing it to fall wide and slide down my arms. He untied the casual twist at my waist and slipped his hands inside, forcing the shirt to fall free. With hands at my waist, he continued to kiss me, drawing my mouth deep, lapping long at my lips and filling my mouth with his tongue again. A finger slipped under the thin shoulder strap and removed one side, and then the other. Hitching his thumbs in the sides, just under my arm, he rolled the material downward to expose my strapless bra.

How I longed for sensation, that tingle I should have felt, but Tommy took care of that. His mouth moved over the top of my cleavage, taking his time to suck at my skin and run his tongue over the swells. He unhitched the bra, exposing my tattooed tits and taking a long look.

"I hate cancer," he whispered, his voice catching on a croak. "But you are so beautiful." He paused, swallowing as he stared at my breasts. "And it changes nothing." His mouth returned to attending each breast with tender kisses and light pecks before he dropped to his knees. He dragged the remainder of the dress to my hips and slid it to the floor, tapping an ankle. I stepped out of the material and stood before him only in the strappy heels. A calloused fingertip traced over the design across the top of my foot before he looked up at me, his eyes wide and obsidian black.

"I didn't get to finish what I started at the bar. I knew there wasn't enough time, but now I plan to savor every drop of you, and you're going to come so hard, darlin'." He parted my thighs, skating a hand upward and delving two fingers into my core. Releasing me with a moan, he licked his fingers and pressed my legs further apart. I gripped the dresser at my back for balance as his head fell between my naked thighs, as he returned to parting me with his tongue. It was different this time, slow and languid, as if he swirled and dug for every last drop of a favorite treat. The flatness of his tongue lapped at me, and then returned to slip inside me. My legs quaked again, but this time it wasn't the thrill of the race but the torture of the tease. I looked down to find silver-and-ink-colored hair between my thighs, and it unsettled the tremors deep in the pit of my stomach. I released one hand to comb fingers through his hair, and he purred against my sensitive folds.

"Tommy," I whispered, warning him, but he already knew. This man I'd known only days already read my body better than anyone ever had, and his attentions picked up the pace. He hitched up one leg, wrapping it over his shoulder as I balanced on one heeled foot. I gripped his head at my thighs, and within seconds, I came, so sweetly, so slowly, so surprisingly long, I nearly cried. The sensation was nothing I'd felt before, and emotion poured from me as I rode the orgasm at his lips. Kissing me tenderly inside each thigh, he pulled back and blew a kiss to my privates.

"Fine wine, just like I pegged," he said, and I chuckled softly at the memory. Oh, how I hated to leave this man, I cried inside, warning my heart in equal measure not to fall in love with him. My practical side said you don't fall in love within days, anyway.

He stood slowly, coming for my mouth again with a searing kiss before turning me toward the bed. When the back of my knees hit the mattress, he gently pushed me and I fell back. The springing felt carefree; the bounce made me young. I stared in wonder as he undressed, taking his time to torture me with a striptease of T-shirt, jeans, and boxer briefs. He'd already kicked off his boots, and he removed his socks as I scooted up the bed.

"We have one small problem, darlin', and I hate to mention it now, but I must." I paused, and he stilled, waiting at the end of the bed. "I used my only condom on you at the bar. I didn't think to grab another one."

I nodded as I stared at him, an impasse of indecision, because I honestly didn't know how he wanted me to answer.

"I don't suppose you're on the pill," he questioned, and I chuckled in response, shaking my head. There hadn't been a need to be. David fixed all that after Masie. Besides, the chemo removed any other possibility of pregnancy.

"I haven't been without a condom in twenty years, beautiful. I'm clean. I'm tested, and all that shit." I nodded and continued backing up the bed. Separating my thighs just the slightest encouraged him to start crawling, making his way up the mattress over me. I was wanton and desperate for him, but more importantly, I felt wanted by him in the way he looked at me. He gripped himself as he neared my entrance, pausing just outside, teasing me with his tip.

"You sure about this, darlin'?" he whispered, peering down at himself. Hesitating a moment, he added, "I feel like I've never wanted anything more than to feel the heat of you surrounding me."

"I want you, Tommy Carrigan," I replied, and nothing could have prepared me for how quickly he slammed into me. I gripped the sheets in tight fists, and he slipped in to the hilt. His heavy sacs hit the underside of me. Releasing the bedcovers, I reached for his shoulders, stroking down the slight hills and over the deep swell of his biceps as he slowed his thrusting to a steady rhythm. My palms sculpted his body, skimming his sides and wrapping around to his muscled back. I reached for the glorious globes of his ass and pressed upward, willing him to go deeper, harder, faster. He continued to take his time before increasing in a manner that had us both catching our breath. If I thought I'd made love to Tommy Carrigan last night, he was making love to me tonight. He tried to kiss me, but we couldn't keep the pace so instead he concentrated on filling me. Tension built in equal measure between us and I clenched, the release desperate to hold him. Instead, he pulled out quickly, spilling over my lower abdomen.

I watched as he came, the milky substance coating my belly. He rubbed some of it around my loose waist and then pushed the rest upward toward my breasts. Skating between them, he painted me with the seed of his release before he skipped up to my lips and forced a finger into my mouth. I sucked on it, licking the salty flavor and removing the stickiness. He withdrew his finger and stared down at me.

"You didn't," he admonished, knowing I hadn't come again.

"I'm okay," I stated, the words being true. He'd already given me two orgasms in the span of four hours. He'd given me more in the last six days than I'd had in three years. I wouldn't fault him this failure, but he dropped onto the mattress by my side, placing me on top of him. My legs parted, straddling near his sac.

"I'm getting soft, but I'm still willing. Take what you need, darlin'. Ride against me to get the rub." I did as he asked, positioning myself so the spot I needed met him. I tried to be tender, but when I wasn't getting the full effect, I slipped my fingers to the place I needed for relief. I came again with a deep shudder, my head thrown forward, biting my lip to keep from moaning.

"You are so damn hot, lady, do you know that?" He exhaled as he rubbed up and down my sides while I sat astride him. I shook my head, feeling too replete to even speak.

"I'm sorry we couldn't do it again for you," I said, finding words as I slinked a finger down his broad chest.

"Darlin', after having an erection for four hours, there was no way I could repeat so quickly."

"Four hours," I giggled, and then horror struck. "Oh, my God, did you—"

"Don't you dare finish that sentence," he warned, his voice dropping. "I've been stiff for four hours thinking of you. No other enhancement needed."

"Oh," I laughed, jiggling him underneath me. He held up a hand, and I reached out to smack it. He cupped mine in his when we connected. "What's that for?" I said.

"A high five. Three times. I knew I could do it."

I gasped, swatting at his chest with my free hand. "Did you just high five me for three orgasms in a few hours?"

"That I did, darlin'." He chuckled under me, jiggling me up and down before tugging me with our clasped hands to fall on his chest and kiss him again.

# 9

## Risky Adventures

**Let's take an adventure**, he texted me the next day. Masie was too hungover to move, and Caleb went to the bar to watch football bowl games. Tommy hadn't stayed the night, although we both wanted him to. He understood. I wasn't ready to subject my children to this kind of a thing—a man in my bed, especially a man who was only a vacation fling. I felt sick to my stomach with the thought.

**Let's do it**, I replied, and he asked me to meet him in the lobby. We drove the coastline, stopping occasionally at designated viewing points to watch for whales or stare at the ocean. After a stop or two, I'd had enough. I didn't want to seem ungrateful, but from how many vantage points could you see the same thing? Tommy seemed to sense my feelings.

"You're bored."

"I'm not," I whined. "It's just…it all looks the same to me."

He nodded and reached for my hand. Tugging it up to his mouth, he kissed my palm.

"Okay, then. More adventure." We stopped at a public beach and walked until we came to the ancient ruins of a Hawaiian fort. The ocean roared at the sharp, jagged edges of boulders and rock.

"Rumor has it, once upon a time a Hawaiian princess had fallen in love with an explorer," Tommy said, still holding my hand. "Her father denied his request for marriage, claiming she was betrothed to another. She refused to acknowledge this truth and promised the explorer she'd run away with him. Something happened the night they planned to escape, and the explorer set sail without her. When she returned to her room in the castle tower, she found a message in a bottle, saying he'd return for her." I stared at Tommy, wondering how he knew such island lore.

"She waited for him. Year after year. She married the other man as promised by her father, but she never gave up hope that the explorer would return for her. He'd see the world and discovered new things, but he'd always want what he once had and desperately missed."

He waited a beat, and I squeezed his hand to continue.

"So, what happened?"

"Story says, she saw him coming one night when the sun was setting, and the outline of the ship crossed the horizon. She raced for the water's edge, calling his name. "Accomandohulacoola," Tommy called out to the waves.

"And?" I encouraged.

"He saw her on the shore, thinking he could swim to her. Diving into the ocean, he didn't resurface. She raced into the water, thinking she could save him, and she drowned."

I stared at him and then looked out over the rolling water.

"That's a terrible story."

"The moral of that story is never dive, but jump in feet first. And don't race to save a drowning man."

"Those are awful morals." My eyes focused on the ocean waves a moment. "Wait a minute—Accomandohulacoola? You made all that up." I turned to punch his shoulder, and he tucked forward to avoid my fist, laughing hysterically.

"Okay, okay, I did. You should have seen your face." He continued to chuckle.

"You're mean," I whimpered, pouting my lips.

"But you love me." The comment stopped us both from laughing, and after a second, he squeezed my hand again. "I didn't mean, you know, just kind of said it."

"I know," I said softly, letting the awkward moment linger. We couldn't be in love, not after a few days, I reminded myself. He kissed my knuckles and turned us for the parking lot.

Next stop, we climbed down a steep rise to where the shore met the rocks. Tide pools filled with the brisk, rushing surface. I wasn't as nimble as Tommy, so I took my time, praying I wouldn't fall in or slip and embarrass myself. To my surprise, he was patient, never rushing me with my hesitant descent, but encouraging me with gentle praise and occasionally holding my hand as a guide. My fear of humiliation passed. We spent some time trying to find anything unusual in the shallow pools but didn't. As explorers, we agreed we weren't very successful.

Returning to the top of the lookout, we drove a short distance to a cove, and Tommy surprised me with a picnic lunch. Sitting on the beach, a gentle breeze blew as we ate.

"You made me a peanut butter sandwich?" I giggled.

"It was all I could do on short notice."

"What if I was allergic to peanuts?" I questioned, teasing him.

"You aren't. I asked Caleb." My breath hitched at the thought that this man asked my son again for permission to take me on a date. I also noted he'd not made me a peanut butter and jelly sandwich, but just peanut butter, which I preferred. I stared at him, drinking in the side of his scruff-lined face. How did I get so lucky to find him? Why did it take me so long to find him? How would I leave him behind?

"So, let's say I was an explorer of sorts," Tommy said, interrupting my thoughts. "And I went off to see the world, but not to discover things. Say it was my job to travel." He paused, setting down his sandwich. "Would you wait for me, hypothetically?" He turned to face me and hesitant, questioning eyes looked directly at mine. A nervous expression filled his face.

"Depends," I teased. "Am I a princess?"

"You're the queen." He smiled slowly, picking up his sandwich again.

"Am I married?" I lowered my voice, afraid of the thought.

"Nope."

"Then I'd definitely wait as long as it took." For some reason, the song I told him was my all-time favorite came to mind—'Wait for Me'— a song he wrote as Lawson Colt in Colt45. The thought gave me pause. "Who was the song about? 'Wait for Me'? Who did you write it for?" I bit the inside of my cheek, knowing I didn't really want a response. It had to be another girl, possibly someone he loved a long time ago.

"No one special anymore," he said by way of a vague answer. That gave me all the details I needed. He did love someone once upon a time.

I couldn't really complain. I'd been married twenty years. I'd loved my husband at one point as well. But things changed. People changed. David and I eventually weren't those same two people who fell in love. I wanted to know more details about Tommy, but watching him crumple up his sandwich wrapper, I sensed the conversation was over.

"How do you feel about a drive?"

I nodded, and we stood, returning to the car. His car was a Mustang convertible. I had no idea of the year, but I didn't care about things like that. There was only one car I'd recognize. Regardless, it was a nice ride as we wound up the curving Hawaiian roads. Tommy reached for my thigh and slowly climbed, eventually teasing me near my core.

"Watch the road," I giggled, pressing his hand away from me. No sooner had he moved his fingers, they returned, finding their destination. He slipped under the band of my bathing suit, inside my shorts. It was an awkward angle and wasn't accomplishing what I thought it intended.

"Open your shorts," he commanded, keeping his eyes on the road but his hand at my heat.

"Tommy," I hissed, uncertain we should be doing this.

"Take a towel and cover your lap, but push them down a little and open up." I did as he demanded, pushing my shorts down my hips. His hand returned, fingers delved and I gasped. This was risky.

"Tip your head back. Close your eyes." Again, I did as he said, letting him lead me to pleasure, but not quite over the peak. Suddenly, the car jerked right. He pulled to the side of the mainly deserted road, hit the hazard lights, and turned to me. Eyes wide under the broad daylight, he worked at my core until I clenched the door handle and the edge of my seat. I groaned as I came, startling a bird in the tree under which we parked. Panting, I turned to him.

"What was that?" I laughed, feeling carefree, spontaneous, and dangerous. He didn't answer, but pulled back on the road, returning to our scenic drive. I reached for him, rubbing at his zipper.

"Darlin', don't start something you don't intend to finish."

I continued rubbing, stroking over the firm bulge that leapt under my touch. He spread his thighs a little. "Eyes on the road," I warned.

Unzipping his shorts, I had just as much barrier as he'd had to me. He wore tight swim shorts under the outer ones, and I struggled to get at him. Freeing only the head, I leaned forward and licked. This warranted another jerk of the car. The hazard lights blinked again, and he shifted in his seat to free himself. I worked hard and fast, lapping at him, sucking deep in my haste to give him pleasure like he had done to me. It was sloppy work, at an odd angle, and I feared I couldn't give to him what he'd given me. His hand came to the back of my head, holding me in place, and I dragged him deeper, swallowing hard, and licking the tight ridges of his length. My jaw ached, but I sucked.

"Darlin'," he hissed, and too quickly, he shot to the back of my throat. I drew back, dragging the length of him with my tight mouth, and he stilled me with his hand. He pulsed once, and then again. Stroking down my back, his hand rested on my spine as I released him. I sat up to see his elbow set on the car door. Thick fingers rubbed at his forehead.

"What's wrong?" I asked, suddenly terrified that I sucked, and not literally. His hand still on my spine, he rubbed upward, and turned for me. Gripping my neck, he squeezed.

"How am I going to let you go?" he said so quietly I wasn't certain I heard him. We stared at one another for a moment before he lowered his forehead, resting it against mine.

"Maybe you could come after me," I suggested, sensing the weight of such a heavy request. "Since I'm the queen and all, and I've been waiting for you, maybe you could return for me."

My neck was tugged back and his mouth crashed against mine. The kiss was desperate. A farewell, and a remember-me, and a don't-ever-forget-me, and I wanted to cry big buckets of tears. But I didn't. I savored each pass of his tongue and the curve of his lips. There wasn't a chance I'd ever forget him.

When we finally returned to the resort, I found Masie still napping despite the lateness of the day. Caleb remained at the bar watching football games, so when Tommy asked me to come to his room, I didn't hesitate.

"I need a nap, beautiful," he said, stripping off his T-shirt.

"Okay," I said, thinking I'd misunderstood the invitation. I stood for the door, but he stopped me.

"Where you going?"

"Well, I thought if you wanted to sleep, I should go." He chuckled as he tugged my own shirt over my head. "Or not," I responded.

"Will you be comfortable in that?" he asked, implying my suit underneath. I wouldn't actually, and I also felt like I needed a shower. Hiking, picnicking, having an orgasm in a car—it all made me sweaty.

"I need a shower," I said after answering with a shake to his question.

"Nap first. Shower later," he said, reaching for a clean T-shirt in a drawer and handing it to me. "Here."

I undressed down to my bathing suit bottoms and tugged on the tee. It was two sizes too big, but comfy, and smelled of him. I sniffed the collar after climbing into his bed, and he wrapped around me. We lay only a few minutes in silence before I felt something press at my backside.

"Can't seem to get enough of you today, darlin', but I'm lazy." His fingers slid between my thighs, and he stroked me again until I came. Then he slipped off his boxers and tugged one of my legs over his thigh. My back still remained on the bed as he lay on his side.

"Ever do it like this, darlin'?" Somehow, I knew he wasn't looking for my sexual history, but more my permission to try this new angle.

"No," I answered honestly. He scooted his body to line up his hard length with my wet entrance. One leg still over his thigh, he slid into me. The angle was different, the sensation unusual, but he filled me all the same. He scooted a little more so we were nearly at a right angle, and reached for my core, toying with me once again. He seemed to be waiting, holding off until I couldn't take the pressure any longer.

"Tommy," I hesitated, surprised with myself that another climax was building so soon. He strummed faster, and I reached for his waist, digging my nails into his side as I tried to meet his pace. I was a whirl of sensations, inside and out. Clenching around him, swallowing him deeply, I pressed upward, holding him into me. His hand reached across my waist and held me firmly to him as he pulsed within me.

We lay there, out of breath and energy, as he rested inside me, my leg still dangling over his hip. Suddenly, he perched up on an elbow.

"Shit," he said, hastily pulling out of me. "I wasn't wrapped."

The haste of his movement and the crassness of his words startled me. Hadn't we done it the previous night without anything? But then I realized his concern—He came inside me.

"I'm sure it's fine," I said, reaching out for his scruff-covered cheek, but the panic in his eyes told me my words did nothing for him. He gripped my wrist before I could touch him. Kissing my palm too quickly, he rolled away from me and shot off the bed. I slowly sat up having an image of him with a hundred other women, all rejected after he shot his load. He'd done the deed, gotten what he wanted, and split the scene. I didn't like the vision nor the feeling that suddenly applied to myself.

He returned with a towel.

"I guess you should shower after all," he suggested, his voice lower, and slightly colder than I'd heard before. There was no *darlin'* or *beautiful* to accompany it.

"Can I shower here or should I go?" I asked, holding my breath with the question, and hating how weak I sounded. He twisted his lips and glanced away from me.

"I guess here is fine." I didn't like that answer, but I didn't think my legs could carry me to my room quite yet, suddenly feeling too *dirty* to traipse the distance. I stood and entered the bathroom, locking the door behind me, willing myself not to cry until I entered the shower. Standing under the spray, I let the tears fall, ruining a perfectly nice day and a slew of sweet words that he never meant if he could dismiss me with his mistake. I washed quickly, knowing I'd wash again as soon as I returned to my rooms. I dressed in my own soiled clothes and found Tommy in bed, the blinds still drawn, and his back to the door. He snored.

I got the message and left.

+ + +

I returned to my room, and after I checked on Masie, I took a long shower despite the draw to my bed.

"You'll have to fend for yourself for food tonight, honey," I said, feigning a headache, as I'd lost my appetite around the time I lost Tommy.

She still looked a little green, and she shook her head to say she wasn't hungry. She sat staring at the television set, but her eyes were dull. She wasn't watching anything, just staring. She looked like I felt—dead inside. I took a Tylenol PM I found in my shower bag and climbed into bed.

+ + +

I'd slept through the night and woke to what I believed to be a new day, a new insight. It was a new year, after all, and I was cancer-free, but I didn't feel the inspiration of a fresh start. I hadn't heard from Tommy through the night, although I shouldn't have been surprised. Moments before we left for the day, he texted me.

**We should talk.**

**Can't. Have plans with kids.**

As a family, we'd had difficulty scheduling all the things we'd wanted to do in Hawaii in a timely manner. The kids had each been allowed to pick an activity as their Christmas present on top of the trip. With only three days left in our vacation, today was our snorkeling and sea turtle swimming excursion. Masie picked this activity. Caleb wanted surfing, which we couldn't get scheduled until the day before our last.

There was no response after that text, and the empty messenger app stared at me, hollowing my heart. I hated the feeling. It was the very reason I hadn't dated much before. Dating led to heartbreak, I told myself. At my age, there were just too many unknowns with someone new. I wanted the history of someone when there was none. I had no interest in playing head games. I'd done it already in my marriage. For twenty years, actually.

I'd had my own meltdowns over the days Tommy and I had been together, but I honestly didn't think this was a big deal. I couldn't be pregnant, I told myself. At forty-three, I'm too old. I tried not to think of special cases I'd read about, and those tabloid ruses of women in their fifties having babies. It just didn't seem like a strong possibility. I was upset with Tommy, but I couldn't fault him his fear. Possibly pregnant, and with a virtual stranger, did sound a bit frightening.

I willed myself to keep my head in the day with my kids. Masie was so excited, and she squealed with each sea turtle we passed, reminding me that she was still a kid at heart—on the verge of womanhood, but not quite there yet. Caleb was convinced he'd seen a shark, and that was my cue to get out of the water. I watched them from the boat in wonder, relishing their joy at doing new things. I wanted the world for them—oysters and all that jazz.

Shortly after they returned to the tour boat, we saw a wonderful display of whale breeching and I remembered seeing one off the shore. Was that only a few days ago? How quickly the time had passed. How much had changed? In so many ways, I had changed. I wasn't who I'd been when I arrived on this holiday. Tommy had changed me, and reminding myself of that fact calmed me.

I hadn't been *me* in so long, I didn't recognize myself when I looked in the mirror. When I smiled at my reflection after my time with Tommy, the tinges of a new me appeared, and a hint of the old me dusted off cobwebs. *Where you been?* That haunting image asked, and I wondered the same thing myself. I'd been waiting, I decided. Waiting for that explorer, returned from the sea with his new ways of thinking, to show me what he had discovered. Through sharing his learnings, I found me. I was drowning before, but now I could swim, or at least be brave enough to wallow in the shallow end. I wasn't anxious to rush home and date, but I realized I needed to try and experiment more often. I *deserved* to take the risk. I didn't want to be alone. In fact, I didn't think I could be as alone as I'd been. I needed to get out more. However, my days and nights with Tommy were going to sustain me for quite a while, and I was all right with that thought.

L.B. Dunbar

We returned to shore and had dinner at a local restaurant known for their oversized burgers and fish tacos. Caleb was continuously texting but Masie remained quiet, as she had been most of the day. When we returned to the condo, Caleb went out almost immediately, while Masie opted to stay in.

"What's going on?" I asked, standing behind the kitchen island as she scrolled the television channels.

"I just don't feel like going anywhere." She shrugged, her eyes focused on the mindless channel surfing.

"Masie, honey, what happened?" She slammed the remote on the couch and looked up at the ceiling.

"I'm such an idiot," she blurted, closing her eyes and rolling her head on the back of the couch. My mouth opened to speak but she continued. "He thinks I'm a kid, and after getting drunk, I'm sure that confirmed it."

"Did he call you a kid?" I assumed we were referring to West.

"Actually, he acted *interested*, but he kept his distance. One minute he came to share music and fell asleep holding me, and the next day it was like I had a disease. Then he wanted to watch a movie, but he didn't even hold my hand. What am I, his little sister?"

"I certainly hope not," I scoffed. West had definitely shown signs of a crush on my daughter.

"Did I say something at the concert?"

"Well, uhm, I'm not certain that matters…" My voice drifted, but my daughter eyed me in that way that demanded I speak. "You said he didn't like you when he offered to bring you home."

"And why didn't he bring me home?" she said, exasperated. "Because he doesn't like me. Not *like me* like me."

I paused, knowing the ice was thin, but I had to risk cracking it.

"He didn't bring you home because he realized if he left the bar with a drunk high school girl it would make the tabloids." Masie sat forward and turned in my direction. Her mouth opened and closed. Then opened again. Then closed again.

"Did I say anything else?" Her voice lowered.

150

"You didn't say anything else at the bar. But you cried in the car on the way home, asking me why he wouldn't kiss you."

"Ugh," she shrieked, covering her face with both hands and falling over to bury her head in the cushions.

"Honey, have you talked to him about this?" Her head rolled in response, still face first in the cushions. "Why not?"

She sat up, her face red, and stared at me. "What is there to say? I haven't spoken to him since that night. I'm too embarrassed."

"It's been practically two days," I said, startled that she'd let so much time pass. "Has he not tried to call you…or text you?" It still astonished me that all kids did was text, never using their phones to make a physical call and hear a voice. I didn't realize I'd been flipping mine, rolling it on the surface of the counter I stood behind as I spoke to Masie.

"He's texted. He's called. I just ignore them."

"Don't you think he might be worried about you?"

"I'm sure Caleb told him I puked my guts out and was hungover." She rolled her eyes and fell back against the couch cushions.

"But to be fair to him, don't you think you should call him and just let him hear it from you?" A slow trepidation filled me with my words. "Maybe he doesn't know what to say? Maybe he does like you but he doesn't know how to proceed, because you're still in high school, or maybe because he's a superstar?" I babbled, guilt slowly eating at me with each word spoken.

"I think you owe him the courtesy of a returned call or text. Maybe he owes you an explanation." The words flew from my mouth while my heart raced. Wasn't I doing the same thing? Ignoring Tommy instead of facing him? Granted, Tommy wasn't actually busting up my text messages or trying to call me, but I had been the one short with him in return. Did I warrant more communication after my response that I couldn't talk? Maybe. Suddenly, I wasn't willing to let Tommy off the hook any more than I thought Masie should dismiss West. West had been chasing her all week. I didn't believe he thought she was a kid, or if he did, he needed to tell her that. But as he was the one still calling her, I didn't believe he felt that way.

"By the way, who gave you all those drinks anyway?"

"Petty."

+ + +

After three unanswered text, and one phone message, I decided I needed more aggressive action. I'd broken down and texted Ivy.

**Tommy's here**, she sent back when I asked if she knew where he was. She opened the door on my first knock.

"I'm so glad you're finally here. He's been a total sourpuss all day." She paused as she closed the door. "No, he's been an ass. There's no way to sugarcoat it. A total asshole all day." She smiled to prove she wasn't upset with me, but harried over her uncle's behavior.

I followed her through the living room and out to the rooftop balcony. Tommy sat in the same chair as the first time I'd been out there, his head rolled back as he stared up at the stars. The rest of the band was present, and suddenly the emboldened woman stalking across the resort wanting answers was nowhere to be found

"Hey Edie, how's Masie?" West asked almost instantly, as I neared their seating. Tommy's head shot up and his eyes met mine—dark orbs that didn't look too excited to see me. The bottle of whiskey on the low table worried me.

"She's good. Maybe you should go see her." West's brow rose in surprise at my suggestion. "She decided to stay in tonight and watch a movie."

"Oh, Loverboy," Petty sang out. "Your girl is calling." He'd snatched West's phone and dangled it in his hand. Petty held it back out of reach and West tried to lunge for it.

"Do you have a girlfriend?" I asked, concerned that I'd just suggested he visit my daughter when another girl was calling him.

"No, but he wants one," Petty snickered, wiggling the phone further out of reach.

"Are you jealous because you don't have one?" I asked, and the slow *ohs* and sharp bark of laughter told me I'd hit a nerve for Petty.

"Maybe, you wanted my daughter for yourself." My voice was rising and suddenly so was my temper. My fist clenched at my side. "Is that why you gave her all those drinks?"

The patio went silent as Petty lowered the phone, and West paused to look at me over his shoulder. The next moment time sped up as West lunged for Petty, clocking him in the jaw, knocking his head back against the seat. Gage stood to grab West off Petty while Tommy leapt to his feet

"What the fuck were you thinking?" Tommy snapped. "Giving an underaged girl alcohol, not to mention a girl your bandmate has interest in?" He grabbed Petty by the collar and dragged him upward. Jared stood, trying to get his arm between his bandmate and their manager.

"Let go of him, Tommy," Jared pleaded, attempting to push back at the older man.

"I'm sick of his shit," Tommy snapped.

"Then quit!" Jared hollered, and suddenly I realized Tommy's bad mood had to do with much more than me.

"You wish," Tommy barked back.

"Do it," Jared demanded.

"You know he can't," Gage said, still holding back West. "And you don't mean that, Jared."

I watched in wonder, not understanding any of what I heard.

"I do mean it, Gage. I'm tired of his old man ways and knocking around Petty. It isn't necessary."

"Jared," Gage warned.

"No, I've had enough. You know my reasons, and he does, too," Jared said, glaring back at their manager. Tommy released Petty instantly, swiping a hand through his hair. He stepped back and looked at me, his eyes wide.

"Apologize," Gage demanded.

"Fuck off," Jared replied, but it was then that I noticed Tommy and Gage were locked in a stare down.

Tommy swiped a hand through his hair again, looking out over the balcony.

"Family always says sorry," Gage demanded, and I remembered this hint of why Ivy was adamant Gage apologize to me.

"I'm sorry, Petty. You know I love you although you piss me off." The words were stated harshly but contrite.

"Jared," Gage commanded.

"No," Jared said. "He's been a fuck-off all day, and I'm tired of it." Jared grabbed the bottle of Jack and stalked across the patio, entering the living area. Gage stepped forward as if to follow his best friend but Tommy stopped him.

"Just leave him be. He's right."

"He didn't mean he wanted you to quit," Gage said.

"He did. But he also knows you need me too much for a while longer." He wasn't arrogant. He just seemed to be stating a fact. This band was rising to the top from what I'd been told, but they weren't there yet. This was going to be their year, Tommy had explained to me.

"We'd never get rid of you," Gage said, his eyes lowering. Tommy slowly nodded, twisting his lips.

"You might." At this, Ivy stood to speak, but Gage wrapped an arm around her waist. He muttered something in her ear, and her open mouth shut. She looked at her uncle with sad eyes, and I wondered what all I was missing. West still stood next to Gage, released from being held back. Silence swirled around us, so I spoke to West.

"I think my daughter might be waiting," I whispered, although it was loud enough for them all to hear. He looked at me, blinked once, and ran for the door. Despite the tension, I had to giggle. Gage shook his head behind Ivy, and she smiled back at me.

"And you." Tommy pointed at Petty. "Apologize to Edie for getting her daughter drunk. Then you owe West and Masie an explanation." He waved his hand as if dismissing Petty, who stood, muttered a weak *I'm sorry*, and left the patio as well. Gage tugged Ivy toward the living room, which left Tommy and me alone. We stood at a crossroads. He swiped through his hair and fell back into the chair.

"I'm sorry you had to see all that, darlin'." I sighed with relief that he'd called me *darlin'*, and instantly, my heart screamed *you're forgiven*, but I still wanted the words.

"Are you okay?" I asked, lowering myself to the couch seat at his left.

"It's been a shit day," he said, throwing back his head, and staring up at the sky again.

"Why?"

His head sprang forward. "First, my girl wasn't in my bed. Then she doesn't have time to talk to me. Next, I've got to spend the day with these ungrateful fuckers, trying to figure out a plan for when we return. Which reminds me we're leaving soon and brings me back to you not being in my bed."

I stared in disbelief. *What?*

"You freaked out about…" I couldn't bring myself to say it. "You know." I wiggled a hand before me.

"Not gonna lie, I did. But then I fell asleep, and you snuck away."

"Why didn't you call me?"

"I did." I held up my phone to show there were no messages. He pressed the button labelled recent and showed me the eight attempts to call me.

"Why didn't you leave a message?"

"And say what?" he snapped, anger still coursing through him.

"I don't know, like, hey, I freaked out and I'm sorry. Or don't worry, I'm sure it can't happen."

Tommy slowly sat forward, resting his elbows on his thighs, clasping his hands.

"Why can't it happen?" His voice was low as he asked.

"Because I had cancer." His head shot up as he blinked at me. "And because I'm too old." My voice rose.

"Edie, beautiful, you are not old, and even with cancer, stranger things have happened. Even if you were pregnant, do you think that's why I freaked out?"

"Of course," I shrilled, letting my hand slap my thigh.

He sat up and scratched at the scruff under his chin. "Darlin', you getting pregnant might make me the happiest man in the world, but here's the thing that freaked me out: if it happened, I'd still be me. I'd still have to travel and follow these asses all over the world, and I'm sensing you've already been that route, of being alone as a parent. I couldn't do that to you, but I can't quit them."

"You thought all that in sixty seconds?" Silence fell between us. The ocean waves rustled in the background. I lowered my eyes and picked at the hem of my sundress. There was a compliment in those words, but there was also something unsaid. If something happened to me, he'd want to be involved, and that meant a lot to me. The thought was sweet. I nodded and gave a soft snort before responding again to him.

"I'm not worried." That's all I had to add. I wasn't. He tipped his head, directing me to come to him, and I stood. I stopped before him, and his hands grabbed the back of my knees, forcing me to straddle him. I cupped his face after I sat on his lap.

"It's been a shit day, Edie." Calling me by my name emphasized the seriousness. "And I've missed you." His mouth reached up for mine, slowly dragging my lips with his. A tug. A peck. Then his tongue pressed forward, and he was in his capturing mode where he conquered my mouth and demanded my tongue. I kissed him back as if it had been weeks instead of hours. I'd missed him, too. Missed him so much, I wanted my kiss to give him all the words I couldn't say. I wanted him to feel how much I missed him.

"No more freak-outs, darlin'," he muttered to my lips, although I'm not certain if he meant me or if he was reminding himself. "It wastes precious time," he said between kisses.

"Then we better make up for it," I replied back with my lips pressed to his. He stood with me in his lap and I wrapped my legs around his waist. I let out a yelp as his hands hooked under my thighs and he hitched me upward.

"You can't carry me," I laughed, still holding his cheeks, as he stood with me latched onto him.

"I'd carry you to the ends of the earth and back, darlin', as long as you keep kissing me."

I kissed him again while he stood with me wrapped around him, but eventually, he set me down. We decided it would be faster. That way, we could race to his room.

# 10
### Sway with me

Sitting in the warm tub, I looked up as Tommy entered the bathroom, a glass of wine in his hand.

"Thank you, baby. This is sweet," I said, looking up at him, and his face split with a smile. He sat on the closed toilet, and I crossed my arms on the edge of the tub after taking a sip from the glass he offered me.

"You're sweet," he said, staring down at me. We smiled at each other a moment, recalling the make-up sex we just had. He'd been rougher than before, spurring me with precious words as well as the stiff length of him.

*Can't get enough.*
*Don't want to let go.*
*Missed you all day.*

He was sweet, I amended in my thoughts, and I had the same sentiments as him. I didn't know how I'd let him go.

"So," I hesitated, taking another sip of wine and lowering the glass to the floor outside the tub. "Want to tell me what that was all about with Jared?" Their fight had brought out some negative vibes and ugly words. Tommy shrugged and looked away from me.

"You know," I gently pressed. "You can talk to me." While we didn't really have that kind of relationship—the kind where lovers with history share other things besides sex—I wanted him to know he could trust me. He'd already told me secrets about Ivy and the history of his sister.

"Being in a band is like being in a family. Tempers run high. Love digs deep. Hatred can exist although you try to keep it tampered."

"Why would Jared hate you?" I asked, slightly aghast at the thought. Tommy seemed to do plenty for the boys, above and beyond what I thought a manager would do.

"He doesn't actually, but he resents me. He wanted the band to get everywhere on their own, proving themselves. It stems from his old man, but when my sister died and then Cash killed himself, we were all at a crossroads. Collision had been an opening act for Kit with Colt45. I saw their potential for so much more. I went to them with advice, and Gage asked me to manage them. I didn't need the money. I didn't need a job. But I saw what I could do for them. I saw *me* in them. The young Lawson Colt of Colt45, who wanted to take the world by storm."

"You did take the world by storm," I protested, but Tommy only snorted in response.

"My band was a mess. Too high, too fast. We crashed, and Kit was there to pick up the pieces."

"You said you picked them up for her, with her ex…her whatever…when he overdosed." I didn't know if Kit officially married the man who was Ivy's father, but I recalled that he'd died from drugs.

"That's true, too. I guess Kit and I were always there for each other." His head lowered, and I sensed the memory of his sister haunted him.

"Anyway, when I saw Gage getting involved with Ivy, pursuing her, I worried. She wasn't in a good way with her mom dying, and her mother wanting her to finish to school. Taking on the management role meant I could watch over the relationship."

"Is that why you won't quit, like Jared demanded?"

"No. I won't quit because I fronted the money for them. I'm their silent producing partner. It's my money on the line if they don't succeed." The generosity and seriousness of this investment was hard to grasp. Curiosity got the best of me.

"Why did you do it?"

"Because I knew they needed a break. I wanted to give them the one I never had." I didn't fully understand. Tommy Carrigan as Lawson Colt had been very successful in his own right. I sensed he felt like a one-hit-wonder as Colt45, the band from my high school days, but as Kit Carrigan and Chrome Teardrops, they'd been a tremendous success.

"What am I missing?" I questioned.

"My dad was a pastor, and he wasn't a fan of the sinful music I produced. When I left home, I struck out on my own, literally. No support from family until my sister was old enough to escape as well. After all that happened–the struggles of Colt45, the death of Bruce—we realized we had to stick together to make it work. We were our only family."

It was sad to me. My parents had always been supportive of my goals, but I had to admit I had nothing so large as being a famous musician on my list of future plans.

"What was all that *family always says sorry* stuff? It was sweet, but seemed like it meant something deeper."

Tommy sighed and swiped a hand through his hair, looking away again.

"Ivy and her mom had a huge blow out near the end of Kit's life. Ivy wanted to stay home to be with Kit. Kit wanted her to finish school. Kit went into cardiac arrest. Ivy thought she'd never have the chance to tell her mother she was sorry for the selfish things she said. When Kit came around, Ivy asked her mother for forgiveness. Family loves unconditionally, Kit told her, knowing how our own father treated us. And family always says sorry, Ivy amended, knowing you can never assume family forgives you. Ivy holds it as a motto with Gage, and it transferred to the band. Gage always considered Collision his family. Him and Jared and Cash were best friends. After losing Cash, where Gage wanted to apologize for all sorts of things that weren't his fault, he demanded anyone associated with the band apologize to each other when they fought. He never wanted anyone to separate with thoughts of being unforgiven or unloved."

"Family loves unconditionally," I muttered, lowering my chin to my crossed arms on the tub. I admired their closeness, their dedication to each other minus the bonds of blood. They were a special group of people.

"You're a lucky man, Mr. Carrigan," I said. He wiggled his brows and removed the shirt he slipped on to answer the door for room service. He stood and lowered his jeans, exposing his commando style. "What are you doing?" I laughed, sitting straighter in the tub.

"Enough talking," he said, a sharp twist to his words. "I am a lucky man, and I want to get lucky again."

"That was cheesy," I said as he stepped behind me in the tub, and I scooted forward. I didn't have a tub in my condo. The master suite had a ridiculously big double shower that would be enough for more than two people. The kids' bath had a shower stall. I missed a tub, as a warm bath was a luxury vacations demanded. When I suggested the soak, Tommy obliged. However, I didn't see how we were both going to fit in this one. Tommy was a solid man.

"Gonna need to sit up on me, darlin'," he said, lowering into the tub and scooping up my backside.

"I can't sit on you," I gasped, worried the weight of me laying on him in the tub would be too much. He'd already stretched out his legs and lowered me to rest at his waist. His knees rose and bent while my legs crossed and slipped between his. It was a tight fit but I liked it. I'd never bathed with David.

Tommy massaged my shoulders as I held his knees. I tipped my head to his shoulder, and he kissed my exposed neck. My eyes closed. Surrounded by warm water, a temperate sensation inside me from the wine, and the heat of Tommy at my back, I was melting into sweet oblivion. Kisses on my neck increased, the pressure of pecks turning into stronger suction and an occasional nip. His hand lowered, brushing over the coarse hair at the top of my legs.

"Are you hurtin'?" he muttered. "I was a little rough." Make-up sex had been intense, but I found I liked it as he held my legs in the air, feet at his shoulders, and pounded into me as I lay on the small breakfast table. I wasn't as flexible as I used to be, but I'd been able to balance. Surprisingly, we hadn't knocked over the table.

"I'm good," I sighed, slipping deeper into peacefulness under his attention. He hardened at my backside, and he jolted when I purred. Tommy adjusted me so the cheeks of my behind straddled the hard length of him.

"Ever do it like this? In the back door?"

I sat forward, splashing water like a small tidal wave as I choked. "No."

"Ever curious?" He continued, pulling me back to him and returning his mouth to my shoulder.

"I…I don't know." Had I thought about it? Maybe. I mean all the hottest romance novels had it in them, but could *I* do it? I didn't know, and I didn't answer.

"What about toys? Got a Mr. Bob?"

"I…" I was about to answer *it's none of your business*. I blushed recalling my awkwardness at purchasing such a thing, but then I considered who was asking and wondered: "Why?"

He chuckled into my neck, as I'd answered his question with my own.

"Want to know how you'll get off when you go home." It was the first time he'd mentioned home, hinting at the separate directions we would soon take. I didn't want to think about it. I decided not to answer at all. Suddenly, my hips were gripped with two firm hands and he lifted me, slightly. His dick stood upright, and perched at my entrance.

"What the…" My voice trailed off, as he slid me over him with no warning. We'd used a condom when we got to his room, but he was bare at the moment. He groaned as he filled me, pressing me forward to accommodate the sudden intrusion. He stilled as I sat over him.

"Don't want to think of others getting you off, Edie," he said, as he started to maneuver my body, lifting and lowering me over him. He slid his knees beneath mine, forcing me to straddle his thighs in a reverse cowgirl style. I gripped the edge of the tub as he continued to move my body in the manner he wanted. I was full in a different way once again. Every time we were together, the sensation was new, the experience original, and I wondered how I'd survived as long as I had without sex like this. I grunted as he started bouncing me up and down over him. The water sloshed and swirled, lapping at the sides of the tub like our skin slapped under water.

"Fine wine—I like you uncorked." His voice came out choppy as he slammed me down over him. "I love you uncorked," he amended, the words coming out on uneven exhales. Was that a declaration? I decided it wasn't and let him work my body in the way only he could. "Touch yourself, Edie. Get there for me, darlin'." I did as he asked, my fingers touching myself, but also stroking the length of him as he entered me.

"Fuck that feels good," he grunted behind me. He whipped me off of him, and wet warmth jetted over my lower back. Reaching around me, his fingers pushed mine out of the way as he took over attending to me. Slipping into my ripe core and adding his thumb to the mixture, he strummed at me while he squeezed himself behind me. I came almost instantly.

Resting his head on my shoulder, I pressed back, allowing my head to balance on his.

*I love you*, I heard in my head, the words fighting to cross my lips. *I love you, damn it*, when I knew I shouldn't.

+ + +

He stepped out of the tub first, and then handed me a towel. After exiting the tub, he worked the towel over me like a child, drying me off and wrapping it around me. He led me to his bed and pulled back the covers.

"I'll set an alarm," he said, setting up the time on his phone. I climbed under the covers and he tugged the towel off of me. "Naked cuddling," he said, slipping behind me.

"Why aren't you married, Tommy Carrigan?" I joked, but a tad serious in the asking. I didn't understand. He was perfect in so many ways.

"Not my thing," he muttered, wrapping an arm over me and dragging my back to his chest. I wanted more details. I'd already sensed he'd been scarred by love in the past. His songs were filled with pain, but I didn't ask. After what felt like five minutes but was actually an hour and a half, I woke to dress.

"Don't like you leaving my bed, darlin'," he said with a groggy voice, leaving the bed as well to dress.

"Go back to sleep, baby," I whispered, but he dressed regardless.

"Need to be a gentleman and walk you back to your room," he said, reaching out for my hand as he led me out his door.

He kissed me at my door and waited as I swiped the keycard (Isn't it a key card?). When I entered, I saw West standing in the living room, Masie on her feet behind him. They both looked guilty, in a way only teenagers can look guilty.

"West," I addressed him. "Masie, honey, it's getting kind of late."

West nodded and stepped forward without a glance back at my daughter. Her eyes followed his retreat. As he passed me with a short, "Good night," my eyes didn't leave Masie. Her body language screamed of longing, and mine ached at recognizing in her how I felt.

Leaving Thomas Lawson Carrigan was starting to feel impossible.

+ + +

We went to the beach to surf on our day before the last, and some of the band decided to join us. Petty and Jared were practically pros, balancing and maneuvering as one with the water. Caleb, Masie and West were a little shaky. Masie, however, had balance as a former cheerleader, but for all of Caleb's athleticism, he couldn't stay on the board. Tommy told me West was from the East Coast.

"He'd never been on a board before, but he took to it pretty easily when he showed up in California."

"What about Gage?" I asked, sitting on the white beach, watching all these young people enjoying sunshine and surf. Tommy laughed.

"I don't think Gage trusts anything he can't fully control, and since he isn't mightier than the ocean, that would be a no to surfing."

I smiled, staring off at the sea. We watched in amazement, soaking up the sun and letting the day drift. Tommy took a black notebook out of his bag and starting scribbling down notes. He looked up once, out at the sea, and then returned to writing.

"What's that? A little black book," I joked.

"Every man's got to have one," he teased.

"Surprised there are any blank pages in that one," I retorted, feeling a little uneasy at the possibility that he owned an infamous black book, filled with phone numbers, amongst other things.

He glanced over at me. "Green is such a pretty shade on you." His lips curled at one corner.

"Why do you always say that to me?" I laughed, knowing jealousy actually wasn't attractive.

"It means you want only me for only you." My breath hitched. He was so sweet. We stared at one another for a moment before he broke eye contact and wrote more in the book.

"Going to show me what's in there, then? Since I'm jealous and all." He snapped the pages closed with a soft clap.

"Nope," he replied, slipping it back into his bag. Then he turned to me again.

"Have dinner with me tonight, darlin'?" His voice lowered, as if he were nervous.

"Of course," I replied, leaning over and bumping his shoulder. His hand came up to my lower back and he tugged me to him for stolen kisses.

"Dress nice, like that black dress from our first night." My brows rose at his recollection of my body-hugging black dress with the scoop neck.

"Okay."

The day passed quickly, and I took my time to prepare for my final date with Tommy, because that's what this night would be. The next day, we would leave one another. He'd return to California, and I'd go to Chicago, and despite the modern technology of texting and social media, I didn't see how we'd keep up with one another. He was in a rock star world after all, and I was in plastic production.

The restaurant was fancy, with white linen tablecloths and a sunset view, but the only thing I wanted to watch was the man across from me. Dressed in a white dress shirt rolled to the elbows, a gray suit vest, and black jeans, his cleaned-up appearance took his hot factor to a new level of off the charts. We ordered wine. We chatted. It was another official date, and I wanted to believe the future held more times like this, but it didn't.

Tommy had brought me to another place that had a dance floor and music playing.

"Isn't this song typically a tango?" I asked, listening intently to the lulling sound.

"It's 'Sway' by Dean Martin, but Bublé made it popular again," Tommy said, listening as well to the sultry interpretation from the female singer accompanied by a piano. He reached across the table and stood, taking my hand and guiding me to the dance floor without asking me to dance. While he knew my apprehension, I trusted him to lead me. This wasn't the swirling fun of a dive bar and the Bee Gees, this was the serious tempo of a seductive song. A violin was added to the mix. Tommy's hip pressed near mine, and sliding a foot between my feet, he moved me to the lyrics about eyes for only one person and being swayed into seduction. His dancing skills were impeccable, and our bodies rolled together, gliding back and forth. A rippling embrace was the best description.

My fingers curled into the hair at the nape of his neck and his hand rested on my upper back. Chest pressed to chest, he held my hand propped between us. The singer shifted to a more modern song I recognized but couldn't exactly place with my spotty musical knowledge. Tommy began to hum in my ear, as the song had a slightly stronger tempo and a clapping beat. The lyrics asked if the person wanted to fall in love, say the words, *I love you.*

"I love this song," I said by way of catching myself from spilling my emotions to Tommy. The music washed over me as the warmth of his body added to the seduction of the music.

"Mmmm...I write songs," he said, and I nearly tripped on his feet.

"What?"

"The black book. That's what it's for. I wrote many of the successful songs for Chrome Teardrops, Kit and Colt, and Collision. Sometimes, I collaborate with Gage to perfect them." He nuzzled at my ear. "You inspire me."

I blinked up at this man, who had one surprising secret after another. "Can you sing one for me?"

"One day." He chuckled, leaning forward and kissing my neck, returning to hum the current melody.

"You're an incredibly talented man, Tommy. Do you know that? I mean, really know that. You're kind and generous, and a gentleman, and that's a rare talent as well." He pulled back to look down at me. His expressions sobered.

"Don't make me feel like I could love you all the days of my life, Edie." His tone teased, but his eyes remained dark, serious.

"Don't make me *want* to fall in love with you, Tommy." I tried to keep my voice even, steady, but it shook. It was too late, I thought. I was already in love with him.

"I wouldn't," he replied, his eyes opening wide, scared almost, as the chocolate melted to black.

"We shouldn't," I replied, trying to stay strong, attempting to keep my voice light, as I teased him. It was definitely a bad idea to fall in love with each other. But love had already tricked me, and one-sided love was never a good idea.

"But I could," he teased, lowering his voice, raising one brow, and tilting his head.

"Don't say that." My eyes closed, needing to shut him out and catch my breath for a second. I couldn't play any longer. The conversation had turned too serious despite the teasing undertones in our voices.

"Don't say goodbye, darlin'. Not yet." His voice returned to pebbles plopping in a puddle, and I wanted to capture the sound and carry it home in my pocket. My eyes slowly opened, and I combed through the curling hair at his neck. We continued to sway.

*Not ever*, I wanted to reply, but didn't. "No goodbye." I whispered.

Later that night, we made love like we danced, and I melted under him, melding my body to his as he led me in ways I'd never moved before. Unhurried and honey-sweet, his movements were like warm syrup poured over pancakes—deliberate, drizzling, and layering me in sticky goodness and tender sweetness. My orgasm wasn't an explosion of excitement but a tender rush, like water rippling over rocks, trickling slowly as I released and lingering as it flowed, coating my entire body from the tips of my fingers to the back of my neck in a glorious out-of-body experience. As I came down from the high, and he stilled to empty inside me, I knew I'd never be the same. Tommy Carrigan had swayed me, and I loved him.

# 11

## Timing

I recruited Tommy for help the morning of our last day in Hawaii. With a mixing bowl, a stack of measuring cups, and a bag of ingredients, he opened the door to the penthouse for me. I set everything in the kitchen area and followed Tommy to Emaline and Ava's room.

"Good mornin', sleeping beauties," Tommy softly greeted them, and they turned with sheet-creased faces and bedhead hair to look at their great uncle.

"Want to make pancakes?" I whispered, to which Ava sat upright and Emaline brushed back her mop of wayward blonde curls.

"Can I stir?" Ava asked.

"Mix, stir and pour," I offered, holding out a hand for her. The brunette beauty stood in her princess nightgown and walked with me back to the kitchen. Under my direction, the girls measured ingredients, filled the bowl, and stirred. Tommy sat at the island, drinking coffee, and smiling in the atmosphere of excited little girls messing up a kitchen.

"What's going on?" Gage asked, rubbing at the back of his head and standing in a pair of forest green boxer briefs. Averting my eyes, I raised my hands like blinders, whispering loudly, "Daddy's in his underwear," sounding like a child. Emaline giggled.

"Pancakes," Ava announced, and Gage stared at Tommy before looking back at me. I peeked between separated fingers and then closed my eyes, telling myself not to admire his under-thirty body of steel and the strip of dark hair climbing to his belly button.

"I'd say…I could buy you another hour or so in bed." It was a peace offering for borrowing his children for my own reasons this morning. I didn't want to say farewell yet.

Ivy padded down the hall, a robe wrapped around her. "What's all this?"

Gage turned to her. "Another hour in bed." He rushed her, picking her up by lowering his shoulder into her stomach and carrying her caveman-style back to their bedroom.

Tommy and I exchanged a look before I laughed, shaking my head. *Oh, to be so young again*, I thought.

"Are you a grandma?" Emaline asked, and I smiled at the innocence of a four-year old.

"No, sweetheart. Caleb and Masie are my babies, all grown-up, but they don't have any children, so I'm not a grandma yet." Emaline looked at me, confused by the process, but Ava filled in for her sister.

"We don't have any grandmas. Mommy's mommy died and Daddy doesn't talk to his. Tommy's like a grandpa, though." I looked at Tommy, whose face beamed with pride. His eyes lowered, but his smile said it all. He loved these girls like a grandfather.

"You could be our grandma," Ava said, shrugging her shoulder, like what she suggested worked as easy as asking. Tommy's eyes shot to mine.

"Well, I'd be honored to be your grandma, but it doesn't work that way," I said, not willing to tackle the complicated explanation of why I could not be her grandmother.

"Just saying," Ava said, sounding wise beyond her years and equally innocent at the same time.

"Yeah, just saying," Emaline repeated, brushing back her blonde curls. I shook my head with a chuckle, looking away from Tommy. *Just saying*, I'd welcome them with open arms in any capacity to be part of my family.

The door opened, and Petty walked in, followed by Jared.

"Pancakes?" Petty shouted in question, and reached out for me, embracing me in a fierce hug. Rocking me back and forth, he spoke over my head to Tommy. "Can I keep her, Tommy? Please, pretty, please."

Tommy chuckled and then admonished him, "Get off my girl." Petty released me and took a bite off Emaline's plate.

"Hey, that was mine," she whined, and Petty asked, "Want it back?" like the child he could be. He kissed her blonde head and moved to the coffee pot. Jared came up to me next, rubbed across my back, and kissed my cheek.

"Thanks, Edie," he said, and I looked up to find eyes filled with a request for forgiveness. The fight from the other night was forgotten; he didn't need to ask. I adored these young men.

Suddenly, I felt like I was at a play, the final curtain was falling and each of the main characters were taking a last bow. The performance was ready to end, and my heart cried out for an encore. I wanted more time with these amazing people. As if on cue, Gage and Ivy reentered the kitchen, freshly showered. Gage went to Ava first, kissing her head, before picking up Emaline and removing her from the stool. Ivy walked to me. Hugging me, she whispered, "Thank you," and liquid filled my eyes. I pulled her tighter, blinking back the tears. How would I say goodbye to this sweet girl?

Releasing her, I stepped back to flip more pancakes. I'd already texted Masie and Caleb to join us, and I refused to look up when they entered. I couldn't say goodbye to my growing children any more than I could separate from these strangers that had grown so important to me. But Masie was going to nursing school eventually, and Caleb would be leaving for spring training shortly after we returned home.

"You okay, darlin'?" Tommy asked at my side. I nodded without looking up at him. A thick finger tipped up my chin, forcing me to look at him. "Not yet, darlin'. Don't go there yet."

I nodded to agree but time was ticking. There wasn't much longer to *not* go there, but I smiled weakly and returned to making pancakes.

+ + +

We spent the late morning and early afternoon at the pool, soaking in the final minutes of Hawaiian sunshine until the last possible moment. Caleb, Masie, and I had a later flight, but we still needed to shower and pack, return the rental car, and suddenly, a list of final details weighed on me.

"I think I'll head up early," I said, no longer able to sit still, and no longer able to prolong the inevitable. I collected my things and stood to slip on my cover-up.

I looked at Petty and Jared first. "It was a pleasure to meet you boys," I said, nodding as they stared back at me. "Try to stay out of trouble." Jared was the first to rouse from his questioning gaze and stood to hug me. Petty followed. West and Masie had gone for a walk, so I'd wish him well a little later. Ivy called Ava and Emaline to me, and I kissed them each on the head before telling them to be good girls for their mother. Gage surprised me, by enveloping me in a warm embrace. "Don't say goodbye to her," he whispered, and the concern in his dark eyes surprised me.

Ivy's eyes filled when she stepped into me, as did mine.

"My beautiful new friend. Not goodbye," I said. I pressed her back before she hugged me too hard, breaking me into a public display of sobs. Holding her at her shoulders, I gently shook her. "Not goodbye, right? You have my number and my email. You call me. I'd love to see you again." She nodded, unable to speak as her eyes lowered.

"Not goodbye," I whispered and tugged her to me. She returned the hug hard, and I willed myself not to shatter in front of them. I couldn't look at Tommy. He'd already said he refused to say goodbye, but he'd meet us in the lobby to load our car. "See you in a bit," I struggled to say, still refusing to look directly at him as I walked away.

+ + +

"Mom, what's wrong?" Masie asked, as she banged on the bathroom door.

"Nothing," I said, through choking sobs. "Nothing," I tried again, focusing on steadying my voice. "Be out in a few minutes."

I heard Masie walk away from the door and then another door opened. There was a slam in the background and then a sharp rap on the bathroom door again.

"Edie, let me in," Tommy bellowed. *Oh, God, no, go away*, I thought. I couldn't let him see me like this. I promised myself no tears. I told myself I could be strong. I could walk away. I *would* walk away.

"Tommy, honey, I need to get ready to go. I'll be out in a while." We weren't saying goodbye; he told me last night. "Tell Ivy I said safe travels and kiss the girls again for me." Another sob threatened to escape and I covered my mouth with both hands. My voice refused to steady. I had faked a normal tone as long as I could.

"Let me in, darlin'." The handle to the bathroom door jiggled. His voice rose, a touch of agitation to it. I shook my head as if he could see me. *No*, I thought again. *No way*. My hands remained over my mouth.

A thump on the door and it shot inward, opening towards me. Turning to face him, I was horrified to find he'd broken the door, but his expression of wide eyes and open mouth proved he was equally surprised. I was a mess of tears, and I spun away from him.

"Darlin'." He touched my shoulder, and I shuddered, but I kept my back to him. He forced me to turn and pulled me into a hug, tucking me under his chin and into his chest. He let me cry, the tears no longer able to be retained, the sob escaping with a sharp bark. We stood like this a few seconds before he spoke.

"Darlin', do you want to see me again?"

I nodded, afraid my voice would crumble to begging. "But I can't."

"Why?" he said, pushing me back and trying to make me focus on his face.

"I'm going to die." Thoughts of cancer consumed me. It wouldn't be fair to involve him in my history and any potential of relapse in the future.

"When?!" He barked, his eyes wide like I'd left out the details of my doom. Panic filled his face.

"Someday," I cried, tears streaking my face.

"When, beautiful?" he asked, lowering his voice, a smile in his tone.

"I don't know," I said, exasperated. "I'm in remission, but I can't saddle anyone with this," I added, tugging at my short hair. He chuckled, and I looked up, surprised and hurt.

"Who's *saddling*? Besides, I want to ride, Edie." He tugged me to him again.

"I'm being serious," I cried.

"Me, too." He kissed my forehead.

"Why me?" I asked, suddenly changing directions as I continued to think of all the reasons we shouldn't be together, when it was the very thing I wanted.

"Why *not* you?"

"Don't answer a question with a question," I mocked, laughing through tears, sensing I'd reached hysteria in my grief at our departure.

"Okay," he softly laughed. "Timing."

I rolled my eyes, hating that answer. Someone once said the same thing about David. The timing was right, and David was there, so we were together. I got pregnant; that's why we were married. And if relationships were about timing, how many had I missed out on? How much time had I lost? Sensing my displeasure with his answer, he tried to continue.

"Okay, it's because—"

"I can't have children," I blurted.

"You think I want them?" he said in frustration. His brows furrowed. "I'm surrounded by children." He snorted, implying the wayward actions of the band. "Plus, I've been around Ivy since the day she was born."

I sighed, and he tugged me to him again.

"Edie." When he said my name, I knew he was about to say something serious and I immediately missed him calling me darlin'. "Let's ride, beautiful. See what happens. I'm not talking marriage here, just sex and some fun."

I nodded, although I didn't fully like that answer.

"Remember what fun is, darlin'?"

"Actually, no, not until recently," I replied, rolling my forehead against his chest.

"Well, then, that's why I'm here. Fun," he stated adamantly, and cupped my cheeks to press my face up to his. His mouth covered mine, sweet and slow and heartbreakingly tender as he lapped up the salty tears on my lips and drank up my sobs with his tongue. We stood several minutes kissing like this, and I clutched his T-shirt in my fists, holding on to him like my life depended on it. In many ways, I felt I hadn't lived until I met him, which meant my life had just begun, and now it was about to end. How was that for timing?

+ + +

We returned home to blustery, negative degree temperatures and the start of a new year. Masie would finish her senior year of high school in a few short months. Caleb would leave for spring training in Iowa for the farm team of a Chicago MLB team. David was pleased by the Midwest proximity, but spring training would take place in Arizona. To my surprise, he cashed in frequent flyer miles so Masie and I could attend a weekend of games during her spring break. He even gave up hotel points to cover the stay. After the trip to Hawaii, I couldn't afford another vacation, so I didn't turn down the unexpected gift in order to see my son on the verge of the major leagues.

I'd held Masie's hand through most of the return flight. Her tears matched my previous ones, silent and steady. I had nothing left after Tommy let me finish packing. We decided to part ways in the condo instead of risking a repeat of my meltdown by the car in the parking lot. However, he didn't keep his promise and stood next to the Jeep before we departed. He shook hands with Caleb, thanking him for his permission to take me out a few times. He hugged Masie, whispering into her hair as she nodded against him. My heart broke further at his tenderness toward my children. When he hugged me one more time, I thought I'd break in two.

"I—" he started, but I cut him off.

"I'm sorry," I blurted. He pulled back to look at me. "Family always says sorry, and I'm apologizing for that break down up there. We promised to keep things fun and light and I messed it up." I shook my head and tried to laugh off my ridiculous behavior. He smiled slowly.

"Family loves unconditionally," he whispered, and my lips curled in response. His eyes searched mine but I didn't know what he was looking for. My mind was a jumble, and an ache had developed from all the tears. I just wanted to close my eyes and return home, knowing I'd feel as if I'd been in a dream—Dorothy returned to Kansas, a world of color restored to black and white.

When the Uber dropped us off at my townhouse on the edge of Chicago, I sighed as I turned the key. Home was sweet, but Hawaii was sweeter. Instantly, I felt rappelled to the old me. Turning up the thermostat, telling Masie to call her father, searching through the mail, I'd slipped back to who I'd been, as if I'd never left.

An hour later, I noticed a text.

**Miss you already, beautiful**.

I smiled to myself.

**Just got home. Tired. Miss you, too. XO,** I typed.

**Get some rest. Talk soon**.

Minutes later, my phone rang.

"Hello." I laughed after checking the caller ID and answering.

"Too soon?" The rough voice of Tommy filled my ear, and my heart leapt.

"Perfect timing," I replied.

"That's what I like to hear, darlin'." Silence followed, and I continued smiling knowing he was on the other side of the phone. "So, I'm not great at this phone thing," he began. "But I wanted to hear your voice."

"It's okay. I'm happy to hear yours, too, but I'm tired. I need to work tomorrow." I should have taken another day off, but I told myself I'd make it through one day before another weekend started.

"Okay, beautiful. We fly out early, but I'll text you later in the day. Have a good one tomorrow."

I told him the same, and we hung up. The room suddenly felt empty, filled with silence. How was I going to make it through each day?

+ + +

I didn't have time to ponder that question as the alarm went off too early. I prepared for work in a fog of jet lag. Returning to Hartcore Manufacturing after a ten-day reprieve was like walking into a waterfall. The work rained down on me, and my boss, Maximillian Hartcore, jokingly told me I was never allowed to leave again. Only, a serious tone underlaid his tease, and for the first time ever I noticed my boss looking at me. Thinking I had food on my face or spilt something on my dress, I swiped at my lips and brushed down the middle of my outfit.

"You look different," Max said, his eyes roaming my body. My boss was only a few years younger than me. Handsome in his own right, his hair had begun to speckle with gray, but his clean-shaved face remained salt-and-pepper free. His eyes were a pretty, piercing blue, and his smile was more of a smirk. I noticed he was actually rather attractive. Something I was aware of before, but suddenly more aware of.

He'd known David for years, as my ex-husband had been his business accountant. They weren't really friends, but professional acquaintances. When I wanted a new job around the time of the divorce, and needed special consideration during my treatments, David had done a decent thing and suggested the position with Max. I owed Max for his generous gift of the vacation.

"Seems a little sunshine agrees with you." My skin pebbled with the appraising look he was giving me.

*I had sex.* It was as if he could read it on my skin and was curious to keep reading.

"Thank you. The vacation was wonderful. My kids and I really appreciated the time together." The mention of my children seemed to snap him out of his leering stupor, and he looked away.

"Right. Well, if you need anything else, you know to ask." His head remained lowered as if the report before him was the most important paper of his life. "But on that note, could I ask you to stay a little longer today? I'd like to get organized for next week. It's been a shit show without you."

I smiled in spite of myself. It was nice to be needed, and I agreed to stay. I'd gone through the holiday mail, organized emails by priority, and made a list of a few things I thought should be first on his schedule for the next week. Entering his office around five, he motioned for me to take a seat as he finished a call. His eyes narrowed in on me as he concluded his conversation.

"Fine, fine. Next week, then," he hissed, a touch of anger I'd often heard in his voice when addressing some of his business counterparts. He eventually ended the call and brushed a hand down his face.

"Rough one?" I asked, nodding to the phone.

"Long day," he said sitting forward. "Hey Edie, do you like Chinese food?" It was a strange question, considering I'd often ordered lunches for him and he allowed me to add myself on occasion.

"Sure."

"Would you mind ordering dinner for both of us?" My brows pinched, as I answered, "Okay."

"Great. We'll make it a working dinner," he said, pressing back from his chair. "I'll be back in a few minutes. When it's delivered, join me in here." He stood and turned his back to me as he exited his office for his private bathroom. The door shut with a soft click, and I stood to order dinner.

When dinner arrived, Max had been professional as always, but I hadn't noticed how funny he was until he regaled me with stories of the holiday temp who replaced me.

"She got her wrist stuck in the copy machine fixing a jam, but the best was when she propositioned me."

"No!" I gasped.

"Yep. Asked me outright if I wanted to sleep with her." Max was divorced like me. He had three younger children, as he married later in life. I could see the appeal from the temporary assistant's side—Northwestern grad, successful business owner, still-young, millionaire—but I could never image being so bold.

"Did you take her up on the offer?" I asked before realizing what I'd said. Max's eyes widened, playful and gleaming.

"Would you be jealous if I had?" His voice lowered, and that pebbling skin returned. I swallowed before I answered.

"Of course not," I laughed, dismissively swiping at the air. The sexual escapades of my boss were none of my business. Rocking slightly back in his chair, his blue eyes narrowed. He bit his lip. "Green really isn't my color," I added, remembering all the times Tommy mocked me for being jealous of other women's attention to him.

"I don't know, Edie. I think you'd be pretty in any color." The comment caught my breath, and I found Max staring at me as he had when I first entered the office that morning. He smiled slowly, and my heart pattered. Was he coming on to me? I patted at some curls near my ear, dismissing the thought.

"Thank you," I said, lowering my eyes and smoothing down the skirt of my dress. "If we're done here, I'd like to go home. I need to get organized there as well after the trip."

Max sat forward, his eyes still on me. "Of course, Edie. Whatever you need."

+ + +

My hands trembled as I started my car, although I did not feel threatened in any way. I chalked it all up to being overly tired. There was no way my boss was coming onto me, I decided, not after all this time, not at my age. He was younger than me, and David's business associate. I checked my phone while the car heated and noticed three missed calls from Tommy during my working dinner. I immediately called him back, only to have it go to voicemail. I didn't leave a message. I didn't know what to say.

*I miss you.*

*I don't know how I'll survive without you.*

*I want to see you again, now.*

The list was so desperate sounding. Even saying something as mundane as *I hope you had a good day* sounded weak and clingy in my head. I hung up, but dialed again to hear his voice, even though it was a greeting message. I hung up a second time, determining I was the most ridiculous woman on the planet. I wasn't a teenager. I was forty-three, but I felt like a girl again, and not in a good way. Insecurity trickled through my veins.

Around one in the morning, my phone buzzed. I was a light sleeper, and I immediately answered.

"Hey," my voice rasped, heavy with sleep.

"I woke you, didn't I, darlin'?"

"It's okay," I said, happy to hear his voice.

"The time change throws me off. It's only eleven here." Tommy and the band had returned to their homes just outside Los Angeles, California. I had no concept of what that looked like. I'd never been to California.

"It's fine." I shrugged like he could see me and shifted on the bed.

"You in bed, darlin'?" His voice lowered and a tickle rose in my lower belly.

"Yes," I exhaled.

"Describe it for me." I laughed in response, but explained the layout of my room finding it similar to the resort condo. I only had a queen-sized bed at home, but my dresser stood opposite of it, with a chair to the side and a night stand closest to where I slept. The description reminded me of the night Tommy knelt before me, lapping at my core before making love to me. My heart rate increased and my hand slipped to cup a breast before skittering down my belly.

"And what are you wearing?" The question asked with seductive intent caused a chuckle in response.

"A T-shirt and underwear."

"The red ones?" he asked, his voice lowering.

"Nope."

"The purple ones?" I laughed again, curious that he seemed to have memorized my boring, bright underpants. "Don't say the pink ones."

In fact, they were the pink ones, the same ones I'd worn on the night haunting my thoughts.

"Yes," I exhaled again, too breathy, too deep.

"Where's Mr. Bob?" he questioned, and I blushed as he referenced the toy buried in my bathing suit drawer in hopes my children would never find it.

"Too far away," I whispered as my fingers hesitated at the top of coarse hair, curly and crisp near the edge of my legs.

"Darlin,' I want to touch you. Can you do it for me?"

I nodded as if he could see me. I sampled myself, tickling through the hair and pressing the nub that ached for him.

"Whatcha doin', beautiful?" His voice sounded strained, and I was curious if he touched himself. Without waiting for an answer, he spoke again. "Describe it to me."

I should have been embarrassed. I *was* mortified, but I was thrilled at the same time. I was too close to the edge to stop myself, and my legs shook in desperation, the pulse between my thighs beat faster than my heart.

"I'm touching myself."

"That's my girl," he stressed. "Tell me more."

"I'm parting the folds, and I'm wet. Really wet."

"Fuck," Tommy hissed.

"My fingers aren't as good as yours."

"That's right, darlin', nothing feels as good as my fingers on you, spreading you." The comment sent a surge through my middle, and I gasped. My fingers increased the pressure. "Keep talking, beautiful."

"I'm stroking fast, pressing hard. Oh, God, Tommy, I'm so close. So close, baby." I moaned, spreading my legs wide and twirling over the folds, rocking my hips upward, reaching for something deeper.

"Feels good, darlin'. So good. You're almost there, almost there." He was panting through the phone.

"Are you touching yourself?" I asked, my voice too high, filled with surprise, despite my assumption.

"Fuck, yeah, darlin'. Just thinking of you makes me so hard, so needy." He paused for a breath, and it was the only sound from both our sides of the phone.

"Slip a finger inside, darlin'."

"I can't," I whispered.

"Do it, darlin'." His voice came out in a rush, his breaths jagged. I stroked over myself, rubbing harder, picking up the pace.

"I can't," I stuttered, feeling myself on the edge of something, but not getting there. My fingers were coated, the slick sound of my skin echoing in the room.

"You can," he barked, his breath hitching.

"I've never—" I started, but he cut me off.

"Inside. Now, Edie. Now." I did as he said, slipping one finger in deep and I bit back the scream as I came. My back arched off the bed as my finger delved inward. My eyes rolled back, and I forgot the phone for a moment.

"That's it, girl. Keep stroking, keep going. Oh, darlin'. So good, so wet, so sweet." His raspy voice encouraged me, and I rocked on my finger until I was replete.

I exhaled into the phone, resting back flat on the bed. My legs shifted, and my arm swiped along the sheet. Aftershocks rippled through me, and I longed for him to be with me. It was good but not enough.

"Miss me?" he questioned, his voice near a whisper.

"So much more than you know," I replied, a tear slipping from my eye. "So much more."

# 12
### Sex. Period.

**I got my period**.

I stared at the text I'd sent, knowing tone was difficult to read in a few rushed words over a screen. However, I wanted him to know he had nothing to worry about. We were nearing two weeks apart, and my period was almost two weeks late. I didn't tell Tommy that, but remembering his freak-out over coming inside me, I wanted to let him know. This was a good thing. Honestly, at forty-three, who wants to get pregnant again, and start the cycle of life over? But strangely, a small part of me was disappointed, and so my rash text was sent by my crabby mood.

I didn't wait for a reply. He was two hours behind me, and most likely, still sleeping. His schedule was one social activity after another, plus days filled with band practice and extinguishing shenanigans from the boys. My first call had actually been to my doctor. I'd made an appointment based on my growing nerves, but needed to cancel. Minutes later, Dr. Crain called me. We'd become friends in the professional way doctors befriend patients they see often.

"Edie, what's going on?" Elizabeth asked. Brushing a hand over my hair, I blushed despite her inability to see me.

"I thought I was pregnant." The silence that ensued dropped the bomb slowly. *Kerplunk*. "But I'm not."

A pause followed those three little words, and I swallowed the ridiculous lump in my throat.

"Edie," she said low, soothingly like only a doctor can. "I don't think that's possible, and you know all the reasons why. Your period needs time to regulate after the treatments you've endured. We've discussed this."

"I know," I huffed, knowing she was right, and my panic was unreasonable.

"What made you think you could be?"

I snorted into the phone, a nervous huff following.

L.B. Dunbar

"I didn't think you were sexually active," Elizabeth added.

"I'm not." It was true, being almost two weeks without Tommy.

"Well," she giggled. "Then you know it takes two for that to happen. Do we need a refresher in the birds and the bees?" she teased.

"No," I laughed along with her, feeling foolish. "It's just…" I stopped myself from speaking. I didn't have close girlfriends. Not ones that I would share such intimate details with about my newly restored and suddenly vacant sex life. Elizabeth's pause hinted that I should tell her. I could speak to her, but this wasn't a clinical thing. There wasn't a diagnosis for what was going on inside me. I was in love. No doctor could detect that, but my heart was breaking with our separation. I just didn't see where Tommy and I could go from where we were—two separate places on the map.

"Look," Elizabeth filled the pause. "You could still get pregnant. You haven't reached an age where you can't. But the likelihood is less, and after all your body has been through, highly unlikely." She paused for more effect. "Is this something you want?"

"No," I exhaled. It wasn't. I was at the opposite end of the spectrum. On the verge of being an empty nester, but still, the thirty seconds of thought at a new life, growing inside me again, filling my days, did squeeze at my heart.

"You know, lots of women go through what you're going through. It's called adjustment disorder. Things are changing at an increased pace. The divorce. Cancer. Caleb leaving and soon Masie. It's understandable that you're having trouble adjusting to the changes. I can prescribe something for that, if you'd like?" My head was shaking before she finished her question.

"No," I said, a bit too adamantly. I took enough pills as it was. I didn't need something else in the mix that I'd have to regulate with diet or other medications. "No. I'm okay. Just a freaky false alarm."

"Okay. Well, if you need something, or think you do, you can call me."

I nodded again as if she could see me, thanked her, and hung up. Then I noticed I'd missed a text message: **What's this?**

My phone buzzed in my hand, and I answered. Hello wasn't even out of my mouth when he growled.

"What kind of message is that, darlin'?"

My mouth fell open at the accusation.

"Uhm, you were there. I don't think I need to spell it out, but I wanted you to know you have nothing to worry about."

Silence followed a moment, and I chewed at my lip. Time had dragged since we'd parted and yet had strangely sped up. The days always seemed like they'd be long, and then I'd been so busy at work the time passed. The nights were unbearably strained, as I missed him too much. I didn't wish to fight, but I was on edge about our relationship. Did we have a relationship?

"I told you I wasn't worried."

"You were," I interjected, sharper than I intended.

Silence followed once more.

"You okay, darlin'?" I swiped at my growing hair. I'd gotten a cut to shape the growth, and I'd even purchased some new clothes, feeling different about myself after the vacation. But that day, I felt like my old self. A bit frumpy, a lot irritable, and just outright frustrated with life in general.

"Yeah," I lied, letting my voice fall. "I didn't sleep well last night." That wasn't true either. I usually felt drowsy the day before my period, and I'd fallen asleep early.

"Do you need anything?"

I chuckled without humor. As if he could do something, I thought. He's in California. I hated my negativity, and hated myself for even starting this conversation. I needed to stop this. "Nope, I'll be good in a few days. I'm at work, and I'm sorry if I woke you, but I can't really talk. Talk later?"

I could practically see him chewing his lip, wanting to say more but respecting that I'd mentioned work.

"Okay, Edie." He hung up, and I cringed at the use of my name. He only said it when he was upset or serious.

Hours passed and around three, the front receptionist called my desk. "You have a delivery." My brows pinched. I never received packages, so I assumed she misspoke, meaning it was something for Max. I decided to take the three flights down to the front desk, stretching my legs that ached a little and twisting my back which ached a lot. I needed some ibuprofen.

Arriving at the desk, I found a beautiful display of red tulips and a plastic bag from the local pharmacy.

"So, where's the delivery?" I asked, looking over the counter for a box or mailing envelope.

"It's there," Grace pointed, implying the bag and the flowers. "You got flowers and this bag." She tapped the plastic with her pen. Opening the bag slowly, I found several items inside—chicken soup, a heating pad, a bottle of ibuprofen, a bottle of Midol, and a Kindle gift card.

"What the heck?" I laughed outright, pulling out the contents one at a time. I stared at the collection, and then reached for the card attached to the flowers.

*I drew the line at tampons, darlin'. Hope you feel better soon.*

I laughed harder as tears sprang to my eyes. My heart raced and I hugged the small card and envelope to my chest. I gathered my things while Grace wiggled a brow at me.

Walking back to the executive office, I set the flowers on the corner of my desk as Max came out of his office.

"What's this?" he asked. "Special occasion."

"Not exactly," I said, staring at the red collection of spring flowers.

"Got a boyfriend?" he asked teasingly in a sing-song voice, like a school boy.

*Did I?* I thought. I didn't know how to answer that. Tommy wasn't a boy, and he was more than a friend. Were we simply long-distance lovers? I didn't know.

"Just a..." I couldn't speak. I felt Max's eyes on me, so I swallowed and added. "A friend."

The lie made me feel cheap.

Adding to my poor day, minutes before the work day ended, Ivy called me. I decided to take it, worried that something was wrong as she typically didn't call me during the days.

"Hey, honey," I started. Ivy's voice choked on the other end of the phone. "Ivy, what's the matter?" My heart raced, and I instantly thought of Tommy, worried something had happened to him.

"I'm pregnant," she blurted, and tears echoed through the phone.

+ + +

Ivy and I spoke for nearly an hour while I sat at my desk despite my colleagues leaving the office.

"Gage doesn't know yet. He's not going to be happy."

"Why not?" I asked, my voice rising in surprise.

"The tour is coming. He's already upset that I said I wouldn't join him. Ava starts first grade, and I want her to be home, going to a regular school, on a schedule."

"I see. And he doesn't like that idea?"

"He doesn't mind. He sees where I'm coming from, wanting to give the girls a stable life after mine wasn't, but he still thought I could take her out of school here and there and join him on the road."

"Ah," I sighed. Gage had this unnerving need to have Ivy always with him, and while I understood young love, and all that, it was bordering on possessive. He was smothering her.

"I don't know how to tell him."

"You aren't going to do anything rash." Panic rushed through my voice.

"No, of course not. I want this, it's just…"

"It's just what, honey?"

"I thought with Ava going to school, I was one step closer to a little freedom. I was hoping to get a job." I blinked. Ivy didn't need a job. Her husband made more than ten heads of household, but before I even questioned her comment, I understood. Ivy suffered that suffocation from Gage.

"What were you going to do?"

"I've kept my musical therapist license renewed. I always thought I'd do something along those lines. Work not-for-profit or volunteer. Nothing major. Nothing rigid. Just something more than purple dinosaurs and singing backpacks."

I laughed knowing exactly how she felt. Ivy had gone from college to marriage, with a baby barely in between those two events. The same thing happened to me.

"Ivy, you can still do this. Hire a babysitter. You need to get out. It will be better for you and the baby, especially if you feel trapped."

"I don't feel trapped," she replied, her voice stronger than normal.

"Okay, trapped might be the wrong word, it's just—"

"I'm sorry, Edie. I didn't mean that." *Family always says sorry.* "I'm just so worked up about this."

"I think you should tell Gage everything. Tell him about the baby. Tell him about wanting a job, that you need something for you. You'll work it out." I tried to be reassuring. I remembered being her age, being overwhelmed and so young.

"I'm losing myself, Edie," she whispered, and my heart broke.

"Don't let that happen. Don't." I wanted to reach through the phone and shake her, and then hug her because she needed that hug, and so did I.

+ + +

My boss asked me to join him for drinks at the end of the week. He'd never offered before, and I never would have dreamed of accepting, but I needed that drink. It had been a rough few days. Tommy and I still spoke each night, but it felt different. Time was rearing its evil head. Distance was not making the heart grow fonder.

"I really appreciate your invitation," I said, looking around me, wondering where the other office staff was. Max said it would be casual—a few people from the office just hanging out at the end of a winter work week.

"I feel like we don't know each other as well as I'd like," he said, taking a sip of his double whiskey on the rocks. "I mean, I know about David, and…" His voice trailed off, avoiding the word cancer. "But I don't know the other things. What do you do for fun? What music do you like?"

I took a large swallow of my wine, gulping more than sipping, as the question caught my breath. It was something Tommy might ask.

"I'm not really good with music. I find I love it, but lack the knowledge to know who sings what." I laughed off my own deficiency, guilt seeping into the conversation for some reason.

"There's a concert in a few weeks. Ever hear of The Nights?" I had, and I loved their music. "I have two tickets. Would you like to go?"

I took a deep breath. Should I do this? Tommy and I never discussed being exclusive, but I'd expect the same of him. I wouldn't want him to take someone to a concert, but he probably did. Not to mention, Max was my boss. My very handsome boss, who I noticed more and more was looking at me in a way that was more than just appreciating my organizational skills.

"You can think about it if you'd like? It's in two weeks."

"Thank you. I'd like to get back to you. I just want to check my home calendar," I offered, trying not to make it an adamant no and hurt his feelings. On that note, my phone buzzed.

**Where are you?** It was Masie.

**Out for drinks. What's going on?**

**Out for drinks? You never go out,** she reminded me. She was correct, and I was starting to think I needed to change that fact.

**Well, tonight I did.** I paused a moment and sent another reply. **Was there something you needed?**

**I have a surprise for you. You need to come home.**

**Soon.**

**Now, Mom.** While texting didn't inflict tone, I didn't care for Masie's.

"Everything okay?" Max asked, nodding toward the phone.

"I'm so sorry. This was so rude. I'm not sure. My daughter's asking me to come home. I hate to ignore her. It won't be for much longer that she's home. She graduates in May."

Max's eyes roamed my body. "It's hard to believe you have a high school senior."

"I also have a twenty-two-year old son." I laughed.

"And you had him when you were twelve?" Max's eyes widened as he chuckled. "I'd forgotten." His warm smile and roaming appraisal was flattering, but surprising. His roving eyes didn't ignite me like Tommy's did, but a flicker burned. He was just being complimentary, I told myself.

"I should probably go," I said, slipping off the stool and reaching for my wallet.

"This is on me," he said, reaching for his wallet inside his back pocket. "But you have to promise to do it again."

My head shot up, and I caught his baby blues sparkling.

"Okay," I said, my voice unsure, but willing myself to take chances. "Have a good weekend."

"You too," he said, and as I walked away, I sensed his eyes on me. I might have swayed my hips a little more than normal.

+ + +

"Tommy?" In all his rock star glory, he stood in my living room, wearing dark jeans and a gray V-neck sweater. My breath hitched, and I wanted to catapult myself over the coffee table and tackle him to the couch. Instead, I exhaled his name, and he stepped around the low table. With Masie as our audience, he simply reached for my hand and brushed his lips against my cheek.

"Darlin'," he breathed against my jaw.

"Can I spend the night at Daphne's?" Masie asked, forcing me to flinch under Tommy's touch. Daphne was Masie's closest friend and a bit of trouble.

"Are her parents home?" Masie rolled her eyes in response, but a few weeks before the winter break, her parents hadn't been home. There was definitely drinking and boys involved before Daphne's older brother broke up the party.

"Mom," Masie drew out. I looked at Tommy and back at my daughter, torn between being the diligent parent and the sex-craved woman this man had turned me into. I wanted nothing more than him alone in my house, but my need for responsibility gnawed at me.

"Are you sure? You don't have to leave." My eyes shot to Tommy and back at her. Tommy nodded, and I realized I'd already missed some conversation. "Is West with you?" The question was insensitive. Masie hadn't heard from West, and the dismissal stung.

"We just chatted about him. He's not here, beautiful." Tommy winked at me, and I turned back to Masie, noticing a bag already packed and at her feet.

"Fine, you can go."

Once Masie left, I was suddenly nervous. My hands stroked my hips as I stood before Tommy, who had taken a seat after Masie grabbed her bag and left.

"What are you doing here?" I asked, lowering myself to a chair near the couch.

"I have business here. Came to see my girl," he said, sitting forward, elbows bracing on his knees. "Is that all right?"

"That's amazing," I said, swiping a hand over my head. "I'm just so surprised." In fact, I was absolutely dumbfounded to see him sitting on my couch, in my living room, in Chicago. Quickly, I stood again.

"Would you like something to drink? I have wine." My voice trembled as I turned for my kitchen leaving him behind. My hands shook. Entering the kitchen, I gripped the edge of the counter, pressing my head forward to rest on the upper cabinet.

"What's wrong?" His soft gravelly voice spoke directly behind me, and I turned to face him.

"I don't know." I laughed anxiously. "I'm so surprised...and...nervous." With that, he stepped forward, filling my space, cupping my jaw and lowering his mouth to mine. My body slowly thawed. His mouth was molasses drizzled into sweet cookie batter, and I licked at his lips, not wanting to miss a drop. His lips led mine, and he tilted his head, increasing the pressure, accelerating the intensity. My hands rose to his biceps, finding the sweater foreign when I'd seen him so often in T-shirts. Slipping up the hills of his shoulders, I found the curl of his hair at the nape of his neck, and my libido kicked in. I pulled myself to him, pressing firmly against his chest and breathing him in with my mouth. He was oxygen, and I hadn't breathed in weeks.

"There's my darlin'." He chuckled against my lips, returning to kiss me with that aggressive appreciation only his mouth gave mine. "Still got your period?"

Nearing the end of my flow, the question should have killed the moment, and in some ways, it did. It was a reminder of our awkward and brusque conversation earlier in the week. "Why?"

"Always a question for a question," he teased, coming for my mouth another second before pulling back. My lower lip was nipped between his before releasing me. "Let's shower."

The comment surprised me until he stepped back and led me to the staircase. Did he want to…? While I had my period?

"Uhm…" I paused as I blindly climbed the stairs behind him.

"Uh-oh," he teased, leading me into my room after sticking his head into the doorway of Masie's and then Caleb's rooms. "Seems like I have some uncorking to do. My fine wine has been stoppered, and she needs a reminder of how sweet she tastes."

"Oh, God, you can't do that." His brow rose as he chuckled in response. I'd misunderstood. He meant me, as a whole. He turned on my shower, and then stepped back, watching me. His bulk filled my bathroom, and a space I considered a little haven suddenly seemed closed in and tight with his presence. I didn't move, like I'd forgotten what to do.

"How you feel about that shirt?" I looked down at the crisp white blouse. It was fine enough. I wasn't really a blouse woman, and it had been a little annoying and restricting, but it had been part of my new clothing purchases. Suddenly, two hands snuck into the opening at my neck and tugged. Buttons flew, and the fabric ripped. My mouth fell open.

"There she is," he groaned, looking from my neck to my waist and back to stop on the nude bra I wore. His hands slipped around my sides, tugging me close to him and capturing my lips once again. The kiss loosened me up. My arms wrapped around his neck.

"I'll give you a minute. Do what you need to do and then step into the shower." His directions surprised me once again. We hadn't showered together before, and I wasn't sure how this would work, but I did as he said. Stepping under the warm spray, I took a few deep breaths, releasing it slowly and willing my heart to stop hammering. This was Tommy. I wanted him here. I wanted him.

Seconds later, he stepped into the shower, and I lost my breath. Literally. I couldn't breathe at the sight before me. His tan had lessened, but only a little. The hair on his chest curled. The lower hair led to a treasure I couldn't peel my eyes from. Already stiff and upright, I swallowed as I took in the pleasure of admiring him covered in water.

"You are a wonder, Mr. Carrigan," I said, my voice husky and rough.

"You are a beauty, darlin'." With those words, he stepped forward and kissed me again. The hard length of him hit my belly, distracting me instantly, and I wrapped my fingers around the ridged shaft.

"Fuck," he growled against my mouth. "I promised myself I'd go slow, but I've missed you, darlin', and those hands feel too good." I gave him a gentle tug, and he groaned, the sound echoing off the shower tile. He spun me so my back faced him.

"Edie, baby. I can't wait. Can this first time be fast? I'll go slow next time, darlin'." His hands cupped the globes of my backside, and I leaned forward to balance my hands on the steamy tile. A finger slipped through the crack, slowly dipping deeper and lowering to the edge of my entrance. I clenched, uncertain this was a good idea. "Still want to experiment back here one day, darlin', but tonight is a reunion of other parts."

L.B. Dunbar

He stepped forward, and the tip of him caressed my core as he swept back and forth a few times.

"Are you sure about this?" I said, my voice low and shaky with nerves. I'd never done this before. David was repulsed at the thought, although I sometimes found I was equally excitable even with my period. Tommy didn't answer me before he slammed into me. The assault was a little awkward, and a tad rough. I wasn't ready in the way I should be, but as he slid forward and I pressed back, he filled me.

"Let's get one thing straight, darlin'. You feel me in there?" His voice deepened, demanded, and I nodded, my hand curling into a fist against the slippery tile. I felt him, all of him, and it felt better than anything in a long time. My eyes closed at the pleasure. Uncorking was a good metaphor. Tension released as we connected.

"Answer me," he bit, and my eyes, which had closed with heavy lids, snapped open. His hand came to my shoulder while the other rested on my hip.

"Yes, I feel you," I choked as he slid back and then reentered me as if to prove his point. He was in deep.

"I'm bare in there, Edie, because I don't give a flying fuck about your period or if you're pregnant or if you're not." He stilled, and my eyes widened, taking in the tile I'd seen every day for three years as if it were the most interesting thing in the world. "All I care about is you. And me. Us."

I nodded, my head lowering as he continued to torture me by pulling almost to the edge and then leaping forward with a heavy thrust.

"You feel me, darlin'?" he repeated, his words filled with meaning.

"I feel you." I swallowed as my voice caught with the next invasion of my channel.

"Where, Edie? Where do you feel me?" I blinked. Did he want me to describe this? The hand at my hip slipped forward, and his fingers lightly stroked at the sacred spot that would trip me over the edge.

"Deep inside me," I moaned. He pulled to the edge and stalled. My head rose, and I peered over my shoulder as best I could.

"Where else?" he hissed, holding out from filling me again. His fingers stilled as well.

"My heart," I whispered, and he slid inward, the thrust so fierce I lurched forward, and my hand slipped off the slick tile. I jackknifed forward, but he caught me with an arm around my waist. We both groaned at the increased intensity.

"That's right, darlin'. You feel me in your heart like I feel you in mine." He continued to hammer at me, and his fingers developed a matching rhythm. My body gave into his, and I came with a scream. The echo resounded in the shower and both his hands gripped my hips, tugging me back and holding me still as he pulsed inside me, washing my insides as he spilled his seed.

Jagged, rasping breaths forced my racing heart to skip a beat. *My heart* that felt him, that beat for him, sped inside my chest, trying to hold onto him, hoping to never lose the race to be his.

+ + +

We dried off, and Tommy dressed in only his boxer briefs. I'd typically wear flannel pajama pants and a sweatshirt in the colder months. Not a sexy image, so I dressed as I had in Hawaii in a nightshirt and panties, cursing the precautionary pantyliner. However, after what we'd done, my inhibitions were gone. Tommy had broken all the barriers.

"I'm exhausted, darlin'. Mind if we turn on that TV and snuggle a bit?" I climbed in bed next to him. He held out an arm, and I curled in close, resting my head on his chest, listening to his heart patter.

*You feel me in your heart like I feel you in mine.* The words warmed me, and I melted against him again. After a few minutes of TV, my mind wandered. I didn't typically watch television, despite the one in my room, and I had no idea what he was watching. It seemed mindless.

"What's wrong, darlin'?"

"Nothing," I said, rolling to press a kiss to his chest. I lay back. It seemed strange to do something so mundane as cuddle in bed and watch television. We hadn't done that in Hawaii, something so *normal*, something many couples do. Were we a couple?

"You're doing it again," he said, and I shifted my head to look up at him.

"What?"

"You're going all stiff next to me instead of molding into me. What's happening here?" He looked down at me, as his arm raised and bent to rest beneath his head.

"I just…it seems a bit surreal that you're in my house. In my bed. And we're laying here." His arm lowered to his side as he gazed at me.

"Want me to leave?"

"No," I said, shaking my head against his chest, scratching my cheek with the coarse hair of his chest. "No, absolutely not."

He chuckled. "Okay, beautiful. You don't need to beg me to stay. I wasn't leaving unless you physically kicked me out, anyway." He swiped a hand down my cheek and leaned forward to kiss my forehead. "But I'm sensing there is more."

"It's…well…I don't really watch TV."

He chuckled under me again. "Okay, so what do you do?"

"I read."

"Latest mystery thriller?" he asked, and my heart leapt that he'd said the same thing to me on the night we met.

"Not exactly," I answered.

"Well, get the book. Can you read while I watch this show?"

"Sure," I replied, a bit too excited as I sat up, reached for my e-reader and returned to my original position. How strange it seemed to move around, nearly-naked and uninhibited. How strange it was to balance my tablet on his chest.

"This isn't working," I muttered, feeling embarrassed and a bit ridiculous that I thought I could pull off reading next to him. What was I thinking?

His arm stretched behind me. "Roll."

"What?"

"Roll, so your back is to my side. I can still hold you, but you can balance that thing on the bed." I did as he said, shifting so my back pressed against his side, my head resting on his arm. Eventually, he bent a knee, and I slipped a leg over his, our inner thighs touching. He watched his show. I read my book, until I came to a particularly steamy scene. The words made my heart race. The pulse between my thighs beat, and I clenched. His leg slowly moved upward and my thigh pressed over his.

I continued to read, the rhythm increasing, and the words titillating. Could people really do that? I wondered as the story took my imagination to a new level. I hadn't noticed that my leg was slowly dragging over Tommy's, my inner thigh stroking his, letting the faint curly hairs at the top of his leg tickle the inside of mine.

Despite the movement of my body, I kept reading, the words continuing to stroke my imagination and create a mental picture so vivid I clenched.

"Whatcha reading over there?" The sultry tone of his voice ratcheted the pulse between my thighs.

"Nothing," I rasped, feeling my face flush. I stilled my body, hyperaware of his thigh beneath mine and the weight of his leg at my core. I had my period, a light flow, but still…

"Your fine ass just rubbed my hip, like it wanted something."

"Oh…I…the scene is hot," I said, with a giggle. My eyes had drifted, so I started at the top of the page again, but my body betrayed me, reacting in the same way. His thigh pressed upward, my core resting flat against the heat of his leg. Without thought, I lightly squeezed, the pulse at my center beating faster than my heart. Tommy's arm curled, and he pushed the tablet down. His leg nudged harder, firmly pressing against a suddenly needy spot.

"You getting off on my leg, darlin'?" My face heated, but my throat moaned. The sound escaped me before I could catch it.

"I…I don't know," I purred, allowing my body to take over, rubbing my center against the firmness of his thigh. My backside curled into his hip, and I developed a rhythm of rocking over his leg and rolling into his side. He shifted, pressing the length of him against my backside, and I whimpered. The tingles inside my belly had moved from flutters to flight. I was getting so close, and ridiculous as it sounded, I was about to get off on his leg. His hand gripped my hip, and he moved with me, letting me lead.

"Tommy," my voice hitched. He groaned behind me. "That's it, darlin'."

"Tommy," my voice rose an octave, disbelieving this was happening. That I'd gone this crazy as to take his leg.

"Mmmm…right there, baby," he said, his voice that dropping sound of pebbles in a pond. *Plop. Plop. Plop.* And I drowned. My hand sought purchase on the sheets. My thighs clenched together, rubbing his leg. This was insane, I thought, but my body disagreed, and I came and came. My heart hammered and breaths shallowed. As I slowed, Tommy pressed me to the bed and climbed over me. The hot length of him nestled against my core, damp and spent from what I'd done.

"I want inside again."

I nodded lazily. "We might want a towel or something."

"Get one," he demanded, rolling to the side and I raced for the bathroom. Once there I removed my underwear. Back by the bed, I draped the towel over the sheets and lay down. He climbed over me instantly, entering me swiftly, and we both groaned in unison.

"I've missed you so much, beautiful," he said, stilling once he was inside of me and brushing back the sweaty hair on my forehead. He pumped into me, short jagged presses as he spoke. "Can't go so long without you." He kissed my nose and balanced back on an elbow to continue the sharp pulsing. "Why is Chicago so far away?"

With that I laughed, jostling him inside me, and his eyes widened at the pressure. We didn't speak after that. He took what he needed, filling me again, before collapsing on top of me.

"Edie…" he said my name, so serious, so hesitant, but when I looked at him, he only smiled, one side of his lip curling upward. Whatever he was going to say, he changed his mind, but I worried he could read my thoughts. Because my mind said, *I love you, Tommy Carrigan.*

# 13

## Leather and More Lies

We spent two wonderful days exploring the city, a city I loved and had lived in all my life, but didn't know half as well as him. He'd been here before, on tour, and I remembered seeing him at that club back when I was in high school.

"I bet you were a feisty one," he teased as we talked about that night. "You should have introduced yourself."

"You wouldn't have noticed me. In fact, you didn't." I teased in return, recalling dancing in front of the stage, back in the days when I did dance. Tommy's voice washed over me, and I remember thinking this man is going to be a star someday. And he was.

He took me to an underground jazz club on Saturday, where we danced like we did the night before I left Hawaii. The next day we went to the Athletic Club for lunch and looked out at the cold lake, chunks of frozen wake floating on the surface. We even went ice skating at Millennium Park, although I think he was more comfortable on his own two feet instead of blades. The city was alive for me with Tommy at my side, and I wondered once again how much I'd missed in life, while I'd been waiting for him.

On Monday, I had to work. Hartcore Manufacturing was near the airport, although the warehouse was downtown. There had been talks of moving it out of the city, but the incentive to keep the city property kept increasing. I could have driven Tommy to the airport, but he told me it was out of my way as it was past my office. We parted ways when he was picked up by an Uber.

"Not goodbye," he said, as he pressed his lips to my forehead.

"Not goodbye," I repeated, swallowing down the lump in my throat.

Once at work, I fired-up my computer. With the early hour, I decided to sneak a peek at social media. To the right, in the headlines, was an image I couldn't ignore. My eyes gravitated to it instantly. My finger shook as I clicked on the picture. An article instantly popped up, filling my screen with details of Tommy Carrigan and another woman.

*Have Lawson Colt and Deanna Kaye decided to reunite?*

The headline startled me, and I stared at the word.

*Reunite.*

My eyes roamed the article.

*Seen here in a Chicago airport, rumor has it Lawson Colt and Deanna Kaye planned a secret getaway to spend time in the city where they met. Sources close to the former fashion model tell us she still loves him after all these years. Lawson's people refused to comment. The former lead guitarist for both Chrome Teardrops and Colt45 has remained single ever since the couple split fifteen years ago. Maybe first loves never die, as Colt once bellowed in his infamous song, 'Loved Nevermore.'*

I clicked to minimize the image and the article. My stomach roiled. Bile rose to my throat. The taste of regurgitated milk filled my mouth. I stood and ran for the bathroom. Gripping the sink, I willed myself not to be sick, although the nausea nearly overwhelmed me. I hadn't been this shaky since my last treatment. Looking up, my reflection showed I'd paled to a sickly white. My lips were too bright, and my eyes watered, blurring the blue color.

"He couldn't have," I told myself, but I had nothing else to believe. Once again, he had omitted the truth. Pressing off the cool tile, I rinsed my hands and patted my cheeks. I returned to my desk and pulled up the article again on my phone. Copying the link, I forwarded it to him in a text message.

**Reunited?!** I typed under the article link. I threw my phone on my desk and sunk my head into my hands.

"Everything all right?" Max's concerned voice washed over me like a damp cloth, the sensation warm and tender, but making me shiver. My eyes watered, and I blinked rapidly, refusing to look up. "Edie?" The way he said my name, brought the liquid again.

"I'm okay. Just something I read online. A sad story." I smiled weakly, attempting to recover.

"You have a good heart," he said, as he entered his office.

My heart? *You feel me in your heart like I feel you in mine.*

There had to be an explanation. But it was hard to swallow that he'd lied again. Omitted. Had he been married? It wasn't a big deal that he was divorced, but he hadn't told me the truth. Again.

My phone buzzed.

"Darlin'," he started, but I cut him off.

"Don't. Don't you darlin' me. I asked you. No, begged you, to never lie to me again."

"I didn't lie."

"You didn't tell the truth," I shrieked, lowering my voice as I looked up to see Max watching me from his office. "You didn't tell the whole truth. Again." I repeated, my voice almost a whisper.

A sigh filled the phone, and I pictured him swiping through his hair. I didn't care. I didn't want to think of him nervous and sexy.

"It's not what you think."

"What I think?" I gasped. "The only thing I can think is the article is true as I don't know any other truth."

"Darlin', you can never believe the fucking press. Never. They took an innocent image and skewed the whole thing."

My heart dropped to my stomach. He'd all but admitted he'd met her.

"Who is she?" I hated that I asked. I hated that my voice cracked, sounding needy and sad.

"She's Deanna Kaye, former model for DHX." I had no idea what that meant. I didn't even care. She was a model, and I was...in manufacturing. My elbow slammed on my desk, and my forehead lowered to my palm. I didn't want to know what she did. I wanted to know who she was to him.

"Look, we were married all of three seconds. It didn't mean anything, and that picture means nothing now."

"You were married!" I hissed into the phone, eyes jumping up to Max again, who thankfully wasn't watching me come unraveled. "You didn't tell me." In fact, I recalled him specifically saying it wasn't his thing.

"It doesn't matter."

"It matters to me."

"Why?"

"Did you love her?" *Damn it!* I kicked at the underside of my desk and met Max's eyes. He stood, stalking for the door of his office. "You know what, don't answer that. I'm at work. I can't do this now."

"Edie—"

"I have to go," I muttered, my eyes on Max's as he walked through the entrance to his office, his hand working at rolling up his shirt sleeves, exposing strong forearms. I didn't want to be rude to Tommy, but I had to get off the phone. I clicked off.

"Edie, are you sure you're okay?" Max walked all the way to my desk and sat on the edge. Eyes pressed on me—other eyes—those of the people in the outer offices watching as Max never spoke this intimately to an employee, even if I was his personal assistant. "You can talk to me. You know that, right?" he offered, and the generosity almost broke me. I sat up straighter, swiped my hands down my pencil skirt and smiled too large, too forced.

"I really appreciate that Max. Honest. It means a lot to me, but I'm fine." A shaky hand smoothed at my growing hair, and Max's eyes watched my fingers. I lowered them, hiding them under my desk.

"If you're certain, how about meeting in my office in five? I have a few things to be scheduled this week."

I nodded. He stood from my desk, and I watched his backside as he entered his office. It occurred to me, I knew more about my boss than Tommy. I was in over my head with the former rock star. What I needed was normal man—a stable, considerate, no-holding-back-the-truth man. To my shame, Max turned and caught me staring at him. My face pinked, and his lip curled. My phone vibrated on the desk, and I instantly looked away from my teasing boss. Reading Tommy's name, I closed my eyes. I couldn't answer him. I had work to do.

+ + +

Twenty minutes later, Max's office phone rang. He didn't even say hello when he noticed who was calling.

"Sure," he answered, his eyes looking up at me. Holding out the phone, I stared at him. How could the phone be for me in his office?

"Edie," Grace's hushed voice hissed through the phone. "The most gorgeous silver fox is here to see you. Girl, you have some explaining to do."

"Who is it?" I asked, knowing full well who might be standing in the lower office, but still shocked that it could be him.

"He says his name is Tommy Carrigan, but girl, he looks just like an older Lawson Colt." She hummed into the phone, and I shook my head. He *is* an older Lawson Colt, I wanted to scream.

"Thank you," I said through gritted teeth. "I'll be right down."

Looking back at Max, I found him watching me.

"I'm so sorry. I'll just be a few minutes."

His brows pinched, and he nodded once, dismissing me. I turned for the door, attempting to walk in even, normal paces, one foot in front of the other. But the second I cleared Max's office, I was nearly sprinting, my heels clicking as I walked as quickly as my tight pencil skirt would allow. I banged on the elevator button, tapping my foot as I waited. When it opened, I huffed "Finally," although the inanimate object couldn't care less about my galloping emotions. My insides coiled like a tempest, half-thrilled, half-angry. When the doors to the elevator opened on the ground floor, the tempest hit land like a hurricane, and my legs shook. Tommy stood just outside the double doors, facing me, waiting. His hair stood on end, as his fingers had run through it.

Stepping forward, I said something that was the furthest from my mind. "You missed your flight."

"I'll take another one." He looked over his shoulder at our audience of Grace. Reaching for my elbow, he tugged me to the side. "Let's get out of here."

I twisted, pulling my arm upward, and releasing his grasp. "I can't do that." Some people needed to work for a living. I was one of them.

"Why not?"

"What do you want?" I countered. His lips curled in a smile as I answered his question with a question, but then they went flat as he took in my expression.

"Fine," he huffed. "I met Deanna here in Chicago over fifteen years ago. It was one of those instant attractions. A one-night stand and we got married." I stared at him. That wasn't enough information. It wasn't even comforting information, and I sensed he was omitting again. My arms remained crossed, my hip out as I waited. His eyes looked away and he took a deep breath.

"She said she was pregnant. She claimed it was mine, and I did what I thought was the right thing and offered to marry her."

My mouth popped open, an audible gasp echoing through the windowed lobby. My stomach, which already churned, circled again, and the nausea returned.

"You have a child?"

He shook his head. "She lied."

My arms fell, and I stood taller. My brows pinched in question, but the anguish on his face said it all. He'd wanted to believe she was pregnant. He wanted his own child, and it hadn't happened.

"I'm sorry," I said, my voice scratchy and lowered. I was sorry *for him.*

"She was a model. Six years younger than me. I should have known better. She didn't want a kid. It would have ruined her figure. We were only married a few months, long enough for the tabloids to eat us up and spit us out. It was eventually annulled."

"What about the airport?" His head shot back to mine.

"It's an airport. She was heading out. I was coming in. The paparazzi must have snapped the picture as we greeted each other." His voice was filled with irritation as he explained. That greeting included a hug. His hands on her shoulders. Her hands on his jaw. It looked intimate, longing, and something else. Did they once love each other? Instant attraction? Hadn't that been us? I was ready to ask everything when the hard sole of a man's shoes tapping over a tile floor drew my attention. Max walked directly up to us, determination on his face, as he came towards me. He stopped at my side, and I took a moment to compare the two men. It was a life-size display of "This or That", like one of those games on social media. The man with a suit, or the man with tattoos. The clean-shaven, sensible short hair look, or the scruffy jaw with hair to his collar. The millionaire businessman, or the millionaire musician. My eyes flicked from Max to Tommy and back.

A battle of wills stood between the two. Max came to my side, and unprecedentedly, placed his hand on my lower back. It was a display of possession as he spoke to Tommy, but asked the question of me, "Are you all right?" Tommy took in the position of Max, the placement of his hand and the nearness of him to me.

"She's fucking fine," Tommy replied, and Max's hand tightened on my back.

"Edie?" Max inquired, his voice rolling over my name and I turned to look up at him.

"I'm fine, Max. I'll be back upstairs in a minute."

"Who the fuck is this?" Tommy barked, and my head snapped back to him.

"This is my boss, Max Hartcore, the owner of the company," I hissed through clenched teeth, cursing in my head how unbelievable this situation seemed.

"And you are?" Max asked, extending a hand. Tommy gripped it and held a moment.

"I'm Tommy Carrigan." Tommy looked to me, waiting for me to clarify who he was, but I didn't know anymore. Every time I turned around there was a new piece to the puzzle of him, and too often I was dazed by the sex to see clearly how the pieces never matched. Tommy released Max's hand, and swiped his other one through his hair again.

Looking away from me, he muttered, "Fine." He took a step back, twisting toward the door. "Great," he mumbled. I reached out for him, but he took another step before I could reach him. Turning completely, he headed for the double glass panes.

I spun to face my boss. Max's expression held a smug look, his mouth curled in an ominous smile.

"I just need another minute." My eyes pleaded with him, and to my surprise, his fingers came up to my hair. Brushing short curls behind my ear, he lingered a second. "A minute," he said, his eyes searching my face. My heart hammered. Then he stepped back, and I twisted to find Tommy walking out the door.

Quickly, I stalked after him, cursing my skirt for the tightness at my thighs, preventing me from actually sprinting.

"Tommy," I yelled after him as he hit the curb. His phone was in his hand, and he was typing. "Tommy, wait."

He spun to face me. "What the fucking hell was that?" I'd never heard him so angry, not like that, not at me.

"He's my boss."

"He wants to fuck you." My mouth fell open, and my arms crossed, cupping my elbows.

"He does not," I stammered, shocked and appalled by the comment.

"Don't be so stupid, Edie."

"Excuse me?" My mouth fell open again, my eyes wide and staring in disbelief. Who was the stupid one? Oh right, me, for thinking he cared about me, for hoping he'd no longer hold the truth from me.

"He totally wants all over you."

"How did this get turned around to me?" My arms released and slapped at my hips. The chilly, late January air finally hit me. My body shivered.

"Go back inside," Tommy snapped. "Go back to work." I crossed my arms again, rubbing up and down my sweater sleeves.

"I don't want you to leave like this," I said, lowering the wall a little. He looked out at the street, narrowing his eyes.

"Look, Edie, being apart is hard. It involves trust." He sighed and looked back at me. My body was beginning to tremble, but it wasn't the cold winter air. Shock was kicking in. He was going to break up with me. We weren't even dating, and he was going to break up with me.

"You want the truth, Edie? I wanted that baby, the one she never had. And I wanted her to love me, but that wasn't love. Tricking a man into thinking he's going to be a father—that was treachery. Did I love her? I don't think so, but I've written songs about it, about heartbreak and lost love and ruined dreams. But it wasn't her. It was the emotion after a tragedy, but not her."

His whole body twisted, and he removed his leather jacket. Wrapping it around me, the soft material was heavy over my shoulders, but the heat of his body lingered in the fabric, warming me. His scent filled my nostrils.

"Darlin', I love you, but if you don't trust me, there's nothing between us."

My eyes shot up to his. I couldn't even blink. The cold seemed to freeze my eyelids. He couldn't mean it. He couldn't have even known what he said.

"What?" he asked, growing nervous as my eyes remained wide and dazed.

"You...you just said you loved me." I blinked. "But of course, it was just a slip. I mean..." Hands cupped my face, and he stepped into me, his lips stealing any other words. This was his kiss—aggressive, pressing, and demanding. He parted my lips, commandeering my tongue, and took his time to cover every inch of my mouth. Pulling back, he looked at me, and I shivered.

"You can be so stubborn, darlin'," he said, ignoring my comment and adjusting the jacket. I didn't speak.

"I didn't want to do this here. Not like this. I had it all planned out, repeating it over and over in my head, but it never came out." I continued to stare, not taking his meaning. "I love you, Edie. I know it's been a bit fast, and I said *don't make me love you*, but you can't seem to help yourself. And I can't help myself either. I love you."

Tears welled in my eyes, blurring him from my sight.

"Darlin'?" he questioned, pressing his thumb against my cheek and swiping at a tear that threatened to freeze in the chilly air.

"I love you, too," I said, my voice shaking from the cold, but more so from the words. "I think I loved you from the first touch, but I definitely loved you before I ever left Hawaii." His mouth returned to mine, searching, seeking, savoring. It was in his kiss. All the longing, the miles and hours between us, and I didn't want to separate again, but we had to. A car honked, and he pulled back from me.

"That's my Uber. I need to get back to the airport." He lowered his head to mine. "Are we good, darlin'?" In many ways, I thought we had so much more to discuss, but this was enough. For the moment, it was enough.

"We're good."

"I love you," he said again, giving the collar of his jacket a little shake. "Trust, beautiful."

I nodded, moving to remove the heavy coat. "Keep it. I don't need it in California. It will be my excuse to come back."

My brows furrowed, and his finger pressed the crease. "What's that look?"

"I want to be the excuse for you coming back," I said boldly.

"You'll never be an excuse, darlin'. Always my reason." His lips curled with the comment, and we gazed at one another a moment.

"I'm never going to be able to surprise you. I can't just fly off to California." I looked down at my boot-covered toes. "I couldn't afford it. How is this going to work?"

"Darlin', you surprise me by saying you love me. That's all the surprise I need. You love me, and you want to see me, that's all you have to say, and I'll send you a ticket."

"I love you," I said, my lips curling, my face splitting between my sudden happiness and the cold sorrow of his departure.

"I love you, darlin'." He kissed me once more and slipped into the car. Driving away, he might have left me his jacket, but he took a piece of my heart with him.

L.B. Dunbar

+ + +

"I don't know how you do it," I said to Ivy over the phone. My heart shattered inside me, clogging up my insides with the sharp pain of missing Tommy. It was unbearable. I couldn't see how our relationship could continue with only phone calls and no schedule to see one another.

"You get used to it. Separation becomes a norm of your life."

I didn't like that answer. I'd already been with a man who travelled often, missed much, and was hardly present when he was home. A long-distance relationship was the last thing I thought I'd have at my age, but I couldn't see any way around our situation. He lived in California. I lived in Illinois.

"I just miss him so much." I couldn't believe I'd admitted this to his niece, but I had to tell someone. It seemed inappropriate to tell my children how I longed for a man who wasn't their father, even if they were old enough to accept our divorce.

"I know." Ivy's voice lowered, and I realized she'd lived her whole life with separation—from her mother, her lover, her husband. Shaking off the sad direction of our phone call, I asked her about other things.

"How did Gage take the pregnancy?"

"He was disappointed that I couldn't travel with him, but he's always excited about babies." The idea seemed contradictory to his hard ass personae.

"Did you speak with him about the musical therapy work?"

"I did. He wasn't overly receptive, but..." She paused as sarcasm filled the line. "I found the perfect place. Edie, I don't have all the details, but it's a not-for-profit school, and it needs some funding. It isn't in the best location, and it seems to be desperate. It needs a director after the last one misappropriated their funds. I'm looking into a...secret...with them."

I lowered my voice in conspiracy with her. "What's the secret?" I whispered.

210

"I'd like to buy the place." I sat straighter, eyes widening even though she couldn't see me.

"Can you do that?"

"I'm researching it. Their board wants to just disband, but I see its potential. It's kind of exciting." The enthusiasm in her voice was infectious. Her desperation to be involved and take over the school, whatever that might mean, was nearly palpable.

"It sounds interesting. Can I help you somehow?" I had no idea what I could do from Chicago, but I'd aid her in any way I could.

"I don't know," she chuckled, her laughter filled with fear and passion. "But I'll definitely keep you in the loop."

"Is anyone helping you now?" I hoped Tommy was supporting her if Gage wasn't.

"I hired a lawyer. He's working on the legality of things." Her voice rose again with anticipation. She wanted this project.

"I'm so proud of you." Silence followed the statement, and I worried I'd lost her. "Ivy?" I questioned, thinking the connection was cut.

"Thanks, Edie. That…that means a lot to me. A lot." Her tone had shifted, and the weight of her appreciation hit me in the chest. This is what Ivy had wanted, someone to be proud of her, like her mother would have been.

+ + +

Over the next two weeks, Tommy and I talked nightly, and Skyped often, including some risky, sexy time over the wires.

"Darlin', whatcha doin'?" he asked me one night when Masie was at her dad's, and Caleb had taken off for team meetings in Iowa.

In an exhibitionist sort of way, I took more risks with Tommy than I'd ever taken before. I slipped out of view, stripped, and re-dressed. Reappearing before the screen, his dark eyes turned to obsidian.

"Is that my jacket?" He swiped through his hair, pressing his face closer to the screen. "I'm so fucking jealous of that leather." He sat back, and his hand lowered below the table where his laptop sat.

"Open it a little more." I parted the jacket, exposing a hint of breast, and then slipping lower, revealed a touch of thigh. He swallowed, and I watched the roll of his Adam's apple. "Fuck," he groaned.

I moved the laptop to rest on my bed. Crawling toward the screen, I laid on my side, facing him. I shifted the jacket to cover me like a blanket. The sharp sound of his zipper ripped over the wires. We'd gotten a little out of control one night, and he showed me himself as he took care of his business. I drew the line at holding the phone between my thighs as I worked myself.

"I don't need this on some foreign internet porn site," I had teased.

I rolled to my back. The sound of gentle vibration echoed in my room, and I heard Tommy's breath hitch.

"Is that…Mr. Bob?" he choked. He couldn't see what I was doing. Everything was under the jacket, but with the weight of the material, the scent of him surrounding me, and Mr. Bob between my thighs, it was as if Tommy were present. Not quite, but close enough. His voice increased my arousal, encouraging me with dirty words, and I rolled my head to focus on his face as I took my own pleasure with a little battery assistance. We came together.

"Fuck, you're better than porn, beautiful." He reached for something outside the screen and wiped his fist.

I laughed, rolling to my side to face him. "Not quite."

"My private porn star," he muttered. His laptop rose and movement rattled my view of him. The mattress dipped, and he settled on his own bed. Setting the computer in the same manner as mine, he lay facing me, propped up on an elbow. The position was awkward, with computer screens and not so perfect angles, but it was as close as we could get.

"I love you, darlin'," he said, his raspy voice lowering.

"I love you, too, baby."

His plump lips curled. "You know I love it when you call me that." We just stared at one another a moment. "I wish I was there."

"Me, too. I'd kind of…it's been hard for me." I swallowed down the nerves to speak my mind. "I wish we lived closer. I want to see you. In person." His eyes opened wide, and I worried I'd said too much. As if *I love you* wasn't revealing enough, but they were only words. Admitting to my desire to live closer, spend more time with him, be near him, seemed more exposing.

"Hang on." He disappeared and returned with his phone, lying back down. "What time do you get off work on Friday?"

"Around five." I hadn't told Tommy that I accepted The Nights concert ticket. I told myself it was nothing. Max was younger than me by a few years, but we were close enough in age. We'd been chatting more often about personal things, as well as business, and the attention was refreshing. He seemed tortured that he only had his kids twice a week and every other weekend. He said his ex-wife had been his best friend, and strangely they remained amicable despite their separation. It didn't change the fact he still missed his children. He was alone, like me, and I'd convinced myself a concert wasn't a date, just two lonely people listening to music. It wasn't that I wanted to date someone other than Tommy, but I didn't want to be alone any longer.

"Can you get off work earlier?" Tommy addressed me, but stared on his phone, and I grew a bit agitated that I lay under his leather jacket, replete and warm, while he played with his cell phone.

"Why?" He chuckled at my response, and my phone pinged on my dresser. Flipping his phone to face me, my eyes narrowed, but I couldn't read the information.

"Grab your phone, darlin'." I sat up and reached for it. Opening up the text messages, he had typed, **Check email**. Clicking over to my email, I found a confirmation message from an airline.

"What's this?" I snorted, staring as I read the information. Friday afternoon flight from O'Hare Airport to SFO, San Francisco International Airport. "You sent me a plane ticket?"

"I told you, you say you love me and you want to see me, and I'll bring you here. I'll be in that area this week." He was proud of himself; it showed in his expression. "It's the first time you asked." He'd been waiting for those words from me, and I wanted to kick myself for holding out on saying anything sooner.

So much for the concert.

That Friday, I was going to California for the first time in my life.

# 14
## California dreaming

His mouth crushed mine as he met me at the airport. It was almost embarrassing, but it had been weeks since our lips had been together, and he devoured me, publicly.

The coolness of San Francisco accosted me in a good way. I'd left behind zero-degree temperatures, so I was thrilled to shed my heavy jacket. Tommy took my bag and held my hand as he led me to his car. The vehicle wasn't exactly what I pictured him driving, and I stared at it.

"Is that a '65 Mustang in robin egg blue?"

"You know cars, darlin'?" I knew even less about cars than I knew of music, but *this* car I recognized.

"This is my dream car," I sighed, swiping a finger along its curved edges as I passed to the passenger side.

"Oh, yeah?" His voice teased, husky and puddle-plopping. "What did you dream of doing in a car like this?" I looked up to find his eyebrow wiggling, hinting, and I laughed.

"I'd dream of you doing me on that hood." Tommy stared at me, bracing his hands on the trunk where he'd just placed my suitcase. He stalked toward me without a word, his face dropping. When he reached me, he almost knocked me over as he pressed me into the passenger side door and kissed me hard. He wasted no time, lowering his hips and grinding into me.

"God, I've missed you, beautiful," he said, and my heart skipped a beat. He opened my door, and I sat on the leather seats, rubbing my hands up and down the worn canvas. It was a beautiful car, a musician's car, and one that cried badass and carefree. He lowered to his seat and started the engine, which purred. Pulling onto the highway, I got a glimpse of the hazy surrounding area.

"Fog," Tommy clarified. "It isn't a joke." Neither was the traffic. Chicago didn't even rival this standstill. Eventually, we broke free as we seemed to be travelling north.

"Where we headed?" I asked, hinting at my unasked question. Why wasn't he taking me to his home in LA?

He drove with his right hand, and his left hand ruffled the bands at his wrist—a set of wooden brown beads, a solid silver bangle, and a leather strap. Jiggling them, he seemed nervous.

"I thought I'd take you some place special." His eyes shifted to me before returning to the road.

"Okay," I smiled.

"Yeah?" His lips curled.

"Sure."

"We're going to Napa. I know a vineyard inn there that's private." He was elusive, and it sounded romantic, but the privacy thing struck me.

"Are you worried that people would recognize you?" He shrugged and replied. "It happens."

Another thought occurred to me.

"Are you worried people would see you…with me?" His head spun to face me, briefly blinking in shock before gazing back out the front window.

"Are you serious?"

"Yes." The pause lasted a beat. "I mean, look at me." I waved a hand before myself. "And look at you." I dismissively flung my hand in his direction as my heart dripped like candlewax to my stomach. "We don't exactly match."

"What?" His voice rose, irritation lacing the edges.

"I mean, you're all leather and I'm not even lace. I'm just cotton and occasional pearls." Come to think of it, I hadn't worn my pearls since I met Tommy, but that was beside the point.

"Darlin', what the fuck are you talking about?"

"You're Lawson Colt and I'm just Edie Williams," I said exasperated.

"First," he bit. "I am not Lawson Colt. I'm me, Tommy Carrigan. And second, you're more than just pearls, although you're just as precious and pure. I like that about you. It makes you different than the bullshit I see."

"Different," I sighed, my shoulders lowering as I stared out the window.

"Yes, *different*, in a good way, in the best way. You aren't assuming. You aren't scheming. You aren't money hungry, or gold digging, or even recognizing of who's who. You're just you, and I love it. I love you," he said adamantly.

"I just worry that I'm not enough."

He sighed as he swiped a hand through his hair. The silver shimmered in the sunshine. "Are you trying to pick a fight with me?"

"No," I scoffed, startled by the accusation. The hint sounded precariously similar to something David would say to me and that dripping-wax heart melted. He shifted so his left hand held the steering wheel and his right hand reached for me. Taking my hand in his, he lifted it and kissed my palm.

"Edie, you're everything I need." The comment gave me momentarily ease, so I let my worries flicker away.

After an awkwardly silent ride, we arrived at The Vineyard Inn, the ironic name of a quaint and secluded resort. The older couple who owned the place told us they had been married for over fifty years. I loved their wrinkled faces and the sly smiles they gave one another. Hard work and long love made them beautiful.

That night, we had a very quiet dinner despite other patrons in the restaurant. An eerie feeling surrounded me as I scanned the couples. I was quickly learning the guests were not there to intermingle but to not be seen.

"This place is famous for the rich and *famous*," Tommy explained. He nodded toward a couple. "Movie director. She's not his wife, but his assistant." Peering over my shoulder, I tried not to stare. Their age difference had to be over twenty years.

Shifting his eyes to my right, Tommy continued. "Movie industry exec and a girlfriend, also not his wife." I briefly took in the more age-appropriate match. Then Tommy tipped his head toward the bar. "World champion MMA fighter. That *is* his wife." The brunette beauty giggled softly behind the bar as she served her husband a drink. "Her grandparents own the place," Tommy clarified, and I remembered the older couple who registered us.

"Just be thankful the first wives' club isn't in session this weekend."

"What's that?" I laughed nervously, sipping my Californian rosé to disguise the dread creeping over my skin as I awaited his explanation.

"A group of barracuda women on the rebound from their divorces. They're first wives of the famous and they come here to celebrate their *freedom*." He air-quoted the second statement. "They have no shame."

I suspected Tommy had been the recipient of such a celebration. Moreover, he'd probably brought a woman here previously for its privacy. The place suddenly didn't hold the romantic appeal I had imagined, knowing I didn't qualify as the second wife, but more likely a third or fourth woman he'd brought here. I took another sip of my wine to divert my attention.

The weight of his stare pressed on me as I remained quiet. "You don't like it."

"I do," I said too emphatically. "It's just a bit surreal. I feel like I'm having a clandestine affair instead of a romantic weekend away." Then again, we were lovers. Nothing more.

Tommy sat back, his head bobbing. He tugged at his plump lips with his teeth and a hardness filled his eye. I'd hurt his feelings, and I laid my hand on the table, but he didn't reach for me. My feelings hurt instead.

"So, what did you have planned for this weekend?" he asked, swaying the conversation.

I took a deep breath as I withdrew my hand, lowering it under the table as if ashamed of myself. "I was supposed to go to a concert."

Tommy's brows shot up in excitement. "Oh yeah, who?"

"The Nights." Tommy whistled low in response. "That's some serious shit, that band." He leaned forward, crossing his elbows on the table. "How'd you get that ticket? And why didn't you tell me?"

I didn't speak for a half a second, but I watched as his brain clicked.

"Were you going on a date?" He teased, but his dark eyes narrowed.

"No," I sputtered. "No, not exactly." His eyes widened.

"Well, what *exactly* was it?" he spat, his head lowering as he realized his voice rose too loud in the hushed surrounding.

"Just a friend going with a friend."

Tommy's eyes narrowed on mine. "What friend?"

I chewed at my lip, tugging so hard, it burned. "Max."

"Your boss?" He sat up and slapped a hand on the small table, jiggling it under the pressure.

"Yes." My voice was so low, it was hardly a whisper. Tommy signaled for the check. When the waitress came to the table, he told her our room number and stood without a glance at me. I stood as well, thanked the girl, and followed his large stride. I didn't race to catch him. His anger filled the void between us, and it was all my fault. I shouldn't have been honest. Actually, I shouldn't have accepted the concert invitation, but I'd been alone so long, so often, and I didn't see anything wrong in wanting company, even if it was my boss. My attractive boss, who might be paying too much attention to me.

I followed Tommy into the room, where he stood with a hand braced on the wall. He stared out the window, despite the darkness of the night.

"I'm sorry. I shouldn't have accepted."

"You're damn right you shouldn't have accepted." He pressed off the wall and spun to balance against it with his back. He glared at me across a small room that felt just as wide as the miles between us.

"You don't have to raise your voice."

"Raise my voice?" His teeth clenched. "I'm pissed. What else should I do?"

I stared at him. "Maybe tell me what this is." I waved a hand between us. "Tell me what we have."

"I love you, Edie, isn't that enough?" It was. But it wasn't.

"Where are we going? Is this a relationship? Are we exclusive? I don't really know what you're doing when you're socializing for business. You went to the Grammy's, for God's sake."

"I explained that," he huffed, exasperated with me. He had explained. The band had been nominated, and the tickets distributed long before I was even a thought to him.

*"I didn't predict you, darlin'"*, he had teased, making light of the fact I came into his life after the nomination. It didn't bother me that I didn't go, but it was another reminder that he was famous, and I wasn't anywhere near him. I had no idea what he did at that event amongst the beautiful people, but I could only imagine.

"You did," I replied, not wishing to argue about something I had no control over. We glared at each other a moment, an impasse of crossed arms and strong wills. "So…"

"So?"

"What are we? Are we a clandestine affair, is that why we didn't go to your house? Are you hiding me from someone?"

He huffed as his arms flared and then smacked on his jean-clad thighs. "I thought it would be romantic."

"And it is," I said, stepping toward him, but realizing our disagreement was ruining it. "But I wanted to see your home. I want to know where you live, so I can envision you there. I want to know how you decorate, where you grocery shop, where you take your runs." My heart raced as my voice stressed the things I desired to learn about him. His shoulders sagged and his head lowered. His arms returned to cross over his chest. "I'm sorry that I've ruined this." I plopped down on the edge of the bed. "I just wanted to learn more about you and your real life."

It was too intimate to want those details. Did he prefer bananas or apples? Potatoes or pasta? Orange juice or water? I lowered my head, a war within my mind of all the mundane things I wanted to know, as if I could capture his history and speed it towards the present, making up for lost time and years of never knowing him. It was a ridiculous thought.

I sensed him walking, and my eyes closed briefly, preparing for him to walk away.

Then another thought occurred. I seemed ungrateful for this weekend, when I wasn't. He'd flown me here. He'd brought me to this beautiful inn. We were alone. I wanted him…I just wanted a little more of *him*, the man, not the extravagance. Shaking my head, I realized I made no sense to myself. I was being foolish. I should just live in the moment.

He surprised me when he sat in a chair diagonal from me. His elbows rested on his thighs and his hands cupped together.

"You really want to know those things about me?" His voice lowered, somber and hesitant. Looking up, I saw him staring at his fingers.

"Yes," I sighed, breathless. His eyes met mine.

"Why?" Startled by the question, I had only one answer.

"Because I love you. That means I want to know everything about you. At least, for me that's what it means."

He nodded slowly and sat back in the chair, his arms shifting to the rests. He seemed lost in thought, his mind drifting away, and I worried he wanted to return me to Chicago.

I stood and crossed the short distance, folding to my knees before him. My hands covered his thighs.

"I'm sorry. If you want to send me home, you can."

"I don't want to send you home, darlin'," he said, reaching forward and brushing my growing hair behind my ears. His eyes roamed my face. When he looked at me like that, I felt naked—not undressed, but exposed, like he wanted to see inside my soul, like he questioned who I was, and what I wanted from him.

There was only one way I felt I could reach him. My fingers hesitantly stretched for his belt.

"Edie?" The seriousness of his voice spurred me on. I unclasped the buckle, and he shifted his hips. Next, I slid down the zipper. Tugging at the sides of his jeans, I jostled him like a rag doll. He lifted his hips enough for his pants to free the thick shaft. My mouth watered, and I brushed my fingers up the ridged length, circling the tip with a delicate stroke, and then holding him upright. I rose up on my knees and lowered my lips, swallowing him deep, sucking hard and swirling my tongue. He jolted in my mouth, the wetness increasing the slide. My cheeks hollowed, drawing him deeper, tugging at the firmness as he filled my mouth. I forced back the gag reflex and lowered myself further until he reached the back of my throat. A hand came to the back of my head, and he held me steady. Tangling my tongue over him, I pulled back only to lower rapidly.

He hissed without endearment or my name, his fingers folding into my hair. I opened wider, swallowed deeper, and sucked harder. He pulsed in my mouth without warning, the first jolt surprising me, but I took what he gave. Eventually, his hand stilled on my head, and he gently tugged at my hair. I released him and gazed up at him. He stood, cupping me under my arms and dragging me two steps before we fell to the bed, not speaking the entire time. As we tumbled and then bounced, he wrapped his arms around me, holding me close, but far enough so he could see my face.

"I don't want to send you home, darlin'," he said in that quiet, low voice he could sometimes have. "I want to make my home with you."

The words startled me. "What?" The shaky question quietly squeaked.

"I want to take you to my home, but if I did, I'd never want you to leave." I didn't believe what he was saying. Not that he wanted to imprison me, nothing like that, but more…was he asking me to move in with him? That was crazy. We'd only know each other six or seven weeks.

"Next time," he amended. "Next time, we'll go to my house." The answer worked for me, as his mouth took mine. His hands skimmed my body, reaching for hems and lowering waists, and any other questions I had about us were lost in the sex. This was my problem. The sex was a thick smog that clouded my decisions.

+ + +

We spent the rest of that night huddled under the blankets talking and kissing.

"Mmmm. You like that don't you?" Tommy asked, as I stroked fingertips over his scratchy jaw and kissed his neck. My feet were tucked between his thighs and I moaned in response. Those scruffy cheeks brought me strange comfort and contentment warmed my insides.

"There are so many things we should talk about," he said after another kiss, "but I just want to linger at your lips." On this comment, I pulled back, the contented feeling cooling inside me a little.

"Like what?" My eyes searched his face, and my heart tip-toed toward my stomach. My emotions were on a rollercoaster, and I couldn't get myself to settle into enjoying the ride.

"I want to know more about your marriage, but then again I don't. I want to know what he did to make you the way you are, but then again I want to forget he had you first." His fingers brushed over my hair and his eyes followed the motion.

"I'll tell you anything you want to know." His words were so sweet, my own voice struggled to speak.

"I don't know if I want the answers," he said, finally looking directly at me. My brows pinched, completely uncertain what he might ask. His mouth opened and then it closed.

"Sometimes, there are questions that don't need an answer." He returned to caressing my hair and curling his fingers around my ear. "You're with me now, and that's all I need to know."

My brow pinched again, but his lips took mine, clearing away the discussion. More smog, I thought.

+ + +

The next night he said he had somewhere he wanted to show me. We drove through the early evening darkness and wound through forested roads. The lush coastline surprised me, as most of my limited impression of California included palm trees and sandy beaches, not open fields and conifers. Eventually we turned off the two-lane highway and crept up a narrow path through thick-trunked trees, pulling to a halt at the top of a cliff. Turning off the headlights, we were surrounded in darkness.

"Whoa." I giggled at the severity of black around us.

"Give your eyes a second to adjust." Tommy opened his door and came around to mine. Holding it open, he extended his hand and helped me step out of the car. I looked up at the night sky, and my breath hitched. Millions of stars dotted the heavens. Under the slightly cool evening air, the image looked magical. Tommy had rounded the car for the trunk and returned with a blanket. Spreading it before us, he guided me to sit between his legs.

We'd had a nice day. Late breakfast. Wine tasting. Lounging in the room. The time passed, lazy and pleasant.

"I love you," he whispered at my ear and something in his voice made me turn.

"I love you," I said back, keeping my voice quiet as if I'd disturb the peacefulness around us. He swallowed at the words and kissed me too briefly.

"You've lived in Chicago your whole life, right?" I nodded, but he continued. "Ever consider moving?"

I pulled back, startled by the question. "All the time," I laughed. "It's cold there in the winter."

His eyes glinted despite the darkness, but something serious lingered in them.

"It is cold there, but I'm being serious. Ever think you'd move somewhere else?"

"I guess I hadn't given it much thought." I shrugged. Any Midwesterner considers moving during sub-zero temperatures. We joke about it during an April snowstorm, but seriously considering a move, that I hadn't done. Then my brain tapped itself and reminded me not to lie, because I had contemplated it, for about sixty seconds. I allowed myself the impossible dream that Tommy Carrigan would want to transplant me to California.

"My job is in Chicago," I blurted as if he could read those wayward thoughts. "Caleb is in Iowa, which is near enough, and Masie still has to graduate high school. I keep hoping she'll stay close to home for college." I did hope she'd be close, but she'd been leaning toward the West Coast. Her graduation was another reminder I'd be even more alone sooner rather than later.

"You mentioned that," he said, massaging at the nape of my neck. "You know, essentially, you'll be an empty nester."

The thought made me feel old, and a little no-longer-needed, as if my purpose as a mother had ended. I nodded reflectively, remaining silent under the eerie quiet of the dark night.

"Does that make you sad, darlin'? You're very quiet."

I exhaled before I spoke, preparing to share more honesty with him. "I hadn't ever considered I'd spend the middle years of my life alone. David said it would be the time we'd travel, see the world and have an adventure. He'd tease the kids that we'd be happy to see them leave us, so we could do what we wanted with our lives. But the truth was, we never had adventures to begin with. We didn't have grand plans. I didn't know where his comments stemmed from," I paused, uncomfortable that I mentioned David so casually. "I never foresaw travel in my future. Hawaii was a once-in-a-lifetime trip."

Tommy kissed my neck, and his smile lingered. "Yes, it was, darlin.'" He nipped my neck again. "But you aren't alone." The words caressed my skin, and I shivered. His arms wrapped around me, holding me tighter against his chest. We both looked up at the stars, wanting, wishing.

"California is a lovely place," he sighed behind me, and his shoulders released a hidden tension I hadn't sensed.

I smiled to myself. "Yes, it is."

"Want to move here?"

I tried to spin to face him, but he held me fast, my back still pressed against his chest. He didn't allow me to look him in the eye to gauge the seriousness of his question. I twisted to look at him over my shoulder. "Why?"

L.B. Dunbar

He chuckled, his head shaking in the dark. "Always a question with a question." I wanted to point out he sometimes avoided answers with *that* answer. His arms squeezed me, and his mouth lowered. Another too-brief kiss covered my neck.

"You're igniting dreams I didn't know could exist for me, Edie Williams."

I giggled a little. "You're quite the fantasy as well, Mr. Carrigan."

He purred at my ear. "Speaking of fantasy…" His voice drifted as he shuffled behind me and stood. Reaching down for my hand, he tugged me upward as he bent forward to retrieve the blanket. He threw the blanket over the hood of his car and then spun me until I backed into the front bumper.

"Wha…" The word wasn't completed before his mouth covered mine in that signature, capturing kiss. He gently pressed against my body, molding me to his as I lowered to the hood. Releasing my lips, he pulled back slightly as his hand travelled to the waist of my jeans.

"I want to make all your fantasies come true, darlin'," he whispered, his voice not as playful as it typically was, but a combination of earnest and urgent. His fingers struggled with my jeans. The button. The zipper.

"What are you doing?" I chuckled as flutters tickled my belly.

"Fulfilling my own fantasy, beautiful." His lips met mine, momentarily distracting me. He pulled back abruptly, working my jeans and underwear down to allow cool air to hit my thighs and a scratchy car blanket to tickle my backside. Fingers filled me, and I arched at the welcome intrusion. "Fuck, darlin', this isn't going to be enough."

Releasing me quickly, leaving me empty, he wrestled my jeans to my ankles and then hastily undid his own jeans.

"Taking me on the hood of this car?" I questioningly muttered, my hazy memory recalling the flirtatious tease I threw out there when I first saw this beautiful convertible.

"Oh, I plan to, darlin'. On this car. In this car." There was no time to clarify the specifics as he leaned forward and thrust into me. I moaned as I slid a little with the force, the blanket slipping beneath me on the smooth hood. "I plan to take you places you've never been."

His mouth crushed mine, so I couldn't tell him he'd already done that. He'd already taken me so many places I never dreamed I'd go, done so many things I only imagined doing. He'd been the adventure I never knew I'd have. Hawaii was a once in a lifetime experience, and so was Tommy Carrigan.

# 15
*Ex*tra surprised

By March, the winter weather was getting to me. I hadn't seen Tommy in nearly a month. He travelled to Chicago a second time at the end of February, but the physical distance and longevity of time between visits continued to wear on me. He said I wasn't alone, but I felt more alone knowing he was out there and I was over here. We chatted often like teenagers. Some nights we sexually played. Other nights we talked about life, but the separation was draining on me. I was too old to consider that this was the full extent of our relationship. He lived in a whole different world in California, one that revolved around social activity, and the frenzy only increased the closer the boys got to their summer tour.

Ivy had been upset to learn I'd been in California.

"Why didn't you tell me?" she whined.

"It was a spur of the moment surprise. Besides, we didn't even stay near L.A. We went to Napa." I tried to sound cheerful about the weekend getaway, making it appear as if Napa was too far away to be so close to her. I'd still been disappointed and a bit discouraged that I hadn't seen his home.

"Why didn't he bring you here?"

I sighed in response. I still hadn't gotten an official answer to that question, and my overactive imagination told me he held more secrets.

"I don't really know," I said, my voice lowering. He said it was because he'd keep me there, but I choked on another thought. Maybe he didn't want me to see his world. I didn't fit with him. It was something I thought of often, and yet each time he called me, the negative thoughts erased. Nevertheless, I tried not to imagine a future with him, because I couldn't envision us together. I swallowed hard at the thought. We'd never discussed how to end this, if things didn't work out. We'd never had that conversation I'd read about where lovers agree when it's no longer working for one person, they would let the other person go. I'd be crushed if he simply walked away.

"Well, it sounds romantic," Ivy said, her voice quiet, encouraging, as if she could read my thoughts. "He's been working so hard with the band lately. He must have wanted a weekend away, keeping you all to himself."

"Probably." My voice trembled, I wasn't convincing her any more than myself. I nodded like she could see me and quickly swiped at a tear trickling down my cheek.

Thankfully, the conversation shifted to the music therapy school and her progression with the lawyer.

"I would have loved to show you. Do you think Tommy will bring you out here again soon?"

"I don't really know, honey. I don't know when I'll see him again. We don't really plan things. Besides, I have a trip to Arizona at the last week of March." The words sounded pathetic. Again, I mentally questioned what type of relationship we had. Were we just long-distance lovers? What kind of relationship was that?

I had a strong suspicion I had a better-located, more-attentive, possibility in my boss, if I wished to date locally. However, Max's attention cooled after I cancelled the Nights concert. He still flirted on occasion, and complimented me more than he had in the past. Or maybe I hadn't noticed in the past, too absorbed in healing myself after the cancer treatments. Or maybe sex revived me, and the experience glowed off my skin, announcing I was ready to share myself with another person in a physical manner. I laughed at myself. The only person I wanted to share anything with was Tommy Carrigan.

+ + +

Masie's spring break coincided with spring training games for Caleb. David not only offered miles and points for this trip, but he'd had slightly renewed interest in communication with me because of the trip. I wasn't naïve enough to not be suspicious. My inner knowledge of him told me to hold on; the other shoe would drop eventually. However, he sounded sincere at moments, and I wondered if he felt the same as me. Our children were outgrowing us.

"It's the last time we can really be together as a family," he said, hinting at Masie's impending high school graduation. I wanted to scream that the last time we'd been a family was over three years ago, and officially longer than that, but an eerie sensation prevented me from arguing. David teetered on the brink of being an absentee dad, and I feared that Masie's graduation would sever ties with his daughter. He didn't know how to communicate with his children, unless they were doing something he wanted them to do. Thus, Caleb had a connection with his father because of baseball. Masie, not so much.

I was worn down by work, the weather, and the wayward thoughts of Tommy when we finally left for Arizona. I needed the long weekend respite Max allowed me to take, and looked forward to time with my children. The sunshine alone would do me good, I decided, and I went into the trip full of hope for rest and relaxation.

"You look different," David said, eyeing me as we stood in the hotel lobby. I didn't see my ex-husband often. He'd been one of those men on the edge of model good-looking. Angular cheeks. Sparkling eyes. A dimple in his cheek that melted panties. It stung me that he was aging well: fine lines by his brown eyes, salt and pepper mixing in his once dark hair. But the swollen jowls of his neck told me he still indulged in too much alcohol.

We hadn't flown together, but we coordinated enough to meet at the airport and ride to the hotel together. His eyes continued to skim over my body, taking in the skinny jeans and fitted T-shirt I'd worn, and the flip-flops at my feet.

"You look good." He spoke as if the comment surprised him, and I hated him a little more. There were so many times I'd look at him and try to remember I once loved him. Then he'd say something that would remind me why I no longer did.

We were called forward to register, and I beamed heat into the back of his head, noticing a slight balding that strangely pleased me. He'd traded me in for a younger model on a whim that ended before we divorced. I'd never recovered from the betrayal. His freedom meant he partied harder than previously. My head shook, willing away thoughts I didn't want to envision because I no longer cared.

"Where's my room?" I snapped as we stood by the concierge desk, checking into the hotel, and I watched the desk clerk slide one envelope to David.

"I only had enough points to book one room." If David had hit me over the head with a baseball bat, I'd be less surprised.

"You what?"

"Do you know how expensive it is here at this time of year? Not to mention how full most of these places are because of the pre-season games?" He tapped the keycards on the counter and took the pen from the pretty young thing working the desk. After signing a receipt, he slid a card to me.

"I can't believe this," I muttered, turning for my bag. Masie stood a few feet back from us, typing on her phone. The sight reminded me to text Tommy. He wanted to know we arrived safely and checked in. He wasn't pleased with my travelling with my ex-husband but he understood the concept of family, no matter how loosely ours was linked.

**Made it here.** I sent.

**What room you in?**

Without considering the question, I replied: **323**.

The elevator dinged, and we each entered, pulling our suitcases behind us. I lost connection for a second in the lift and slipped my phone back in my bag. Entering the room, I silently seethed as I noticed the two queen-sized beds and rather tight space. Clearly, Masie and I would be sharing a bed, but the thought of being in the same room with David made me uneasy. Had I known this was the arrangement, I would have booked something myself. I sat with a huff on the edge of a bed.

Hardly a minute passed before a knock came to the door. David looked around at our bags, taking stock that we brought up our own luggage. Shrugging, he walked for the entrance and opened it.

"Who the fuck are you?" The slight accent and gruff tone, sharp on the *k* sound could only be one man. I stood and turned for the door.

L.B. Dunbar

"Tommy?" A smile broke on my face at the welcome surprise of him, however, my expression quickly shifted when I saw the look in his eyes. Cold black steel.

"What the fuck is this?"

"This is my room," David interjected. "And you clearly have the wrong one."

"Where's your room, darlin'?" Tommy asked, ignoring David, and attempting to pass him for entrance into the small space. David's hand came up and pressed toward Tommy.

"What do you think you're doing?" The calmness to his defensive tone almost made me laugh. The comparison between the two men was night and day. Lion and mouse. Sunshine and snow. Tommy was black T-shirt and dark jeans—broad, powerful, confident. David, on the other hand, was thick from alcohol, demeaning in tone, but weak in presence with his golf shirt and khaki pants.

"I'm getting my girl," Tommy announced, brushing past David and strutting to me. His hands cupped my face, and while I anticipated a kiss, none came. His cold eyes searched mine, thick thumbs stroking over my cheeks.

"What's going on here?" David barked behind Tommy.

"Where's your room, darlin'?" Something shifted in Tommy's eyes, the darkness lightning to confusion.

"I don't have one. I didn't know he only booked us one." A hand slipped from my face. The other stilled its caresses. His eyes shifted to coal again.

"For the two of you?"

"For the three of us." I waved a hand out at Masie, who stood between the beds, watching this awkward interchange between her mother, her father, and her mother's lover. Tommy turned toward her.

"Hey, Tommy," she said, waving weakly.

"Hey, girlie." A smile returned to his tone as he addressed my daughter. He turned back to face me. "I have a surprise for both of you." His hand released my face and reached for my hand. His other hand reached out for my luggage. "Masie, honey. Grab your bag."

232

"Wait a minute," David demanded, standing before the open door, his back to it with hands on his hips. He looked like a retired superhero: overworked, underwhelming. "Just *who* are you?"

"I'm Tommy Carrigan," he stated proudly, looking back at me. "Her boyfriend." My mouth fell open at the announcement. It was the first declaration of any label between us, and I stared at the side of Tommy's face as he addressed my ex-husband, who muttered a strangled, "What?"

I giggled with nerves, tightening my hold on Tommy, so I wouldn't break into hysteria at the awkwardness of this introduction.

"And where do you think you are taking her?" David inquired louder, and I laughed outright at the inquisition. He sounded fatherly, like he wasn't. Not to mention, it was none of his damn business.

"She's coming to my room. I have space for Masie, too."

"My daughter is not sleeping with a stranger."

"Good thing I'm not a stranger." Tommy glanced at me after this remark. "Why am I gettin' the feeling he's never heard of me, Edie?" The use of my name was not a good sign, but his fingers squeezed mine.

"I don't really talk to David," I offered, ignoring the glare of my ex-husband. The truth was, I didn't, and because of that, I didn't feel the need to explain my *boy*friend to my ex-husband. Tommy's lip twisted, and I sensed this conversation wasn't finished, but he let it rest for the moment. He turned to Masie.

"I have a suite with separate rooms, so I hope you'd feel comfortable in that space."

Masie reached for her suitcase, and Tommy had his answer. For a moment, my heart pinched for David. His fists fell from his hips at the betrayal. Even his daughter didn't want to stay in a room with him. I worried for a moment the rejection would send him to alcohol for solace, but I couldn't let myself be concerned. I closed my eyes, reminding myself that David had made his choices, and they didn't include his family. I could not take responsibility for his decision to drink. I'd already bore that burden, and I had learned to let it go

"Let's meet in the lobby at seven for dinner, okay, Dad?" Masie offered as way of a peace offering. David nodded and stepped back. Tommy passed first, holding onto my hand as if I'd slip away from him. As I passed David, he reached for my arm, and I stopped.

"Are you sure about this?" David's eyes shifted to Tommy, assessing him. If I could read his thoughts, I imagined he asked what a woman like me saw in a man like him. Silvered hair, longish to his collar. A ring on his forefinger and those bracelets on his wrist. Tattoos lacing up his arm. Looking from Tommy to David, I answered: "I've never been more certain in my life."

+ + +

The anger coming off Tommy filled the elevator, and Masie remained quiet as well. Marching down the hotel hallway, single file, I felt like a woman walking to a death sentence, the tension between us heavier than a chain gang rope. On the inside, I rattled with the notion that I'd stood up to David. While I'd done it in the past, the way in which I confidently walked away from him, holding onto Tommy, surprised even me. Previous attempts at defending myself seemed like small victories compared to the battle I just won.

Tommy opened the door of the suite and stepped aside, allowing me to enter first. A man stood from the couch facing the windows and turned toward us. Long bangs, black hair and bright blue eyes stared at me with a hesitant smile.

"West?" Masie bumped into me, and the shriek startled me to move. I stepped to the side so my daughter could walk around me and toward Weston Reid. He remained behind the couch, rubbing his hands anxiously up and down his thighs.

"Hey," he said on a strangled sound. Masie looked at me, and then she raced around the couch, nearly catapulting toward West, who laughed as he caught her. The two stood in an embrace, swaying back and forth for a moment before Masie broke the hold. A hand pressed into my back.

"I hope you don't mind," Tommy murmured. "He wanted to see her."

"What are you doing here?" Masie's voice rose with her excitement as she stared at West.

"Tommy said he was coming to surprise Edie, and I asked if I could tag along. We've been so busy but Tommy told Gage to give me a few days off. Plus, I wanted to see Caleb play," West replied, reaching out to stroke a long lock of Masie's hair.

"Oh my God, Caleb," I said, covering my mouth and turning toward Tommy. "I need to call him." I fumbled for my phone, struggling through the mess in my bag and retrieving it from the bottom of the abyss. It was then that I saw Tommy's response to my room number.

**Surprise.**

My brow pinched. "Why didn't you tell me you were coming?"

"I wanted to surprise you," he said. "But I guess I'm the one surprised."

"I can explain," I offered, hating the taste of those words in my mouth. After a deep exhale, and a hand down his face, Tommy replied: "I was hoping so, but first, the suite has two rooms. I was thinking West would have one and I'd have the other, but I'll understand if you and Masie want to share."

Tommy looked sheepishly at Masie and back at me. "I don't think the hotel has other rooms available, but I can look into it," he added.

"Masie can have my room, and I can take the couch," West sweetly offered.

"This is all my fault," I muttered, a moment after realizing West implied I'd be sleeping with Tommy in the other room. I couldn't do this in front of my daughter.

"Because you didn't tell me you were staying with your ex-husband?"

"Because I didn't know I was staying with my ex-husband. I knew better than to trust David to handle everything." I swiped a hand over my longer hair. I'd had it cut again into a stylish swipe, longer at the bangs but still trimmed up the back. Tommy's eyes roamed over my hair.

"I like it, darlin'," he said. "You look beautiful." Without thinking, I stepped toward him, reaching for that scruffy jaw I adored and tugging at his face to draw him to me. It was my turn to capture his lips and kiss him like I'd never let him go.

"I've missed you," he said after I released him.

Masie jokingly groaned in the background. "Ewwww, minor here."

"I love you," I mouthed to his handsome face. The curl to the corner of his mouth told me I was forgiven, for the moment.

# 16
## Declarations of Commitment

We passed on dinner with David and Masie, for obvious reasons, and West went in my place. While I initially thought we would go out to dinner, Tommy opted to stay in and ordered room service. When it arrived, I set my phone on the table, but it vibrated against the surface.

**I can't believe you are allowing this.** The text from David didn't surprise me. Most issues, according to him, were my fault. My thoughts deepened to decide he meant the sleeping arrangement, and guilt ate at my stomach that Masie had to fight my battle with her father.

Tommy set the serving plates on the small dining table and poured me some wine. Looking over at me, he asked, "Everything okay?"

"Yeah, just David."

Thick hands set the bottle down and reached for the phone in my hand. He glanced at the text and then tossed my phone toward the couch.

"Talk to me, not him," he demanded. Instantly, I sensed we were headed for a heavy discussion, and I took my seat. Taking a hearty sip of wine, I glared over the rim to find Tommy watching me. "I'm biting my tongue, darlin', but it's starting to ache."

"I know," I said, lowering my head, staring at my plate. "But I wish you wouldn't."

"Wouldn't what? Bite my tongue? I'd like to bite yours, but only once I have answers," he teased without humor.

"What do you want to know?"

"Why doesn't he know about me?"

"I told you, I don't talk to David. We don't share these things."

"Like that you have a boyfriend?"

"I definitely do not discuss dating with my ex-husband," I snipped, my voice harsh, and my heartrate rising. "Besides, I didn't know you considered yourself my boyfriend until you told him."

Tommy slid his chair sideways, angling his body toward me.

"I told you I love you. What did you think that meant?"

"I don't know," I muttered, shrugging my shoulder and flipping the fork on a linen napkin back and forth for something to do. A thick hand covered mine, enveloping it, and then tugging me towards him. He patted his thigh, and I stumbled onto his lap.

"Darlin', those three words are treasure, not a rash statement to get in your pants. If I say them, I mean them, and that means I'm committed to you. Do you understand me? I'm not saying them casually, not saying them to get you in my bed, which I miss, by the way. I'm saying them because I feel them." He took my hand and pulled it up to his chest, pressing it against the firm pec that thumped under my touch. "Do you not feel the same, beautiful?" His voice lowered as did our collective hands and sadness coated the words.

"I do feel the same, it's just…" Liquid filled my eyes and the emotion of the altercation with David caught up to me.

"Just what?" His voice hardened, fear mixed with irritation.

"I don't like the separation. I don't want to sound needy or desperate, but I just want someone more present. I know we talk all the time. And I love the attention you give me. But I just thought…I thought if I ever dated again it would be with someone within the same state as me." I sighed, feeling like I'd said too much but relieved a little to let the weight off my shoulders.

"Why haven't you said something before?" he asked, shifting me on his thigh and I decided my weight was too much for him. I scooted off his lap and sat facing him again. My hands reached for his knees.

"I didn't want to lose you. I still don't. But this is hard for me. You're so busy, with a crazy schedule and night life, and I don't know what you're doing—"

"I tell you what I'm doing," he snapped, and I started at the curt sound in his throat.

"I know, but what I mean is…aren't you lonely without me?" My voice broke on the question, fear filling me that he wasn't lonely because he filled the absence with others. A traitorous tear dripped off my nose.

"Edie." He exhaled. "I think maybe I'm used to being alone. I can't say I like it, but I can handle it because I've been alone for so long. I'm not attached." At the words, I pulled back my hands.

"That's not what I meant," he said, reaching out for me, catching my fingers before I sat back. "I mean, I *wasn't* attached to anyone, so I would come and go without concentrating on the loneliness. My life centered around the band. But having you in my life has changed all that. I'm shifting, darlin'. I miss you like a piece of me is missing each time we say good-bye or hang up the phone or go too many hours without speaking. It's a strange feeling, Edie, but one I don't want to give up, even if it's all I get."

Another tear fell, uninhibited this time.

"I wish we were closer, darlin', I do, but for now, it has to be as it is." I nodded. He was right. I knew he was right, but it didn't make it any easier to accept. He'd joked about me moving to California. The sunshine. The mild temperature. Him. But I never took the teasing as a bona fide offer. "I wish you'd told me how you felt. You don't have to hold back with me."

I snorted unattractively.

"What is that?" Tommy demanded.

"Tommy, why are you even with me? You could have anyone. Someone more like Deanna Kaye."

He released my hands and sat back, staring at me a moment.

"Darlin', do you think I didn't notice how your ex sized me up? I don't give two shits about him, but that doesn't mean I can't read his thoughts. He doesn't think I'm good enough for you. Do you know how that makes me feel? How I know he's right in a million ways? My world is upside-down and backward most days, with shit I'd never want your innocent heart to see or bear. I question why you're with me just as much. The only thing I'm confident of is it's not because I'm a former rock star or affiliated with Collision. You've already proved that to me with your atrocious musical knowledge." His eyes sparkled, and his face relaxed. "So, what do I have to do to prove to you that I want only you? That I'm sitting in Arizona, fighting with you over your worth, because you are worth everything to me, huh?"

More tears fell and I swiped at my cheeks. I didn't know how to respond. It wasn't like I had a checklist. I just had trouble accepting what we were doing, but I realized I was wasting precious time when we *were* together by having this conversation. I reached for his hand and tugged him toward me. He leaned forward, his eyes aiming for my lips, but as he got close, I stood.

"Darlin'?"

I gently yanked at his hand and stepped forward, guiding him to follow me. A few more steps, and I was suddenly scooped up into his arms. Kicking my legs and laughing as my arms wrapped around his neck, we were almost to his room when the main door of the suite opened.

"Get a room," West teased, Masie bumping into his back.

"I have one," Tommy hollered, but something in my face must have told him I couldn't do this with Masie in the room. I couldn't let him take me to his room with my daughter watching us.

"Put me down, please," I whispered. He stopped and set me on my feet.

"Maybe you're embarrassed of me after all, darlin'," he muttered as he spun away from me and returned to the table. Sitting down, he dug into a cold dinner while I'd completely lost my appetite.

+ + +

West and Masie left shortly after their return as West said he knew somewhere he could take Masie that didn't require her to be carded. As soon as they left I was on Tommy, literally. The door closed and I crossed the suite to straddle him, gripping his face, nails dragging through his salt-and-pepper scruff.

"Don't ever say that again," I growled, trying to tease down my serious tone. "I am not embarrassed by you, and I don't know why you would even say that. But I need you to respect that I'm not a groupie, and I'm not like the boys in the band. I can't run off in front of a group, knowing that *they* know I'm about to have sex with you. And I especially can't do it in front of my daughter."

His hands curled around my wrists, and he tugged out of my grip.

"I'm sorry, darlin'. I shouldn't have said that. I was...frustrated." His mouth came to mine too briefly, and as he pulled back, I cupped his cheeks again.

"Well, time to *un*-frustrate." My mouth came to his and demanded he open for me, swiping across the seam of his lips and begging his tongue to play with mine. He kissed me back, opening for me as he gripped my hips and pulled me fully onto his lap. His hunger built and mine matched. I was starving for him.

Standing, I held out my hand, leading him once again toward the bedroom. Within seconds, he was before me, tugging me along and slamming the door, flipping the lock.

"I'm not taking chances this time." My shirt was over my head by his hands, and my fingers worked his belt buckle and zipper. We crossed the room disrobing one another until my knees hit the bed, and he pushed me backward. I scooted up the mattress, and he followed like a predator after prey. When my head hit the pillows, I stopped, and he lowered over me. His mouth found mine as he positioned himself at my entrance, but I pressed his shoulders, hinting that I wanted him to roll to his back. He flipped us, and my legs spread, straddling over him. I sat back and held him upright, stroking him.

"Darlin', if you don't get me inside you, I'm gonna explode all over your hand." Giggling, I pressed up on my knees, balanced on his tip, and then slammed down to envelop him. We groaned in unison as my hands came to his abs. Slowly, I rolled over him, developing a rhythm that held him deep within me. His hand slipped between us and his thumb caught me, pressing in a circular motion. Something came over me, and my hips rocked faster, my channel clenched harder, and my eyes closed with the sensation of losing control. Tension rolled off of me, and a new tension built. His name became a litany of hyperventilating puffs of air mixed with the struggle to cry his name.

My toes curled, and my thighs clamped at his hips. I held still and threw back my head. The release was sweet and spiraling, and I was still coming when he sat forward and flipped me to my back. Braced on his hands, he hammered into me, thrusting and delving, wild and reckless like we hadn't been before. "Faster" and "harder" crossed my lips in a whisper. "Fuck, darlin'," crossed his. The bed squeaked with the rapid motion, and the headboard banged on the wall. He stilled, and that internal pulse of his release set me off again. My hands gripped the globes of his ass, forcing him to remain inside me. Moments later, he collapsed on top of me.

"Sweet Jesus, that came from my toes," he muttered into my neck. I giggled, as I understood the feeling. "I don't like to fight with you, darlin', but if that's how we make up, I'll fight you every day for the rest of our lives."

"How about if we don't fight and just make love like that the rest of our lives?" A moment passed as the words lingered, the reality of their meaning settling around us like pillow feathers floating to the bed. Tommy's head popped up and he stared down at me.

"I'd make love to you the rest of our lives, if you'd let me," he whispered.

"I'd let you." My quiet voice answered. I'd let him have anything he wanted if he kept looking at me the way he was in that moment—like the rest of our lives was everything he wanted.

+ + +

The next day we went to watch Caleb's game. Tommy and West had obtained tickets, and I could only image what favors were pulled to get entrance to the sold-out stadium. We sat mid-section along the first base line, as Caleb was a first baseman. He waved when he saw us and signaled for Tommy and West to approach the dugout. A manly handshake and a slap on the back from Tommy, and the same for West, showed how much of a bond my son had made with these men in such a short time. After Caleb played the New Year's Eve concert, his love of music renewed, and I noticed he took his guitar with him to training even though it had sat in his room at home during college, untouched. A dream died when he no longer touched those strings. He hid his passion from his not-so-understanding father, eventually dismissing it altogether to concentrate on sports in high school.

David spotted Masie and I, and made his way to our seats. He nodded at me, his eyes drifting away as he sat next to Masie. She was typing on her phone, disinterested in the stats her father read off to her about the players. Tommy and West made their way back to our row, pausing at the end of the aisle for David to stand as customary at a ball game when people have seats in the same row. David eyed the baseball jersey of Caleb's team that Tommy wore, open and exposing a white T-shirt. West wore a matching one, buttoned up and hanging loosely outside his jeans. A backward baseball cap covered his dark hair. David turned to me.

"What is this?"

"Dad, you met West at dinner, and you already met Tommy," Masie said as way of intervention. David sat back and twisted his legs, hardly allowing room for West and Tommy to enter the row of narrow stadium seats. Masie and I stood, and I stepped over a space so West could sit between Masie and me. I remained standing, letting Tommy go around me, but he stopped in front of me. Our bodies pressed together in the tight space, and his hand came up so quickly, I hardly registered his intention until after his mouth took mine. The kiss deepened, and I melted into him before I remembered where we were. A flash snapped to my left. Tommy released me, but kept his eyes trained on my lips.

"I think someone just took your picture."

"I hadn't noticed." His lips curled, and he bit the corner. My smile slowly matched his.

"You're a bad man, Tommy Carrigan," I teased.

"I think that's why you like me." He winked as he finished passing me and folded into his seat. His arm slung behind me over the stadium chair, and he toyed with my shoulder while the team finished their warm-up. David's eyes bored into the side of my head, but I refused to look at him. He once found me undesirable, but a very desirable man just proved something it took me a long time to accept—David was wrong. My hand came to Tommy's thigh, and he looked down at it over his jeans.

"Making a statement, darlin'?" he teased. I rolled my head to face him, my smile growing.

"Weren't you?"

"Abso-fucking-lutely, beautiful." He chuckled, and I shook my head as I laughed as well.

+ + +

Someone had taken our picture, and a few days later, I was the mystery woman on Tommy's social media. Speculation was that I was a one-night stand in Arizona where Lawson Colt was on family business. To my surprise and relief, Masie was completely blocked from the position of Tommy in the photo. Weston Reid, bass guitarist for Collison, and my high school daughter were of no interest.

"Don't let it get to you," Tommy commented through Skype after we all returned to our respective homes.

"I'm more worried about you. What will happen when they discover I'm in manufacturing, not modeling?" I was mostly blocked as well by Tommy's hand cupping my face. There would only be a handful of people who could recognize me, and they'd have to be stalking Tommy like I did to see the photo in the first place. I laughed at my joke, but Tommy's face drew near the computer screen.

"You're fucking beautiful, and every man within a fifty-mile radius wants in your jeans. And if you were a model, men would want you for your fame and not your personality, which is off the charts gorgeous."

I stared at him, blinking rapidly.

"You say the damnedest things sometimes, you know that? I'm just speechless."

"Well, get used to it. Besides, I have better use for those pretty lips than talking."

He *was* a bad boy.

"So when can we see each other next?" We hadn't had much alone time in the shared quarters with Masie and West. West eventually did take the couch, and Masie and I bunked together, only I found my daughter curled over a sleeping West in the early morning. Innocently dressed, they were wrapped around one another and my heart pinched at the youthfulness of love.

"April 22," Tommy said at the same time I said, "April 15."

"Can't do the fifteenth, darlin', I have a meeting in New York."

"I have to bring Masie to California for a campus tour at Santa Clara University."

"I thought she selected Marquette," Tommy replied, knowing I'd hoped she'd decide on a school in the Midwest. Marquette had been one of her choices, but Santa Clara University offered her scholarship money we hadn't expected. David promised her he'd cover the rest, if that scholarship came through. I couldn't turn down the opportunity for her, even if I was anxious that David wouldn't hold up his end of the deal. I'd never be able to afford the school on my salary.

"She did, but I told her we could look at Santa Clara. I'm hoping she hates it," I teased.

Tommy scoffed. "Darlin', one look at California and she's going to love it here." I bit my cheek, tempted to tell him I wouldn't know. He'd been to see me twice, and the one time I went there, he whisked me off to Napa Valley, which was beautiful in its own right, but not the portion of California I wanted to know better.

"You know that's only like five hours away from me. So, you're coming all the way here, and I won't be here." A hand wiped over his face. "Can't you reschedule?"

"She has a day off of school, so timing-wise it worked best. Plus, she has to decide by May first. What about you? Can't you reschedule?"

"Can't, babe. We've been waiting for this meeting for months. It finalizes the tour."

The tour kicked off in June, and I sensed the stress each time Tommy mentioned the details. Forty-three days on the road. I couldn't imagine.

"Well, another weekend." I sighed, pasting on a false smile with my fake cheeriness. After the April date, Masie had prom, graduation, and a slew of parties and activities commemorating the end of high school. I didn't have a free weekend until June, when the tour started. "I'll get to see Ivy this time," I added. Excitement filled me at seeing my young friend and learning more about her secret project, which she still hadn't announced to her husband. She knew I was coming before I told Tommy, assuring me that I'd at least see her house as she offered a place for Masie and me to stay. Tommy's brow pinched at the mention of Ivy, and that old feeling of something kept from me crept through me.

# 17
## Secret Therapy

"Isn't it beautiful?" The rundown building before me wasn't exactly something I'd consider architecturally stunning, but the old church had potential. Ivy stared at me as if desperate for my approval, and I didn't want to disappoint her.

"It's got possibilities," I murmured, my hands tucked in my jacket pockets as I surveyed the building once again. I wasn't convinced this was the safest of areas, but my knowledge of Los Angeles was limited to my first official visit. Masie and I flew into San Jose on Thursday evening, took her campus tour on Friday morning, and then flew to LAX in the afternoon. My heart dropped, knowing Tommy was probably somewhere in that airport taking off at the same time we landed. Ivy picked us up, refusing to allow us to stay anywhere but at her modest home along Malibu Beach, and when I say modest, it's with full tongue-in-cheek. The home was gorgeous, set along the coast with an endless view of the ocean. White sand was her backyard and the glass exposure hid nothing. It was breathtaking.

Tommy had offered his house, but I refused on principle. I didn't wish to intrude without a proper introduction to his home from him.

"I know, right?" Ivy squeaked, her excitement hardly concealed as she tugged at my arm to follow her. A realtor had already sold her the location, and lawyers were involved in the details of her future music therapy school. "It's perfect." The sigh in her voice was nothing other than pure love for this facility and a dream coming to fruition.

"And how is Gage taking all this?" I asked. A dismissive wave gave me my answer. As my baby-bump-friend waddled to the front entrance, fear harbored inside me that her husband wasn't going to share her enthusiasm, especially after he found out she hid all the details from him.

Pulling me into the church, construction plans were pinned to a wall, sketching out the division of the massive space into therapy rooms for both small and large groups.

"It has the perfect acoustics, but also all these niches for intimate study." Her face beamed with the thrill of helping others in a way someone raised in music might enjoy—by sharing the gift. With hands clasped reverently beneath her chin, she walked slowly through the open forum, eyes wide as if she could already envision the layout. I sighed behind her, my shoulders falling, but not in defeat.

"Your mother would have been so proud."

Ivy spun to face me. "Do you think so?" Her voice was small, child-like even, as she awaited my answer.

"Without knowing her, I'd say she'd be over the moon." Ivy's face lit up, and her sheepish smile grew. She exhaled in subtle pleasure. "I bet your uncle would be proud as well." Ivy's smile faded a touch, and her head hung.

"I just can't seem to find the right time to tell him. Any of them. They're so wrapped up in the tour, which is where they should be. In fact…" Her lips twitched as if she fought the return of a smile. "It's been perfect for me, because they've all been too absorbed to notice I'm busy." A tiny giggle escaped as if she'd gotten away with mischief, which she had.

"Aren't you worried they'll be upset that they didn't get to be a part of this? That they didn't get to help you?" With those questions, Ivy's curled lips flattened.

"Actually, no. They wouldn't be a *part* of anything. Gage would take over, and Tommy would direct, and I'd be lost again."

I drew in a deep breath at her sudden outburst, understanding once again Ivy's strong desire to do this, to do something on her own, for herself. Being five months pregnant didn't seem the ideal time, but what did I know?

"I wish there was some way I could help you," I offered, letting my eyes drift upward to the dust mites tumbling through the sunshine, dancing before the dirty windows.

"Really?"

My head fell forwards and I peered at my young friend. "Of course. I'd love to help if I could."

Ivy chewed at her lip for a moment as if considering something. Her mouth popped open and then closed. Her eyes lowered before she spoke.

"Actually, I could use a manager."

"Good idea, with the baby coming. It sounds like this will be up and running around the time you give birth. I don't know how you'll manage both jobs at the same time. Motherhood. Music Therapist." Knowing that Ava started first grade in the coming fall, Ivy still had Emaline at home, refusing a full-service nanny or daycare. With another baby on the way, opening the school would be a double whammy of full-time responsibility.

"The timing isn't ideal, no, but again, it's why I'd need a manager. Someone I trust to run the place and look out for it if I couldn't be here. Or…run things while I was here, but if I was indisposed because of the baby." Ivy and I had one of those strange conversations about breastfeeding that women of children seem to have with complete strangers, as if baring one's breast to feed a child is some kind of unwritten bond. Nodding, I agreed with her plan.

"So…" Her voice drifted as she watched me, my head still rolling in different directions taking in the large, sacred space.

"So?" I shrugged, returning to look at her.

"Would you consider it?"

The world seemed to stop moving. The flutter of ancient doves flapping in the hollow room rippled through my ears. The flutter echoed like the beat of a tambourine. I couldn't have heard her correctly.

"What?"

"I'd like to offer you the position of manager. I'm sure I can match your salary, as I'm sure that's the biggest issue…" Her words faltered as I focused on her, unblinking, unbreathing.

"I live in Chicago." Ivy nodded to agree with me.

"You could move?" she questioned, and she had the decency to glance away in hesitation.

"I—"

"With Masie accepting the scholarship at Santa Clara University, and Caleb now in the minor leagues, travelling all the time, I thought you might be willing…interested…available…to move here. Masie would be close by…" She paused watching me as the words softened. "And Tommy's here, too."

"Honey," I sighed. "Please don't use Tommy in this if he has no idea about the school. Not to mention, your uncle has never implied he wanted me to move here nor has he asked me other than as a joke. I've never even seen his home." My voice rose, and my hand slapped at my thigh, exaggerating my rising frustration. Here I was, thousands of miles from my house, only a few miles from his, and I had no concept of where he lived.

"With his lifestyle, he's hardly there anyway," Ivy said, dismissively waving away my concern. "He keeps an apartment in LA." The words were spoken casually, as if nothing unusual was said in the combination.

"His lifestyle," I muttered. Her eyes opened wide.

"Oh, Edie, I didn't mean anything. I just meant he's so busy, and he's hardly around. He has a place for when he…" Her voice drifted once again, as if she'd said too much.

"What's in LA for him? Or should I ask who?"

Ivy's brow rose as she stepped towards me, her hands reaching for my forearms. "No, no, it's not what you think. Tommy's totally in love with you." While we'd said the words, and he was adamant they meant something deep to him, I still couldn't process the depth of them. He didn't say I love you in a pretentious way, but he almost said the phrase too easily, too comfortably. As a woman who hardly heard the words in my marriage, I had trouble accepting their full meaning as anything other than something casually said, like *I love pumpkin pie*. Skeptical of Ivy's explanation, I let the conversation pass, but something still lingered in how she said what she said. What was she leaving out? If it wasn't what I thought, what was it then? However, I wasn't here to probe her for Tommy's secrets. I was here to witness hers.

"Anyway, I appreciate your offer. I'm honored and surprised. I mean, why me?" It was a rhetorical question but Ivy seemed prepared to answer.

"I told you in Hawaii, I feel like you were sent to me. Like my mother wanted me to meet you, and I can't shake the feeling. I like you, Edie, and I feel like I can trust you. I obviously do as you're the only one who knows about this adventure other than my lawyer, the contractor, and now Masie." Masie heard all about Ivy's plans after our campus visit. Masie's excitement for California was fueled by Ivy's.

"You're going to love it here," Ivy promised Masie. "And I'm right here if you need anything." The encouraging hug that followed told me Masie was sold. California bound she'd be come August, and it made me feel even more like the empty nester Tommy called me.

"I know it's a lot to consider," Ivy's words broke into my thoughts. "But I don't want you to tell me no yet. Can you think about it? Just let it simmer a bit?" Her hopeful tone pinched at my heart. My eyes closed a beat, and my shoulders sagged. I had trouble saying no, and it led to most of my issues with David.

"I'll think about it."

The squeal that followed rang to the heavens and could have raised the roof off the steeple. A fierce hug enveloped me, and it was hard to remember I was only considering the slim possibility.

+ + +

Something tickled my neck, and I woke with a start. Dark, playful eyes peered down at me as mischievous lips curled.

"Mornin' darlin'." I blinked in surprise as the weight of his body covered mine, obstructed by the blanket over me. I slept in a guest room of Ivy and Gage's, and my head swung to the other side of the bed where Masie was supposed to be. "She fell asleep on the couch in the media room," Tommy explained with a smile.

"What are you doing here?" My voice croaked in the early morning.

"Took the red eye overnight. I just couldn't stand the thought that you were here, and I was out there. I had to get to you." My lips curled, my insides warming at his sweet words.

"I like seeing you first thing in the morning," I whispered, swallowing after the words escaped. Each time I saw him, I was reminded of how much I missed him.

"We need to rectify that," he muttered, drawing close to my lips, but only brushing his lightly over mine. "I might keep you out here." He was teasing me, but I had to admit my heart raced with the possibility. With Ivy's offer still playing over in my mind, I hated that Tommy was a huge reason I was holding back. I didn't want to appear as if I was chasing him. For once in my life, I wanted to be the one chased. The possibility of him giving up his lifestyle for Chicago and me was out of the question, though. There was that word again—*lifestyle*. What was he hiding from me? Was he a player and I'd been played? It was hard to believe that was the reason I hadn't been to his home as he overpowered me with kisses after taking the red eye back to California to see me. His hand slipped under the blanket, outlining the curves of my body, skimming downward for covered treasure, and all questions about potentially moving disappeared.

An hour later, I met Tommy in the kitchen. The open concept was massive yet welcoming, with light colors of white and gray. It was the perfect beach set-up, with a view of the bright day and the roaring ocean. Masie sat on a stool between Ivy's girls while Ivy stood on the other side of the island cooking breakfast. Gage watched his wife over the edge of his coffee mug. He was an intense man, but I also sensed he'd never purposely harm Ivy. He smothered her, but he loved her.

"Mommy says you're going to school here," Ava said to Masie. The comment brought my attention to my daughter. I didn't know she'd made a decision, and if she had, I was a bit disappointed she told Ivy before telling me.

"Well, I'm still thinking about it," Masie answered, sheepishly eyeing me.

"You'll be here," Gage interjected, a telling tease in his tone.

"So, I heard you're getting a new school," Masie said, deflecting the question away from her. Her excited voice filled the kitchen, suddenly quiet beyond the perk of the coffee pot and the sizzle of bacon.

All other sound seemed to dissipate, including my breathing. I froze in mid-reach for my glass of orange juice and noticed the slightest pause in Ivy's motion to flip a pancake.

"I'm going to be in first grade," Ava announced, and my shoulders relaxed at the innocent response saving us all from a sudden awkward revelation.

"First grade? No way! I thought you were already in sixth grade," Masie teased.

"I'm going to school, too," Emaline replied, her head shaking adamantly to emphasize her participation in something similar to her older sister. "I'll be going with Mommy."

This time the quiet weighed heavy, the echo of silence after Emaline's announcement ringing longer as Gage slowly lowered his coffee mug, Ivy set the spatula on the counter, and I stepped to Ivy's side.

"What's going on, darlin'?" Tommy asked, noting my sudden proximity to Ivy.

"Nothing," Ivy and I said in unison.

"Mommy's getting a school," Emaline offered, her attention still focused on the pancake before her.

"Oh, God," Ivy muttered as I whispered under my breath, "Shit."

"Babe?" Gage questioned stepping towards his wife, and her eyes closed, knowing this was the opportunity she'd been searching for, albeit inopportune. Unfortunately, there was never going to be a right moment. It was time.

"I have something to tell you," she said, her voice lowering. Tommy's eyes met mine, but I quickly avoided his questioning glance and set my hand on Ivy's back. Gage noticed the movement and reached for his wife's shoulders.

"What's wrong?" His eyes searched her face. "Is the baby okay?" A hand lowered to Ivy's belly.

"Yes. Oh, God. It's nothing like that." She sighed. "It's just...I bought a school." The words tumbled out of Ivy, and her eyes closed at the sight of Gage's eyes widening in shock. This could only go one of

L.B. Dunbar

two ways for Ivy, and I held my breath: he was going to hate it or love it.

"Tell me about it," Gage requested, and I took a sigh of momentary relief. Tommy's eyes burrowed into the side of my head, but the need to protect Ivy didn't allow me to meet his glare. Honestly, I was afraid to look at him. Ivy explained how she'd kept up her music therapy license and had been considering using it again. When she noticed the floundering school in the news, she inquired what it would take to restore the organization. She explained to Gage that she needed something to do. She loved the girls and being his wife, but she wanted something more.

"I'm your something more," he said selfishly before swiping a hand down his face.

"That's just it. You have your music. The band. I want something more for *me*." My heart broke as my young friend tapped her chest, the desperation evident in her voice. She needed this or she'd break. Ivy Everly had a quiet, confident strength, but she was teetering on the edge of cracking in that fortitude.

"Maybe we should give you two a moment," I offered, pressing Ivy toward Gage, hoping to encourage them to speak privately elsewhere.

"This is your fault, isn't it?" Gage snapped, looking at me over the shoulder of his wife. "You put her up to this, didn't you?"

"I—"

"Check your tone, mister," Tommy interjected in response to Gage's accusation.

"Edie wasn't involved," Ivy whined. "This isn't about anyone else. This is about me, Gage. Look at me," she snapped at him. His eyes briefly shifted to her before returning to mine.

"Everything was fine until you met her. I don't get it. Life was good. Now my band manager is jet-setting off to Chicago. My bass guitarist wants time off to visit your daughter. Just what the fuck?"

"Gage," Ivy hissed, her eyes shifting to the children. On that cue, Masie picked up Emaline and reached for Ava's hand before guiding the girls out of the room.

"Darlin', why am I suspecting you knew something about this?" The tone of Tommy's voice told me he questioned Gage's accusation. He considered it a possibility. A sudden chill bristled over my skin.

"Ivy told me of her plan, and I think it's a wonderful idea. If she wants to do this, you should both support her. It's very...noble." Ivy peered at me over her shoulder, giving me a slow smile of gratitude.

"I support her just fine." Gage glared at me. "I support you, babe." He looked back at his wife, cupping her face in his hands. "I give you what you need, right? What else do you want?"

Ivy's eyes widened, the excitement returning, detecting false sympathy in Gage's tone. "Well, we need some sponsors and—"

"Not for the fucking school. I mean, what do you need? From me? For us?"

Ivy and I might have blinked in unison, in confusion. Was he not listening to her?

"What I need is your support *of me*," Ivy clarified, suddenly realizing Gage's tone had nothing to do with understanding her desire for the school.

"You have my support. I give you everything you ne—" She tugged her face from his grip.

"Are you listening to yourself?" I snapped, knowing it wasn't my place but suddenly protective of Ivy's dream. "She's telling you what she needs *is* this school. What she wants to do is give kindness and help others. It doesn't involve you other than to love her."

"Darlin'," Tommy warned.

"It doesn't involve you either," Gage snapped. "Or so you say."

"Actually, it will include Edie. She's thinking of becoming the school's manager." A chill rippled through the room as if a threatening breeze before a thunder storm. Tommy's mouth hung open before he swiped his fingers around his lips and closed them.

"Darlin'," Tommy questioned. "You moving to California?" I was afraid to look at him, afraid to see his eyes. Fear slithered through me, and when I glanced over at him, my assumptions became reality. He didn't want me here.

"I don't think so." The low tone forced Ivy to spin toward me, her back to her husband.

"You said you'd think about it. Edie, please. I can't do this without you." Her fingers reached for mine, curling into them and holding onto me like a lifeline.

"How long have you known about this, Edie?" Tommy's tone hardened around my name.

"Since she got the idea."

"Which was when?" Gage growled.

"In January," Ivy answered, lowering her eyes, knowing a truth that omitted all the details could be just as powerfully wrong as a lie.

"You didn't say anything," Tommy returned to me, the irritation in his voice growing. Then he spoke to his niece. "Ivy, girl, are you sure this is the time for something like this? With the concert tour? The baby coming?"

"It's the perfect time, Uncle Tommy."

"I disagree," Gage said.

"Well, you don't have a say, as it's already purchased and under construction," Ivy snapped, the further admission startling both men. Tommy's eyes narrowed at me, realizing I knew a lot more about this project than the *idea* of a school. The shock on Gage's face was like a slap to his scruff-covered cheeks. Ivy had never been so direct with him in my presence. His head shook as he looked up at me.

"And just what do you get out of this?" Gage snorted, his nostrils flaring in anger.

"Gage, you're out of line," Ivy warned, her voice low.

"What is it you want from her, Edie? Notoriety? Money?"

Too stunned to answer, I stared at him. My eyes would have filled with tears if I wasn't so angry at the accusation.

"I don't know why you're involved," Gage continued, despite his wife's second warning. "Who do you think you are? Giving her ideas that she needs something more. Encouraging her to take this risk and in her condition. You aren't her mother."

The words hung in the air like the crack of a whip. Sharp. Pointed. The sting resonated through me, but I was more concerned for Ivy, who took an audible gasp. My poor friend, who'd made this decision because she'd lost her mother. Because she felt distanced from the band's life. Because she didn't want to lose herself. I'd encouraged her, and I'd assured her, had her mother been alive, she'd support her. But I never, ever assumed a role of replacing her mother. I'd actually fought against any misconception of that thought. In that moment, Ivy's pain was as palpable as Gage's words.

"You've gone too far," Ivy muttered to her husband, her voice eerily low. She brushed past him and headed for the sliding glass doors to the deck. Not bothering to close them behind her, she raced for the stairs and the beach below. Gage followed after her and I spun for the counter, bracing my hands on the surface.

"Why didn't you tell me?" Tommy asked.

"It didn't seem my place to share her secret." I exhaled, my shoulders shuddering.

"She's my niece. Practically like a child to me. I think you should have said something."

"That's the thing. She's a woman, and she wants to be treated as such," I said, looking up at him, hoping he'd understand.

"Are you telling me how to treat my family?" He blinked, surprised.

"No, I'm telling you, as a woman, that she wants things for herself that revolve around her, not just her children, or her marriage."

"You should have told me, Edie." His voice lowered to a tone I couldn't decipher.

"Like you tell me everything?" I whispered harshly. "This is hardly the world's greatest secret." I don't know where the words came from, but the sharpness was because of my growing anger. I'd just been accused of things I'd never imagine doing—taking advantage of them.

Masie came into my peripheral vision. "Mom, I don't want to interrupt, but we need to get going." A quick glance over the stove at the clock revealed we had twenty minutes to get our things collected for the airport. I nodded at my daughter, who disappeared almost as quickly as she entered the room.

"Look, this isn't the end of the world..." I began but Tommy raised a hand to stop me.

"Maybe it needs to be."

Disbelief caused me to blink several times as I stared at him.

"What are you saying?" My fingers curled around the edge of the countertop, my nails digging into the hard undersurface, needing stability.

"I'm saying, I think it's time." His eyes closed as he spoke, shutting me out of his vision. "My family is everything to me, Edie, and keeping something from me in regards to them is a hard limit for me. It's about trust, and you've broken mine." I glared at him. After all the things he'd kept from me, *continued* to keep from me, he was accusing me of breaking trust. Was he seriously breaking up with me over this—his niece opening a therapy school? Or was it the possibility that I would move here? Or was it his Californian lifestyle, that mystery I wasn't allowed to know, that I might infringe upon if I were closer? The statement was clear. There was no place for me in his world. Any fight I had drained out of me, puddling on the tile floor. With strength I didn't feel, I spoke.

"If that's what you want," I whispered, pressing off the counter. He turned his head towards the beach view, refusing to look at me, and I rounded the counter to exit the room.

# 18

## What the doctor ordered

Without a word to Ivy, Masie and I flew home. Still stunned that this was the cause to the end of my relationship with Tommy, I stared out the airplane window, hollow inside like the clouds outside. The end of my marriage hadn't paralyzed me as much as the sudden, unexpected end with Tommy. The accusations stung. The distrust incomprehensible. All my concerns that things would eventually end had come true. Unfortunately for me, I never considered it would be over something like Ivy's therapy school.

Understandably, I didn't fit with Tommy Carrigan, but in many ways, he'd been good for me. He'd restored in me some things long-suppressed and awakened other things I'd never known I wanted.

He'd been just what the doctor ordered.

When I went for my six-month check-up with Dr. Crain, her words resonated with me.

"I don't have to tell you how fortunate you are, Edie," she had reminded me. I had survived the battle, for now, through treatments and a mastectomy, and after that appointment I had the all-clear for the foreseeable future. In many ways, I was blessed, and I didn't take my life for granted after all I had been through. Elizabeth's medical guidance and personal support had been unparalleled, considering I went through a divorce at the same time as my diagnosis. Because of our friendship, borne through sharing such an experience, she had the ability to speak candidly with me. "You've been given more time. Take advantage of it."

The implication was clear. I'd been given a second opportunity to do what I wanted with the life I had. I was free of David, despite the loneliness of being divorced. The weight of no longer being married had taken time to lift, until I recognized the burden I bore with him and the relief I felt at no longer being attached to him. It didn't lessen the awareness that I was alone, but I was also my own person again. Tommy Carrigan had been the baptism of my rebirth. He'd let me see what I desired and that I could be desirable to another person. I missed him. Lord, did I miss him, because he'd brought to light things I didn't know I wanted, things I'd never been comfortable demanding. He made me feel alive, and I had to credit him with giving me the experience of a lifetime.

And finally, the tears came.

Elizabeth diagnosed it as part of that adjustment disorder I'd experienced in January. My emotions were a mess from all I'd endured over the last few years. The loss of Tommy, coupled with the future loss of Masie through her graduation and subsequent move to California, left me feeling adrift, like bark floating down a rapidly moving river. Time was speeding up, and I couldn't get a grasp on where I wanted to go next. In addition to my other losses, I missed Ivy.

"I'm so sorry," she pleaded once we final spoke. "I expected him to overreact, but nothing like he did."

I nodded as if she could see me, her words a reminder of all that Gage said.

"You know I'd never take advantage of you, Ivy—"

"I never for a moment thought you were," she interjected, cutting me off from any more explanation. "I can't believe he said that." She paused a beat. "If anything, I took advantage of you, wanting you to give up everything for me and move here to help me. And I'm so sorry about Tommy. He'd completely overreacted as well." The heavy exhale after she spoke made my heart sink. Ivy carried a weighty burden.

"Tell me you're still continuing with the school?" I asked hesitantly, hoping to deflect the conversation away from Tommy.

"Absolutely, and my offer still stands. I haven't tried to find a manager, as I'm hoping you'll still consider helping me, despite my uncle and his stubbornness." She chuckled softly, but I found no humor the situation.

I actually had considered Ivy's offer more often than I should have. I'd been working in my current position for years. I was good as a personal assistant. Organization was my middle name, but the more spontaneous my life had become because of Tommy, the more disheartened I was at the mundane routine of dressing for work, going to work, and coming home from work, all with the sole purpose of making money. I hadn't ever had convictions like Ivy; however, my life had changed. I was learning from her, and the idea that I'd been given a second chance returned to me.

"Honey, I think *because* of your uncle, I should continue to decline the offer."

"Edie," she whined. "This is exactly what I feared. Please don't make it about them. This is still about me. I want you here. I trust you, and that's exactly what I told Gage and Tommy." The comment reaffirmed that Tommy and Gage both thought I had ulterior motives and I said as much to Ivy.

"They don't trust me. The irony is, I'm the one who would lose on this venture. I'd be giving up my home, the place where I've lived my whole life, a secure job, and a confident doctor."

A short gasp filled the line. "You're okay, right? Is something wrong?" The concern grew with each word expressed.

"I'm fine, honey. In fact, I have a clean bill for now. Medication for five years and regular check-ups. I'm all good."

Ivy exhaled a quiet, "Thank God," before adding, "You know I don't believe what Gage said. I don't think you're trying to replace my mother."

"I know," I replied, a weak smile on my lips. I believed Ivy, and a moment of silence passed as we both thought of her mother's plight.

"It's a risk, Edie. The move and everything. I explained all this to Tommy. You would be giving up way more than you were getting from this arrangement, and I was the selfish one to ask." She paused to add, "We'd find you the best doctor out here, by the way."

"Aw, honey, you should have been a lawyer. You're setting up a good argument, but I'm still going to decline. I can't explain it, but I don't think I can be around your family knowing how they feel about me."

"Tommy loves you, Edie. I know this for a fact. He still loves you, he's just...he's just Tommy."

Despite a failed marriage, I knew enough about love to know this was not it. Distrust on this level, the lack of defense from me, this wasn't love. But my heart lied to me, reminding me I still loved him.

+ + +

"Mom?" I didn't have time to ponder my lacking love life in great depth as Masie called my name. It was prom night, and my daughter was attending alone. To my surprise, she wasn't asked, but she didn't want to miss this tradition. She was actually relieved not to have the pressure of attending with someone on a friends-only basis.

"I don't want it to be weird," she'd said, insinuating that even a male friend might have expectations for prom night hook-ups, another rite of passage for some. I shuddered at the thought of my baby girl giving herself to someone only because of a date for a high school dance.

As I entered her room, I stared at my beautiful daughter on the verge of womanhood. In every way, her body was already there, but my heart couldn't reconcile that my little girl was nearly an adult. Through my cancer diagnosis, chemotherapy treatments, and doctor appointments, she'd grown up, but then again, she'd always been on the responsible side.

Her hands smoothed down her yellow dress, which wasn't a color I would have guessed her selecting, and yet, she looked like a modern-day Belle from *Beauty and the Beast* in the slim-fit dress, with her acorn-colored hair piled on her head. A sixty-second thought included *if only she had a date to share the festivities*, but then pride filled me in her decision to brave the ritual alone. She'd be surrounded by people who adored her, even if one in particular wasn't her companion for the evening. She had a strong head on her shoulders, despite occasional shenanigans like getting drunk on New Year's Eve. She was a confident girl blossoming into a driven woman. She knew what she wanted, and she planned to go for it.

As she spun to examine the back of the dress in her full-length mirror, I couldn't remember ever being that confident, that headstrong, that ready to take on the world, but if I ever was…one day I suddenly wasn't. I don't know when it happened, when I decided to take life so seriously, became too safe. Possibly it was the responsibility I received in having children. Maybe it was the commitment to my lackluster marriage. It had never been my job. A job was financial security, but for me, it wasn't personal fulfillment. It was simply something I did. The thought brought me full circle to Ivy's offer. Working with her would include doing something—something for a greater good—and that might make all the difference for me.

The doorbell rang and Masie looked up at me. "Did Caleb change his mind?"

We both knew Masie wanted him to see her off tonight, but it just wasn't possible, as baseball season had officially opened. David was scheduled to arrive an hour ago, and Masie had given up hope. The calling of my name initially meant she was ready to head to Daphne's for pictures. I swear, prom photography was worse than wedding photos.

Descending the stairs before Masie, the doorbell rang again. It couldn't be Caleb, unless he'd forgotten his key. A dark head of hair was the only outline I could make out through the opaque glass of the front door. Opening it, my eyes widened and my mouth hung, his name about to fly out when a finger slipped over his lips to silence me. I stepped back to allow him entrance as the click of Masie's heels on the hardwood staircase warned us of her descent.

"Quick," I whisper-hushed. "In here," I offered, motioning toward the living room to the left of the staircase. He'd be momentarily hidden until Masie reached the bottom step.

"Who was it?" she asked, patting at her head, tucking a wayward curl behind her ear and then returning it to hang by her cheek. The smile on my face couldn't be contained, and I motioned with my eyes toward the living room.

"Wh…" Masie froze, staring at the handsome young man dressed in a classic cut black tuxedo that made him look older than his years.

"Masie." His voice sounded rough, and he cleared it with a fist to his lips before speaking again. "Masie, I wondered if you'd go to prom with me?"

She hadn't replied, but the quiver of her lip worried me. "Don't cry, baby, answer him," I said, feeling guilty at witnessing his proposal, yet I couldn't pull myself away. This was a grand gesture. My eyes drifted to the open door, desperately hopeless in my search for another presence, someone to witness this. A royal blue Mustang was the only thing parked before our town home.

"I'd love to go to prom with you," Masie said, swiping at a tear threatening to trail down her cheek. Stepping forward, he presented Masie with a wrist corsage of yellow roses, and she looked up at him in additional surprise. "I don't have anything for you."

"I only want you to be my date, Masie. That's all I need." My heart clenched at his declaration.

"I'll get my camera," I lied, slipping into the dining room, hidden from their view, allowing them a moment alone. Their conversation continued.

"I can't believe you're here." Masie paused. "What are you doing here?"

"I hope you don't mind. I didn't know if I could pull it off until the last minute, or I would have warned you."

"I'd never need a warning to see you."

"I was worried someone else might ask you last minute." His voice lowered and the dress sole on hardwood told me he stepped forward.

"No one else asked me," Masie murmured. The snap of plastic signaled the opening of the corsage from its container. "I still can't believe you're here."

"I didn't want you to go alone. I hope you don't mind me crashing?"

"You can crash me anytime you want, West," my daughter replied, and my hand covered my heart. Weston Reid crushed it in the romance department.

# 19
### Oh, baby

Masie graduated from high school. Caleb played minor league baseball. And life went on. Months passed without contact from Tommy.

Summer came, as did Collision's concert to Chicago. It was mid-July, and Masie would be leaving soon for college. West sent two tickets for Masie and me, but I told her to take Daphne instead. I couldn't stand the idea of going and knowing Tommy was there somewhere but not wanting to see me.

I called Ivy on the night of the concert instead.

"How are you doing, mama?" I teased.

"I'm as big as a house. I can't see my feet, and I'm exhausted."

I giggled at her misfortune. The joys of pregnancy seemed a lifetime ago. We chatted about the therapy school, the final touches of construction to be completed any day. A grand opening was scheduled for the same weekend Masie moved to Santa Clara in a few weeks. Ivy intentionally scheduled it so I could attend.

*"You don't have to do that," I said, thoughts of seeing Tommy making my stomach churn.*

*"I want you here, Edie. It's important to me."*

We continued to talk about some sponsors Edie received, one being the infamous Nights, whose concert I missed months ago to visit Tommy. Then Ivy groaned.

"Ivy, you okay?"

"Jesus," she moaned. "I don't know where that came from." She giggled uncertainly.

"Everything okay, honey?"

"Yeah, just a back spasm or something. This baby is laying on my spine. Gage swears it's a boy trying to spoon me. He's jealous already of our unborn son, because he knows a little boy will be the love of my life." She giggled, masking a longing I hadn't heard before in her voice. Another soft groan filled the phone.

L.B. Dunbar

"Ivy?"

"It's nothing," she grunted, attempting to speak again. "So, anyway, I had a generous donation from the Nights, and an anonymous one from someone affiliated with them as they...*shhhiiit*..." Ivy hissed.

"Ivy, are you having contractions?"

"I don't think so. It's a little too early. I'm not due for a few more weeks. Gage promised me he'd be home for the baby."

Sarcasm erupted within me, but I kept it to myself. Gage might be almighty, in his opinion, but he wasn't a god when it came to due dates. Ivy hoped to make it through the grand opening before giving birth, however, the timing could never be planned perfectly, and the stress of her therapy school, along with the absence of Gage, could induce labor early.

She moaned again followed by an elongated, "Fuck."

"Ivy, you're freaking me out." I nervously chuckled.

"I'm freaking out, too. I think my water just broke," she said, hysteria filling her voice before she burst into tears with a steady chant of *no, no, no, no, no.*

"Is anyone there to help you? I thought Gage hired a sitter-slash-housekeeper to be with you?"

"He did. I fired her. She was too pretty." I laughed outright. Ivy wasn't that shallow, and never acted insecure, but now wasn't the time to argue about the dismissal of assistance because of her appearance.

"You need to call 911 and then call Gage."

"I'll never get a hold of him," Ivy moaned through the phone. "He's on stage." Glancing at the clock on my nightstand, Ivy was correct. The concert in Chicago had started twenty minutes ago.

"Try his assistant?" I offered, not even knowing if he had a personal assistant.

"That would be Tommy. He'll be too engaged."

"Well, *un*-engage him. Send a 911 text or something."

"Edie," Ivy laughed my name. "I'll just call 911."

"Okay, right. Okay, good. Keep me posted." We hung up quickly, and I paced my room, feeling helpless and frustrated that my young

266

friend was all alone having a baby. Gage was estranged from his family. Ivy didn't have extended family other than the band, and they were all on stage. She should have had her husband present. She should have had her mother there for her. And with that thought, I did the craziest thing I'd ever done.

+ + +

With a quick text to Masie, I told her I'd lost my mind. **I'm heading to California. Ivy in labor. Can't get ahold of Gage.** I had no idea how I thought I'd help Ivy. It would take hours before I got to California, but I had to do something. Even if Ivy got in touch with Gage, he couldn't get to her until the show was over, even in the best scenario.

**Texting West.** Masie replied. **So exciting.**

I didn't know how texting West would help, but I didn't scoff. I was already boarding on ridiculous, literally. I entered the plane, saying a swift prayer for safe delivery of both Ivy's baby and myself to California.

I arrived at an ungodly hour and raced for an Uber, calling out the name of the hospital. When I entered the registration area, inquiring about Ivy, my adrenaline came to a screeching halt.

"We don't have an Ivy Everly admitted, ma'am." I stared at her, blinking. She had to be here. Where else could she deliver? Dawning came slowly that Ivy could have been taken to any number of other hospitals, but with her status, I assumed she'd be taken to the one she requested. I slammed a hand on the registration desk.

"I'm sorry, ma'am. Are you family?" The question struck me as odd. Why inquire unless…Of course, only family could be admitted.

"Yes." I breathed. "I'm her aunt." The lie didn't choke me like I thought it might. If I had continued my relationship with Tommy, the possibility could have been real. *Could have been.* I didn't ponder the lost possibility.

"And your name?"

"Edie Williams." Without thought, I blurted my own name.

"Edie Carrigan, actually," a deep Southern drawl commented from behind me, and I spun to face Tommy. My breath hitched. He should come with a warning. His silvery hair was slicked back, as if endless amounts of fingers had swiped through it. His dark eyes were lit and slightly tired, the tell-tale sign a touch of purple on the undersides. My mouth dropped open, frozen by the sound of my name mixed with his.

"Edie Carrigan," he clarified. "I'm Tommy Carrigan. I'm on the list. Hell, I made the list." He chuckled, winking at the female registrar. His instant charm was a reminder of all I didn't know about him, and my heart pinched.

A warm hand came to my back, pressing me forward toward a bank of elevators.

"Whatcha doing here, darlin'?" The question stumped me, and I answered with the obvious.

"Ivy's in labor." He nodded with another soft chuckle. "How did you get here so quickly?"

"West. That pansy had me hold his phone, not wanting to miss out on finding Masie in the crowd. It kept vibrating in my back pocket, and I finally pulled it out. I couldn't unlock the screen but the first few messages told me all I needed to know. I left immediately."

Silence wavered between us as we rode up to the maternity ward. Awkward tension filled the lift. Heat radiated off his body, and mine responded with an internal cry of longing.

"I was sorry to learn you weren't attending the concert," he murmured. My head shot up at the comment.

"I thought it best to let Masie's friend attend in my place." He nodded, and the conversation stilled again. The elevator signaled our arrival, and we stepped off. Tommy led the way down the hall, offering our names to a blushing nurse. We followed her directions, and Tommy knocked softly on the door.

"Hello, baby girl," he murmured, his voice drifting behind me as he allowed me to enter first.

"Edie," Ivy called out, exhaustion filling the sound of my name. With two quick steps, I was at her side, embracing her while she broke into a sob. Hushing her, I stroked over her hair as I held her against my chest. "Shhh, honey. You did good," I said, taking note of the little bundle, swaddled and sleeping in the clear bassinet on the other side of the bed.

"Why you cryin', baby?" Tommy asked, and Ivy shook her head, pulling back from me to swipe at her cheeks. A smile lit her face.

"I don't know," she said, giggling as more tears streamed down her face.

"It's all the hormones, sweetheart," I soothed, rubbing a hand up her arm as she fell back on the pillows. She gave me an understanding look, tears still flooding her eyes as she nodded at me.

"Ten fingers and ten toes?" Tommy inquired, peering into the bassinet but making no move to pick up the sleeping babe.

"Everything's good," she whispered and a knowing glance passed between the two of them. "Thank you for bringing Edie to me," she added, addressing her uncle.

"Oh, baby, Edie and I just ran into each other downstairs."

Ivy's head swung between the two of us. Her brow pinching. "But you—"

Tommy raised a thick palm and Ivy stopped. He shook his head, hanging it slightly, and a strange unease came over me. Then the baby squeaked. I stepped around Ivy's bed, getting a closer look at the new babe.

"Can I get him for you?" I asked, excitement filling my voice at the prospect of holding an infant. Ivy nodded, her lips curled in appreciation. Scooping up the newborn, I nuzzled into his head, rubbing my cheek against his fuzzy hair before pulling back to look at dark blue eyes peeking up at me. "Hello, handsome," I cooed.

"He's just perfect, Ivy." I stared down at his tiny, squished up nose, minute mouth, and wide eyes. A single tear slipped down her cheek when I glanced up at her, and her smile broadened. Realizing I might have overstepped my bounds, I glanced over at Tommy. He was family. Maybe he should have held the baby first.

"Want to hold him?" I offered, but he shook his head at the same time Ivy sweetly giggled.

"Babies aren't Tommy's thing," she mocked, holding out her hands to take her son. Pressing the child into her arms, my body felt lighter, relief washing through me that all was well.

"You okay, darlin'?" Tommy asked, and I nodded as a tear escaped. I brusquely swiped at my cheek, not trusting words to answer him. A warm hand rubbed up my back, and I shuddered.

"You're shivering, darlin'," he added, his voice that puddle plopping sound that made my belly flutter. I nodded again, unable to respond, afraid any words would open the floodgates of my adrenaline release. His hand continued to stroke up my spine, soothing me as I continued to tremble.

Suddenly, the door burst open. A harried-looking Gage rushed to his wife, reaching for her cheeks and kissing her in that demanding way I'd seen him use before. Knowing the moment was intimate, I turned away, only my eyes wandered to Tommy, who was watching me. A slow, weak smile curled my lips.

The baby squeaked again, and we both turned to the kissing couple. Gage pulled back and looked down, as if he'd completely forgotten why his wife was in the hospital.

"Say hello to Daddy," Ivy crooned to her son, kissing his forehead before looking up at Gage.

"Did you decide?" Gage questioned, his eyes hopeful as he gazed at his wife. I glanced back at Tommy, uncertain of the question. Tommy watched his niece with just as much curiosity.

"Granger Thomas Everly, welcome to the family," Ivy announced in a hushed tone.

Tommy gasped, his eyes filling, his hand stilling on my back to clutch at my sweater.

"Granger?" I questioned.

"Granger is Gage's real name, and of course, Thomas, for Tommy," Ivy explained, a loving expression filled her face as she watched her uncle. I turned to find him swallowing hard before he pinched at his eyes.

Without thought, my arm slipped around his waist, and he tugged me into his side, a place I'd missed too much.

# 20

## Moments of truth

"You look dead on your feet," Tommy commented after I excused myself from Ivy's room. After a few additional words of congratulations, I decided it was time to give the young couple and their new addition some privacy. Tommy excused himself at the same time and followed me out the door.

"I'm a little overwhelmed." I chuckled, swiping fingers through my longer bangs. I'd let the curly Qs and crazy Cs of my hair remain, allowing a stylist to shape them more distinctly and trim my bangs in a way to flatter the waywardness. Tommy's eyes followed the movement, his mouth opening to speak when I added, "And a whole lot tired."

"Where you staying?" he asked and I stopped walking.

"Oh my gosh." I laughed. "I have no idea. I didn't even bring a change of clothes. I grabbed my purse and called an Uber, searching flights on the way to the airport. It's the craziest thing I've ever done." Looking up at him, I knew that wasn't really true. The craziest thing I'd ever done was let a virtual stranger drag me into an empty ballroom and finger me. As if Tommy could read my thoughts, one brow rose, and a smile broke over his face.

"Anyway, I didn't plan any further than getting here." I looked away from his intense gaze and easy expression. I couldn't allow myself to remember all the things we shared as I stood in his presence. I'd break into tears again, the emotion of Ivy's delivery and my rush to get here suddenly hitting me.

"Darlin'," Tommy hesitated. "I was wondering if I could take you somewhere." My brows pinched at the nervous tone of his invitation, and for some reason, I couldn't deny him.

"Okay," I weakly responded, allowing myself to blindly follow him when there were so many unasked questions and unanswered explanations. I didn't have the will to fight with him, though. I was just too damn tired all of a sudden. So, when Tommy placed his hand on my back again, I let him lead me from the hospital.

+ + +

"We're here," he whispered, his voice low at my ear as my heavy lids opened slowly. I'd fallen asleep in the backseat of the car. A private driver met us outside the hospital, and I don't think we made it out of the parking lot before I sunk into the soft leather and closed my eyes. I woke at the sound of his voice tickling me, a thrill rippling through my body as my head rested against his heart. Somehow, I'd ended up against his chest, his arm around me where he repeatedly curled my hair around my ear.

A nervous energy vibrated off Tommy as he removed his arm from around me and opened the door. Stepping out, he reached for me and directed me toward a massive, modern-looking mansion. A large set of cement steps led to a double-set front door, but the thing that caught my attention was the ramp installed at the side of the entrance. I looked up in question.

"Welcome to my home," he said, his voice shaky as he spoke. Taking my hand, he led me to the front door and pressed a code into a keypad. A snap popped the door open, and Tommy pressed forward. The entrance wasn't gregarious, but definitely spoke of wealth, with an elaborate chandelier brightly lighting the foyer and a set of stairs that led sharply upward. It was a combination loft-effect and Hollywood-eclectic, but not distasteful. It also wasn't what I envisioned of Tommy's home.

He led me past the staircase to a drop-down living room that might have housed my entire townhome. The space was massive, with the largest leather couch I'd ever seen facing an entertainment unit above a fireplace. The brick façade was white, as was the couch, and my brows pinched as I scanned the room. The room looked clean but untouched. There weren't many personal effects, and for a moment I felt as if I'd stepped back in time. The place reminded me of a 1970s ranch: sprawling, angular, and not very welcoming.

"I have something to tell you, Edie." The seriousness of his voice and the use of my name immediately put me on alert. I gazed up at him as he stepped before me. He swiped a nervous hand through his hair.

"I have so much to say. I don't even know where to start." He paused. "Would you like a drink?" He took two quick steps in the direction of a large credenza that opened to display a fully-stocked bar, complete with glasses and a backlight illuminating the variety of alcohol.

"No, thank you," I murmured, and he paused, turning back to me.

"Mind if I do?" I waved dismissively, knowing whatever he was about to tell me must be serious if he needed a drink at nine in the morning. The thought made me realize it was eleven at home, and I'd been awake more than twenty-four hours other than the cat nap in the car.

He walked back to me, offering a seat on the pristine couch. Sitting next to me, he held the cut-crystal tumbler in his hand, not taking a sip, but staring at the amber liquid.

"This was my sister's home. I inherited it upon her death." The words struck me, and I took another look around the room. It explained the barren whiteness. He sighed. "I didn't have the heart to sell it."

Silence spilled between us and it took great patience to wait out further explanation.

"Shit, this is harder than I thought," he muttered, raising the glass to his lips and taking a hearty gulp.

"You must miss her," I said, by way of something to say, trying to understand what I didn't.

"You have no idea," he mumbled, leaning forward, his elbows resting on his knees. He swirled the glass in his hands, allowing the liquid to dance along its edges. He peered over at me. "She was my best friend," he offered as way of explanation. Then added, "But it's more than my sister's home. It's where Lawson lives."

His eyes bored into me, willing me to comprehend, but I had no idea what he wanted to say. The first thought escaped, setting bile churning in my stomach.

"You have a child?" The question choked me, and his head shook. "No. Kit had a son." If Tommy asked me to play guitar I couldn't have been more surprised. There hadn't been one mention of an additional child, a sibling to Ivy.

"He has cerebral palsy and lives in a wing off this main room." His eyes scanned the space. "I don't have the heart to remove him from the only home he's ever known. He has round-the-clock care, and he's well provided for."

"Tommy—" I questioned, still not fully comprehending.

"Kit did everything she could to protect him—his identity, his condition. She didn't want any unwarranted sympathy for herself or for him. She didn't need his birth to be a media circus, propagandizing his condition and Kit's sexual history. She was a God-loving woman, and she believed Lawson came to her because it was His will. She had the strength to handle it, and thankfully, the resources."

"What about Ivy? Does she know?"

Tommy rolled his head to look at me. "Of course. Lawson came after Ivy. Kit had been through so much: the rejection of our father, the death of Bruce, raising Ivy as a single mother. Then she got pregnant from some roadie. It was a short-lived relationship, over before Kit recognized she was pregnant."

He paused, allowing that information to soak in.

"So, he lives here, and he's well-cared for. Does Ivy visit him?"

"On top of raising her family, and now this therapy school, she comes to see him at least once a week. Making time grew more difficult with the younger children and the demands of following the band."

"Gage kept her from her brother?" I shrieked, but Tommy shook his head.

"No, nothing like that. Ivy followed us those first years, and it separated her from Lawson. With her own children becoming a priority, Ivy's attention grew divided, but she's always been a loving and understanding sister. She couldn't share him with the world. Kit didn't want any attention on Lawson, knowing life was difficult enough for him." He sighed, his lips curling into a weak smile. "When Ivy was little, she would go into his room and jingle on a tambourine. She'd give him music sticks—you know those ribbed kind—and he'd bang them together. I think that's where the music therapy comes from." Tommy swiped a hand through his longer hair. "Lawson has this bark-ish kind of laugh. Ivy'd giggle in response, and he'd grow louder. It's like her laughter was music to his ears, and Ivy glowed, knowing she made him happy. Kit melted every time she saw it. That strength in Ivy is just…" Tommy blew out a breath, unable to properly credit his niece.

"Is he ambulatory?" I asked, considering the ramp near the front door which I recognized as wheelchair accessibility.

"He isn't. He's an adult, and over time, he couldn't fully support his own size. He's wheelchair-bound. He communicates, but through a sound machine, computerized with images, as he can't read or speak."

Tommy was silent a moment, his head hanging down as he took a final pull from the glass in his grasp.

"Tommy, is this why you didn't bring me here?"

"God forgive me," he mumbled, "I just couldn't. This just seemed like too much to share." He sighed. "I had my own place. Something much more modest, before Kit's diagnosis. It was my room-to-breathe space. But when Kit got sick, I moved in. I inherited the place, and I keep it for Lawson."

"Ivy says you have an apartment in LA?"

"I do. It's over the studio, and I crash there when I've been working long hours. Other times I crash at Ivy's. Sometimes I go to Chicago." He smiled weakly again.

"Why?" My brows pinched with the question.

"My place is lonely, darlin'."

"Tommy." Sadness filled me as my shoulders sank.

"I should have had you sign a NDA," he teased, humor lacking in his tone.

"You already know I'll sign whatever you'd like," I assured him. "Only a sick person would exploit Lawson and Kit's situation."

"Oh, there are plenty of people out there who would love this story." He paused, looking directly at me. "I didn't believe in you, darlin', and I'm sorry." The apology made me sit up straighter. "Ivy wanted to tell you. She trusted you. Hell, she thought I already had. But this…this was a heavy burden, and I didn't trust myself to share it with you. It's not about me; it's about Lawson and Kit. It's about family."

"Family," I said softly, agreeing with his concern but heartbroken that he didn't trust that I would protect his family as much as my own.

"I trust you, Edie. I have from the moment I realized you had no idea who I was. Just something about you screamed safe—and scary—to me." He reached over and pressed a wayward curl around my ear.

"Scary," I snort-laughed.

"I didn't trust myself, darlin'. I wanted to give you everything, but that meant giving you all of this, too. And I feared for them, even when deep-down I knew the secret was safe with you. Maybe that safety scared me, too. I worried I'd get too close, draw you too near, and then when you left, you'd break me."

"Where would I go?" I laughed, humbled and humored that he thought I'd be the one to leave him. "I don't really want to be without you," I admitted, my voice lowering along with my eyes. "But you said some really hurtful things, Tommy."

His head hung. "I did, darlin', and I'm sorry. Truly sorry. I'd understand if you kicked me to the curb, but I'm hoping you don't. I'm hoping you can give me time to prove I don't want to be without you, either. I overreacted, beautiful. I panicked." His eyes drifted up to mine. "Family's all I have and I thrive on being in charge of them, being in the know. I'm used to putting out fires from the boys, but not trouble from Ivy. It just…" His voice faltered. "It just threw me off, but I understand now. And by the time I thought about what I'd done, the tour started, the boys needed me, and once again I put them before myself, before what I wanted."

A hand came to my knee. "I want you, darlin'. You and me. And I think it took you walking away for me to realize you're the piece of me that's been missing. The loneliness I cover, that feeling I deal with, it's because I didn't know what I'd been missing was someone like you." His hand moved from my knee to cup my face.

I bit my lip, loving the words but fear trickled through me.

"What is it, darlin'? What's happening in that pretty head of yours?"

"I want to believe you're sorry. I want to understand where you were coming from, but you ripped my heart out, Tommy. You jumped to conclusions and didn't let me explain."

"I didn't mean to hurt you. I'm saying I'm sorry, but I know apologies take time not words. Family always says they're sorry, though." A weak smile curled his plump lips. "And I wanted you to hear how sorry I am."

While the logical side of me told me to kick him to the curb, like he suggested, my heart screamed for me to take the risk. A risk like that insane woman who let a stranger finger fuck her in an empty ballroom.

"I forgive you." His smile grew and a moment passed with only our eyes connecting us.

"Is it crazy that I want you to move to California after only knowing you a few months?" He chuckled, setting his empty glass on the low coffee table, and turning back to face me.

"Not as crazy as the fact that I would have said yes if you asked me." The words hung between us.

"Darlin'?" he questioned, his brows furrowing, his expression a cross between serious and curious.

"What changed your mind? Why are you telling me all this now?" I asked, changing the direction of the conversation. My hand waved to indicate the room and Lawson.

Tommy reached for my hand, drawing it over to his lap. Thick fingers curled around mine before flipping my palm to face him. He stroked over the tender pad with the tips of his thick digits, and a ripple shimmered up my arm.

"I planned to see you in Chicago. I thought you'd come to the concert, and I'd get your attention afterward. In fact, Ivy knew my plan to tell you everything and grovel at your feet if I needed to." Dark eyes sparkled, before returning to my hand. "I've missed you, darlin'." His words warmed my insides and my belly fluttered. "I think the thing that clarified everything for me was seeing you in that hospital waiting room. I accused you of telling me how to love my family without recognizing you already loved them."

"Family loves unconditionally," I said, a tear trickling down my cheek. My free hand swiped under my eye and the movement broke Tommy's concentration on my palm. His head shot up

"I'd never hurt Ivy or take advantage of her or you..." My assurances were cut off when his mouth took mine, nearly knocking me backward in his aggressive approach. His lips captured mine, drawing them into his before his tongue invaded my mouth, reaching for mine. He'd released my hand, so I reached for the salt-and-pepper scruff at his jaw, nails scraping over his stubble without thought.

"Like that, don't you, darlin'?" He chuckled against my lips.

"I do like that," I mouthed against him.

"Well, I love you, Edie." I pulled back, startled, and he repeated himself. "I love you, and I want you to move to California. Next stop is my place. My real place, but I had to share this with you first. I had to know that this," he waved out at the stark white room, "was okay with you. Secrets of the rich and famous."

I cupped his jaw again. "Maybe before we see your place, I could meet Lawson?"

"God, woman," he muttered, his mouth capturing mine as he pressed me back against the cushions. "First, I want inside you. That's home. Then you can meet my charming nephew." His hand skimmed down to the waist of my jeans as I reached for his. He had me on my back, his legs already between mine, but we were definitely not close enough.

"If your nephew's half as charming as you, I might stay here with him instead." I laughed.

"Never," Tommy growled against my mouth, his fingers forcing my jeans down my hips at the same time. "You're with me."

# 21
### Family always says *I'm sorry*

"I think you should take the job with Ivy. I think you'll be good for her. She needs someone here with her." Gage ran his hands through his hair, a tell that he was nervous. Ivy sat on the couch in their open concept living room, the baby resting in her lap. Tommy and I stopped by to see Ivy and little Granger the next day. The plan was to return in three weeks, when Masie moved into her dorm. We'd be driving cross-country to move her things. Tommy said he'd be up for a road trip, despite finishing the summer tour around that time.

I stared up at Gage from my seat next to Ivy, shock coming off her in waves.

"Family always says sorry, and I'm sorry for what I said, Edie. Truly." His eyes closed, his sorrow was visible even without his eyes on me. He opened them in a flash, staring at me with pain in his pupils. "Never should have said what I said to either of you." He looked down at his wife, his toes tapping at hers. I glanced over at Ivy, not realizing that the fight they'd had months ago wasn't fully resolved.

"I'm selfish," he said. "Ivy knows this, and she accepts it, but that doesn't mean she lets me get away with it." He knelt before his wife, surrounding her legs with his arms. He kissed his son's head before looking over at me.

"Ivy's been explaining the music therapy school to me, and I'm looking forward to spending time there as soon as the tour ends. We have to make up two dates for the birth of this little guy." He kissed Granger again. "But then, I'm home. I'm all in." Pressing up on his knees, reaching for Ivy, and she leaned forward to kiss him.

"All right, darlin', we need to get going," Tommy said, and Gage looked up at me expectantly. I wanted to take Ivy's offer but there was still one offer I needed. We hadn't made it out of Tommy's sister's home, spending the past twenty-four hours alternating between make-up sex and napping. I constantly argued with myself that good sex wasn't a

L.B. Dunbar

reason to give up everything I knew. Not able to respond to the question in Gage's eyes, I leaned for my young friend and hugged her hard.

"We'll talk soon," I whispered.

+ + +

Tommy's studio apartment included a galley kitchen and an extra-large island in the corner of a large great room. Floor-to-ceiling windows illuminated the second-story warehouse space. Record awards filled one wall. His bedroom was off to the left. Galvanized silver, rich browns, and white walls accented the place. Scanning his masculine set-up of leather couch and large, flat screen television, I met Tommy's eyes. He looked hesitant.

"I love this," I said, my voice hardly a whisper. His shoulders relaxed as he stepped toward me. Tender fingers stroked my cheek.

"Did you mean what you said, darlin'?"

"What was that?" I smiled, feeling strangely at peace in his place, comfortable with his touch on my face.

"You'd move here, if I asked?"

"Yes," I whispered, not trusting my voice, not believing the possibility of his asking.

"Then I'm asking, beautiful. I'd like you to take the job and move in with me."

I could hardly contain my smile, but my logical side overruled my heart.

"Don't you think it's a little fast?"

"Not as fast as I'd like. I don't want to wait three more minutes, let alone three weeks, but I understand," he teased, his eyes melting to liquid chocolate. I didn't speak, and the pad of his finger stroked over my bottom lip. "Sometimes fine wine needs to breathe. You've breathed enough. Now it's time to savor you—every day, Edie. Every damn day."

His mouth covered mine and all sanity left me, just like that first time. A sane woman might not have done what I did that night, nor would she do what I was considering doing this night. But I didn't consider myself insane, either. I was in love, possibly for the first time. This time around things would be different. I had to trust in myself and trust in Tommy, which I did. When he pulled back and stared into my eyes, I knew the idea of living without him outweighed my fears of giving up everything and moving here. Not to mention that the job offered by Ivy sounded more purposeful, more self-fulfilling, more beneficial to others, and I was ready for something like that in my life.

"I don't want you to leave," he said, his voice gravelly.

"I can be here as soon as mid-August." The timing would be right, with Masie's move, and allowing for a reasonable notice at work.

"Sounds like perfect timing," Tommy offered, a smile breaking across his face. For his part, he needed the concert tour to end.

"What's next? After the tour?"

Tommy shrugged. "There's always something with those boys, but I'm looking forward to some time off with my girlfriend." His lips covered mine again, and there was no more discussion.

# Epilogue
## Holiday in Hawaii

"This is where it all started." Tommy smirked, rolling his head to look over at me as we sat at the edge of the pool, our feet dangling in the cool water while we soaked up the Hawaiian sun. It had been on the edge of this pool, one year prior, that I saw the tall, dark, and brooding man, dressed in black from head to toe, as if he were a security guard. The memory made me giggle, considering his present attire of bright orange board shorts with giant palm leaves printed at odd angles. Either way he dressed, he still gave off that aura of protective alpha, and I adored the care he gave to me.

When I gave my two-weeks' notice, Max hardly contained his surprise. When I told him I was moving to California, to be with the man I'd met during my trip to Hawaii, his forehead furrowed in disappointment.

"To think I helped support that trip," he had muttered, recalling the gift he'd given me. He hadn't spoken in anger but shock. He surprised *me* by adding, "If I'd gone with you, maybe you'd be staying here to be with me instead." It had been the first blatant comment that he'd been interested in something *more* with me, and I realized an opportunity had been lost between us. Then again, my *more* sat next to me on the edge of the pool.

In addition, nothing could have prepared me for David's strong reaction to my decision.

"You're what?" he'd barked into the phone, when for some strange reason I felt I owed him the courtesy of explaining I quit my job and planned to move across the country. "Is this about that tattooed dude in Arizona?" The venom in that question reminded me, I owed David nothing. I was free to live my life the way I wanted it to be.

Who knew my forty-third year would be a whirlwind that changed everything? New location. New job. New love. All after-effects of having cancer, a killer disease that decided to rest for the moment and allow me a second chance at life. Love wasn't on the prescription pad when I got the clean bill of health, but it certainly had been the pill I needed. I could have continued my life as it was and been fine, but like Tommy joked, why always settle for wine, when some days call for champagne?

Our trip to Hawaii would certainly qualify for celebration. We'd returned to honor Ivy's annual tradition—as a family. Thankfully, Masie and Caleb were included in this special occasion. Shortly after moving to California, and moving into Tommy's studio apartment, he asked me to marry him.

*"I thought you said marriage wasn't for you,"* I teased, recalling his words despite the catastrophic marriage he'd had in his youth.

*"Just hadn't met the right lady,"* he replied, tackling me onto his couch. *"And you haven't answered my question? Have I misread something, darlin'? Did you not want to do the marriage thing again?"* His eyes held that hesitant gaze, one I'd seen more often than I originally witnessed from such a self-assured man, because therein lay the truth: Tommy Carrigan was just a man, who had once been a rock star, and he had doubts like every other man.

*"I'd love to marry you, Tommy Carrigan."*

*"So, let me ask again, and we keep all the other stuff out."* He winked, acknowledging that his proposal had been overshadowed by his previous marriage and mine.

*"Edie Williams, I'd love for you to be the fine wine I sip every day. I warned you to not make me fall in love with you, but I don't think you could help yourself. From the first moment I saw you, you were irresistible to me, and I want to continue to worship your irresistibleness for the rest of my days. Will you marry me?"*

*My head nodding before he finished the question, he paused, awaiting the word. "Yes. Yes, yes, yes."*

*"Mmmm...You know how much I love it when you say that word to me,"* he hummed into the crook of my neck before sliding off of me to kneel on the floor. He slipped a ring out of his pocket.

L.B. Dunbar

*"Well, I love you," I said, while righting myself on his couch. He remained on his knees before me, reaching for my left hand. "I love you, too, darlin'." His voice dropping in that pebbly sound as he slipped the ring on my finger.*

Sitting by the pool, I stared down at that ring, glistening in the sunshine. His hand covered mine, and he brought my fingers to his lips, kissing over the knuckle below the ring. We were getting married the next day—a beach wedding, surrounded by immediate family.

"Tomorrow," he muttered, looking up at me under hooded eyes. "And every tomorrow after that."

Did you enjoy this story? Please consider writing a review on major sales channels where ebooks/books are sold. Also, if you liked this book, you might also enjoy any of my other work:

# More by L.B. Dunbar

## Silver Fox Former Rock Stars
When sexy silver foxes meet the women of their dreams.
*After Care*
*Midlife Crisis*

## Romance for the over 40
*The Sex Education of M.E.*

## The Sensations Collection
Small town, sweet and sexy stories of family and love.
*Sound Advice*
*Taste Test*
*Fragrance Free*
*Touch Screen*
*Sight Words*

## Spin-off Read
*The History in Us*

## The Legendary Rock Star Series
Rock star mayhem in the tradition of King Arthur.
A classic tale with a modern twist of romance and suspense.
*The Legend of Arturo King*
*The Story of Lansing Lotte*
*The Quest of Perkins Vale*
*The Truth of Tristan Lyons*
*The Trials of Guinevere DeGrance*

## Paradise Stories
MMA chaos of biblical proportion between two brothers and

the fight for love.
*Paradise Tempted: The Beginning*
*Paradise Fought: Abel*
*Paradise Found: Cain*

**The Island Duet**
The island knows what you've done.
*Redemption Island*
*Return to the Island*

**Modern Descendants – writing as elda lore**
Modern men of Greek god mythology.
*Hades*
*Solis*
*Heph*

# (L)ittle (B)lessings of Gratitude

Words cannot express my gratitude for Loving L.B., my Facebook group. You Lovelies rock day in and day out, and it's my pleasure to hang with you. Extra love and affection to Ashley, Chantell, and Karen for beta reads. A triple scoop of Tommy for Joanne Schwehm, Bestselling Author of the Prescotts. Darlin', your suggestions were invaluable to me. Hugs to Sylvia for all the things.

Shannon, four years, twenty-one books, and five covers later, you are still with me, and I'm forever grateful.

Kiezha, I'll never forget that your help pushed me to a new level.

Karen, a second helping of appreciation for being my second set of eyes, always.

Thank you to the ultimate silver fox, although, damnit, he still has more dark hair than gray (it's all in that sexy beard), Mr. Dunbar. You're my rock star. And of course, MD, MK, JR and A, my babies who I'll motherly converse about any day.

+ + +

# About the Author
www.lbdunbar.com

L.B. Dunbar loves the sweeter things in life: cookies, Coca-Cola, and romance. Her reading journey began with a deep love of fairy tales, medieval knights, Regency debauchery, and alpha males. She loves a deep belly laugh and a strong hug. Occasionally, she has the energy of a Jack Russell terrier. Accused—yes, that's the correct word—of having an overactive imagination, to her benefit, such an imagination works well. Author of over a dozen novels, she's created sweet, small town worlds; rock star mayhem; MMA chaos; sexy rom-coms for the over 40; and suspense on an island of redemption. In addition, she is earning a title as the "myth and legend lady" for her modernizations of mythology as elda lore. Her other duties in life include mother to four children and wife to the one and only.

+ + +

# Connect with L.B. Dunbar
I love to chat with readers, so feel free to find me in any of these places.

www.lbdunbar.com
Stalk Me: https://www.facebook.com/lbdunbarauthor
Stalk Me More: Instagram @lbdunbarwrites
Read Me:
https://www.goodreads.com/author/show/8195738.L_B_Dunbar
Follow Me: https://www.bookbub.com/profile/l-b-dunbar
Tweet Me: https://twitter.com/lbdunbarwrites
Pin Me: http://www.pinterest.com/lbdunbar/
Get News Here: https://app.mailerlite.com/webforms/landing/j7j2s0
AND more things here
Hang with us: Loving L.B. (reader group):
https://www.facebook.com/groups/LovingLB/